.44

ALSO BY JIMMY BRESLIN

Can't Anybody Here Play This Game?

The World of Jimmy Breslin

The Gang That Couldn't Shoot Straight

World Without End, Amen

How the Good Guys Finally Won

ALSO BY DICK SCHAAP

Turned On

R. F. K.

Instant Replay
(*with Jerry Kramer*)

I Can't Wait Until Tomorrow . . .
'Cause I Get Better Looking Every Day
(*with Joe Namath*)

The Perfect Jump

JIMMY BRESLIN
and
DICK SCHAAP

THE VIKING PRESS   NEW YORK

Copyright © Jimmy Breslin and Dick Schaap, 1978
All rights reserved
First published in 1978 by The Viking Press
625 Madison Avenue, New York, N.Y. 10022
Published simultaneously in Canada by
Penguin Books Canada Limited

LIBRARY OF CONGRESS CATALOGING IN PUBLICATION DATA
Breslin, Jimmy.
.44.
I. Schaap, Richard, 1934–   joint author.
II.   Title.
PZ4.B8425EO   [PS3552.R39]   813′.5′4   78–3864
ISBN 0–670–32432–9

Printed in the United States of America
Set in VIP Primer

ACKNOWLEDGMENTS
Chappell Music Company: From "Rich Girl" by
Daryl Hall. Copyright © 1976 by Unichappell
Music, Inc., and Hot-Cha Music Co. International
Copyright Secured. All Rights Reserved. Used by
permission.
Harcourt Brace Jovanovich Inc.: From "Buffalo
Bill's" from *Complete Poems 1913–1962* by E. E.
Cummings.
UFO Music Publishers: From "Parasite" by Nick
Drake. Copyright © 1978 Warlock Music Ltd. All
rights reserved. Controlled by Island Music (BMI).
Reprinted by permission.

AUTHORS' NOTE

This is a novel. It is based on historical realities — the Son of Sam killings in New York City in 1976 and 1977 — but it is not itself historically accurate. It is not supposed to be. Many people were hurt by Son of Sam, directly and indirectly, and to avoid hurting those people further, and to protect those who shared their experiences and their thoughts with us, we have invented people, places, and dates, everything except the terror. The terror was real. This is a novel. It is not factual. We hope it is truthful.

— Jimmy Breslin
— Dick Schaap

New York City
February 1978

1

Connie Bonventre spread her outfit on the bed so that she could study it. She had picked a black Milliskin top, backless, with a scooped front, cut low on the sides, just barely covering the breasts, the outfit held up by anatomy and two thin straps that tied at the back of the neck. The Milliskin top, a mixture of nylon and spandex, cost almost twice as much as the conventional, all-nylon Danskin, but Connie felt the new material was worth it; the Milliskin was brighter, shinier; the spinning lights above the disco floor would bounce more brilliantly off the Milliskin. To go with the black top, she had bought a white skirt, very tight, with one dramatic slit that ran to her upper thigh. She had purchased the skirt in Manhattan, at a small Lexington Avenue shop called Disco-tique; she preferred to buy her skirts in boutiques because, almost always, the skirts available in department stores were slit only to the knee. She had laid out a pair of gold shoes, the toes drastically pointed and the spiked heels four inches high, and, to match the shoes, a gold pouch that she would tie around her waist with a rawhide string. She never carried a purse to discotheques anymore. If you put the purse down when you got up to dance, someone would rip it off. The pouch was safer, it was decorative, and it was just large enough to hold the essentials — cigarettes, lipstick, money, keys, and proof of age. She had borrowed proof from a friend. Connie was going to be eighteen in two weeks, and, a week later, she would graduate from Sacred Heart High School.

Connie stood naked, fresh from a bubble bath. She had patted herself dry, oiled her legs, patted baby powder on her waist and crotch, then sprayed herself, generously, with Ciara, a cologne whose fragrance she considered sexy. She stepped away from the bed and turned toward a large mirror hanging above her dressing table. She admired her body in the mirror, her legs firmly muscular after three years of ballet, tap and modern dancing, her breasts as firm as she could hope for, considering their size. She began to move in front of the mirror, hearing the disco music in her head, reacting to it, enjoying the reflection and wishing that perhaps someday she could dance naked like this, natural, uninhibited, in a discotheque. She carved the air with her hands, acting out the dance, and her fingers brushed across her nipples, and she smiled. Connie felt good. She had just heard, earlier in the day, that she had finally been accepted by New York University's School of the Arts. She had been admitted to the Professional Actor Training Program.

She stopped moving now and leaned forward and, starting to frown, examined her face. She liked her body better. Her teeth, she was convinced, were too large, her cheeks too full, and the top of her nose, just below eye level, was absolutely flat for half an inch, the permanent reminder of a broken nose she had suffered when she was ten. She had been standing on her older brother's shoulders, diving into a YMCA pool, and her first ten or fifteen dives had been fine. The next one was too good. She sliced into the water too sharply, sank too swiftly to the bottom, and cracked her nose hard against the floor of the pool. She came up bloody and crying, and now, as she ran a finger across the bridge of her nose, she wondered whether plastic surgery might make her face prettier. She imagined herself with a smaller, more graceful nose, a nice WASP nose, and the thought made her smile. The smile exposed her oversized teeth. Studying the mirror, she tried to smile without showing her teeth, or with only a little tooth showing, but she could not do it. Each time she attempted a smile, Bugs Bunny emerged. What's up, Doc? Connie thought.

Her face, she knew, was perfect for comedy. It was a genuinely funny face —not *ugly*-funny, *laughing*-funny. Her eyes were large, full of wonder, and she looked like she was having a terrific time even when she wasn't. When she had auditioned for NYU, she had delivered April's monologue from *Company*, and her portrayal of a beautiful but dumb airline stewardess had been very convincing, even though, in truth, she was neither beautiful nor dumb. For the second part of her audition — and she knew then that the audition, not her school marks, would determine whether or not she got into the Professional Actor Training Program — Connie had played Agave, from Euripides' *Bacchae,* the scene in which Agave comes down from the mountain, carrying the head of the son she has just slain. The director of the NYU acting program, a man who laughed easily and wore a belt laden with pouches, one for his tobacco, one for his pipe, one for his glasses, one for his pen and notebook, had been impressed by Connie's sudden shift from April to Agave, just as she had hoped he would be. The final part of her audition called for a song, and instead of going for one of the standard audition numbers, she decided that, since her voice was neither especially strong nor especially musical, she would pick a song to be acted, a song whose content, properly phrased, would have impact. She chose Ophelia's song from the fourth act of *Hamlet,* not the dirge she sings for her father but the bawdy "St. Valentine's Day Song":

> *Tomorrow is St. Valentine's Day*
> *All in the morning betime,*
> *And I a maid at your window,*
> *To be your Valentine.*
>
> *Then up he rose, and donn'd his clothes,*
> *And dupp'd the chamber-door;*
> *Let in the maid, that out a maid*
> *Never departed more.*
>
> *By Gis and by Saint Charity,*
> *Alack, and fie for shame!*
> *Young men will do't, if they come to 't;*
> *By Cock, they are to blame.*
>
> *Quoth she, before you tumbled me,*
> *You promised me to wed.*
> *So would I ha' done, by yonder sun,*
> *An thou hadst not come to my bed.*

Connie walked into the bathroom and began to make up. She had spent two summers working with a street theater in the Bronx, and from the professionals who occasionally volunteered their time and skill, she had learned more about makeup than most of her friends.

She started with a light foundation cream, then highlighted the very top of her cheekbones. From there, she worked down the face, going from light to dark, applying brown-out to her cheeks to try to make them appear smaller, to give herself a hollowed look. Next, she turned to her eyes, beginning with an eyelash curler, a metal-and-rubber contraption that took hold of the lashes, squeezed them, and curled them. Then she put on three different colors of eye shadow, starting right on the eyelid and working up to the bottom of the brow, from a light blue to a dark, almost blue-black to an eggshell white. She used black pencil on the lid itself. Then she applied a few dabs of Blush-on, on the forehead above each eye, on the nose, and on the chin, and, finally, her mascara, thickening and darkening and lengthening her eyelashes. She paused and studied her face for dramatic effect. She approved. She picked up a brush and, for twenty strokes on either side of the part down the middle of her head, she ran the brush through the long brown hair that spilled onto her bare shoulders.

Back in the bedroom, she dressed slowly, enjoying the ritual. She stepped first into the Milliskin leotard, savoring its silky feel. She pulled it up and tied the straps behind her neck. She liked the way the top flattened and firmed her breasts. She reached down to her crotch, where some of the fabric had gathered, tugged the stretch material away from her skin, and spread it evenly, without bulges or unnatural bumps. She ran her hands down over herself, first to smooth the material, then simply for pleasure, touching her breasts and her stomach and her hips, letting her hands slide across the body suit and onto her thighs, pleased by the change in surfaces. She felt sensual. She felt free. She did not have to wear a bra, nor panties, with the one-piece Milliskin top. She had considered wearing a Danskin body suit, which came with three snaps at the base of the crotch — snaps that were very helpful for peeing and for petting — but she chose the leotard for comfort, walking and dancing and sitting. Sometimes, when she sat wearing the body suit, she felt the snaps pressing against her. She had learned, too, that when she did want to go to the bathroom, the Milliskin was elastic enough to pull out of the way, and when she wanted to be touched, the same procedure worked. Besides, she enjoyed being touched through the material, responding to the blend of nylon and spandex and finger.

Once she was happy with the leotard's feel and its fit, she stepped into her white skirt. She whirled, watching in the mirror as the skirt flew up, revealing her thighs and the black leotard from bottom edge to waist. Her buttocks shone. She stopped, patted down the skirt, slipped into her spiked heels, tested her balance quickly, then tied the rawhide string of the gold pouch around her waist.

She went to her dressing table, opened her jewelry box and took out two pairs of inexpensive gold-plated earrings, one pair of hoops and one pair of studs. She took one hoop and slipped it onto her left ear. She took the matching hoop and slipped it through the pierced opening at the base of the lobe of her right ear. Then she took one of the studs and, probing, on her right lobe, about a quarter of an inch above the original hole, she found another opening. She attached the gold stud. She put the stud's mate into a third hole another quarter of an inch up on her right lobe. The top two holes on the right ear were new. Her girl friend, Kathy Grasso, the one she was going out with to celebrate her acceptance at NYU, had pierced Connie's right ear only a few weeks earlier. Kathy had taken half a dozen ice cubes, wrapped them in a towel, then held the packed towel against Connie's ear for twenty minutes, freezing the surface. Then she took a sewing needle, lit a match and held the needle in the heart of the flame for thirty seconds, till the heat threatened her fingers. Using the sterilized sewing needle, Kathy twice pierced Connie's lobe, seesawing the needle a few times to widen each aperture, then put a pair of earrings through the holes to keep them from closing up. The process had been more painful than Connie had admitted.

Black top, white skirt, gold shoes, gold pouch, gold earrings, strikingly coordinated, Connie needed only a few last touches. She brushed her teeth, then took a lip pencil, traced a very thin bright-red border on her lips and filled in with a brownish-red lipstick. Finally, she picked up her gold necklace with the small gold horn. Her grandmother had given her the horn. "It will keep away the bad spirits," her grandmother had said.

Connie had laughed. She knew all the old woman's superstitions. If you put new shoes on a table, it is bad luck. If you dream about a funeral, it is good luck. If you dream about a wedding, someone is going to die. Connie did not believe in the superstitions, but she had to admit that in the six months since she had begun wearing the horn, she had not had a single one of the headaches that used to devastate her every few weeks. When non-Italian friends asked her what the horn was for, she said, "It keeps away headaches."

She snapped on the necklace and glanced down at the horn. She was ready now. She was armed for the disco night. The previous night she had dreamed of a wedding.

He picked at the large scab on his left elbow. He was alone in his dark, nearly empty room, sitting on the only chair, an office swivel chair, and his fingers had settled on the scrape on his left elbow. He pried the scab up from one side of the scrape, wincing as he did it, and then quickly pressed the scab back down.

Blue bedspreads were nailed over the two windows in the studio apartment. They were thick enough and dark enough to strangle even direct light trying to enter the room. In a small alcove, the third window, was covered with a gold tablecloth whose design made it appear to be a religious vestment. Some light seeped through the gold cloth, but not enough to disturb the darkness in the rest of the apartment, number 9M at 743 Hudson Terrace in the City of Yonkers.

When he had first moved in, only a few months earlier, the windows were uncovered, and Bernard Rosenfeld could look straight out at the Hudson River at its most beautiful point. The river is a mile wide off Yonkers, and on the far side stand the Palisades of New Jersey, gray in winter, but now spring green, awesome cliffs rising high out of the water. If Rosenfeld moved to the windows and pushed aside the bedspreads and looked down, he could see, or sense, something more powerful than the Palisades. At the foot of the apartment house in which he lived was a narrow street of wooden houses, and behind the houses a hill, and at the bottom of the hill, hidden by foliage, was a backyard. Sam Thornton's backyard.

Sam Thornton's dog was in the backyard. The dog was a black dog, and he stood motionless and saw everything and heard everything and knew everything. The foliage made it impossible for Rosenfeld to see the dog. But he knew the dog could see him. The dog could see through the trees. Bernard had put up the bedspreads and the tablecloth to keep the dog from looking into his apartment, to keep away his eyes and his howls, too, but, of course, it had not worked. How could it work? The dog could see through the trees and through the bedspreads, and he could see through the walls when Bernard went into the bathroom and tried to hide. The dog would see, and then the dog would command. He would look up from Sam Thornton's backyard and howl for blood.

Bernard knew that Sam Thornton, who lived in a gray wooden house badly in need of painting, was more than six thousand years old. Bernard knew that Sam Thornton was six thousand years old and bloodthirsty and relentless. Bernard knew all this, even though he had never actually met Sam Thornton and had never spoken to him, not directly. Only through the dog. Sam Thornton, Bernard was positive, made the dog howl for blood, and the howling was so persistent, so persuasive that one day, in response, Bernard took out a red pencil and printed on his wall in big bright letters: "SAM THORNTON IS MY MASTER."

"I am a servant," Bernard said as he sat in the dark and stared at the bedspreads that shielded him. "I must do what I am told." He heard the dog howl once more. Rosenfeld spun around on his swivel chair. He leaned on a breakfront between the alcove and the kitchenette, and he began printing in large neat letters on a yellow legal pad:

SAM'S DOG HOWLS FOR BLOOD. I CAN'T SAY NO. THE EVIL KING EVERGREEN MUST GET WHAT HE WANTS. BLOOD FROM A PRETTY PRINCESS.

He spun back and looked at the bedspreads. There was no sound now. But he could feel the dog looking at him. Hot red liquid eyes burning in the dark. He sat and waited for the dog, silent now, to command him.

"All in the Family" had ended, and Salvatore Bonventre moved toward the television set to switch to Channel 11 to watch the Yankee game. He would only watch a little of the game. He did not enjoy it the way he used to. Too many black players now, not like the great teams with DiMaggio and Rizzuto and Berra and Billy Martin. Sal Bonventre limped to the television set in short, uneven steps. The limp was the price he had paid to escape from Brooklyn in the 1950s.

He was working then, as now, for a textile house in Queens, as a dyer, spending all day on his feet, mixing chemicals, sweating among vats of boiling water, with no air conditioning. One day, one of the janitors in the shop, trying to clean up early to get out early, accidentally swung his broom against a vat in front of Sal Bonventre, and the vat overturned, and the boiling water splashed onto his right leg, from the knee down, seeping into his workboots and burning deep into his ankle. The water penetrated to the bone. Sal had been rushed to a small local hospital, and after three weeks in bed, and two operations for skin grafts, and bandages changed too carelessly and too infrequently, had emerged with permanent scar tissue and a permanent limp. Had he been treated in a better hospital, by wiser doctors using more modern facilities, he might have come out walking perfectly. But he had no bitterness toward the hospital, or toward the doctors who had tried to help him, or even toward the janitor who had knocked over the vat. None at all. As the victim of a partially incapacitating industrial accident, Sal received a lump-sum payment of $5000 from the Workmen's Compensation Board. He took the $5000 and made a down payment on a $15,000 house in the Pelham Parkway section of the Bronx.

Sal Bonventre picked an area where trees still were a common sight and blacks a rare one, where most of his neighbors, like himself, were born of families which had made the pilgrimage from the south of Italy to a city neighborhood. Sal was born and raised and married and began a family of his own in the Bushwick section of Brooklyn. When the blacks and Puerto Ricans first infiltrated the neighborhood, Sal thought of Long Island. Then a sister persuaded him to move to the Bronx, where he now felt comfortable, where he heard familiar shouts in the streets, where he could raise his children without worrying about them all the time. Joseph was six when Sal and Gina Bonventre, his parents, moved to the Bronx; Anthony was born a few months later, and Constance six years after that.

The house Sal Bonventre bought, on Westervelt Avenue, not far from Pelham Parkway, was perfect for a family of five. There were three bedrooms upstairs, one for the parents, one for the sons to share, and one for the daughter. Downstairs, there was a living room, a dining room, and a kitchen. The house was built of red brick, with a basement at street level. Thirteen steps led from the sidewalk up to the front door, guarding a hallway that ran straight back to the kitchen. The dining room touched the kitchen, and in front, just off to the right, was the living room. Sal Bonventre spent most of his time in the living room, watching the television and dozing off in his favorite armchair, a big soft blue one, protected, like the rest of the furniture in the room, by a plastic cover.

Once he had shared the room — and the television — with his children, but now his sons, who used to watch the Yankees with him, were gone. Joseph, the older, had become a priest, and Anthony a film editor, and while some of the kids in the neighborhood had done much better financially — legitimately by building $200,000 homes in Connecticut or by selling Cadillacs in Harlem — Sal was proud of his boys. They both worked hard; both believed in what they did. Joseph had entered the seminary when he was seventeen; Anthony had become a messenger for a film company, a can-carrier, at the same age, then had worked himself up to being an editor.

Now only Connie was still at home, for a few more months or a few more years, and she was Sal Bonventre's favorite. He did not know how she had gotten so smart, but everyone said that she was brilliant, that she could memorize a speech or a scene from a play faster than anyone else at Sacred Heart. Connie was always cheerful, always surrounded by friends. As a child, she had gone to neighbors' houses, putting on plays for them, and at Sacred Heart she had had the good fortune to encounter an unusual nun who recognized and encouraged her theatrical talents. Everyone liked Connie. Sal loved her. He loved her so much that the only time in his life he felt bad about his limp was when he went to school to watch Connie in a play. He tried very hard then to take long, even steps.

Connie came down the stairs from her bedroom and walked into the living room. She walked slowly. She did not want her mother and father to notice the slit on the side of her white skirt. Sal looked up from the baseball game. "Where you going dressed like that?" he said.

"To a dance," Connie said.

She knew it was better to say "to a dance" than "to a discotheque." Her mother and father knew dances; Joseph and Anthony used to go to dances. Her mother and father did not know discotheques.

"So late?" said Gina Bonventre.

"Oh, Mama," Connie said. "Things don't get started till late. It's Saturday night."

Sal shook his head. "Who you going with?" he asked.

"Kathy. Kathy Grasso."

9

"That's good," the father said. "You come home with Kathy, too. You come home by one o'clock."

"We won't get there till after ten," Connie said, "and the music'll just be starting. We'll be back by, oh, two-thirty."

"You be home by two. Your mama doesn't go to sleep till you get home, and she keeps me awake, too. I want to get up for mass tomorrow. You get up and go to mass, too, it won't hurt you."

The doorbell rang, and Connie leaned over, kissed her father, kissed her mother, then moved toward the door. She opened it, and Kathy Grasso, short and black-haired, wearing makeup and costume to match Connie's, stood there, giggling. "When you get to be a big star," Kathy said, "will you introduce me to Al Pacino?"

"Really," said Connie. "And Robert DeNiro."

"We'll take them for a ride," Kathy said, "in my father's Cutlass. He's letting me use it tonight."

"Good," said Connie. "Are we going to New Rochelle? We going back to the Short Giraffe?"

"No," Kathy said. "I want to try someplace different."

"Okay."

"I've heard about a place in Queens, in Bayside. It's called Jinni. It's supposed to have great music, a great DJ, great dancers."

"Oh, wow," said Connie. "You know how to get there?"

"It's easy," Kathy said. "We just take the thruway over the Throgs Neck and it's only about ten minutes from there."

The two girls came down the thirteen steps from the Bonventres' door and walked to Kathy's father's Oldsmobile. Kathy slipped into the driver's seat, and Connie, from the passenger side, into the so-called death seat.

He picked at the scab again. Huggy made him get this scab. Rosie had scraped the elbow four days before, when they had him helping to lift the immense sheet metal air-conditioning duct off the truck, Huggy's truck, which was at the rear entrance to the unfinished Texaco office building in the town of Harrison. There were five of them unloading the duct from Huggy's truck. They were on the bull gang, which is what they call apprentices in the Steamfitters' Union. Everybody was lifting the duct except Rosie. His fingers were on the bottom of the duct, but there was not enough pressure on them to make the fingers red.

"Rosie, you're fuckin' everybody," Huggy yelled at him.

Bernard Rosenfeld put his head down so Huggy would not talk to him again.

"I said you're fuckin' everybody!"

"I'm lifting," he finally called to Huggy. He tried to make himself sound as though he were straining.

"Liftin', my prick!" Huggy shouted.

Rosenfeld was paying so much attention to Huggy that he didn't notice the other men shifting and the bottom of the duct suddenly rapped his left elbow. It hurt him and he let go of the duct and began to hold his elbow.

"You fuck!" Huggy yelled.

He tried not to talk to Huggy, but Huggy was coming directly toward him.

"I hurt my arm," he told Huggy.

"You fuckin' hump!" Huggy said.

Rosenfeld started to cry. When Huggy saw the tears, and saw Rosie's chest heave as he tried to suppress a sob, Huggy shook his head and walked over to the bull gang and took Rosie's place lifting the duct off the truck.

For the rest of the day, Huggy stayed away from Rosenfeld. Once, in the middle of the afternoon, he heard Huggy shouting and he thought that Huggy would be coming to see him. Rosenfeld went into a corner of the loading area and cried heavily. How could Huggy come and bother him? Huggy had caused all the trouble. Rosenfeld rubbed his scraped elbow. Why didn't Huggy understand that he had caused this, that he had hurt his elbow?

The sudden barking of the dog caused his body to jump. The swivel chair creaked. Bernard Rosenfeld took his fingers off the scab and leaned forward. The barking turned into yips. Yip-yip-yip and then the last yip broke into a bay which moved higher and became a ceaseless howl into the night, a howl that came through the trees and the windows and the bedspreads and lodged itself in Bernard's head. The howl became so loud that he put his hands to his ears to keep the noise out, but his hands didn't help, because now the dog was inside his head, howling, commanding him to hunt.

Bernard Rosenfeld stood up and walked through the darkness to the foyer, where he flicked a switch that brought on two sixty-watt bulbs in a ceiling fixture. The studio apartment, with its white walls, was now in pale light. Khaki socks hung over an open closet door. He reached up and felt them. The socks were still damp. He walked over to the bed, where he had left his other socks, his black socks. The bed was a box spring and mattress on the floor covered with a yellow comforter, with a design of a guy smoking pot stitched in black thread. On top of the comforter were about two dozen magazines, sixty-cent detective magazines. The black socks were partially covered by one magazine. On the cover was a frightened girl, cowering with a pink sheet around her, long bare legs spilling out of the pink sheet, while standing over her was a man who was bare from the waist up. The man held a gun. Rosenfeld turned to the page he had been reading earlier in the day. His eyes ran down the fields of type until he came to the one paragraph:

> She was now lying on a gynecological-examination table, her feet in the stirrups and her wide-spread thighs held apart by straps. Her hands and arms were also secured by straps, and the matrons were breathing rather hard.

When he had first read this, at about noon, he had dropped the magazine and put his hand inside his open fly. Now, as he read the scene again, there was another stirring between his legs. He put aside the magazine. He had no time for it; he had to go to work. He looked at his watch; it was getting close to ten o'clock. He could feel the dog's eyes burning into him. He went over to a black Styrofoam toolbox on the floor and took out a small plastic bag. He opened a cardboard box of bullets in the kit and took out seven of them. They were large brass cartridges with a lead slug as thick as a man's little finger. He put the bullets into the plastic bag and put the bag into the pocket of his jeans. On the floor alongside the toolbox was a green plastic garbage bag. The brown wooden handle of a gun protruded from the bag. He twisted the green plastic and closed the opening. He shut off the lights as he left the apartment.

The moment he stepped into the hallway he became confused. Two young black women were down at the end of the hall, waiting for the elevator. He did not want to ride in the elevator with them. They would look at him, and he could not look back at them. Or perhaps they would say something to him. He could not do this today, even with white people. The prospect of getting into the same elevator with black people caused his breath to catch. He turned around and pretended to be opening the door of his apartment. He could feel that the women were still in the hallway. He went into his pocket, pushing his fingers past the bullets, reaching for his keys; he took them out and inserted one into the lock. The two women were still at the elevator. His chest began to pound. They were standing there deliberately. They knew he wanted to take the elevator, and they were standing there and taunting him. He had put the key into the lock, but he had not turned it. If the door opened and the dog saw him coming back into the room, the dog would be mad at him. Bernard could not take that pressure. The last time that Bernard had not done what he was told, he had been tied up in the backyard and beaten. It had hurt. He did not want to be hurt anymore.

At the sound of the elevator doors opening, tension ran out of the drain at the bottom of his stomach. He watched the two black women get in. Relieved, he walked back toward the elevator. Immediately, he became apprehensive again: what if somebody else came out of an apartment and he was still waiting? At the elevator bank, he found he was fortunate: the black women had taken the car down only two floors. It rose quickly and he stepped into it, a nervous bundle of suet with a green plastic garbage bag in one hand.

His face was one of those which frequently give ethnic-conscious New Yorkers a problem: Is this Jewish or Italian? The two strains usually live alongside each other, mix continually, and now look alike. A tough Jew looks like a tough Italian; a soft Italian looks like a soft Jew. Rosenfeld had a soft appearance. He had a fat neck and round shoulders. Chubby thighs and a large rear end caused him to walk with the suggestion of a waddle. At five-foot-ten and 210 pounds, he was at least forty pounds too heavy. The face was round and almost pink. There was a slight hook to the nose. The eyes were large dark-brown pools that seemed to have mirth, or tears, just under the surface. His hair, black and wiry-wavy, was receding badly on the left side. A bald spot showed in the back. He was twenty-three. He would be bald by thirty-five.

He walked quickly through the new-shabby lobby of the apartment house and went up a flight of steps to the sidewalk. His car, a cream-colored Galaxie with a black top, was parked a few yards up the block. As he got into the car, he pushed a black sneaker off the driver's seat. On the seat alongside him were a pair of jockey shorts,

13

an empty cranberry-juice jar, a green toothbrush, a bottle of Canoe, and a road map of Queens and Long Island. He added the green plastic bag to the clutter.

As he started the car, his soft eyes suddenly became low wood fires.

Yonkers is a gray river town which begins where New York City's Borough of the Bronx ends. Old red-brick factory buildings, many of them closed, line the riverbanks. Staring from the street corners, from the doorways of boarded-up shops, and from the windows of old frame houses is the query to Yonkers' future: the faces of the black unemployed. Because the old frame houses, once gracious, have been cut up into so many small apartments, nearly all of them have ugly fire escapes on their fronts. The newer apartment buildings, such as the one in which Bernard Rosenfeld lived, are filled with transients: Yonkers is a good place for a person to get lost in. As he drove away from 743 Hudson Terrace and turned onto North Broadway, Bernard Rosenfeld was a person whose face was familiar to only a few people in Yonkers, all of them living in his apartment building, or in the building next door. And only one or two people could put together his face and his name.

He drove along Broadway, through the silent business district, down to the brink of the Bronx. On a side street, he pulled up in front of a small trailer set back in a lot alongside a Sons of Italy building. The trailer had been converted into a diner. He walked up to the trailer confident that only the counterman would be there, and the counterman had a harelip and therefore could not articulate, which left Rosenfeld free from the humiliation of conversation; words usually struck Rosenfeld like thrown bricks. At the trailer, he ordered two hot dogs, potato chips, and a Dr. Pepper. He paid for his meal and walked to the front of a sporting-goods store, which was in the next building. He ate the two hot dogs and looked at the hunting rifles on display in the window. The store was his favorite; a week before, he had walked in, bought two boxes of .44-caliber bullets, and walked out without having to say another word. According to New York state law, the store was supposed to keep records of everyone who purchased ammunition, but so many years had gone by without anyone from the state ever asking to see the records that the store owner had simply stopped keeping them.

Rosenfeld got back into the car and put WPLJ, a rock station, on the radio. The music was from an Earth, Wind, and Fire album. His right hand tapped the dashboard as he drove into the Bronx, then across the Bronx until this great necklace of lights, the Whitestone Bridge, appeared out of the darkness. The bridge rises 142 feet above the night-darkened water of the East River. It stretches out for 2,310 feet, connecting Queens to the Bronx. As he drove up to the bridge, he took three quarters from a plastic tray on the dashboard and got into the exact-change lane. He dropped his quarters into the mesh basket and waited for the gate, a thin wooden arm, to rise automatically and allow him to pass. He stared at the gate, and when it did not rise immediately, his body shifted in agitation and his hands tightened on the wheel. Then the gate went up. As he drove past it, his head jerked and he spat at the gate. Then he drove over the bridge and came down into Queens. He followed the Cross Island Parkway to a green sign that said: "Northern Boulevard."

"Pretty Queens girls!" said Bernard Rosenfeld, his voice rising. "Pretty Queens girls!" He knew why the Queens girls were prettier. Sam had told him. The water in Queens was better and that made the girls more beautiful.

Jethro Tull's "Thick as a Brick" was on the radio as Rosenfeld's car rolled through the section of Queens called Bayside. In this part of the borough, as it runs toward the first massive suburb, Nassau County, Queens seems to be a green belt threatening the identification of New York as an urban center.

Rosenfeld drove along Northern Boulevard for a few blocks, then turned onto a side street, onto 218th Street, and for a couple of minutes, he cruised in easy, familiar rectangles. For more than a month now, ever since he had come back from Houston with the .44-caliber revolver, a souvenir of a visit to an old army buddy, he had been out every night, driving around. He had been learning the streets of Queens and the streets of the Bronx, and he had been learning the people, too, the habits of the young and the old. He had been out hunting.

He parked on Forty-seventh Avenue. He put the green plastic bag inside his sport shirt and got out and started to walk in the night on the quiet, empty street. He walked close to the frame one-family houses, so that the maples lining the curb kept the streetlights from falling on him. The people in this section of Queens are mostly Catholics, homeowners, nearly all middle-aged, and they are in bed on a

Saturday night at an early hour, sleeping with an iron gate pulled down inside themselves in an attempt to keep the morning, Sunday morning, from reaching them before it has to. On Sunday there would be the job of going to mass or, much worse, the all-day depression which would follow nonattendance at mass.

As Rosenfeld walked toward a parked car, there was for just a small moment a great rise within him: two heads appeared to be in the front seat of the car. Now, he looked at the silent houses and almost wanted to scream for all the people to come out, for all the people to see the hand of God. Inside his right temple, there was a small heat, a cardboard match just struck. As he came closer to the car, the flame became brighter, a wooden kitchen match, and the heat spread through the side of his head, and it was just starting to make noise, the first crackling of a good log, when he saw that there was nothing in the car, no people, just a pair of headrests. The fire in his head went down, and he shook his head, half-smiling, and walked on. And now, in a low voice, he began talking to himself again.

You've been howling for it, and tonight you're going to get it. Blood, all the blood you can swallow. Suck on blood, Sam. How do you like it?

He reached Northern Boulevard and turned onto the main thoroughfare. Shiny cars crouched like sleeping animals in darkened auto show windows. A line of one-story attached shops sold storm windows, aluminum siding, television sets. Red-brick bank buildings, designed like religious monuments, stood at the corners. He watched the boulevard traffic as it moved along. A large green bus, with only five or six people in it, dawdled along close to the curb, shuddering as it hit potholes. Out in the middle of the boulevard, the night cars rushed along, causing a warm wind which was similar to the air coming out of the back of a vacuum cleaner. The night cars in Queens are Cadillacs, Buicks, and Oldsmobiles, with the youngest drivers in Firebirds, the tails perched high atop great racing tires, the double exhausts barking loudly each time the souped-up motor is brought above cruising speed. By day, Queens streets are filled with delivery trucks, Fords, and old Volkswagens. But the nights belong to those whose lives are poured into vehicles which expand the sense of power-importance.

In front of him, in the middle of the block, was a metal goose-necked light stanchion. It rose out of the cement curb at a spot in

16

front of an appliance store. His eyes were fixed on the lamppost as he walked. He started to veer away from it, to walk in the shadows along the building line, but he changed direction and went up to the stanchion. As he approached it, he held out his left hand, the palm flat, and then, as he walked past the metal lamppost, he slapped it.

He checked his watch; it was 10:20 p.m. Ahead, at the end of a long block of darkened stores, was a pool of light under the front awning of a discotheque. The place was windowless, with an imitation fieldstone façade. A blue neon sign said "Jinni." As the black metal front door to the club opened, sound came blaring out into the street. A young boy and girl emerged into the bright light under the awning. As Bernard Rosenfeld watched them, another cardboard match was lit in his skull. The match became wood, and suddenly the first melted wax of a flaming candle dripped down the inside of his temple. The boy had his arm around the girl's back, and the girl's shoulder-length brown hair spilled down almost to the boy's arm.

He stopped in the shadows. He watched the boy guide the girl out onto the boulevard, stop in the middle to let the traffic pass, and then go to the other side, to a Buick parked at the corner. The car was pulling away as Rosenfeld continued walking toward the discotheque entrance. The sound of laughter made him stop. He stood in the shadows again. A crowd of young people came around the corner and went into Jinni. The last one to go in was a large black-haired guy in a dark suit and a red shirt. The sidewalk under the awning was, for a moment, empty.

Kathy Grasso and Connie Bonventre walked up to Jinni, two young girls tripping into the light under the awning. Kathy went through the door first, and for a sliver of a second, Connie Bonventre was alone. As she moved to go up the stairs and into Jinni, the slit in her white skirt parted. Her leg, all the way up to the thigh, the top of the thigh, gleamed in the blue light. Her long brown hair swung across her bare shoulders. Then she was gone.

He walked through the shadows and went past the light stanchion without looking at it or reaching for it. The green plastic bag wrinkled as he reached inside his shirt and put his right hand tightly on the .44-caliber Bulldog revolver.

2

The moment Connie Bonventre stepped through the black metal front door, and paused, to taste the sounds and sights, Frank Parisi spotted her. A new face. Frank knew everyone who came to Jinni regularly. He knew the kids from Pelham Bay Park in the Bronx, and from Douglaston in Queens, and from Coney Island in Brooklyn. He could tell where they were from just by looking at them and listening to them for a little while. If a fight broke out, and one guy said to another, "Awright, Richie, I got your back," then Frank knew that the two guys, covering each other, were from Brooklyn. "If they were from Douglaston," he said, "they'd probably run. They're mamas' boys."

Jinni—the name came from Arab folklore and meant a supernatural being, either good or evil—was Frank Parisi's second home. The bartenders and the bouncer and the waitresses were like family. He came to the discotheque five nights a week, Wednesday through Sunday. Sometimes, he would stay only an hour, or two hours, and then move on to another spot, The Magic Castle, or Icarus, looking for a different beat or a different crowd or, restless, just looking to keep moving. Sometimes he would stay at Jinni all night, from ten or ten-thirty to three or three-thirty. He was one of the few customers in the place who could bridge the gap between the dancers and the drinkers.

The dancers came to dance. On weekday nights, they would drink Cokes and chew gum, and on weekends, when they had to pay a $5 cover charge, which entitled them to two free drinks, they would still chew gum and use their chits on Cokes or, perhaps, nurse a rum-and-Coke or a Seven-and-Seven through the full evening. All the dancers really cared about was a new step, a new move, a new gesture, the evolution of the Hustle; they were in constant competition, using a partner to play an individual game, each of them dreaming of being the best. Once in a while, they took a break from the dancing. They went outside, walked around the block, sucked in fresh air, smoked a joint, and then came back in and whipped through work-outs that would have wiped out O. J. Simpson. There were some guys who could go fifteen straight minutes, full out, but the most durable dancer, among the regulars at Jinni, was a girl. She could go thirty minutes and wear out three partners. She didn't do it too often because she didn't like to sweat too much.

The drinkers, the guys, came to hunt. They stood at the bar, drank up the cover charge quickly, then drank some more. They leaned toward scotch, toward real whisky. They tended to be better-looking than the dancers, and to have more money in their pockets; they didn't have to buy a new pair of shoes every week. They were also slightly older, as a group, most of them perhaps twenty-one to twenty-four, instead of nineteen to twenty-two. (In Jinni, anyone over twenty-five was conspicuous.) The drinkers were the rappers, better talkers than the dancers — not that the conversations in Jinni got very profound. Where you from? You come here often? You like to dance? Lemme light your cigarette.

The girls who hung around the bar were not exactly bashful. The girls on the dance floor might be so horny they had to go to the bath-room and wipe themselves after each number, or they might be virgins, but there were no virgins at the bar. What would you like to drink? I'd like a Slo Comfortable Screw. That was actually the name of a drink — a mixture of sloe gin and orange juice and Southern Comfort. Subtlety was not the strong suit at Jinni. "Why don't we go sit where it's comfortable?"

Jinni was divided into three separate areas. There was the dance floor — with muted, multicolored lighting, spotlights bouncing off spinning, reflecting globes, striving for a psychedelic effect — bordered by patches of a short wooden fence, something for the dancers to lean on when they needed to rest. Then there was the bar, bigger than the dance floor — and more profitable — the lighting still multicolored, but brighter; people on one side of the bar could see the people on the other, could pick out their prey. One end of the bar overlooked the dance floor. The third section, as big as the bar area, was a lounge, a collection of vinyl-covered couches and cloth hassocks. It, too, overlooked the dance floor; it was here that dancers, resting, and drinkers, hustling, collided. Magnified snapshots of the regulars at Jinni were projected on walls decorated with plastic palm fronds, soft lights created an exaggerated atmosphere of intimacy, waitresses in leotards darted about with trays of drinks, the nonstop beat of the disco music made lip-readers out of everyone, and in dark corners, on the vinyl-covered couches, guys and girls who didn't have their own apartments, who couldn't afford a motel room, got to know each other as best they could. Most of them stopped at a certain point, and moved outside to a parked car, their own or a friend's, or, if they knew the people who worked at Jinni well, went downstairs to the basement, to a well-worn cot. But some had no modest qualms. One night, Frank Parisi was sitting on one of the couches, half-drunk and half-stoned, when a girl he knew came over, deftly unzipped his fly and pulled out his cock in one quick motion, then sat down on his lap. She kept moving in time to the music. So did her boy friend, who was, at the time, busy on the dance floor.

Frank Parisi was both a dancer and a drinker, a rare breed. He was twenty-one years old, six-foot-two, slim but muscular. He had brown eyes, wavy black hair, and a small trim mustache that curled just around the edges of his upper lip and prompted girls to tell him that he looked like Mark Spitz. He had three brothers and three sisters, and his parents, even though they had come to the United States as children, were old-fashioned people. Frank's sisters were never allowed to go out on a date unless the boy first came to the father for permission, answered a battery of solemn questions — What do you do for a living? What does your father do? Where do you live? Do you want to marry my daughter? — and then brought the two sets of parents together. On the first date, the boy and girl would go out with all four parents. If they went to a movie, the girl would sit at one end, the four parents in the middle, and the boy at the far end. The system was ridiculous, in this day and age, but it worked very well. Two of Frank's sisters were already married to young men who loved them, worked hard, and earned a great deal of money.

Frank worked in a garage that was owned by one of his uncles.

Frank's father managed the place, and two of Frank's cousins worked there, too. The garage was close to an upper-middle-class residential area and catered to housewives who would bring in their own cars and their husbands' for service. Frank and his cousins catered to the housewives, too. One of his cousins loved to get laid in the backseat of a car perched on top of the hydraulic lift. The car would rock precariously, adding to the excitement. This particular cousin also liked to get laid on the floor of the garage and on the desk in the office and, if the customer was very special, in a motel room. Then he would give the customer a bill that said: Tune-up — $45; oil change — $8; gas — $13; labor — $25. The cousin did not charge for overtime.

Sometimes Frank's father would get very angry and scream, "Are we running a business or a whorehouse?" But most of the time he tolerated his nephews' and his son's adventures. After all, sons were different from daughters. Sons could do anything they wanted, as long as they showed respect. They could not bring shame into their own home because that was disrespectful. Once, the father caught Frank in the basement with a girl, both of them naked, and he whipped Frank with his belt because the son was not showing the proper respect for his own home.

Frank was sexually precocious. He got laid for the first time when he was eight or nine, he was not sure which. That was also the first time he got drunk, on beer. A girl who was sixteen took him under the bleachers at a high-school stadium and fucked him. She had no particular interest in him, but she enjoyed what they were doing very much. He had found, as he got older, that many girls had the same attitude. The girl who had sat on his exposed lap in Jinni, for instance. She would take him to her apartment and climb in bed with him and moan and say, "I love you, I love you," but Frank knew it wasn't true. "She don't love me at all," he explained to his friends. "She loves *it*. Her boy friend, she loves *him*, but she don't love *it* with *him*. It's crazy."

As soon as Frank saw Connie Bonventre walk into Jinni, he knew he wanted to fuck her. He liked her body. He liked the long slit in her white skirt. He liked the black brilliance of her Milliskin top. He liked the way she moved. He watched her walk to the bar, order a drink and begin to react to the music, and he could tell, just from the way she swayed, that she was a good dancer. He walked up to her. "Hey," he said, "didn't I dance with you one night at The Tides?"

Connie Bonventre looked puzzled, but pleased. She smiled. "No," she said. "I don't think so."

"You forgot me?" Frank said. "Jeez, I didn't think you'd forget."

He had found the ploy a successful one — his own variation on the Don't - I - Know - You - from - Somewhere theme: Don't- I- Know- You- from- Somewhere- Where- Good- Dancers- Go? Frank had no trouble coming up with the names of discotheques. He had visited almost all the best spots in Queens and Long Island in the five years since he had begun disco-dancing. He had, at first, been a very poor dancer, but one of the girls who loved *it* had volunteered, in return, to teach him how to dance. She was very patient, spent dozens of hours teaching him every step she knew, then, at a popular disco, sent him out to solo. Frank picked a girl he had been staring at for months, one of the best dancers, and asked her to join him. They went out on the dance floor and began to move. She kicked one way; he kicked the opposite way. They were supposed to be kicking the same way. What the hell's the matter with you, Frank thought. Don't you know how to dance? The pair kept getting messed up, and other dancers stopped and watched and laughed. "Hey, Frank," one of them said, "you know what?"

"What?"

"You're doing the girl's steps."

His teacher had taught him perfectly, but she had taught him her steps. He was so angry he threatened to stop fucking her, but she apologized and said she had made an honest mistake; she hadn't realized what she had done. Frank calmed down and switched the steps around and quickly became an accomplished dancer. He became sort of a hero of the local disco-culture when he improvised some new variations on the Rope, a modification of the Hustle. Girls liked dancing with him.

They also liked being with him. He was never short of cash — he had been earning good money in the garage since he was sixteen — and he always dressed well. In the winter, he wore custom-fit silk suits, Italian-made, tapered, perfect for his thirty-two-inch waist. He bought them at an import house in Brooklyn. "You are what you wear," he liked to say. Now, with summer approaching, he was wearing a $55 sport shirt and a pair of cotton slacks with a satin lining, cool enough for serious dancing. He also wore a pouch around his waist; the pouch held his money, his comb, and his grass.

"You dance real good," Frank said to Connie, as he let the crowd press him against her at the bar.

She did not retreat. She kept moving to the music, pressing back. "How can you tell?" she said.

"The way you move, that's all."

"Really?" She was moving quicker now, brushing against him, grinding into him provocatively.

The beat, gentle in the early part of the evening, was starting to grow more frenzied. In his glass booth overlooking the dance floor, Patsy, the resident disk jockey, worked easily, efficiently, blending one record into the next, switching from Phono 1 to Phono 2, mixing the music so skillfully that the dancers never missed a step and only the most sophisticated listeners could tell that one number had ended and another begun. Patsy was one of the main reasons, perhaps *the* main reason, for the success of Jinni. He had all the newest records, American groups and foreign, records that weren't stale, that hadn't been played over and over on the radio. But his style was even more important than his stock. For five hours each night, from ten to three, Patsy was like a pilot at the controls of a throbbing 747, cool, decisive, precise, surrounded by gauges and instruments that would awe and confound an outsider, his Bozak mixer, his McIntosh amplifier, his Technics turntable with the speed adjustable: Patsy could play a 33 RPM record at 32 or at 34 if he thought that off-speed might create a better feeling, a stronger mood. Patsy was a master of mood, and he was flying now — he had slipped outside for some smoke during the previous record — and he was conjuring up a fine soulful mood, turning on the dancers and the listeners and even the drinkers, everyone in the place. He was playing a number called "Bite Your Granny," by a group called Morning, Noon, and Night, and while not more than two or three people among the hundreds jamming Jinni could identify either the number or the group, they were all caught up in its beat. At the bar, the underaged blonde everyone called the Nymph sipped scotch; she had asked, as always, for Chivas, and she had received, as always, bar scotch. "Mellow," she said, sipping scotch and chewing gum at the same time. The two Vodka-and-Grapefruit-Juices — labeled by their usual drinks — sat with their tall icy glasses, one of them a skinny girl with no breasts, the other chunky with an enormous chest, both wearing V-neck blouses, one showing nothing at all, the other revealing a foot and a half of cleavage. There were ridiculous hats and necklaces that said "FOXY," and while some of the young girls looked delicious, others looked as if they had been deprived of only one thing at home: a mirror. It was a carnival of bad taste.

"Wanta dance?" said Frank Parisi.

"Sure," said Connie Bonventre, and she let Frank guide her through a sea of flesh to the dance floor. He was right; she did dance well. She knew the latest moves in the Hustle — the shorter steps, the dramatic gestures, the sharp turns. She whirled, and her white skirt flew up, and her Milliskinned bottom caught the reflections of a dozen lights, and the round, glowing surface helped Frank Parisi dance his best, more than a dance, a pantomime of sex.

For ten minutes, Frank and Connie danced, and then he cued her for a break, a few minutes, long enough for a scotch for him and a Tom Collins for her, then back on the dance floor for ten more minutes of temptation and promise. "Let's go outside," Frank suggested. "Let's get some air."

"I could use that," said Connie, and as she felt Frank's hand slide along her ass, she turned to her friend, Kathy Grasso, and said, "I'm just going to go outside for a few minutes to get a little air. I'll be right back."

Kathy smiled. "Have fun," she said.

Rosenfeld walked quickly through the blue light in front of Jinni and went into welcome shadows at the corner. He turned right onto 218th Street, going along the side of the discotheque. Halfway down the building, there was a side door, another black metal door. It was closer to the music than the front door, so close that the music thumped against the door and caused it to vibrate.

At the end of the building, there was an alley leading to an open kitchen doorway. He walked near the curb, so that he would be out of the light as he went past the alley. He could see into the kitchen. Standing in front of stacks of dirty glasses were two dishwashers, in black T-shirts, and a man who was obviously the boss, a tall guy with a nose that seemed to have been bent by a tire iron. He wore a suit with a flamboyant blue plaid.

"So?" the boss said in a loud voice to the two workers.

When neither of them answered, his voice rose. "So, I just axt you, why did you use my fuckin' name with those two girls?"

The two didn't answer.

"I told you never to use my fuckin' name!"

Bernard Rosenfeld thought of Huggy swearing at him and reached for the scab on his left elbow. He walked away from the alley and went past frame houses with large fans whirring in the bedroom windows. Summer had come early, before the end of May.

He reached the intersection of 218th Street and Forty-sixth Avenue, a block south of Northern Boulevard. One street light spread a faint glow over the intersection, a glow which could not counter the deep shadows from the trees. On one corner, the northeast corner, there was an empty lot that had been turned into a parking field for Jinni. On two other nights, Rosenfeld had spent long hours prowling about the lot, waiting for a command. But no command had come. There were too many cars, too many chances for trouble.

Now Rosenfeld looked across the street, to the far side of Forty-sixth Avenue. The Continental was there. It was there just as it had been during his earlier trips to Bayside, sitting less than one hundred feet from the corner, parked directly in front of a house, swallowed in a blot of darkness created by two huge maples. He knew they would be in and out of the car all night; he had stood and watched them. Man and woman. Count the heads in the car. Two heads. Look away and back and count the heads again. One head. Watching this last week, he had become so distressed — one hand pulling at his face, one going inside his pants to squeeze his cock — he had had to leave.

Tonight, he told himself, tonight he would do it, he would end this long, terrible part of his life. Tonight he would be happy. He would do as he was told. The dog's hot red liquid eyes became a pilot light in his head again. He resumed walking. Down at the next corner, Forty-seventh Avenue, two blocks south of Northern Boulevard, he cut in between a tree and the hedges of a corner house and turned right. He remembered that the sidewalk flagstone would end five or six yards up and that he would be on a simple dirt path for a while. "Don't trip," he told himself. His feet, unsurprised, came down on the dirt. It was as easy in the dark as in the daylight. He strode to the next corner. As he crossed it, he looked up toward Northern Boulevard. A few cars were going by. Then he continued along Forty-seventh Avenue until he was in front of a house with low pine bushes, which gave off a sweet, wintry smell. The cream-and-black Galaxie was parked at this spot.

He had time to spare, and he spent it by driving. He remained on side streets, going up and down rows of sleeping one-family houses. He had become familiar with most of the side streets in this part of Queens. He felt they offered him protection. Police cars on a run always use main thoroughfares. To rush down a side street, where the car must slow at each corner, is too dangerous and takes too long.

As it was, Rosenfeld knew, the police had trouble getting to a place quickly. He knew that the police department always claimed that it would react to an emergency call in three minutes. But he also knew that it usually took much longer than that for the police to respond. When he was an auxiliary policeman in the Bronx, he used to listen to the lectures about response and then he would go to a phone booth and dial the 911 emergency number. Several times, particularly after midnight, the lines had been so overloaded with calls that a recorded voice had said to him, airline-reservation style, that the call was being held electronically and would be picked up by the first available police-communications person. He then had waited a minute, often longer, before the call had been answered. Several other times, it had taken as many as sixteen rings to get any answer at all from 911. In actual time, he knew, sixteen rings comes to one minute and fifty-two seconds. When he was an auxiliary policeman, he did not like it to take so long.

He drove the streets with the radio beating into his ear and with the dog watching him. He knew the dog could see him, see him right now. The dog would be inside Sam Thornton's house by now, but that didn't matter. The dog could still see Bernard. See him and reach out and touch him if he wanted to. Bernard's body came forward into the steering wheel as he felt the dog's paws on his back.

He took Northern Boulevard out to 255th Street, almost at the Nassau County Line. He was at a red light in front of a bank, and he stared out the passenger window at a metal light stanchion. Something crept across his stomach. He held his left hand to his mouth. His teeth clamped down on his index finger. He bit harder. The thing crawling across his stomach grew larger. He looked away from the light stanchion. His eyes were pulled back to it. He bit into the finger so hard that his hand shook. He pulled the finger out of his mouth and opened the car door and slid out and walked up to the light stanchion, his left hand out, the palm flat. As he walked past the stanchion, the hand slapped it.

He turned around and came back to his Galaxie and drove up to Jinni, turned into 218th Street, passed the parked Continental, and then turned onto the side street, Forty-seventh Avenue, and again parked in front of the house with the pine bushes. It was a good sign, the parking place still being there.

"Thank you, Sam," he said. He got out of the car carrying the green plastic bag. The bag had bunched up by now, revealing the brown wooden handle of the .44-caliber Bulldog revolver.

"Sam the Terrible," he said softly. "I'm your creation, and I'm going to do my job."

He retraced the route he had walked an hour earlier. When he came around the corner and started along the building, the owner and his help had resumed their argument in the kitchen.

"I told you I want to know, you know?" the owner, the one in the plaid suit, said.

"I told you already," the other voice said.

"Told me what?" the owner fired back.

"I said I told you."

"You told me bullshit!"

He walked diagonally away from the sound of the voices, toward the parking lot. In the lot, he stood between a couple of cars. He liked the idea of standing there, camouflaged by the night, further concealed by the cars. From that spot, he could look across the hood of a car, a black Oldsmobile, and see the start of the alley leading to the kitchen and also part of the lighted sidewalk in front of Jinni. When he turned and looked the other way down the block that ran from Forty-sixth Avenue to Forty-seventh Avenue, he saw that there were four cars parked diagonally across from him. The cars probably belonged to people in Jinni; those who lived in the neighborhood inched their cars up the narrow driveways between houses and into wooden garages each night. As he stared at the cars, his hands tightened on the wooden handle of the .44.

Now he looked at the Continental, which was just across Forty-sixth Avenue, on the same side of the street as he was, perhaps forty yards away. One hand came off the handle of his gun and went to the scab on his left elbow. He forced the hand to go back to the gun handle. To get breath, he opened his mouth and pulled in the night air. Inside him, the dog howled, howled so loudly that, for a moment, Bernard Rosenfeld closed his eyes against the noise.

Bobby Yankosek and his girl friend, Ginny, were walking down the block, young people together, boy and girl holding hands. When the two of them stepped off the sidewalk and began crossing the street toward the parking lot, Rosenfeld walked out of the lot and went across Forty-sixth Avenue. When he glanced back, he saw that the boy and the girl were heading for the Continental. Rosenfeld moved away, went three-quarters of the way down the street, and stopped in front of a silent house that had yellow aluminum siding. He watched as Bobby and the girl parted, Bobby staying in the street and approaching the driver's side of the Continental and the girl walking to the passenger's side, the side against the curb. Rosenfeld's ears hummed as he watched the couple climb into the car. The girl's hand brushed at her skirt as she slipped in.

The plastic bag crackled as he gripped it tighter. Once the two young people were inside the car, girl on the sidewalk side, girl with blood, he began padding up the sidewalk toward the Continental.

"Scumbag!"

The owner and one of the workers were out on the sidewalk now. The owner had the young guy by the front of the black T-shirt. The owner's open hand came down hard on top of the young guy's head.

"I told you —" the young guy wailed.

"You told me bullshit!" The owner's hand rose and came down again. The slapping noise could be heard up and down the block.

"Shit!" the young guy shouted. He was almost crying. "You're shit!"

This produced another loud slap. "Say it again, motherfucker." Another slap. "I said, say it the fuck again."

Rosenfeld stood motionless as this went on. Minutes went by while the argument rose to shrieks and then subsided into indecipherable babble. A furnace door opened inside his temple and there was complete heat. Orange and red flames whipped about, and in the center of the flames was the dog, hot red liquid eyes, and he howled for blood.

Up the street, the owner swung once more at the young guy, who broke away, holding the side of his head, and began running, right up to where Bernard Rosenfeld was standing, waiting, fighting for breath. Rosenfeld saw the young guy heading straight for him.

Rosenfeld pivoted and walked across the street and walked away, back down toward Forty-seventh Avenue. He turned at the corner and heard the young guy go padding by him, racing and panting.

The furnace door was closed and the heat was subsiding. But still the dog howled.

"I couldn't," he said to the dog.

The howl was louder now.

"I said I couldn't. But I will. I will."

And now he could see the dog roaming the inside of his head, the hot red liquid eyes and the open mouth with sweating red and yellow pus teeth, and now the eyes narrowed, and the dog raised his head and his cry became a shrill compelling call for blood.

As Frank Parisi guided Connie Bonventre away from the dance floor, toward the black metal door at the front of Jinni, a guy standing at the bar reached out and touched Connie's arm. "I could watch you dance all night," he said, with a half-smile, and then he leaned forward and kissed her on the cheek.

Frank saw the move and turned on the guy. "Hey, you crazy?" Frank said. "Leave her alone."

The guy backed away, retreating against the bar. He was obviously older than most of the customers, perhaps twenty-nine or thirty, and he had deep, narrow eyes and thin eyebrows. His hair was wavy, almost curly, and his lips soft, almost feminine. Frank had never seen him in Jinni before.

"A creep," Frank said, and Connie shivered and nodded.

Just before they reached the front door, Frank stopped at a small table where each new arrival had to purchase two drink tickets for $5. Jess DeStefano, the muscular bouncer, an Italian Arnold Schwarzenegger, was standing next to the table. He kept order just by standing there.

"Hey, Jess," Frank said, "can I use your car a few minutes?"

"To drive?" Jess said. "Or to sit in?"

"Sit."

Jess nodded. "Bobby's out there now," he said, "but when he gets out, it's yours." He looked at his watch. "It's ten after twelve. It's yours till one. I won't send nobody else out."

The bouncer's car, a silver Continental Mark IV, was community property, a motel room on wheels. Jess DeStefano was only nineteen years old; he was the strongest teenager in Queens, and he was also the friendliest — to his friends. He could not do enough for them, and if they wanted to use his car while he was busy keeping the peace in Jinni, they were certainly welcome to it. Jess himself did not smoke or drink or use drugs or care very much about girls. He preferred pumping iron. He was not the least bit jealous of his friends who borrowed his car for blow-jobs, for smoking grass, and for snorting coke.

"You do coke?" Frank Parisi asked Connie Bonventre as they emerged from Jinni and paused, for a moment, under the club's blue neon sign.

"No," she said. "It scares me."

"Smoke?"

"Sometimes."

"Hey, how old are you anyway?"

"Eighteen . . . *almost* eighteen."

Frank whistled. "Seventeen," he said. "I never would've known. I thought you were, you know, older. Twenty, twenty-one."

Connie took the remark as it was meant, as a compliment.

"My friend's car's parked around the corner," Frank said. "We could go sit there, you know, and smoke a joint. I don't have my own car. They took away my license for speeding."

"What kind of car do you have?"

"Foreign car."

"What kind?"

"Porsche," Frank said, hanging his head. "I don't like to say it 'cause, you know, it sounds like bullshit. I mean, guys are always saying, 'I'm using my friend's Volkswagen 'cause my Ferrari's being repaired,' and they're full of shit, you know. But, yeah, I do have a Porsche, only it's sitting in the garage and I'm here."

Frank walked Connie toward Jess's Continental, and as they approached the parked car, they could see two heads above the dashboard in the front seat. Then they could see only one head. Frank took Connie's hand and led her across the street. "We'll get a little more air," he said. They walked all the way around the block, past Jinni once more, then turned down the side street, approaching the Continental just as two people were getting out. "How ya doing, Bobby?" Frank said, and Bobby Yankosek grinned and said, 'I'm stoned, good and stoned," and then his smile disappeared and he said, "Hey, some weird-looking guy stuck his face up against the window of the car a few minutes ago. Scared the shit out of me."

"What'd he look like?"

"I don't know. Scary."

"Older guy?"

"Yeah. Thirty, maybe."

"I think I saw him in the club. Just a creep."

Bobby and his girl floated away, and Frank politely held the passenger door of the Continental open for Connie. He waited till she had slid inside, then closed the door behind her. He walked to the driver's side, and climbed in behind the wheel. He switched on the overhead light, found the cigarette lighter and pushed it in. Then he turned out the overhead light, took a joint out of his pouch, lit it with the lighter — carefully, to avoid wasting too much — then inhaled deeply, drawing in air and smoke at the same time. "Want a hit?" he said, and as Connie nodded, he handed the joint to her. As she held it to her mouth, tightening her lips on the end, Frank's hand fell gently to her thigh. He slid his hand down, softly, and she turned to him, smiling.

The first two steps had been slow. But then he had his body in rhythm and he walked quickly, watching those two heads through the back window of the car, the inside of his own head afire, the dog excited now, yipping and howling, unable to stand still, and he stepped around the maple trees and saw them right in front of him, the back of that lovely head, all that long brown hair, framed by the car window, and the gun, freed from the green plastic bag, came straight out and his knees broke and brought his body into a half-crouch, brought it level with the passenger window, and he exhaled and, with only his right hand on the gun, pulled the trigger and the noise of the gunshot overrode the howling of the dog. The car window exploded into ocean foam. He could not see through the foam. He concentrated on looking through the bullet hole in the window. Looking right at the brown hair. Again, the gun roared and jerked upward and took his hand to the left. He brought it down, aimed at the holes in the windows and fired again. The wooden handle of the gun had a hump to it that made it too big to hold easily, and this time the gun nearly

31

jumped out of his hand. His fingers desperately gripped the gun and he fired at the window again and again, emptying the last two bullets in the .44, and then he was in terror that he had missed. But now he saw the blood streaming out of the brown hair, blood that Sam could drink, and the dog was walking away, walking out of his mind and back inside Sam Thornton's house, and Rosenfeld spun from the car and started to run down the block.

The plastic bag, discarded, fluttered to the ground as he was running. Running, running, running in the night with his right hand stuffing the gun into the pocket of his jeans. He cut the corner onto Forty-seventh Avenue and thought automatically about the end of the pavement. His foot was true as it hit the dirt, and he slowed down now, and moved without noise down the block, crossed the street, and went halfway down the next block. He came to his car. A man was getting out of a car directly across the street. The man had his back to him. The man shut the car door. He tugged on the handle. Something was wrong. The man, still with his back to Rosenfeld, opened the car door again and toyed with the inside lock. He slammed the door again. Satisfied, the man walked up to a nearby house and went inside without looking around. Rosenfeld waited in the winter-sweet smell of the pine bushes, then stepped out, slid into his car, and started off. He drove straight for several blocks, made a right turn and was on the service road to the Clearview Expressway. At Northern Boulevard, the maze of lights was red. He stopped and waited for the light to turn green. He did not believe in going through red lights. Then he took the ramp running to the expressway and followed it to the Throgs Neck Bridge. He had done his job. He had gotten blood for Sam. Now he was hungry for eggs and French fries in a diner on South Broadway in Yonkers.

He wished that he were home watching a movie on television. Watching a movie and waiting for his son, James, to come home with the car. Nineteen years old and he can't go anyplace without a car, Dom Carillo thought; freaking kids in their cars, you stay up all night worrying about them.

A nudge broke his thoughts. "Hear that?" John Maloney said. Maloney, tall and straight-faced, was the chief of detectives.

Carillo looked up. The entire room full of men, two hundred of them, was laughing. At the front of the room, a pink-faced man, eyelids half shut, expanded in the laughter.

"He's something," Maloney said to Carillo.

"Do I know it," Carillo said. He wondered what movie was on television tonight.

At the microphone, the pink-faced man, Jack Leahy, chief of the Retired Detectives Association, picked up his subject again: "When the Irish first got here, they got all their power from the saloon owners. Anytime you had a problem, where did you go? Right to the saloon owner. He took care of it. He was the one who went to the politicians for you. Now the Italians, they done it a different way. They done it with bookmakers."

Maloney chuckled and clapped Carillo on the shoulder.

"Hey," Carillo said, "do I detect a note of bigotry here?"

"Oh, come on," Maloney said. "It's not bigotry. It's the truth." Maloney began to laugh loudly.

Carillo made a sound analogous to a laugh. As he forced this out, he looked down at the tablecloth and wondered if getting ahead was a personal expenditure he could still afford: How many asses do you kiss before you become a punk?

Leahy rambled on. "And as I look around me tonight and I see the man you're honoring, Eugene Murphy, I remember back to Manhattan South. He wasn't called Eugene then. He was called 'Wall Locker' Murphy. Yup, that's right, that was his name. It seems he had a certain form he followed when he questioned an alleged perpetrator. His own lie-detector system. The Wall Locker. He would take the guy and stuff him into this locker he had out in the hallway. Then Murphy would slam the door and, goodness me, the wall locker would tip over and go down the flight of stairs to the basement."

A voice boomed out from the back of the room. "Murphy!"

"Yes?"

"Just in case they change the rules, do you still have the wall locker around?"

A big cheer went up. John Maloney, shaking with laughter, reached for the bottle of Red Label on the table. "Oh, boy?" he called out to a waiter. "Be a good fella and get us some ice, will you?"

Carillo shifted about in his seat. Here comes the sloppy part of the night, he reminded himself. Whisky and bullshit. He looked across the room. Ralph Dattolico, from Brooklyn, was sitting there equally bored. In a department that has become fifty percent Italian, the Irish still hold on to the top jobs, as if by birthright. An Italian practically has to qualify for pope before the Irish police bosses give him anything. Carillo's rank, deputy inspector, was only a step above captain. Everything in the department up to and including captain is civil service, with promotions determined by exams. The appointed spots above that are usually as political as the Dublin Dail. It took two years of haranguing by the Columbian Association, the Italian-American group on the force, to budge the Irish commissioner into naming Carillo a deputy inspector.

"Have a taste," Maloney said to him. He poured a considerable amount of whisky into Carillo's glass. Carillo stared at it. He knew he was safer with heroin than he was with a drink this big at this hour, a quarter to one. He shrugged and was going to pick up the glass when a high whine came from the beeper on his belt. The first thing he thought of was his son, James, in the car. The second thought was that the call had come just in time. The last thing that occurred to him, as he got up from the table, was murder.

"What can you do?" he said to Maloney.

Maloney waved him off and lumbered along the wall toward the table where Wall Locker Murphy, the guest of honor, sat.

Dominick Carillo, deputy inspector of detectives, the top man in Queens Homicide, walked across the dance floor and slipped out of the room. In the hallway, waiters were walking in and out of the other catering rooms in the building, Antun's Catering on Springfield Boulevard in Queens Village. A fountain sat in the center of a large circular lobby. Two girls in pastel dresses sat on the edge of the fountain and looked at a bouquet of flowers one of them held.

"Bored?" Carillo said.

"No, gee, it's been a terrific wedding," one of them said.

"We're just planning what comes next tonight," the one with her said. They both giggled with meaning.

Carillo walked into the office and nodded to the owner's son, who was tabulating a stack of bar checks. Carillo picked up the phone and called his office.

"Fifteenth Homicide Division, Detective Clark," the voice on the other end said.

"Inspector Carillo."

"Hey, Inspector. How's the racket going? I'll bet you it's a good —"

"You called?" Carillo said.

"Yeah, well, we got two people shot. Man and a woman. In a car. Northern Boulevard and 218th Street. Actually 218th and Forty-sixth Avenue."

"When was this?"

"We got the call, what, ten, fifteen minutes ago?"

"I'll take a run over," Carillo said.

As he walked out of the catering hall to his car, Carillo had both hands on top of his head, patting his short, black hair. If you looked closely, the hair was more than short; it was at the brink of sparseness. Mornings, Carillo would look down and see black hair running in the water on the shower floor. The rest of the day, rather than tug at an ear or scratch the chin, his hands were at his hair, trying to pat it down, to keep it firmly planted in his head.

Man and woman in a car, he said to himself. Guy with somebody else's wife. Or a narcotics beef. Either one. Probably narcotics. The wages of sin. At least, he reminded himself, the call wasn't about his son up against a telephone pole somewhere. That goddamn kid and his cars. Carillo got into his gray 1974 Impala and drove down an avenue for a couple of minutes and then turned onto the Clearview Expressway. He was at the southern end of it. He had a quick run up to Northern Boulevard.

"Inspector!"

"Uh huh."

"Right around the corner, Inspector."

Carillo stood under the awning at Jinni carefully pinning his gold badge onto the lapel of his tan suit, the best suit he had, $155 on sale at Barney's. He intended to keep it in good condition. The last suit he bought, a gray pinstripe, lasted exactly three nights. He ripped the elbow of the jacket on a file cabinet somebody had left open in the office. Some Irish slob bastard just left it open.

At first, standing under the Jinni awning, Carillo appeared older than his forty-three years. Large, soft-brown eyes had deep smudges under them. Pouches, actually. They had been there since he was a kid; sometimes in high school, the teachers thought he was somebody's parent. The Roman nose had a bump which came from a thrown rock rather than from heredity. Carillo was six-foot-two and carried 210 pounds on a frame that had the symmetry of somebody far lighter, of a person weighing perhaps 175 pounds. But a bulge at the beltline, which was particularly noticeable when the jacket was unbuttoned, showed that Carillo could use some exercise and diet. The front had the beginnings of true middle age.

Still, when he finished pinning on the badge and he looked at the officer and said thank you with a broad, warm smile, years fell from his face.

When Carillo saw television lights on the car under the maple trees, his lips pursed in distaste. A rope was strung across the street with a sign on it saying, "Keep Out! Crime Scene." The rope, stretched between telephone poles, should have prevented anybody from walking to the car. But here, inside the rope, was a television crew, poking lights and cameras almost into the car itself.

Carillo walked up to a squad car which was parked with its roof light twirling. A patrolman was at the wheel.

"Officer."

"Yessir."

"I want everybody who is not Police Department out of that area immediately."

"The television, too?"

"The television first."

Carillo waited by the rope until the television crew and a couple of newspaper reporters and spectators were cleared off the street. Then he stepped over the rope and walked up to the car. It was surrounded by uniformed policemen and a couple of detectives. A cop opened the door on the driver's side. Carillo looked at the cop's hand on the door handle. *He knocks out the door on me.*

He tapped the patrolman on the back.

"Yessir?"

"What are you doing here?" Carillo said.

"There was two people in here and —"

"I know that. I asked what you were doing here."

"Takin' a look to see if the —"

"Are you with the Homicide Division?" Carillo said.

"No."

"Then I'm sure there are some worthwhile things for you to do around here. Such as going up to Northern Boulevard and not allowing any cars to come onto this street for any reason. We'll have a lot of spectators around here and I don't want to be bothered with them. Thank you, Officer."

The patrolman, deprived of the chance to play cop, walked away. Carillo looked into the car on the driver's side. The front seat was being taken apart by a homicide detective, Walter Gallagher. He was looking for slugs. The red-vinyl seat covering was wet with blood. Gallagher, who was in a short-sleeved sport shirt, had blood halfway up his arm. The dashboard looked as if somebody had splashed a pail of blood onto it. The crevices around the dials and the chrome handle of the cigarette lighter all glistened with blood.

A younger detective, his face covered with freckles, came over to Carillo. He was Johnny Dwyer of the Fifteenth Homicide Division.

"Kids," Dwyer said.

"How young?" said Carillo.

"They say the boy's twenty-one, the girl's a little younger. Maybe eighteen. Apparently they came out of the discotheque a little after midnight. Somebody back there in the kitchen says he thinks he heard shots fired at about that time. He's not sure. Says he looked out and saw nothing. A guy going to his car found them. About twelve-twenty. They took them down to Flushing Hospital."

"Who's down there?" Carillo asked.

"You mean at the hospital?" Dwyer said.

"Yeah, the hospital."

"Well, we were just —"

"You mean you don't have anybody down there trying to interview them?" The force in Carillo's voice caused the others around the car to look at him.

"We will right now," Dwyer said.

Carillo's face became expressionless, which was how he showed great anger. There were two things Carillo insisted upon: that the scene of the crime be untouched and that a detective get to the hospital and interview the victims right away, in the emergency room. Once, he had these rules pasted on the office wall, and then he had them removed after too many of the men complained about being too experienced for such high-school treatment. Now, Carillo told himself, the signs were going up again.

The patrolmen on the scene were excited. This was a big event in their business, a double shooting, and they wanted to be at the center of whatever was going on. In the meantime, they touched things, stepped on things, and failed to keep outsiders from stomping around the scene. Carillo's detectives had done nothing to prevent this tonight. His stomach tightened.

The hospital made him more furious. How many times had he said it? A detective had to go into the emergency room and interview the victim. Right in the emergency room, right at the point when they are through working on the victim for a moment, and they're waiting to take him up to surgery. A detective with balls has to walk in. He has to know that the nurse is right when she tells him, "No one can speak to this patient." He has to know he is wrong, and he still has to walk by her and go up to the patient and lean over and say, "Who did it?" Either you do it then or you probably never do it. If the doctors get him out of there, the detective won't see the victim for days, if ever. At best, after an operation and anesthesia, who knows what the victim will remember? Or care to remember? For the eleven months that Carillo had run the Fifteenth Homicide Division, he had preached these rules. Apparently, nobody had listened.

Carillo moved around the car. The smashed window on the passenger's side disturbed him. It reminded him of auto accidents. His entire life, it seemed, from patrolman on up, had been spent looking at these foamed windows which so often meant death. Goddamn kid driving his car, driving me crazy, he thought. Carillo counted the heads around the car. Two detectives and three patrolmen still standing there and looking at the car as if it were a ball game.

"How many men do you have out canvassing for witnesses?" Carillo asked Dwyer.

"Well, let's see. We have —"

"There's five more for you right there," Carillo said, pointing to the cluster around the car.

A station wagon from the Forensics Division pulled up. Four detectives in sport shirts tumbled out, carrying black cases. They took over the job of scouring the car for fingerprints and any scraps of anything that would constitute first a clue and later, perhaps, evidence. Carillo grunted. At least this part was being taken care of properly.

Carillo walked over to Dwyer. "What is it, narcotics?"

Dwyer shook his head. "The owner inside says no. They were just two kids. He doesn't even think they knew each other before tonight. He knew the boy, not the girl. They just came out here to use the car. The car belongs to the bouncer. He lets kids use his car. They come out here for purposes of smoking marijuana, I guess."

"And for blow-jobs," Carillo said.

"Well, I guess so," Dwyer said.

"Where's the owner?" Carillo asked.

"Up in the place. Fellow by the name of Billy Lee. He's half-connected to the wops —" Dwyer's lips stopped moving as he realized what he had just done. Carillo's face became expressionless. Then he walked away without speaking.

The discotheque was empty inside. The ceiling lights were on, harsh unshaded lights to help the kitchen workers, who were cleaning up the place. The blue carpeting was covered with cigarette butts and crumpled bar napkins. The rectangular bar was covered with glasses that had napkins and cigarette butts stuffed into them. A young guy in a black T-shirt was picking up glasses and putting them into a rack under the bar. Carillo moved his hand back and forth, clearing a space in the rubble.

"I will," he said to the kid behind the bar.

The kid behind the bar kept putting glasses into the sink.

"I said I will," Carillo said.

The owner came out from the back. "Stevie, will you give the man what he wants?" he said, in an annoyed voice.

A big hand came out to Carillo. "I'm Billy Lee, I got the joint. How are you?"

Carillo did not take the hand. "I'll have a Rémy Martin," he told the bartender.

"Something to keep the heart pumpin'," Lee said.

"It's past my bedtime, something better keep my eyes open," Carillo said.

"I'd have one with you," Lee said, "but my stomach's too jumpy. Geez, what a night we was havin'! Couldn't fuckin' get in the front door. Now, bang! They cleared out of here so fast."

"What was it about?" Carillo asked.

Lee waved a hand at Dwyer, who was using a phone at the end of the bar. "I was just tellin' him, two legitimate kids."

"Sure they were legitimate?" Carillo said.

"Yep."

"Tell me how you know they were legitimate."

Lee's head came closer to Carillo's. "I'm talking to you, Inspector?"

"All right."

"Believe me, when I tell you there was no connections, I mean, that's the truth."

"How do you know?" Carillo asked.

39

Lee rolled his head from side to side. "Because I'm with the outfit and I'd know."

"All right," Carillo said. He swallowed most of the brandy. He held the glass up and looked at it.

"Somebody's boy friend get mad?"

"I told him what my doorman says," Lee said, pointing to Dwyer again.

"What does your doorman say?"

"He says they just met each other tonight. Two legitimate kids. The one kid comes from Howard Beach. Legitimate kid, works for a living. The girl come here from the Bronx with her girl friend."

"What were they doing in the car?" Carillo said.

"Doing what they had to do."

"That's all?"

"What else could there be when you're nineteen, twenty? Hey, Inspector, you know. How much wrong could you do when you're only twenty?"

He's right, Carillo thought. He finished the brandy and looked past Lee and began telling Detective Gallagher to make up a master list of witnesses, people in the neighborhood, people awakened by shots, and have it ready for him by the time they got back to the office. Carillo then looked at his glass and said nothing. It was his way of dismissing Lee. Carillo never thought these people deserved even the courtesy of hello and good-bye.

It was a half hour later, out on the street, when Detective Dwyer came up to Carillo.

"The girl died," he said.

Carillo was expressionless.

"The boy will be all right. He's in shock now, a bullet in his thigh. But he'll be all right."

"Did we talk to either of them?" Carillo asked.

"No," Dwyer said. "But we'll have the boy soon. In an hour maybe."

Detective Gallagher walked up. "You know how I feel about this?" Gallagher said. "I got a daughter this age. I mean, isn't this a lousy shame?"

"It's worse than that," Carillo said. "Nobody was at the hospital to talk to her."

3

As soon as he woke up, Danny Cahill reached for the phone. He had to work, and the idea of it made him feel exhausted. All day long, and particularly at night over a drink, Danny Cahill told everybody who would listen, himself first, how good he was. But each morning when he woke up, his first thoughts were how long it would take him to write his column for the New York *Dispatch*, four to five hours on a typewriter, and how hard it was to think of words and put them into a line. If you're so good, Cahill always asked himself in the mornings, then why does it take you so long to do? The answer was obvious: he was not as good as he boasted. Cahill never faced this answer. When he came to it, as he had on this morning, he immediately would reach for the phone and start talking to people, as he did now.

"What's doin'?" he said when a harried voice, that of Ben Rubin, a judge, answered.

"I'm shaving," Rubin said.

"So what do I care?" Cahill said.

"I do, and therefore I'm going to hang up and go back to shaving," Rubin said.

"How's Sara?" Cahill asked. He knew his market: Rubin began talking. Rubin, fifty-five, was a bachelor. For several years he had been taking out a thirty-two-year-old divorcée. Rubin could talk of nothing else. Now, having been asked the question, he forgot about shaving and spoke for ten minutes about Sara.

"A judge," Rubin concluded, "I'll tell you what kind of decisions I

41

have to make. The only decision I am going to make today is whether or not I should kill this Sara."

"Don't worry about it," Cahill said.

"What do you mean, 'Don't worry'? This woman is killing me."

"Ben, she's too young for an old guy like you," Cahill said. "Let's be truthful here. You're an old guy now. In five years, you'll be sixty. You know what she'll be? Thirty-seven. How the hell would that work?"

"The age has nothing to do with it," Ben said.

"Yes it does. Pretty soon you'll be too old to have children," Cahill said.

"Why, you son of a bitch," Rubin snapped.

"Ben, I got to get off. I have to help out with the kids," Cahill said. "I got a nice large family. Be around me when I'm an old man."

Cahill hung up elated. He had driven truth from his mind, always a victory, and replaced it with that warm feeling which comes with doing well at another's expense. If somebody were to do this to Cahill, if somebody were to start the day by telling Cahill that he has too much love of seeing others fail to be a good fellow, Cahill would require medication. Take it, he could not.

He called to one of his six children, "You get me the freakin' paper yet?"

"Yes," replied Patrick, the fourteen-year-old. Patrick was lying. He had not gotten the paper yet. He was, naturally, his father's favorite. "You go get it," Patrick told his nine-year-old brother.

"Bring it up to the bedroom, Patrick," Cahill shouted.

"Sure. In a minute."

Cahill always insisted upon reading a late edition of the *Dispatch*. He did not like to read an early edition, because in the early editions the printers murdered him. His column came out as a festival of typographical errors. He knew this was no accident. He had been having trouble with printers for a long time. Early in his career as a columnist, when he was working for the New York *Herald Tribune* and the Typographers' Union was threatening a strike, Cahill had written an unusually vicious column about the printers and their leader, a man named Bertram Powers. From then on, the ancient elevators that bounced between the city room and the composing room were always filled with graffiti about Cahill. And typos occurred in his column with far greater frequency than, say, in the column of the sportswriter who gave the printers fistfuls of free baseball tickets.

Cahill prayed each night for the arrival of total automation in the composing room. And, to back up the prayers, he sent bottles of scotch to the editors who read through the first edition, caught the errors in his column, and corrected them.

"Here's the paper," announced Patrick a few minutes later. "I went to get it so early this morning I almost couldn't remember where I'd put it."

"God bless," said Cahill.

The columnist leaned back against his pillows. He filled most of a double bed. His hair was at war with itself, a miniature race riot, black versus gray, evenly matched, every individual strand running off in its own direction. His brown eyes were, by now, permanently bloodshot; he looked like he had a hangover even when he'd gone a week or two weeks, as he sometimes did, without a drink. He had given up smoking cigarettes many years earlier, but he had retained his cough. He smoked cigars now — short, square foreign cigars called Villigers. At forty-six, his face was still — remarkably — cherubic, but the rest of his body had grown up. It was hard to believe, glancing at his belly, that he had once played football in high school, and boxed as an amateur, but it was much harder to believe that he still swam a mile or more almost every day of his life.

For a quarter of a century, he had been earning a living with his hands — with his typing fingers — and with his ear and his instinct for the essence of a story and his gift for getting people to sound in print as they sound in person. But he was able to keep this ability off balance by thinking about it too much. The greater he told himself he was, the more unsure he was of what he could do.

Cahill grew up in a middle-class section of Queens, but he made it sound as if it were a spawning ground for Murder, Inc. He boasted that, as a teenager, he had caddied for Frank Costello, the gangster. "Best loop I ever had," said Cahill. "Gave me fifty bucks to take my girl to the junior prom." Actually, late one afternoon, he had shagged golf balls for two men practicing their irons. At the end of the hour, the caddy master gave Cahill an extra $5. Cahill ran to a bar where he waited for the bus home and he began drinking 10-cent beers with his money. The caddy master came in and told Cahill that Costello was one of the men who had been hitting the iron shots. The first chance Cahill had, when he was older and knew there was no caddy master around to contradict him, he began to tell the story in the $50 version.

43

Cahill did not like to admit that he had attended college for a year, Long Island University, or that his mother had been a high-school English teacher. He insisted that he had no knowledge of grammar — "I ain't very smart" — and he made certain that all of his writing sounded as if it were coming from the side of his mouth. Once, in *Newsweek* magazine, it said that Cahill's work had a touch of Runyon, a touch of Hemingway, and a touch of the poet. Cahill loved it. "Next to me, everybody else is nothing," he announced at the bar.

But the morning did not go away. Once, with a bad hangover causing the doubts to be greater, Cahill comforted himself by saying that no matter what he had or did not have, he always could work hard enough to communicate. He could communicate to the educated and the uneducated, the rich and the poor, the black and the white. He got through. He made people notice him and react to him.

"What the fuck is this?" he said, leafing through the main section of the *Dispatch*. "They got me buried back on page four. What the fuck happened? Carter quit? The Pope die?"

He turned to page three, and at the top of the page, he saw the headline: COUPLE SHOT IN PARKED CAR — GIRL DIES.

He read the story:

A man crept up to a parked car in Bayside, Queens, shortly after midnight this morning and fired four shots, killing an attractive teenager and wounding her male companion.

The assailant fled into the darkness without saying a word.

Police said that Connie Bonventre, 17, of 5734 Westervelt Avenue, the Bronx, was killed when the first bullet, fired at close range, crashed through the window on the passenger's side and struck her in the back of the head.

A second bullet entered the thigh of Frank Parisi, 21, of Howard Beach, Queens, who was sitting in the driver's seat. One slug ricocheted off the door. The fourth shot was found lodged in the front seat.

Parisi and Miss Bonventre had been dancing a few minutes earlier in Jinni, a discotheque on Northern Boulevard. They had just sat down in a car that belonged to Jess DeStefano, an employee of the discotheque.

Miss Bonventre, a senior at Sacred Heart Academy in the Bronx, came to the Queens discotheque with a friend, Kathy Grasso. The

44

two girls were celebrating Miss Bonventre's admission to New York University.

Detectives said they believed that the murder weapon was a .45-caliber automatic, but were not able to confirm this, pending ballistics tests. . . .

Cahill threw down the paper. "Who cares?" he said. "Some two-bit murder in Queens, and they play it over me. They got to be crazy. Some cunt blown away by an ex-boy friend. Happens every night."

He was good and angry. He was in perfect shape to write his column.

Father Joseph Bonventre, who was twenty-nine, sighed. He had just gotten his mother, Gina Bonventre, calmed enough to sit erectly when a young girl, faltering, handkerchief to mouth, hands trembling, stepped into the chapel through a side entrance. When the girl's eyes focused on Connie Bonventre's wax face in the casket, the girl screamed through the handkerchief.

The first of us to die always leaves a glimpse of life with no sun.

A low growl sounded within Gina Bonventre. Her son, sitting next to her, took her hand. The hand was cold and shaking.

"All right," Father Joseph said.

His mother's growl began to ascend in a spiral: from a groan to a moan, and the moan rose until it was vibrating in the mother's nostrils and she opened her mouth and screamed. Her head flopped to one side. Her other son, Anthony, who was twenty-three, ran from the side of the room and fell on his knees in front of her.

Father Joseph Bonventre stood up and held his mother's face between his hands so the head would not droop and she would be looking at him.

"Ma," he whispered.

The eyes were shut as the mother cried that her daughter had been taken from her.

"Ma!" Father Joseph said loudly.

The eyes opened. They were wet and brown and terrified and frightening. A thousand years of Sicilian hurt and anger raged across the corneas.

Father Joseph Bonventre was numb. He wanted to mourn, he

45

wanted to smash his fist into the wall and cry for the death of the person who had murdered his sister. But he knew that his role had to be different. He had for months been in turmoil over the Catholic priesthood and its celibacy. But now he had to rely on everything his religion ever had taught. For it was his job to help his mother.

"Ma, we have to think of something," he said. "We are the ones *she* should pray for. Where she is, she's safe and happy. Where we are, we're unsafe and sad. She is in so much a better place. Please, Ma, be happy. Connie is in heaven."

"Who did it?" Gina said.

"Ma, think of Connie and pray that she prays for us."

"Who did it?" Gina screamed.

This brought Sal Bonventre limping hurriedly back to his seat alongside her. He had been outside having his first cigarette since the funeral chapel opened at one in the afternoon.

"Mother," he said to her.

"I'm not her mother anymore," his wife said. "She's gone. Dead! And I want to know who did it. Do you hear me? I want to know *WHO KILLED MY DAUGHTER!*"

Her voice was a scream that silenced the entire chapel. Actually, there were three chapels converted into one to hold the great crowd, over five hundred of them on this night.

"WHO KILLED MY DAUGHTER!!!"

The next night, at eight-thirty, Sal Bonventre was standing inside the funeral chapel talking to a neighbor when he saw them come in. Three of them, the one old and the other two young and chewing gum. The old one, bald and small, wore a pearl-gray suit. The younger ones, in their early thirties, had on denim suits with flowered sport shirts, the collars worn outside the jackets, California style.

Sal knew the old man for years, from Troutman Street back in Bushwick. The old man couldn't read a newspaper and he sold drugs. His name was Carmine and for all the time Sal Bonventre knew him, Carmine preyed on young girls, girls as young as thirteen. Sal Bonventre wished the three would say their prayers and leave. He was offended that the old man, who lured high-school girls into his Cadillac, would be standing at his daughter's casket.

The old man walked over to Gina Bonventre. He slapped a hand across his chest.

"You could cut out my heart," he said to Gina.

"What a shame," one of the two younger ones with him said.

"What a shame," the other one said.

The old man said to Sal, "Come downstairs for a smoke with us."

Father Joseph Bonventre said, "My father will be all right here."

"Yeah, I'm staying here," Sal said.

Gina Bonventre stiffened. She glared at her husband. "Go have a smoke," she snapped.

"He'll stay right here," Father Joseph Bonventre said.

"Well, then I'm going to have a cigarette," Gina said. Her son and the old man helped her out of the chair. When her son tried to go with her, she held up her hand to stop him. "You stay here," she said firmly.

Her son Anthony, seeing his mother with Carmine, left a knot of relatives and came up, his face in a scowl. The mother waved this son away, too. She walked with Carmine and the two younger ones, with her husband trailing, out of the packed funeral parlor and down the flight of stairs to the smoking lounge. There were eight or ten people in the lounge.

"Could we have a little privacy?" one of the guys with Carmine said.

The people jabbed their butts into the sand-filled ashstands and shuffled out of the room.

"My own heart," Carmine said to Sal. Whisky fumes steamed from his mouth. "My own heart got cut out, you understand? I remember her, geez, a little girl goin' to the store."

Sal stiffened. This drunken buffoon watching his little daughter.

Gina Bonventre sat on a couch. One of the young guys gave her a light.

"This is Ninni and this is Rocco," Carmine said.

"Pleased," one of them said.

"Pleased," the other said.

"Now, who did a thing like this?" Carmine said to Gina Bonventre. "Just tell me who could of done such a thing. What rat bas —"

"Tony did it," Gina said to her husband. "Tell them, you know he did it."

"Who Tony?" Carmine said.

Sal Bonventre ran a hand over his face. "I don't want to say," he said.

"Sal!" his wife snapped at him.

"I told you, I don't want to say."

"Why you not tellin' me?" Carmine said.

"Because," Sal said.

"Hey. We got all these niggers runnin' in the streets, right?" Carmine said.

"Yes," Sal said.

"And how many niggers do the cops catch?"

"Nobody," Gina said. "The *melanzanas*, they get like flies."

"So how do you think they going to catch the dirty rat-bastard that did this to your daughter?"

"This is different," Sal Bonventre said.

"You say it's different. What makes you so sure?"

"Oh, I don't know," Sal said.

"What do I have to tell you about what happens?" Carmine said. "They even arrest a guy like this, he kills your daughter, what happens? He gets a lawyer. The lawyer could mess around with the thing, and the guy shot your daughter never has to go to court himself. The lawyer goes for him."

Gina pushed herself off the couch and stood up. "Sal, you tell or I'll tell."

Sal Bonventre's anger rose as he looked at Carmine. This baby-raper. But Sal also believed that Carmine was right, that the lawyer would go to court and his daughter's killer would stay home. Money walks and bullshit talks.

"Tony Gallo once slapped my daughter around," Sal said.

"*Slapped* her?" Gina said. "You call that a slap?"

"Who Tony Gallo?"

"From First Avenue and a Hundred and Twentieth Street," Sal said. "I went to see his father about it, and that was all right. But then we had more trouble —"

"My husband said he'd kill him. And the kid said he'd kill my daughter."

"When is this?" Carmine said.

"Last year," Sal Bonventre said. "When he slapped my daughter, I went to the kid's old man and I told him, you know, do the right thing. So the old man took care of it. He works for the Sanitation. So now this here kid of his comes up here and moves in with this here broad and —"

"*Butan!*" Gina said.

"Well, she is a slut. She got kids of her own and all. Anyway, this Tony kid, Tony Gallo, he's living with this slut up here and then he decides he wants to see my daughter again. And this slut he lives with catches him on the phone or something and now the slut is screaming at my daughter on the phone, and I say, 'Let me do something here.' I go to the kid, I catch him in Westchester Square one night and I tell him, 'Tony, you stay away from my daughter or I'll kill you.' You know what he says? He leans out the car window, he was sitting in his car, and he says, 'Hey, I'll shoot your daughter.' That's what he said. Before I could get a hand on him, he drives away."

"When is this?" Carmine said.

"December, January," Sal Bonventre said.

"What does this kid do?" Carmine said.

One of the young guys, the one named Rocco, spoke. "He jerks off, I know the kid."

"You know?" Carmine said.

"I know."

"He could kill this girl?" Carmine said.

Rocco pursed his lips and closed his eyes for a moment. "He probably thinks he says it, he has to back it up."

The other young guy, Ninni, cut in. "A complete jerk-off," he said.

Carmine shrugged. "So why don't we go to this kid and ask him if he did it?"

Sal Bonventre stiffened again. For three full days now, since the moment the police woke him up to tell him that his daughter had been murdered, he had been asking himself about Tony Gallo. The detective who had come to the wake, Dwyer, had asked him names of people who, for any reason, didn't like his daughter and he had thought of telling Dwyer she had had a little trouble with this Tony Gallo. But Sal had decided not to tell the detective about the kid threatening his daughter. He was unsure of his memory. And now, here in the smoking room, Sal Bonventre still was confused. Did the boy threaten Connie because he had threatened the boy first? Was it fair to say the boy had killed his daughter? If these gorillas here went after the boy, he knew they surely wouldn't bother to look for another side of the story.

"I think he killed my daughter," Sal Bonventre said. The words just came out of him; at first he didn't even know why he said them.

Then an anger rose from his stomach and suddenly his mind was filled with the image of Tony Gallo, in his red Firebird, pointing a finger at him and saying, "Hey, I'll shoot your daughter," and then driving off with a sneer. Now Sal knew that this was the reason he said that Tony Gallo had killed his daughter. He said it, Sal Bonventre told himself, because Tony Gallo *did* kill his daughter.

"We'll go now," Carmine said.

"What do you do?" Sal Bonventre said.

"We do what we have to do," Carmine said. He went over and took Gina in his arms. Sal Bonventre almost grabbed him and pried him loose. "Don't worry, Mama," Carmine said. "Whoever shoot your daughter, he's —" Carmine nodded to Rocco and Ninni, and they left.

Two days later, early on a warm Friday morning, Alex Gregoretti was carrying coffee from the Puerto Rican's store to his job in the body-and-fender shop on Southern Boulevard in the Bronx when he heard his name called. Behind him, sitting in a red Cadillac, were Ninni and Rocco. Rocco, behind the wheel, yawned.

"What's doin'?" Alex said.

"We just want to axt you somethin'," Rocco said.

"Sure," Alex said. He put the coffee down on the car hood and leaned through the window to talk to them.

"So what's doin'?" he said to them.

"Nothin'," Rocco said. "We just got this thing here, the old man, you know, he was supposed to do somethin' for a kid and he loses the kid's address and nobody knows where to find this here kid and the old man don't want the kid to think he forgot him. So he axt us to find the kid for him, so we look around; we can't find him. Tryin' to do the kid a favor, you know. We can't find him to tell him. Then somebody yesterday says to us you know where he is."

Rocco smiled and held his hands out, palms up. "So, we come here and we axt you. That's what we're doin'. We're sittin' here and we're axtin' you. That's all. No big deal."

"Who is it?" Alex said.

"Some kid . . . Tony Gallo."

"He's in New Mexico," Alex said.

"Where New Mexico?"

"Geez, I don't know," Alex said. "I know he was around here last week."

When he saw the two of them react to that, Alex became nervous.

"Maybe he's still here," Rocco said.

"No, he went back," Alex said. Then he thought for a moment. "Say, you know who knows? Angelo the Baker. He got Tony the spot down there. With some real-estate thing."

"Angelo the Baker?" Rocco said.

"You mean Fat Ange?" Ninni said.

"Yeah, Fat Ange the Baker."

Rocco reached out and patted Alex on the cheek. "All right, good boy. You're a sweetheart. We'll tell the old man what you done. Thanks."

As Alex was getting the coffee off the car's hood, Rocco leaned out the window and said to him, "Say, do us a favor, don't say nothin' — you know?"

When the car pulled away, Alex walked back to the Puerto Rican's store. He had to use the telephone. He knew that he had done something bad when he had told them that Tony Gallo had been home last week. But he had no choice. If they asked him a question for Carmine, they had to get an answer. He had tried to help Tony Gallo by mentioning Angelo the Baker. But he knew Ange wasn't nearly heavy enough to help Tony Gallo if he was in real trouble with Carmine's people. Oh, there was trouble, all right. Alex knew that. People from East Harlem, where he lived, can detect this kind of trouble as easily as Gloucester fishermen sense a storm. Alex went into the phone booth to call Tony Gallo's brother.

4

Johnny Dwyer was angry with himself. He knew he should have gone straight to the hospital when Connie Bonventre and Frank Parisi were shot. The odds were he would not have gotten a word out of Connie before she died, but he should, at least, have tried — for a name, a description, a motive, anything. He had been a detective for six years, long enough to know, without Deputy Inspector Carillo telling him, that his first move had to be to talk to the victims. Forget about witnesses or physical evidence or anything else until after you talk to the victims.

He wanted to make up for that dumb mistake. Carillo was always needling him, always pushing him a little harder than he pushed anyone else in the Fifteenth Homicide Division, and he wanted to show the inspector that he was as good as any other detective in the division, or maybe better. He didn't have a single decent clue in the shooting of Connie Bonventre, but he was going to crack this case.

Dwyer phoned a friend in the Bronx, another homicide detective. "Look," Dwyer said, "do me a favor, will you? Look around. See if you can find out anything about the Bonventre shooting. The wise guys know anything? Anybody got a beef with her — or with her old man? So far, I'll tell you, I got nothing, no reason for anybody to kill her. You hear anything different, let me know, okay?"

Dwyer hung up. Just my luck, he thought. I couldn't get a hanger. I had to catch a mystery.

Johnny Dwyer did not like unsolved crimes. Mysteries were terrific for Kojak or Colombo, but for him, and for ninety-nine detectives out of a hundred, a hanger would do just as well: a guy standing over a corpse with a smoking gun in one hand and a signed confession in the other. That was the kind of case Dwyer liked: man commits crime, man is apprehended, man is convicted, man is incarcerated — case closed. That's what a cop was for.

Dwyer had wanted to be a cop ever since he was a kid. He had lived on the same block as a precinct house in the Flatbush section of Brooklyn, and, like most of the kids on his block, he had a fifty-fifty shot at either side of the law. He chose his side early. When he was nine years old, he tried to swipe a baseball glove in the schoolyard, and a cop passing by caught him. Instead of taking him to the station house or, worse, to his father, the cop bought him a soda and talked to him. The cop was the first grown-up to talk to him outside of school or church. Johnny began hanging around the precinct house, running for coffee and doughnuts. The cops liked him. When he started playing high-school football, a skinny 150-pound halfback with some speed and more guts, the cops used to come to his games and cheer for him.

When he got out of high school, he wasn't old enough to take the exam for the police force and he wasn't smart enough to go to Harvard and he wasn't rich enough to retire. He decided to join the army. He had a good time for five years. After basic training, he spent a year and a half in Paris and learned to speak passable French without a Brooklyn accent. Then he spent two and a half years in Italy and learned perfect Italian. He also acquired an Italian wife. They had six months together before the army decided to give him a chance to learn another language — Vietnamese. He spent almost two years in combat, long enough to learn that he could kill and that he didn't want to make the army a career. When his tour of duty ended, he went home to Brooklyn with his Italian wife and, his first week back, took the test for the police force. Then he took a job in the post office.

Two weeks later, he got a phone call. "This John Francis Dwyer?"

"Yeah."

"You the one who took the police examination?"

"Yeah."

"How many people know you took the examination?"

"Just my wife — and a friend of mine who's a cop."

"Would you be interested in a special assignment that might be a shortcut to becoming a detective?"

"Sure."

"Come to the Police Academy next Tuesday at two-thirty. I don't mean two-twenty-eight or two-thirty-two. I mean two-thirty. Walk in the main door, walk past the guard, don't stop, turn left, go to the elevator and go straight to the fifth floor. Room five twenty-one. Walk in. We'll see you there."

The following Tuesday, around noon, Dwyer set his watch by dialing the time on the telephone. At two o'clock, he went to the neighborhood of the Police Academy. He waited one block away until two-twenty-nine. Then he walked to the academy, marched through the doors, swept past the guard, onto the elevator, and straight to Room 521. Three men in plainclothes were waiting for him. They did not introduce themselves. They began asking him how he felt about the war in Vietnam. He said that he thought the United States was right to try to stop the spread of communism. He also said that if we were in a war, we ought to try to win it. "What do you think of the antiwar demonstrators?" he was asked.

"Not very much," he said.

"Would you take part in antiwar demonstrations?"

"No."

"Would you take part in prowar demonstrations?"

"No," Dwyer said. "I'm just not the demonstrating type."

The three men asked him several more questions, mostly about his background, and then told him to return at the same time, the same way, three days later. When he returned, three different men questioned him. The line of questioning was very similar. Then they asked him if he would be willing to join the antiwar movement — as a cop. They wanted him to be an undercover radical.

"Sure," said Dwyer.

A week later, he got another phone call. He was told that he had to take a physical to be admitted to the police department. But he was not to take the physical with the rest of the recruits. He was to go to a certain corner in lower Manhattan and wait until he saw a man carrying *Life* magazine under his right arm. He was to follow the man carrying *Life*. He was not to speak to the man. He was to stay fifty feet behind him on the street. Dwyer did just as he was told, and the man led him to an office building, to an elevator, and to an unmarked, tenth-floor office. Within twenty minutes, three different doctors had come to the office and examined Dwyer and pronounced him fit for police duty. After the doctors left, the man carrying *Life* told Johnny Dwyer he was now a member of the New York Police Department. He handed Dwyer his shield. Johnny almost cried. He had been dreaming for almost twenty years of getting an NYPD shield. Then the man with the magazine took the shield back. "You will carry no identification," he told Dwyer. "You will tell no one you are a police officer except your wife. You will be paid once a month — in cash. You will get a phone call telling you where to pick up the money. You will initial a voucher for it."

The next day, Johnny Dwyer turned radical. He got involved in the Rainbow Coalition, a joint effort among the Black Panthers, the Puerto Rican Young Lords, and several white radical organizations. He was quickly welcomed into the movement. The whites, most of whom came from comfortable upper-middle-class backgrounds, were delighted to have a genuine member of the proletariat on their side.

Dwyer spent two years working undercover, an assignment that fascinated him but drove his wife to the brink of divorce. The neighbors all felt sorry for her, married to a man who had no visible means of support, who dressed like a hippie and who came and went at weird hours. The department didn't even bother to give him a cover. The people inside the movement knew that Dwyer was married, and when they asked him why his wife didn't come to the meetings, he explained that she did not share his activist beliefs. This rankled some of the women in the movement, who took to calling Dwyer's home at odd hours and, when his wife answered the telephone, asking for Johnny in the most suggestive possible tones. He tolerated the pressure and the abuse until the weekend he had to go to a rock festival in Connecticut. By the second day, he realized he was the only person at the festival who was getting neither stoned nor laid. Departmental regulations frowned upon both. Dwyer didn't mind being straight, but he hated being horny.

After the weekend, he called his contact at police headquarters and said, quite seriously, that he felt he had outlived his usefulness as an undercover agent. The department was understanding: he got his gold detective's shield and an assignment in Brooklyn to a PIU, a Precinct Investigative Unit. Then he moved up to Burglary and, finally, to Homicide. Along the way, he became a member of an elite unit, the Hostage-Negotiation Team. He took a special course, heavy in psychology, to qualify for the Hostage-Negotiation Team. Only a year before the Bonventre shooting, he had walked unarmed into an apartment where a man was holding a machete to the throat of his own two-year-old daughter, and he had talked the man into giving up first the machete and then the girl.

Six months later, he had come to Queens, to work under Deputy Inspector Carillo in the Fifteenth Homicide Division. There were twenty-four detectives, divided into three eight-man teams, working out of the Fifteenth. For any particular tour, on any given day, allowing for vacations and illnesses, there would probably be half a dozen homicide detectives available. Each of them would, in turn, *catch* a case — be responsible for that case, nursemaid it from the start of the investigation to the end of the trial, if it went that far. It was Dwyer's turn to catch when the 10 – 10 — report of a person shot — crackled over the division radio the night Connie Bonventre and Frank Parisi were shot. The report came at 12:26 a.m., only thirty-four minutes before the end of Dwyer's four-to-one tour, and his reaction was immediate and basic. "Oh, shit," he said.

"You're up," one of his team members called out.

Dwyer and three other members of the team had gone to Jinni in response to the call, all of them hoping for a hanger, none of them expecting to encounter Carillo on the scene or to find a pretty teenager shot through the head. Dwyer had daughters of his own, an eight-year-old and a six-year-old, and most of the other guys on his team had teenage children. Dwyer was young to be a homicide detective, still in his early thirties; his undercover work had accelerated his career.

Within forty-eight hours after his call to the Bronx, within a week after the death of Connie Bonventre, Dwyer got a call back from his friend. "I think I've got something," the friend said. "I checked with a bartender in a wise-guy saloon, a guy who owed me one, and he tells me the old man has fingered an ex-boy friend, a kid the girl stopped seeing nine, ten months ago."

"What's his name?" Dwyer said.

"Gallo. Tony Gallo, no relation."

"What kind of kid?"

"Smartass. You know, sold football pools in high school, dealt grass, figured he was moving up to better things. Anyway, he and Connie were in some kind of neighborhood acting thing together, and they went out a few times, maybe a lot of times. But then she decided she didn't want to go out with him anymore, and, the way I hear it, he got a little upset."

The guy in the Bronx told Dwyer about Tony slapping Connie, and about Sal Bonventre going to his old man, and then about the trouble with the slut he's living with. "I hear Connie's father threatened to kill the kid himself. You follow?"

"Yeah," Dwyer said.

"Anyway some local Don, a friend of the kid's family from way back, arranged for the kid to get out of town before he got hurt. He sent him to New Mexico to work on one of those land-development swindles — you know, beautiful two-acre retirement plot, all that shit, in the middle of some desert. So the kid went to New Mexico."

"How long ago?"

"About four months."

"That knocks him out of the box for our thing," Dwyer said.

"No. My guy tells me the kid came back to New York just a month ago."

"Yeah?"

"And that ain't all. He's disappeared again, and the word around is that he took off for New Mexico two days after the shooting."

"You're beautiful," Dwyer said. "I owe you a big one."

Dwyer went to Carillo and told the inspector what he had learned. He told Carillo everything except he didn't mention the word "Don." He just said "a friend of the family."

"Call the New Mexico State Police," Carillo suggested. "See what they can get for you on the kid."

Dwyer placed a call to Albuquerque and got through to a Sergeant Fail of the New Mexico State Police. Dwyer explained who he was, what had happened, and what he was looking for. "Can you check into the kid for me?" Dwyer said. "Anthony Gallo. Who he's running with, what he's doing."

"Sure," said Sergeant Fail. "We've got nothing else to do here anyway except check on the people you scare out this way. Do me a favor, too."

"What's that?"

"Tell me — what's Pleasant Avenue like?"

"Pleasant Avenue? Beautiful. In Harlem. East Harlem. A lovely spot for murderers, stick-up men, and drug pushers. Why?"

"We got a street out here they call Pleasant Avenue West. Now I know why."

The next day, Sergeant Fail called back. "Found him," he said. "All we had to do was inhale. He's not hard to find. He's doing some bookmaking just to stay in shape. But that's not what's interesting."

"What's interesting?"

"Fella we know has a big gun store that caters to your Eastern cowboys, strictly legal, weapons for sale. He says your man came in a couple of months ago and didn't buy anything. But the guy with him bought a forty-four-caliber Bulldog revolver. That help you?"

Dwyer whistled. The case was turning from a mystery to a hanger. He had a suspect with a strong motive and access to the murder weapon. All Dwyer needed now, he figured, was a plane ticket to New Mexico. Carillo said he thought the department could afford it. Sergeant Fail said he'd meet Dwyer at the airport.

When Dwyer got off the plane in Albuquerque, Sergeant Fail was waiting for him, the biggest sergeant Dwyer had ever seen, at least six-foot-five and 270 pounds minimum. He wore a state police uniform and a cowboy hat. The cowboy hat struck Dwyer as a little strange because Sergeant Fail was, obviously, an Indian, also the biggest Indian Dwyer had ever seen. The sergeant stuck out his hand. "Never Fail," he said. Dwyer had to laugh. "You're shitting me," he said.

"Nope," said the Indian, "and don't complain. You might've ended up with my cousin. He's in the State Police, too. His name's Will."

Dwyer laughed again. He felt very good about the case.

He checked into a downtown motel — "Anyplace you like," Carillo had told him, "up to ten bucks a night" — showered, and changed. He put on a gray-checked suit, a blue shirt, and a tie with an abstract pattern. Dwyer always wore a suit when he was dealing with the public, even with the bottom level of the public. He believed a detective should wear a suit over his holster and his .38 revolver.

It took only an hour for Sergeant Fail to lead Dwyer to Tony Gallo. "Tony," Dwyer said, "I'm Detective Dwyer, New York Police. I want to talk to you."

"What about?"

"The shooting of Connie Bonventre."

A bolt of fear flashed across the kid's face. "How do I know you're a cop?" he said.

Dwyer pointed to Sergeant Fail in uniform and then pulled out his own gold badge. "I'm a cop," he said. "I am definitely a cop."

"What do you want from me?"

"I want you to make it all very easy for me. I want you to tell me why you shot her and how you did it and what you did with the forty-four."

"You're full of shit. I didn't shoot nobody. And I don't have no forty-four."

"Tony, you were seen with a guy here buying a forty-four-caliber revolver two months ago. Connie Bonventre was shot to death with a forty-four-caliber revolver. You had a beef with her and with her old man. What does that sound like to you?"

The kid began to shake. "Let's get off the street," he said. "I don't want nobody to see me like this. Let's go where we can talk."

"Talk here," Dwyer said.

The kid couldn't stop shaking. His words came out slowly, between deep gulps for air. "I didn't shoot Connie," he managed to say.

"Lot of people think you did," Dwyer said. "Heavy people."

"Shit, man," Tony Gallo said, and he seemed ready to cry. "I heard about them, but, shit, I didn't do it. I didn't."

"What about the gun?"

"I ain't seen that guy with the forty-four since the day he bought it," Tony said.

"What's his name?"

"Philly."

"Philly what?"

Tony Gallo blinked. "I don't know," he said.

Within forty-eight hours, with Tony Gallo held for his own safety, Sergeant Fail and the New Mexico State Police found Philly and the forty-four-caliber Charter Arms Bulldog revolver he had purchased with Tony Gallo. "I didn't buy it for no friend," Philly said. "I bought the thing for myself."

"What for?" Dwyer said.

"To protect myself," Philly said. "From the snakes in the desert. You see the fuckin' snakes here yet?"

The New Mexico State Police sent the gun to its labs for ballistics tests. In three hours, the results were back. In another hour, those results had been compared with information Dwyer was carrying, the results of ballistics tests done in New York on the bullet that killed Connie Bonventre. Dwyer was stunned. The gun and the bullet did not match. Same caliber, same make, but no match. There was no way the New Mexico .44 could have fired the New York bullet.

Dwyer called Carillo in New York and told him the bad news about ballistics.

"There was one other bad thing, too," Dwyer said.

"What's that?"

"The kid had a plane ticket saying he flew back to New Mexico two days *before* the shooting. I thought he could've faked it."

"Yeah."

"But you can't fake ballistics, can you?"

Carillo hesitated. "Maybe they changed barrels in the gun," he said.

"I thought of that," Dwyer said, "and I asked the ballistics people, and they said no way. They said this gun hasn't been touched. It's just the way it came off the assembly line. You know the gun's made in Connecticut?"

"Yeah."

"These are nice people out here. I hope we don't ruin them with Eastern guns and Eastern punks."

"Dwyer?"

"Yes, sir?"

"Come back tonight. No sense having the taxpayers pay for another night in a motel."

A few days later, back in New York, Detective Johnny Dwyer went up to the Bronx to see Salvatore Bonventre. They sat on the plastic covers in the Bonventre living room. "You should've told me about that kid you had a beef with," said Dwyer.

"What kid you talking about?"

"The kid in New Mexico."

"I don't know no kid in New Mexico."

"Well, that's good. But, anyway, we heard about this kid, and we went out to see him, and we checked out reports he had a forty-four-caliber pistol and we checked out his alibi. He didn't have a gun. A guy he knew had a gun. And it wasn't the right gun. And, besides, the kid was in New Mexico the night of the shooting."

"You sure?"

"I'm sure. I've checked it out ten different ways by now, and it all adds up to zero. He's a lousy punk-kid, but he didn't kill your daughter."

"You positively sure?"

Dwyer nodded. "Uh, huh."

Salvatore Bonventre stood up and walked the detective to the door. His limp was worse than ever.

"Thank you," Bonventre said. "Now I got to go tell some people not to take an airplane trip tonight. I may be too late to tell them. That would be a terrible thing, wouldn't it?"

5

He sat on his swivel chair and listened to the dogs howling. For more than two weeks now, from the moment he had arrived home after shooting Connie Bonventre and Frank Parisi, the demons to whom Bernard Rosenfeld was responsible had been expressing their displeasure. More than two weeks, and they were still assailing him. What do they want from me, Bernard said to himself. I gave them blood to drink. All right, the boy did not die. But the boy spilled blood; the demons could lap up the blood from the wounds. What more did they want? The girl had bled to death before the ambulance arrived, one newspaper said. That gave them all that blood to drink, four and a half quarts. To a demon, a pint of human blood is worth 4700 pints of animal blood. They should be happy, Bernard said to himself. Instead, the howling in his head rose, louder and louder, and it told him what the demons wanted: Death, right away.

Bernard became angry. He challenged them. "The bullets got deflected," he said aloud. "How did that happen? It was either you or God who deflected the bullets on me. It wasn't God. I know that. He wouldn't have let me kill the girl. No, it was you. You deflected the bullets. Now you blame me for not killing him."

Their answer was to howl louder. The hot red liquid eyes of Sam Thornton's black dog was joined by others, by an entire pack of dogs, six or seven of them, mouths open, dripping mucous, screams coming from deep in their throats. He went over to his mattress and fell on it, holding his ears. The howling became even greater. He went over to the wall and took a red pencil out of his pocket and printed on the wall, in big letters, "KILL FOR SAM THORNTON." It was on the wall opposite his earlier sign, "SAM THORNTON IS MY MASTER." This had to stop them, he thought. He was signing his life away to them. The answer of the demons was to cause the entire dog pack inside his head to give tongue at the same time, the sound rising until he could not remain still. He began to walk around the dark room, kicking magazines out of the way, his shoulders brushing against the wall. He could not walk the screaming out of his head.

"You stopped me from doing my job!" he shouted. "You deflected the bullets."

The rebuttal from the dogs caused him to grab his hair with both hands. His hair was oily. He couldn't keep his hair clean even if he shampooed it twice a day. They wanted his hair always to be dirty. Each time he washed it, the moment he stepped out of the shower, they threw a cup of oil onto his head, and he would know it only later, when the greasy hair would collect dirt out of the air. He spun around and went out the apartment and down the empty hallway to the elevator. He rode it down to the lobby and walked out to his car.

He drove to the diner near South Broadway. In the light in the open doorway, he could see one customer inside the trailer, a man in a white shirt who had a soda to his lips. Rosenfeld waited outside until the man was finished. Then he went in.

"Hot dog," he said to the man with the harelip.

The counterman nodded.

"Four, no make it five, liverwurst sandwiches."

"What kind of bread?" the counterman asked.

"Any kind. White bread."

"Mustard?"

"No. No mustard. Nothing on it at all."

Rosenfeld chewed on the hot dog while the man made the sandwiches. When the man opened the refrigerator to put the roll of liverwurst back, Rosenfeld reached across the counter and picked up a small grease-blackened meat cleaver. He unbuttoned his shirt and stuffed the cleaver inside, down into the belt.

In the car, he unwrapped the sandwiches. He took the liverwurst from each sandwich and patted it into the palm of his hand. He dropped the bread on the floor. By the time he was finished, he had a large lump of liverwurst, nearly too big for his hand to hold. He drove the car with one hand, going down McLean Avenue, then turning off onto a road that ran past factories and brought him to a dead end at the entrance to Oakland Cemetery. The cemetery sat behind a gloomy tan stone wall. He parked the car and got out, holding the liverwurst, and slipped through a space between the end of the black iron gate and the beginning of the tan stone wall. Inside the cemetery, he walked onto the narrow roadway and he began going up the hill, past gravestones. He kept walking until he could not see the streetlights anymore. Up ahead, the first dog came out from the headstones.

There always are dogs in the cemetery at night; Rosenfeld knew that from the nights he had spent sitting on his stepmother's grave, fingering the new dirt. The cemetery dogs lie on the grass and wait for rabbits. During much of the night in a cemetery, Rosenfeld knew, there are dogs growling, snarling, baying as they chase rabbits. Every once in a while, there are frenzied, prolonged sounds: a rabbit being torn apart. And now, as Rosenfeld walked up the cemetery road, he could see this one dog clearly. The dog had German shepherd in him. Body slung low, ears laid back. Behind the shepherd, two large dirty white dogs came running. He kept walking toward the dogs, and the first, the shepherd, growled. Rosenfeld walked right at him. The white dogs had stopped running and were moving to the side, watching, watching. In the faint light from the moon, Rosenfeld saw tufts of fur rise on the back of the German shepherd's neck. A low steady growl came from the dog. Rosenfeld held the liverwurst in front of him. The dog continued growling. A nose twitch showed that the dog had caught the liverwurst scent. Rosenfeld dropped the liverwurst on the roadway, dropped it out ahead of him, but still within his circle of reach. The dog came scurrying forward, head low, the head tilting to get a better bite. Rosenfeld unbuttoned his shirt and took out the greasy meat clever and brought it around three-quarters overhand, in one motion, and sank the meat cleaver into the middle of the dog's spine. Sank the cleaver in so hard he could feel something snapping. He tried to pull the cleaver back out, but he could not. It was wedged in the dog's backbone. The dog was screaming and thrashing.

The dirty white dogs, frightened, rushed away sideways and went out of sight. Rosenfeld cringed in the howling of the German shepherd. He had to stay there until all the howling in his head was transferred to the German shepherd on the ground. Screaming would flow from his head to the dog's head. For he had just taken his stand against the demons: he had let them know he was not to be tormented. Perhaps he wasn't a general in charge of killing, like Jack Cosmos was, or an assistant to the general, like Sam Thornton, but he was obedient, he did what the demons wanted him to do, and he did not have to be afflicted like this. So he had struck back, he had shown them.

The German shepherd's noise subsided to a whine and then ceased and the dog lay dead. The inside of Bernard's head became silent and cool. It had worked. He breathed the night air deeply. He started to walk back to the cemetery gates. Then a sound came from behind him. He turned and saw the German shepherd, tongue flopping out of the corner of his mouth, standing in the roadway and laughing at him. There was no cleaver sticking out of the dog's back now. Once again, a howl rose inside Bernard Rosenfeld's head. He put his hands to his dirty hair. He knew now that he had no recourse, he would have to live with the howling like a disease, until he could cure it by killing.

He went home and he did not sleep. In the morning, sitting on the chair and staring at the blue bedspreads, he suddenly thought about work. He looked at his watch. It was 8:00 a.m. already, the time he was supposed to be starting work. He got up and went to the shower. He used a bottle of natural herb shampoo, washing his hair twice, but he knew it was no good. The howling inside him nearly blocked out the sound of the running water. He knew that the moment the water was turned off and he stepped outside, they would throw a cup of oil onto his clean hair.

When he got to his job in Harrison, Rosenfeld stood in the mud and gravel outside the shanty for twenty minutes, his eyes disconnected, his fingers reaching for the scab on his elbow, which, by this time, was not there. He couldn't start work until he picked up his brass disk, number 164, in the shanty. It looks like a coat check and serves in the same manner: Pick up the disk at the start of the day to check the body in; turn in the disk at the end of the day and take the body home. Only Huggy could give out the disks. It was nine-thirty now. Rosenfeld was an hour and a half late. He decided to go home. He was halfway back to his car when Huggy's voice came at him like a knife.

"Rosie, you hump!"

He turned around to face this new torment.

"Come here, you hump!"

Rosenfeld walked up to Huggy, saw the hostile eyes, and immediately looked down at the mud.

"Rosie, what are you, a mutt, Rosie? A fuckin' mutt? A dog in the fuckin' street? Your uncle got you on the job here and is this what you do to him?"

He kept looking at the mud and gravel.

"Now why are you gettin' here late, Rosie?"

He could not raise his eyes or form words to say.

"Rosie!"

Still looking down.

"Rosie!"

He was shoved on the shoulder and he went backward. He looked up and saw Huggy's eyes bulging in anger. "I got you the job account of your uncle and you put me on the spot: comin' here late, and you won't even tell me why. Rosie, you hump, I'll —"

Rosenfeld held the back of his hand across his eyes and his body shook. Tears streamed out from under the hand. Huggy froze.

"Wait a minute," Huggy said. Huggy went into the shanty and came out with the brass disk. He handed it to Rosenfeld. "Now get your ass to work."

When Rosenfeld walked into the loading dock, everybody started calling his name.

"Coffee, Rosie."

"Rosie, where the fuck you been? Got no coffee."

"Let's go, Rosie."

"Light, no sugar, Bernie."

He picked up the cardboard box he kept against the wall, and he went around and took coffee orders from the other steamfitters. He wrote the orders down on a small pad he carried in the breast pocket of his shirt. Then he walked over to Vito's lunch counter, a trailer sunk into the muddy earth as if it were there permanently. There was a line of four or five other apprentices waiting to get into Vito's. When Rosenfeld got to the front of the line, just as he was about to step into the trailer, two men from the masons' union came up to him. They were Italians, Marco and Sonny, swaggering, bare from the waist up, tanned already, weeks before anyone else.

"Rosie baby," Marco said. He swung in front of Rosenfeld. The

other one, Sonny, went into the trailer. Marco remained in the doorway, blocking it so Rosenfeld could not step in.

"How are you, Rosie?" Marco said to him. "How are you doin',
Rosie baby?" Marco laughed at Rosenfeld.

They don't know, Bernard told himself. They don't know that I
have a job to do. And he knew that the two stonemasons knew nothing about the organization he did his work for. They thought he
was a clown. Only he, Bernard, knew what he really was.

Six thousand years ago there was a war in Heaven. Not the war in
which Saint Michael the Archangel slashed with his sword and
chased Lucifer out. Bernard's war was the one that happened six
thousand years ago and caused the first holocaust in Heaven. One-
third of the angels in Heaven were contaminated by the Devil and
had to be driven out of Heaven. Not just by Saint Michael, but this
time by the full force and fury of God himself. As each fallen angel
was being slashed out of Heaven, the fallen angel would reach out
and stain another angel. As it was not the fault of the angels stained,
God did not send them to Hell. But they had been changed, stained
forever, and God could not allow them to remain in Heaven. So God
sent them to earth, and the moment these stained angels came to
earth, they reacted badly. They turned against God. They went about
capturing people and forcing them to go out and kill pure people,
innocent people, to defy God. The angels on earth, who turned into
demons, then drank the blood of the innocent people and laughed at
God as they did so. For the demons on earth knew that only one-third
the people who used to be in Heaven were there now. New souls,
therefore, were being greeted with rapture. The idea of this made the
stained angels on earth, by now total demons, deliriously happy because they could kill with impunity, they could kill God's favorites on
earth, the young and the pretty, and there would be no retribution.
Heaven needed new angels, no matter how they arrived.

The demons who had captured Bernard were some of the most
important on earth. There was General Jack Cosmos, who was in
charge of all killing in the tristate area of New York, New Jersey, and
Connecticut. Then there was his special assistant, Adjutant Sam
Thornton. General Jack Cosmos delivered his orders to Thornton, and
Thornton spoke to Bernard through a black dog. Sometimes, when
Bernard did not do exactly as he was told, other demons would be-
come angry. They, too, spoke to Bernard through dogs. Which is

what happened when he missed killing the guy in the car at Jinni the other night. He had upset many of the top demons and they had let him know it by having their dogs scream inside his head.

"Rosie, you want somethin', Rosie?"

The door to the trailer was clear now. Marco and Sonny had left. Inside, the owner, Vito, leaned over the counter and called to him. Rosenfeld put his foot up to go into the trailer. Just then the dog pack inside his head sounded at an intensity which Bernard could not stand. He dropped the cardboard box on the ground and walked away. He went to his car.

6

"Did I tell you what happened yesterday?" Marie Perrotti said.

"No," Madeleine Giordano said.

"I'm at the cash register and this man comes up and he pays his check and I give him the change. Then he hands me a dollar and I don't think nothing of it. I figure he wants change to leave the waitress a tip and I open the register and I start to make change and while I'm doing this, I see the guy walking out. I say, 'Hey, mister, you forgot your change.' And he waves to me and says, 'That's for you,' and I say, 'Oh, no, I'm the cashier, I don't get any tips.' And he says to me, 'Keep it, it's yours.' I'm holding out the money and my boss comes up and he grabs my hand and he says, 'Are you crazy? This is yours.' You know what he does, Maddy? He unzippers the breast pocket — I was wearing my jump suit, you know — and he puts the dollar in and then he pats it. He puts his hand right here." She covered her breast with her hand. Then she pushed in. "Like that. He said to me, 'There, now you keep that.' "

"So he got a cheap feel," Madeleine said.

"No, you don't understand. He didn't even know he was getting a feel. It was that he was opening my zipper in front of all those people and he didn't even care, he was so interested in me getting a dollar."

"And he still got a feel," Madeleine said.

The two sat on the fender of Marie's father's car, which was parked on Country Club Road near Lohengrin Place in the Bronx, where old one-family frame houses and new two-family brick houses sit on narrow streets that seem as alien to a city as Queens does. The streets have trees which, in summer, form an umbrella over the street. There is no country club anywhere near the neighborhood. Country Club Road begins at the busy Bruckner Expressway and runs into the marshland and polluted waters that lead into Long Island Sound. The main street was once known as Slack Place, but an alert builder, in concert with his favorite New York City councilman, had the name changed to Country Club Road because this was much more appealing in real-estate ads. The neighborhood is suburban, a $12 cab ride from Times Square, and on summer nights the streets are filled with young people tired of being cloistered. They roam about, drinking and smoking dope, and the parents' anguish is lessened only by the knowledge that the dreaded niggers are still far away.

On this Sunday night, July 18, 1976, Marie Perrotti, twenty-three, and her friend Madeleine Giordano, twenty-two, had just come from the Premier East, a small nightclub with live music on Tremont Road. The girls wore tight jeans and black T-shirts. "Want to go inside and watch a movie on the TV?" Marie said.

"I'd rather just sit here and wait for my honey to come along," Madeleine said.

"What honey?"

"Any honey that comes along is my honey," Madeleine said. "But tonight I'm waiting for my real honey."

The two were laughing, their bodies rocking back and forth. They did not notice the cream-colored Galaxie that drove past them.

He saw them, however, the two young girls delighted with life, and he knew he had to kill them. Sam must drink their blood. Lap it up from the wounds. The dog pack inside his head was gone. Once in a while, Sam Thornton's dog would appear, the eyes getting larger, commanding him to kill. But Bernard understood the rules: keep hunting and the demons ease off and allow you to try. But the demons make no consideration for anything outside of ceaseless hunting. They howl and nag even when he stops for gas. On the front seat of the car, Rosenfeld had his old cranberry-juice jar, gallon size, filled with water. He knew that he could not tolerate the shrieks which would arise if he so much as stopped for a soda. Rosenfeld drove straight ahead on Country Club.

"Oh, did I tell you about what Uncle Nicky said to Aunt Rose last week?" Madeleine said. "I just found out about it last night."

"What did he say?" Marie asked.

"Well, you know how she's always out at bingo. Or at least she says she's always out at bingo. Well, last week she came home late, three, four in the mornin', and she said she hadda stop and buy coffee for everybody on account of she won the jackpot. She puts a hundred dollars on the table and says to my Uncle Nicky, 'Here, I won the jackpot. Isn't that good? Now I'm so tired and sweaty from the bingo hall that I'm goin' in and take a bath.' And he picks up the hundred dollars and throws it at her and he says, 'When you take your bath, make sure you don't get your bingo card wet.'"

"Oh, he's terrible," Marie said.

"Yeah, but what do you want off my Uncle Nicky? She tells him she goes to bingo."

He drove up Country Club to Parsifal and made a right turn and then ran into Lohengrin Place, which is closer to being an alley than a street. He rode slowly along it, as it sliced diagonally back toward Country Club; he was almost brushing against garbage cans in front of the houses. A fat dog waddled across the street. Sam Thornton, Bernard said to himself. His sign shows up wherever I go. He made a left on Country Club and came past Marie Perrotti and Madeleine Giordano. He looked at them carefully, but they were busy talking to each other and did not notice him.

"He must of won," Marie was saying.

"Why? Because he isn't home yet?" Madeleine said.

"That's right."

"Supposing he lost and he stopped on the way home and met somebody who could console him?"

"You always think of such nice things to say," Marie said. "Here I'm sitting here and waiting for Johnny to come by, I'm sitting here on a car fender, and you're telling me he's off in some plush spot with another girl. Madeleine, that's not being a friend."

"I thought friends was supposed to tell each other the truth," Madeleine said.

"What do I care?" Marie said. "I'm tired sitting here." She slid off the fender and stood in the street and her body began to weave and her hands began to play in the air. Eyes closed, head rocking, she danced. When Madeleine got off the fender and walked up to the stoop of Marie's house, Marie followed her, rocking and dancing.

He passed the first box, Fire Box 3197, which was in front of 5172 Country Club Road. Then he came up to the corner of Robertson Road and pulled into a space alongside a telephone pole. Another firebox was on the pole. He knew that this was Fire Box 3196. He remembered the first time he had been on this block, when he and his friend Lenny Siegel from Co-Op City had gone on both sides of Bruckner Boulevard for a week, learning the locations of the call boxes and their numbers. If they were going to be firemen, they had decided, they were going to know more about the fire department than anybody else who ever came on the job. Over a period of six months, Bernie and Lenny had learned the number and location of every firebox in the Bronx, Queens, and Brooklyn, a total of 13,480 fire boxes.

And now, parked in front of number 3196, Rosenfeld opened the glove compartment and took out his .44-caliber Bulldog. He stuffed it into his belt. There was no plastic garbage bag this time. He got out of the car, untroubled by the demons because he was truly hunting, and walked to the opposite side of the street and then started down Country Club Road. He walked past houses which still had the blue light of television showing in the upstairs windows. He knew he could do nothing to counteract this. If somebody came out after him, he would have to outrun him. It was 1:20 a.m., the nineteenth of July now. If he waited, the two pretty princesses would disappear. The instant the slightest thought of waiting went through his mind, there was a screech which caused his head to shake. Great hot red liquid eyes filled his head. "I do my job, I do my job," Rosenfeld said under his breath. The dog eyes went away and he looked across the street as he approached a spot that would bring him almost even with the house where Marie Perrotti and Madeleine Giordano stood on the stoop. Rosenfeld looked at them. He ran his hand across his stomach, over the gun handle. Because of the cars parked at the curb, he knew that the two girls could see only his head and the top of his shoulders. But the pressure was on him; he had the command; Sam had spoken. He would have to come out into full view. He stared for a moment longer and then he started to walk around a car and out into the street.

"Who's this, Marie?" Madeleine said.

Marie Perrotti looked at the bulky guy walking out from behind the car and into the street.

"I don't know who he is," she said.

"Well, what is he doing here?" Madeleine said.

"Yeah, who is this frigging guy?"

He could see they were nervous. They were standing up now and looking at him and talking about him. As he walked closer, he could see they were more than nervous; they were frightened. He didn't want them to be. Why should two lovely princesses be nervous? He smiled as he came up to the curb, and he said to them, "Excuse me, girls, but could you please tell me how to get to White Plains —"

The words held their attention, had them holding still. *Just stay there, don't move, it won't hurt.* He had the gun out from under his shirt and the two girls froze and he held it straight out with his right hand and he fired from the gutter at the two girls on the brick stoop. The gun came up, up very high, and the hump in the handle twisted in the space between the thumb and forefinger. He brought the gun down and out straight again and he fired again. This time the girls on the stoop were somehow going away from him, backward, starting to turn, beginning the move that would take them inside the door and away from him, and he exhaled and squeezed off another round and the gun twisted in his hand again and this time, as he brought the gun down, he saw one of the girls had pitched onto the steps and the other one had stiffened, then had jumped off the stoop, and her movement distracted him and he hesitated a moment and then he shoved the gun into his belt and turned and began racing back down the sidewalk, running to his car.

For lunch he had the same sausage-and-peppers hero that he had eaten on every working day for months. He was by himself, leaning on a packing case while Huggy and the rest of the bull gang sat on the opposite side of an empty cement-walled room. An unfinished duct system hung from the ceiling. Rosenfeld put his sandwich down and took out two newspaper clippings, one small, the other a large one, folded several times so it would fit into his wallet. He read the long one first. It was from the *Dispatch*. The headline ran all the way across the top of the page. The story said that a lone gunman had shot down Connie Bonventre and Frank Parisi in Bayside, Queens. He particularly liked the part of the story that said, "Connie Bonventre . . . was killed when the first bullet, fired at close range, crashed through the window on the passenger's side and struck her in the back of the head." The first bullet. That was very good. Of course, the story had mistakes in it—it said that he had fired four shots, instead of five, and it said that he had used a .45-caliber pistol, not a .44—but still it was a good story. He read the story as thoroughly as he had read it before leaving the apartment for work in the morning. He read this story three and four times a day. When he finished, he put it into his wallet and then looked at the short story. It ran for only two paragraphs and it said one girl had just been nicked by a bullet and another girl, Marie Perotti, had been shot in the back. Her condition was serious, but stable; she was out of danger. She was cheated, Bernard said to himself. She should have been given the chance to die and go to Heaven. Then he, too, could have been saved from pain. His eyes were red from sitting up all night and facing the demons at their angriest. He put the clippings back into his wallet and reached for his sandwich again.

"Come on, Rosie, let's go to work," Huggy called over to him. The others were starting to pick up things for the afternoon's work. Rosenfeld took a bite of his sandwich.

"Hey, hump! It's time to go to work."

Rosenfeld swallowed such a large piece of the sandwich that it became stuck in his throat. When he was able to moisten it enough to swallow it, the pressure still caused his eyes to close. Immediately, large dog eyes reminded him that he owed blood. He opened his eyes and looked at the sandwich in his hand. He still had a third of it left. Why didn't Huggy give him a break, Rosenfeld thought. Didn't anybody know that he had a job to do?

"Hey, Rosie!"

Rosenfeld sat with his sandwich in his hand and he thought about the clip from Tuesday's *Dispatch*, the small one, the one about Marie Perrotti being stable, and he began to cry.

He shouted to the demon dogs inside his head that he wanted a break, but the demons were ceaseless. Bernard knew he would have to kill again, as soon as possible. He could not let anything interfere with it. The construction job did. As he drove out of the muddy parking lot he knew he couldn't stand this job much longer.

"Spic," Danny Cahill said. Then he read the address, Country Club Road, and he shook his head. "No, I guess it's a guinea. Fuckin' boy friend, probably. Shoots her in the back. I thought guineas always stabbed in the back."

He had the newspaper spread on the bar. Outside, Queens Boulevard was crowded with people walking across to the courthouse. He had read all the major stories in both the *Times* and *Dispatch* at home, and now he was going over the smaller articles. Cahill liked to read in a bar early in the day. "A library where you could smoke," he called it. He took one more look at the two-paragraph story about Marie Perrotti, dismissed it as a boy-friend shooting and turned the page.

"Have a drink," the owner of the place, Shelly Cohen, said.

"Tomato juice," Cahill said.

"You got to have more than that," Cohen said.

"Too early," Cahill said.

"It's after lunchtime," Cohen said.

"No thanks, I got to write today."

"You write better with a couple in you," Cohen said.

"I can't even take a glass of beer before I write," Cahill said.

"When did this begin?" Cohen said.

"All my life."

Cahill stretched his arms. What the fuck was he going to write about today, he thought. Nothing's going on.

When he got home at 5:00 p.m., Rosenfeld kicked off his shoes and pitched onto his face on the mattress. He had not slept since he shot the two girls in the Bronx, forty hours ago. He fell asleep immediately. At nine-thirty, he woke up and stumbled to the bathroom. As he was urinating, he heard Sam Thornton's dog howl. He closed the bathroom door. The dog barked. The dog seemed to be just outside the bathroom door. Another bark. Bernard could hear a paw scratching at the door. "I'm going!" he called out. He had wanted to go back to bed, masturbate, and go to sleep. Now he knew he could not. He took off his clothes and turned on the shower. He had to go out hunting. All of his nights were about to become an empty street with patches of deep indigo and silent houses and, somewhere, a block away, two blocks away, the sidewalk bathed in rose from the neon sign of a discotheque or a bar where young people like to go.

He hunted for seven weeks before he was able to find two that Sam wanted. He had seen the place before, the Eastern Queens YMCA, a low brick building set back from the street by lawns. It was directly across the street from the grounds of Creedmoor State Hospital, the mental institution. On one side of Hillside Avenue, as he drove, was a fence standing in the darkness and behind the fence, far back from the street, the dim lights showing in small square windows with barred cages over them. On the other side of Hillside Avenue was this low brick building, its front a blaze of light, and standing in the windows were young people, some of them very young, but others older, in their twenties. He slowed down when he saw the young people in the lights. The car rolled past the building, and he noticed a parking lot on the side. The parking lot ran up to the backyards of a street of one-family brick bungalows. He parked the car on the street and walked into the parking lot. He was walking on the edge of the lot, along the line of fences of the bungalow houses, when, simultaneously, from two different yards, dogs came up to the fences, snarling and trying to climb over, claws hooked into wire openings. They were tawny German shepherds — the unofficial mascot of Queens homeowners — and their anger caused him to walk back out of the parking lot. Cars were scattered in the lot, some in the deep recesses near the rear of the building. He wanted to check those cars. However, the dogs would not let him. Were the dogs giving him a message from Sam Thornton? They probably were. Every dog in the tri-state area was at the disposal of Sam Thornton and General Jack Cosmos.

He got back into the car and was about to pull away from the curb when a blue Pinto came out of the YMCA lot. Two girls were in it, laughing. They drove up Hillside Avenue and he followed them. The girls went along a business street which was a replica of Northern Boulevard. Twenty blocks later, they came to the bright-gold neon sign of a bar called Pep's Place. It was on the opposite side of the street and the girls swung over and went down a side street, parked, and walked back to Pep's Place. Rosenfeld drove past the Pinto to the next corner, Eighty-third Avenue, made a right, and stopped halfway down a block of brick bungalows. He took a swig of water from his cranberry-juice jar, capped the bottle, took the .44 out of the glove compartment and inspected it. He put his head back on the seat. He knew the street he was on. Eighty-third Avenue and 257th Street, that was Fire Box 3043. Drive straight on Eighty-third Avenue and it brings you back out onto Hillside Avenue. Or, rather than drive straight, turn right and go into a series of neighborhoods that spill into each other. He decided to stay in the car, so he would not be standing around for an hour, maybe more — it was only ten o'clock — waiting for the two pretty princesses to get back in the car. He looked at the gun. If he had done his job right, he thought, if he had not missed the two girls the last time, perhaps the demons would have left him alone for a while.

He wondered why he missed so much. Why did he have to get a gun with a handle that was too big for his hand? It always had to happen to him. Look at that time with the fire helmet, he told himself. He had worked for a long time to get that fire helmet, worked in his grandfather's hardware store on the Grand Concourse in the Bronx. His grandfather paid him $1.50 an hour. On school days, he'd make only $3, and on some Saturdays, he would work long enough to earn $15, but his grandfather would give him only $10 because it was a small store and he said he had to fight to make a decent living. His grandfather never had anything in the store where it could be found easily, Bernard remembered. Yet his grandfather and the customers would become irritated if he couldn't disinter immediately a half-dozen zinc-covered No. 4 screw hooks. "Pay attention and learn," his grandfather would tell him. How could he do this, how could he learn when his grandfather always changed things around and then never informed him when he arrived at the store after school? Sitting in the car, staring at the .44 in his hands, Bernard remembered the woman in the black raincoat who came into the store on a wet, empty Saturday morning, told him she wanted a screen for a frying pan and then, for no reason, became impatient with him.

"It's just a screen that you put over a frying pan," she said.

"Yes, ma'am," Rosenfeld said. He was in the back of the store going through a pile of cartons, and she was up at the cash register.

"A screen so that grease don't come up and splatter all over me while I'm making chicken."

"I know," he told her.

"Grease splatters all over the place. I want a screen that stops it. Not a lid, now. A screen."

77

"I know what you want."

"Ah hah." She said it sarcastically.

The tension the woman created began to bother Rosenfeld. He was going through a pile of cartons and then he stopped and put his head on top of a carton and closed his eyes. "I know what you want," he called out to the woman.

"You do know?" the woman called back.

"Yes, ma'am," he said.

"Then tell me what I want."

"A frying-pan screen."

"Well, don't you want to sell me one?"

"I do. I'm just trying to find —"

"If you'd pick up your head, you'd find one," she snapped.

He looked up and saw that she was leaning over the counter, craning her neck, and staring at him.

"Trying to find one?" she said. She began to cackle.

"What's the matter?" Bernard's grandfather called out from the back. He came pushing through the debris behind the counter. "What can we do for you?" he said to the woman.

Suddenly, the pressure built up. A clot on the brain, he thought. His legs began to swell from the pressure of the clot. Bernard could still remember how he walked out from behind the counter and stood outside in the street, the rain causing the shoulders of his shirt to stick to him, while he tried to understand why the woman disliked him so much. At the time, he remembered thinking that it was as if something had come along and twisted her and pushed her away from him. Later, he was to understand that this was exactly what had happened on the day in the hardware store. Then the same thing happened when he finally got the orange fire hat.

This was in 1969, and he and his father had moved into a four-room apartment in Co-Op City, which is a three-hundred-acre area rising out of the rubble of the North Bronx. Thirty-five cooperative apartment houses, thirty stories in height, stand as the white answer to the blacks and Puerto Ricans spilling across the South Bronx like a wave across sand. Middle-class Jewish people, cabdrivers and garment-center workers and shopkeepers, forty-five thousand people, moved into the buildings. As the place was designed to be a city, a white city in a black borough, the tenants formed community organizations, one of which was a volunteer fire department. It was composed of young people mostly, and their headquarters was an empty carriage room on the second floor of Six Building. The room had a carpet and card tables and was a place to hang out as much as anything else. The management liked the idea of keeping groups of young people from standing in the building entranceways. The friends Bernard met at the volunteer-fire-department meetings began to send away for equipment which would serve as badges of their positions. One day Lenny Siegel appeared with new hip boots. The next day, Carly Bisciglia appeared with fire boots. Rosenfeld saved his money from working in the hardware store and sent away for a fire helmet to Cairnes Brothers of Clifton, New Jersey. The day it arrived, a bright-orange helmet, Rosenfeld took it to the headquarters room, and when he could find nobody there, he went outside the building and looked for his friends. It was March, with a raw, wet wind snarling past the buildings. Bernard walked across the frozen ground to the excavation site where everybody was hanging out. They were walking the foundation walls, which had been put in as the start of a row of shops. Heavy rainfall and melted snow had filled the foundations with water, in one place more than seven feet deep. Bernard walked out on the foundation walls to show the new hat to his friends. He had the hat balanced on his head, not jammed down, and he walked out proudly toward Siegel and Bisciglia. A gust of wind hit Bernard at the knees and in the side and caused him to set his feet in order to keep his balance. The wind increased and the bottom of his raincoat lifted. He put his hands against the coat to hold the flaps down. The fire hat half-blew and half-fell off his head and into the water, seven feet of charcoal-gray water. The front part of the fire hat dipped under the surface of the water, and the inside of the hat, sticking up, became a sail as the wind filled it and pushed the hat out toward the middle of the foundation. There it stopped.

Bernard walked off the foundation and picked up a board. When he tried reaching the hat with the board, he nearly fell off the foundation wall. He stood for an hour, waiting for the wind to blow the hat to within his reach. But each time the wind moved the hat, it only sent it farther out. When the sun went down, he walked off the foundation wall, past a lone streetlight, and went home. All night, he was restless while the picture of the fire hat in the water kept appearing in his mind. Before going to school that morning, he walked by the foundation and saw the hat was still in the middle of the water. When he came home in the afternoon, he and his friends tried to reach the hat with sticks and could not, and then decided to throw bricks at the hat, hoping a brick would propel it toward a foundation wall. This, too, did not work.

And now, sitting in the car, Rosenfeld remembered what it was like when he went to a volunteer fire meeting on that second night that his helmet was in the water. He could feel everybody looking at him and saying, "How could you save lives if you can't even get your own hat back?" He sat with his eyes down and remained silent. When he went to sleep that night, he cried. Why had this happened to him? Why couldn't the wind come along and blow the hat back to him? What was causing the wind to deliberately keep the hat away from him? When he came home from school the next afternoon, one of the boys was waiting for him outside the building. He said one of the construction workers had returned the helmet to the volunteer fire room. Bernard was not elated. It was too late. Something had happened to him that he would never forget: the wind had been against him.

In the car, he stuffed the .44 into his pocket and got out and walked to the corner and turned into the street leading to the avenue. The Pinto was gone. The two pretty princesses had driven away. Numb, he turned around and went back to his car and drove it on the side streets for hours. He got home at 4:00 a.m. to face the demons. It was the wind again, he tried to tell them. The wind that blew my helmet away, blew the girls away. Why did you make the wind do it, he sobbed.

He returned to Pep's Place every night that week and waited for hours, but the people leaving all had their cars parked on Hillside Avenue, in full view of anybody inside the bar, and there was no way to sneak up on them. He gave up on Pep's at three-thirty on a Sunday morning.

On Sunday night, he went to Howard Beach, which is a finger of land probing the broad flat waters of Jamaica Bay. Howard Beach is tormented by the whine and roar and kerosene smell of jet planes, which come in as low as three hundred and four hundred feet high as they land at Kennedy Airport.

For two nights he watched the same boy and girl sit at a wooden table in the parking lot of Rocky's Pizza, a huge brightly lit place on Cross Bay Boulevard, the main street through Howard Beach. He drove past the stand several times while the two sat and talked to each other. Once, Rosenfeld drove his Galaxie into the parking lot, passing within a few feet of the couple. The girl had large brown eyes and long brown hair and protruding teeth. She stared at Rosenfeld and then looked into her soft drink and began to shake the ice. Rosenfeld drove slowly to the rear of the pizza stand. He stopped the car and waited. He put the car in reverse and watched her again as he rolled back. But he did not receive a command from Sam Thornton or General Jack Cosmos. They refused the game he had hunted down. He pulled away from the pizza stand.

7

Three weeks later, on a Thursday night in mid-October, half an hour after midnight, he was driving through Flushing on 165th Street, crossing Thirty-fourth Avenue, when he saw the white Nova parked in front of a row of attached two-story houses. He noted two young women in the front seat. The side wall of his head burst into flames.

"Do you think Rosemary knows anything about Lorraine?" Susan McAuliffe, on the driver's side of the car, said to Jackie Dugan. Dugan was sitting on the passenger's side of the front seat of the white Nova; his shoulder-length brown hair pressed against the window.

"Sure she knows," he said.

"She'd kill Buddy if she caught him with Lorraine."

"Never," he said.

"Never? Huh. Rosemary would go out of her mind if she ever thought."

"If Buddy got the two of them together, believe me, I know what I'm telling you, Buddy would talk them into making a sandwich for him," he said.

"Jackie!" Susan said.

"Don't get mad."

"I don't like to hear that."

"It's true," he said. "He'd get them to do it."

"Well, I don't want to hear it."

Rosenfeld had the gun out in his hand and he was breathing in gasps as he walked toward them. He came up to the car, from behind, and found there was a bush between the sidewalk and the car. The car was parked a full three feet away from the curb. He wanted to walk up to the window and put the gun right against the glass, but the bush was in his way. So he stood behind the bush and held out the gun and fired at the long brown hair on the passenger's side. The dogs panted and his head was afire and the gun exploded in his hand and twisted. The window became foam and now he fired again. There was more howling and he kept firing. He emptied the gun, all five shots, turned, and ran. He was almost certain that somewhere during the firing he had seen an empty place where the brown hair had been. He was certain he had gotten this girl. As he ran, he did not hear the horn in Susan McAuliffe's car sound an insistent call for help.

Early Friday morning, at seven o'clock, he bought a *Dispatch* on Broadway in Yonkers and sat in the car and went through it, but it was the Westchester edition which went to press early and carried no news of a killing in Queens. He did not care if he was late to work. He drove into Manhattan and bought a late edition.

The story wasn't easy to find. It was one paragraph in a list of late bulletins on page eighteen. It said that a young man from Queens received a superficial head wound late Thursday night when a lone gunman fired four shots at a car which was parked on a street in Flushing.

Sam Thornton did not send his dog this time. He came himself. He walked up to Bernard and jabbed a long needle right into Bernard's forehead.

Inspector Carillo's face crinkled as he stepped out of the fall chill and went into the municipal smell of the 104th Precinct, which housed his own homicide unit. The walls had just been painted in the same sick-green color which had been on them for fifty years. On this morning, the first heat of the season entering the radiators caused the paint smell to come out of the walls and hang in the thick air. He walked past the desk, nodded to the sergeant and started up a staircase that had metal tips on the steps and a black iron banister. The staircase was just like the one in Carillo's grammar school, P.S. 117 in South Brooklyn, and in the annex to Manual Training High School. Since age seven, then, Carillo had spent at least part of almost every day in these same stairwells. By this point, the fatigue came before the climbing.

He went up to the third floor, where a card with hand lettering over the doorway announced, "15th Homicide Div." He walked into a large room that had a polished linoleum floor and two windows looking out onto the streets of old one- and two-family houses which make up the Glendale and Ridgewood sections of Queens. A bald, round-faced detective in a yellow shirt spoke into the telephone and put the receiver down on the desk. The bald guy, Sergeant Edward Hanlon, put one fist on top of the other and tilted his shoulders, to simulate holding a baseball bat.

"Chambliss," he said. The night before, Chris Chambliss, the first baseman for the Yankees, had hit a home run which put the Yankees in the World Series.

Carillo rolled up the *Dispatch* and got into the stance of a left-handed batter. He wiggled and then brought the newspaper around like a bat.

"Chambliss," Carillo said.

Hanlon laughed and picked up the receiver and went back to his conversation.

Carillo was about to walk into his office when he saw the three of them at his desk, two detectives and a lean black, head shaved, handcuffed by one hand to the chair. Carillo stepped away from the office quickly. Don't they ever think, he said to himself. Carillo made a point of never being involved in any questioning of defendants unless he had to. If he were ever in the same room with a defendant, the lawyers someday would have the right to bring him to the witness stand. As the head of all homicide investigations in Queens, Carillo could wind up spending all his time in a courtroom. The two detectives using his office should have known enough to take this spade to some other room, Carillo told himself. He shook his head. *Irishmen.*

"He took off his light-blue jacket, put it carefully on a hanger, and sat at an empty desk. He leaned back in the chair and was about to call in for something when he saw the intense looks on the two detectives. The black guy was leaning over the desk, talking to them.

84

Carillo couldn't break it up. He turned the *Dispatch* to the back, to the sports section, and again looked at the pictures of Chambliss knocking down fans as he struggled to get across home plate. Carillo held up the paper. "The only thing between me and him is a curve ball going under my bat," he said.

Hanlon put a hand on the receiver and laughed. For a few moments, Carillo began to daydream about being young and trying to make a living as a baseball player.

He had started doing this in the morning, over his first cup of coffee. The eldest of his four daughters, Maria, said she wanted to go away to college. This caused Carillo to grip the coffee cup so hard that his fingers turned white. He wanted his daughters home. It was all right for those liberals to send their daughters to sleep-away colleges, but that would not be the case in his house. He said nothing to her, however, because he did not want an argument so early in the morning. As his daughter talked, he gripped the coffee cup and remembered the cold rain on the first day he went away from home.

He was eighteen, and it was February of 1952, and he had been signed by the New York Giants to a minor-league contract. On this wet winter day, his father and mother drove him over to the bus terminal in Manhattan and put him on the bus to Florida, to the training camp at Melbourne, with $50 and a new glove.

"So, go out and do it," his father said.

"I'm just afraid of him living alone," his mother said.

"Ma, I told you," Carillo said, "in barracks, Ma. In barracks like the army with a hundred other guys."

What he had told his mother then, Carillo always knew, was right. He was a big strong kid out of Manual Training High School, and he was a baseball player at a training camp. That was a lot different from a girl, an eighteen-year-old girl, leaving the house where she belonged and going to live at some school where, and Carillo always flinched when he thought of it, you have all these kids sitting around dirty and smoking pot and fucking all day. Not any daughter of his. They were going to stay home where they belonged. There were plenty of good colleges in New York City. His daughter could go to Saint John's or Saint Francis. At breakfast, she had mentioned the University of Michigan. She could go to Michigan, all right. Saint John's University in Queens, Michigan. I was a different case, he again reminded himself.

In 1952, Carillo was assigned to the Danville, Virginia, team, and he played so well for them, hitting .305, that he was promoted the next year to the team in Bristol, Virginia, and then to the Nashville, Tennessee, team in a higher league, the Class A Sally League. It was while he was assigned to the Nashville team that Carillo found himself, upon a muggy Florida afternoon, coming up to bat in an exhibition against the Giants' Minneapolis farm team, which played Triple-A ball in the American Association.

Pitching for Minneapolis was a left-hander named Monte Kennedy, who had been up with the Giants, looked good for a while, then had trouble with his control and was sent back to Minneapolis. Carillo batted in the first inning against Kennedy. In his mind, Carillo thought it was the classic match: he was young and on the way up; Kennedy had had his chance and was going down. As Carillo stepped into the batter's box, he glared at Kennedy. Get out of my fuckin' way, Carillo said to himself. He twisted his spikes into the red clay.

Carillo concentrated on Kennedy's left hand. Through the noise and wet heat and body motion and nerves, he still was able to keep his entire body, eyes, shoulders, hips, hands and feet connected only to Monte Kennedy's left hand. Kennedy kicked and threw. The ball was on top of Carillo before he fully understood that it had been thrown. But the pitch was low and outside and as it went past Carillo, he looked up at the sky, trying to appear nonchalant, trying to let them think that he knew all the while that it was not a good pitch.

Kennedy's hands came up to begin the next pitch. His leg came up and forward, and his body after it, straining, the left arm coming directly overhand. The ball was at Carillo just as quickly this time, but he was able to follow it and his body was starting to lean and his hands starting to move, and then the pitch broke. It looked like it dropped a foot. Dropped like a stone. Then it was a hum going past Carillo's knees. It was a pitch he would remember for the rest of his life. For now, sitting at the desk in the 104th, Carillo still could remember looking down at the dirt that day in Florida and saying to himself, He can't make it, and he has a curve like that?

The two detectives shuffled out with the prisoner. One of them said he was sorry he had held Carillo up. "You fooled us, you got in half an hour early today," he said. Carillo kept his face straight. He did not like anybody in his office knowing his schedule so well. He would have to start walking in at unpredictable times. He went into his office and sat down. He reached into an incoming basket and took out a handful of typed forms, the reports of the unusual crimes that had occurred during the night.

The first was a two-page report turned in by the uniformed force. It read:

"At 2135 hours, Oct. 14, 1976, at 351–47 Sutphin Boulevard, second floor, one male black unidentified at this time was found dead of a shotgun wound of the head, that is, the face. Also in connection with this incident three (3) male blacks described below previously were taken to Jamaica Hospital suffering gunshot wounds.

"In response to signal 10-24 from C.U. 'Past Assault,' Police Officer Richard McCabe, shield number 25873, 103rd Precinct Recorder..."

Carillo went back to the first paragraph. He stared at the "described below previously." Then he turned the page and looked at the signature at the bottom of the report: "Robert T. Finnegan, Captain, 103rd Precinct." Carillo's hands pressed against the hair on the top of his head. Described below previously, he said to himself. He remembered the time in grammar school when, for some reason, the family having moved to a cheaper apartment for a year or so, he wound up in Saint Saviour's School with all the Irish from Park Slope. He was afraid ever to say that he had broccoli for dinner because all the flat-faced Irish kids would giggle and call him a guinea. They put all their genius into name-calling, Carillo thought. Once they're finished with that, they're as alert as a chair. Dumb cops. What they really mean when they say that is dumb Irish cops. He put the report aside and picked up the next one, the title on the printed form saying, "Detective Bureau Unusual Occurrence Report."

A short, typewritten paragraph said, "On October 15, 1976, at about 0030 hours at 34th Avenue and 165th Street, Flushing, subject John Dugan, male, White, 23, Flushing, was slightly wounded (top of head) by shot fired by unknown assailant. Subject was seated on passenger seat of parked car. In driver's seat was Susan McAuliffe, 23, of Richmond Hill. Subject was treated at Flushing Hospital and released." Carillo looked at the typed signature. "John Dwyer, shield number 1757."

"Hanlon," Carillo called out.

The bald sergeant, Hanlon, walked in. Carillo held out the Unusual. "You see this?"

"Not yet."

"Take a look at it."

Hanlon stood in the doorway and read the paragraph. "Uh huh," he said.

"I want you to check the area and see if any traffic tickets were given out yesterday or last night," Carillo said.

"Oh, they must of done that already," Hanlon said.

"Well, you do it anyway, just to be sure," Carillo said.

Hanlon looked at the report again. "Hey, Inspector, I'm just looking at the street again. They don't give no tickets in that section. It's all residences. There's no meters or no-parking signs anywhere around there."

"There are fire hydrants," Carillo said.

"What the hell, nobody parks in front of a hydrant around there."

"We don't know that," Carillo said. "Maybe somebody did yesterday. Find out for me, will you?"

He looked down. Why does it take so much talk to get something started, he said to himself. He opened the desk and looked at a sheet with the home numbers of his squad. He wondered why Dwyer hadn't called him last night. He dialed the number, a suburban 516 code, and he asked himself, What the hell does Dwyer use for brain —

"Yes?" the woman's voice said.

"Is Johnny there? This is the office."

"Oh, no, he's still at work," she said. "Isn't he there?"

"Oh, he is still at work? Forget the call then. He'll be around here soon."

Carillo hung up. His lips compressed in distaste. "Broads," he said aloud. He looked in the box for the voucher from the Forensics Unit. Each time a shooting occurs, the forensics, the laboratory people, arrive, sweep the scene, dig out bullets or any other physical evidence, then take it back to the laboratory with them. They give the detective in charge of the case a written receipt for his evidence. When Carillo couldn't find the slip, he became nervous. While he was reading the Unusual the first time, he had been thinking of calling up ballistics and asking them for a rush job; it normally took three or four days to get anything back from them. But now he couldn't even find the voucher for the bullets. And he wanted to know today. He called in Hanlon and asked him to look for the voucher. Hanlon shuffled through papers, then held up his hands. Empty. Carillo

called ballistics, which was located in a laboratory in the Police
Academy building on East Twentieth Street in Manhattan.

"This is Deputy Inspector Carillo of Queens Homicide."

"Sergeant Bauer," the other voice said.

"Sergeant, we had a shooting in Flushing last —"

"We have it," Bauer said. "Your man brought it over here himself
this morning. Gave us a rush delivery."

"Which man?"

"Dwyer — that's his name, isn't it?"

"He's there with you now?"

"No, he left. But we have the evidence. We'll let you know."

"Sergeant, we're waiting for this one."

"I'm working on it," Bauer said.

When Carillo hung up, he reached for his pipe. He was irritated.
Why hadn't Dwyer called him during the night? Then the irritation
dissolved, and the first little bit of tension ran through him.

"Hanlon!"

"Yes, sir?"

"Those traffic tickets from last night!" Carillo yelled out.

Little things. That was all Carillo was sure that he knew about the
business of detecting criminals. Pore through records, look up traffic
tickets, canvass neighborhoods for witnesses. Then go back and
speak to them again. Carillo never had gotten anything done as a
result of a brilliant deduction. Whenever he tried to go for one of
those thoughts, his mind washed up against the front of his skull and
then billowed back, a wave slapping against a wall. The futility of
trying to be brilliant left him with pinpricks of fatigue. And anything
good that ever happened to him as a policeman came as the result of
a visitation of luck which occurred only after hard work.

On the first arrest Carillo ever made as a cop, in 1957, he was
walking the streets at 3:00 a.m. in the Twenty-third Precinct in Harlem. It was a cold, still February night and the temptation was to get
inside a vestibule and keep a little warm until dawn. Instead, Carillo
kept walking in the cold. He was walking on Eighth Avenue, about to
turn into 119th Street, when he saw a man pushing a baby carriage
across Eighth Avenue at 117th Street.

Why you dirty sonuvabitch, having a kid out at this hour, Carillo
said to himself. He started trotting toward the man. The man began
pushing the carriage faster. Carillo broke into a run.

"Don't you go anywhere, I want to talk to you," Carillo called out.

The man stopped and Carillo pounded up to him. The man threw his hands into the air. "You got me," the man said.

Carillo jumped back when the man's hands went up. He fumbled under his coat for his gun. He wasn't sure of what he was doing.

"You don't need no gun, you got me," the man with the carriage said.

Carillo looked into the carriage. It was loaded with meat. At that time, the night-delivery trucks used to leave large stacks of food in the doorways of A & P supermarkets. The notion was, in those days, that crime slept, too, after midnight. Clerks used to come in at 6:00 a.m. and open the stores and haul in the deliveries. There was no question in Carillo's mind that the man with the baby carriage had raided an A & P doorway. He was uneasy about arresting a man for taking food. But Carillo handcuffed the man and brought him to the precinct, where, immediately, he was made to feel like a warrior who conquers children.

"Bringing home the bacon!" one of the detectives said.

When they took the man's name, the detectives stopped jeering. There was a file full of complaints on the man. He was in charge of a fleet of baby-carriage pushers and car riders who had been stripping supermarket doorways at night and selling the goods to bodega owners in the Twenty-fourth Precinct, the Hispanic part of Harlem.

The arrest changed nothing. The stores still had to discontinue night deliveries and many of the supermarkets eventually closed up. But this was not part of Carillo's worry. What mattered to him was that he learned always to take the extra step: if you walk after something instead of hanging around in a doorway, you'll get the break you need. This style was the one which moved him above the rank of captain, which, for an Italian, was the part of the climb where everything became sheer.

Carillo used books to get himself from patrolman to captain. At that point, he knew that no longer would being a monk in a chamber, memorizing scrolls, be of any use. Nor would politics be the answer; he was uneasy and they, the Irish, were uneasy whenever he attempted this. Carillo felt, therefore, that his rank, captain, was to be the end of it, and he presided over the Forty-first Precinct in the South Bronx, a place known as Fort Apache, and then was assigned to the detective division in Manhattan North because, the Irish felt, he had been around the niggers and the spics so long that he understood them and would be a help to the Irish detectives newly assigned to places like Harlem and Washington Heights, which was rapidly going black.

While on duty one day in 1971, Carillo was given a report of a female teacher bludgeoned to death in a teachers' bathroom at De-Witt Clinton High School. By nightfall on the first day, as news of the murder spread into the homes of people coming home from work, the eruption of public opinion could be felt physically. The murder became another limit passed. Now DeWitt Clinton High School was unsafe for Jewish teachers. A high school of the great, crowded, working-class-Jewish area had become, forever, another building in the city to be afraid of.

Carillo was at the scene before the body was moved to the morgue. A red pocketbook was upside down in the sink. A triangular chunk of enamel was on the floor, covered with the blood of the dead teacher, who was in a body bag with her head caved in. Whoever had been in the bathroom with the teacher had blood all over him. Carillo remained there for hours, forcing detectives to go over the washroom from door to windowsill several times. While he stood in the washroom doorway, he overheard two other detectives, assigned to the case by an inspector over Carillo, talking about a possible suspect named Lovejoy. The detectives left, and Carillo kept minutely inspecting the washroom. The three detectives with him were tired.

"When the fuck are we going to finish this?" one of them said.

"When we finish," Carillo said. He had no idea what he was looking for. All he knew was that when he walked away from that washroom, there would be nothing for anybody ever to find.

The next morning, the homicide office was filled with bosses from downtown. The night-long assault of radio and TV, and then the morning *Times* and *Dispatch*, had worried the commissioner and his assistants. Jews were screaming. That is the one confrontation Irish cops know not how to handle. All day long, Carillo sat pulling together the papers involved with the investigation, making out assignment sheets and clearing them with the three and four superiors who were watching every piece of work. After nine hours of this, Carillo looked up. One of the detectives who, the day before, had been talking about the suspect Lovejoy was standing in the room.

"How did you do with that guy Lovejoy?" Carillo asked.

"No good so far. We went to the apartment, but the mother won't tell us where he is."

Carillo was supposed to go home. "Give me the address," he said.

He went to the apartment, a fourth-floor walkup on 167th Street, and he said softly to the woman answering the door, "Ma'am, we have had a terrible death occur, and we need people to help us do the work of the Lord. We need information and your boy could help us. He could help us do the Lord's work." The religious angle worked. Rather than shake her head, the woman said, "If I see him, I'll call you." Carillo went out and had dinner. When he came back, the mother stood in the doorway and said, "You can talk to him, but only if I come with him." Behind her stood a six-foot-four semi-giant with an incongruous baby face. The boy was sixteen.

In Carillo's office, the mother sat alongside her son, across the desk from Carillo. Carillo could see the boy only from the waist up. The boy's first name was Clarence. He said that on the day of the murder he had not been in school; he had gone to a movie with two other kids. He gave Carillo the names. Ernest Wilson and José Vasquez. Carillo wrote down the names. Then he excused himself. He said he had to go to the men's room. When he got outside, he handed the names to a detective and said he wanted Wilson and Vasquez spoken to right away. A half hour later, Carillo was asking Clarence Lovejoy about something else when a detective stuck his head in the office and nodded. Carillo again excused himself and stepped outside.

"I don't know about Vasquez, but he sure as hell wasn't with Ernest Wilson," the detective said. "Wilson's in Attica."

Carillo came back in and sat down at his desk. He shook his head sadly. "I feel terrible," he said.

"What's the matter?" the mother said.

"I feel terrible," Carillo said, looking at the son.

The boy said nothing.

"You know, I'd like to believe you," Carillo said. "Like to believe you. But you told me you were with Ernest Wilson yesterday."

"Was," Lovejoy said.

Carillo shook his head again. "Gee, I'd really like to believe you. Like to believe you. But, you see, Wilson wasn't here yesterday. He was in Attica Prison."

The boy started to say something, but the mother put her hand on his arm. "We not sayin' anythin'. You tryin' trick this poor child.

From now on, we don't say anythin'. My son's a good boy. We want a lawyer before we talk no more."

"That's your right," Carillo said.

"I know it," the mother said.

Carillo said to the boy, "Why don't you take a seat outside? I just want to talk to your mother for a moment. Then the two of you can go home. We'll see that you get a ride. All right?"

The boy got up and lumbered out and slumped in a chair. Carillo leaned forward and started to talk to the mother. Somehow, he had to reach her sense of decency. Maybe the boy had nothing to do with the murder, Carillo told himself. The boy might be lying for an entirely different reason. But he had to find out. He couldn't let this kid go off to the protection of a lawyer. If that happened, Carillo might never see Clarence Lovejoy again. As he leaned over and began to talk to the mother, his eyes strayed for a moment. They fell on the son, who sat slumped in the chair. His long legs were stretched out. This caused the pants to ride up his ankles. The boy had great thick ankles. The knobs pressed against the heavy white athletic socks he was wearing: white athletic socks that were covered with blood.

"Look at the boy's socks," Carillo said to the mother.

She stared out the doorway. She got up and walked out, bent over, and looked at the bloody socks.

"Clarence!"

It was nine o'clock. By midnight, Clarence Lovejoy was being booked for homicide, and at a press conference, the commissioner said, "The case was solved quickly due to the extraordinary work of Captain Carillo." Within a month, he was a deputy inspector. The commissioner was smiling. Maybe Carillo was a guinea, but he was a guinea who had gotten everybody off the hook.

And now, sitting in his office in Queens, Carillo started to go through a sheaf of reports about another murder, the killing of an old man in his apartment in Jamaica. The Unusual report said the man had been bludgeoned to death. Carillo looked for what was left out of the report. Detectives, even in reports, keep something for them- selves. In this case, the report did not say what had been used to bludgeon the old man. This kept Carillo busy while he waited to hear from ballistics. It was only eleven-thirty in the morning, and Carillo knew his wait could be long.

At that hour, in Manhattan, in a dark room on the eighth floor of the Police Academy building, Sergeant Richard Bauer peered into a comparison macroscope. This is an optical instrument which resembles two microscopes joined together. As Bauer looked through the twin eyepieces, he saw something that closely resembled a piece of fieldstone: a gray surface with crevices and irregularities, sitting motionless. A series of lines, patterns of lines, ran from left to right across the gray surface. A thin vertical line, a straight hair, ran down the middle of the gray picture. Bauer turned a small wheel. The right half of the gray field began to revolve. On slides at the bottom of the instrument were two dented smashed lead slugs. The one on the left had been removed from the head of Connie Bonventre. The one on the right had been dug out of the front seat of Susan McAuliffe's car. Looking through the macroscope, the two seemed to be one. But the thin vertical line, the hairline, was the line of demarcation. Everything to the left of the line was the bullet from Connie Bonventre's head. Everything to the right was the bullet from Susan McAuliffe's car. Bauer had been studying the horizontal lines running from left to right across the gray field. The lines did not join. The lines from the Bonventre bullet hit the hairline and then the lines from the McAuliffe bullet picked up, but at different spacing. If Bauer could get a place where the lines came together, he would have a starting point. It would not prove that the bullets came from the same gun, but at least it would give him a place to begin to look. For it would take many lines to match, many irregularities to join each other, right and left, before he would say anything, before he would say the two bullets were from the same gun.

A radio played soft music from a shelf on the wall alongside him. Bauer was motionless, breathing through his mouth, as he hunched over the macroscope. Then he backed away from the macroscope, reached into his breast pocket for a pack of cigarettes, walked out into the hall, and lit up. He stood in the dim hallway, separated from the elevators by a prison-like cage, and took a deep drag. His brain was starting to fuzz. He knew he did not have much longer to work on the bullets today. A ballistics man works at the macroscope in twenty-minute shifts. Over a day, the most he can do is about four hours of work. The concentration required is like that of writing. All the rest of life must be shut out while you live on getting two lines to fit each other. Then two more, and two more after that, and, finally, many, many lines. The horizontal lines on the slugs are the fingerprints of a gun. The grooves and lands, the rifling — the spiral lines inside a gun barrel which cause a bullet to whirl out — are put into a gun barrel by running an instrument called a broach through a newly made gun barrel. A broach is a rod studded with metal burrs. As the broach is drawn through the barrel, the action of metal on metal leaves a set of imperfections on the gun barrel that will be unique to this gun barrel. Any bullet fired from it will carry the markings of these imperfections, the lines that go from left to right on the macroscope. The problem Bauer faced was that the slugs he was dealing with had passed into something else. The characteristics of the slug on the macroscope can be determined by the character of the body it passed through. In this case, on the left, a skull, and on the right, a car window and seat, containing heavy metal springs. Because of this, many times, ballistics can provide no conclusive answers.

When Bauer went back to the macroscope, his eyes saw nothing but the fine rifling lines, going left to right. There were many other marks on the gray field, slashes and V's, from the skull and the car, but Bauer did not know they were there. After four years of matching grooves and lands, he functioned by optical reflex: he saw broach markings, not scratches from skull bone.

It was almost one o'clock when Bauer suddenly became tense. On the macroscope, he had a set of lines, a pattern, which matched perfectly. Or do they match? he asked himself. Are these lines the same? Sure they are, he said. The moment he said that, Bauer pulled up. He stood up, stretched, and flicked on the lights. He knew he was through for the day. The moment you begin reading things into what you're seeing, the moment you begin hoping, then it's time to stop. Have a smoke, drink some coffee, do some filing, and then go home. Go home and go to bed early. In the morning, everything would be fresh. He would be able to tell honestly whether the lines were matching or not.

When Bauer went home at four o'clock, he tried to empty his head so he would not see the gray field, the two bullets, on the car ride all the way up to Suffern, in Rockland County.

At five o'clock, Carillo put down his sheaf of papers and called ballistics.

"Inspector, you know we'll call you when we get something," the man at ballistics said.

"Well, what does it look like now?" Carillo asked.

"Inspector, you know that one man handles one case. I don't know where Bauer is on this. When he has something to report, he'll call you."

Carillo hung up. Outside in the office, Dwyer was hanging up his jacket.

"Dwyer?"

"Here, Inspector."

"What did they tell you at Ballistics?"

"Nothing. The minute I gave it to them, they chased me. They don't let you stay there."

"Well, do you have any idea?"

"No, do you?"

"Me?" Carillo said. "What do I know what they do with bullets?"

For four days, Sergeant Richard Bauer sat at his comparison macroscope and watched the lines. Then he left for his two days off. He got to the Settlers Tavern in Suffern, on the way home, and called his wife and told her to come down and see him; he would not be coming home until he was legless. All during a working week, Bauer finds it impossible to take anything to drink at night. He is too tired, too susceptible, too willing. And it is impossible to work the next day with even the tinge of a hangover. So he puts it all into his days off. His wife came to meet him and they went home at 11:00 p.m.

The day after he returned to work, eight days after the bullet was taken from Susan McAuliffe's car, Bauer reviewed his work on the macroscope. He had both bullets, the left and the right side of the hairline, revolving. He kept watching these rows of lines, patterns of lines, matching each other as if they were a long common line, as if the hairline were not there to show they were separate. He stood up, flicked a switch on the macroscope and then walked into the other office. He picked up the phone.

"Dwyer there?" he asked. He was told that it was Dwyer's day off. He asked for Carillo.

"Inspector Carillo," Carillo's voice came over the phone.

"Sergeant Bauer from Ballistics."

"Yes, Sergeant."

"Both bullets came from the same gun. A forty-four Bulldog. It is made by the Charter Arms Company. Up in Connecticut."

8

Kevin had called and told her where to meet him, but when she arrived, she still was amazed to find him there. His red Capri was parked right up against the boardwalk in the winter emptiness. Laura Davidson parked her car alongside the Capri, stepped out into the freezing afternoon, and was about to run up on the boardwalk and down onto the beach when she remembered to lock the car.

At this part of Rockaway Beach, in Queens, on Beach Thirty-eighth Street, the old wooden bungalows along the boardwalk have been knocked down, leaving block after block of gray-white sand, blinking with broken glass, and made ugly by mounds of old car tires and stained mattresses. Down the block from the beach, on the opposite side of an el trestle, are rows of three-story wooden houses. Some of the windows of the scarred houses are boarded, others covered with plastic sheets ripped and billowing in the wind: welfare insulation. Those who live in the houses, blacks stuck in a desert, casually break into cars left up by the boardwalk, by those white kids who come to surf. Even at 11:00 a.m. on a freezing weekday like this, with the temperature at twenty-three, somebody would walk up from the street of houses, smash the car windows, and begin yanking out tape decks. Most surfers who use this part of Rockaway leave a dog in the car, a big dog usually, a German shepherd or Doberman pinscher, as a day watchman.

Kevin had no dog in his red Capri. Laura glanced in the Capri window as she started for the boardwalk. On the window was a student parking sticker for Cocoa Beach Junior College. In the backseat, a carton was filled with tapes. Laura said to herself, I don't care; if somebody steals them, I'll buy him all new ones. She hurried up the ramp to the boardwalk, her Frye boots sounding on the rotting wood. The anticipation rose with each step. At first, as she came up the ramp, her eyes saw only the iron boardwalk railing. Another step and now there was the waterline, far in the distance, the winter sky hitting the flat cold ocean. She took another step and she saw more of the ocean, with white feathers skipping across it, and Laura started to run and now she could see everything. Here, in the water, right in front of her, perhaps seventy-five yards out, Kevin was sitting hunched over on his board, looking behind him to see if any of the swells would develop into a wave. Alongside him was Tommy Balzer. The two of them looked alike: sun-bleached hair and black wetsuits. Laura Davidson waved. The two surfers did not see her. She clomped across the boardwalk and went down the stairs, avoiding a missing step, and came onto the short stretch of wet, eroded beach. The water washing over the sand pushed along empty milk cartons and plastic bleach bottles. She tiptoed backward to keep the water from touching her boots.

"Yo!"

Out on his board, Kevin Curtin, twenty, had a black wetsuit arm raised. On the beach, Laura Davidson, nineteen, gave a little jump and the right arm of her bright-red down jacket went up in a return salute. She did not notice Tommy Balzer's wetsuit arm waving to her. All she could see was Kevin Curtin on his surfboard. She had not seen him since the last week in August. The wind coming off the ocean caused her to hunch her shoulders. Drops of spray hit her long, thick brown hair. But her mouth remained in a smile of large perfect glistening white teeth.

She stood there for five minutes while Kevin watched the swells build to waves and gathered himself to paddle with them. Each time, at the last moment, he would slap the water in disdain and let the wave he did not like go by. Finally, there was one which built up sufficiently to cause him to drop onto his belly and begin paddling, black arms digging into the water which was beginning to gather white lines. Behind him, the wave rose and frosted at the top and it started to curl as it reached Kevin and then suddenly he was up on his board: crouching, standing on the oblique, the right foot out. He started to ride the wave straight in, the water boiling under the point of his surfboard, and then his body swayed and the feet kicked and the surfboard shot in an arc, from left to right, across the face of the wave, and then he changed direction, plunging straight down the wave while everything broke into foam. He tried to outrun the white water, but he could not, and the board shot out from under him and was tossed high over the wave and tumbled with the white water toward the beach. Kevin disappeared.

"You'll freeze!" Laura yelled.

Kevin Curtin's blond head shot up from under the water. Shaking his head like a dog, he started to push his body through the waist-deep water. Laura Davidson ran along the sand and waited until the water receded in one spot and then she darted across to Kevin's surfboard. She grabbed it and tucked it under her arm and stepped out of the reach of the water. Kevin Curtin splashed out and came up to her. His lips were trembling.

"You've got to be crazy," she said to him.

"I want to get a towel," Kevin said. His feet flopped in his black wetsuit boots as he hurried past her and went up and over the boardwalk and down the ramp to his red Capri. Laura followed with the surfboard. Kevin unzipped the top of the wetsuit and brought out a set of keys which were hanging on a cord around his neck. He bent down and opened the Capri and dove into it. "Be right out," he said. Inside the car, he buried his head in a towel. Laura put the board on the roof of the car. The elastic wires of the surfboard rack were humming in the wind. Inside the car, Kevin contorted himself as he pulled off the wetsuit. He quickly pulled on a white Irish fisherman's sweater. He wiggled into a pair of jeans and jammed his feet into Frye boots. When he came out, Laura had the board already fastened on the rack.

Tommy Balzer came down the ramp with his face twisted in the cold. He handed Kevin the surfboard and flopped into the car. When Kevin finished fastening the other surfboard on top, he opened the car door and flipped his keys in to Tommy. "Meet you home," he said. He slammed the door and walked with Laura to her car, a 1975 Impala.

"Where are we going?" she said.

"For a cup of coffee," he said.

"I could use it, I'm absolutely chilled," she said.

"I'm not?" he said.

"Oh well, you people don't even seem to care. When did you get home?"

"Last night. Real late."

Her excitement rose; he had called her on his first day home. His Christmas vacation was starting before hers.

"How long are you home for?" she asked him.

"For good."

"Oh, wow, you really are?"

"I'm transferring to NYU. I'm taking prelaw courses."

"Oh, wow, that's terrific. When did you decide to do that?"

"I don't know. I just got tired of Cocoa Beach. I mean, it's all right for a while. Then it gets to you. The school gets to you. It's all right if you want to be a cop. But then, you know, it gets to be a hassle. Studying about criminology. You're going to do that, you might as well do it right. Go to law school."

"What changed your mind so quick? When you went away in September, you were telling me how great it was, the surf and all that."

"You want to know the truth?" he said. "For the whole month of September, there were no waves. And then, after that, there didn't seem to be all that many days when the waves were so supergood. I don't know what it was. Whether there were lots of other times last year that we just didn't notice there were no waves — because we were goofin' around and didn't care — or that this year was different, that there really were no waves. All I know is I just got tired sitting there and looking at a flat ocean and then going to school to hear some guy with a crew cut talk about how many jails there are in the country."

"When do you start at NYU?"

"Next month."

"Next month? Wow. I thought you're talking about going in September or something."

"Hey, why waste the time? I made up my mind this time. You see me out here today. Don't get the wrong impression. We just came down here on a goof. We were around warm water for so long. Let's take on the winter. Building character. That's all. Tomorrow I go to the city and register for classes."

"Prelaw," she said. "You can't just sit around getting stoned and expect to get into a law school."

"Don't even talk about it. That's another thing I got tired of. A little is all right. But those guys on the beach down there, sometimes they don't do anything else. All fucked up. Forget about it. After a while, I just wanted to be someplace where people would *talk* to me. At least sometimes. Now — tell me what you've been doing."

"Going to school and waiting for you to call."

"How could I call? We didn't have money for a phone."

"Well, you could've called collect."

"Last year when I did that, your father got mad about the bills."

"I don't care, that was last year. You could've called me a couple of times, anyway. My birthday, you didn't even call me on my birthday."

"I wanted to, but you told me that last year your father — "

"But you should have called me. It was important."

"Why?"

"Because I wanted you to."

"Well, I called you the first time I had the money and that was right today. If it only cost a dime from down there, I'd have called you five times a day."

"Would you?" she said.

"Yes."

"Why?"

"Because I like to talk to you. Didn't I call you right away this morning? I would've called you last night, but we didn't get in until like three-thirty in the morning."

"You could've called me at four o'clock and I would've got up and come over to see you," she said.

"Let's stop in here," Kevin said, pointing to a white shack with a sign saying "Clam Bar." Laura pulled into the empty lot alongside the shack. The front porch, enclosed by screens in the summer, was now protected with storm windows. They sat on the porch at a table with an oilcloth covering and a red tin ashtray. The counterman, in a thick black sweater and stained white apron, brought them coffee and dishes of cherrystones. The clams are raked out of Jamaica Bay by local clamdiggers living in houses on stilts at Hamilton Beach, a cluster of rooftops directly across a finger of water from the runways at Kennedy Airport.

"You'll have to concentrate," she said.

"I know, this isn't Florida," he said.

"It's such a hard thing to do," she said. "When I started last year, I thought I'd just study like I did in high school and breeze right through. Then I got into this Chinese. Wow. I thought I wasn't going to make it. The instructor told me that I was just going to have to empty my head completely and then get with it, breathe it. Don't even live for anything else but the Chinese. Do you know, I don't even remember some of the nights. All I did was go into a trance. But, boy, that's when you're really doing it."

"I'm going to do the same thing," he said.

"You better," she said.

"No, I'm going to do it. I'll handle my mind just like a surfboard. I'll make it do exactly what I want."

He made a curving motion with his hand. She reached out and put her hand on top of his.

"I'm glad you're home," she said.

"So am I." He smiled. "I missed you a lot."

"Then why didn't you even write me?" she said.

"Come on now, that's too much," he said. They both laughed.

They drove home on Cross Bay Boulevard and turned into Forest Park, which runs for four miles, with the exit a block and a half from Laura's house. The walks on both sides of the roadway were empty. At one point, the car came through a depression, thick woods of leafless trees on either side, and then the roadway rose and on the right was a large grove of pine trees, four and five stories high. Laura pulled the car to the curb and started to get out.

"What are you doing?" he asked her.

"I want to see something. Come on."

They walked into the middle of the pine grove. The ground was a carpet of needles. The wind shook the tops of the trees. As Laura walked into the silent, sweet-smelling grove, her head barely brushed against the lowest branches on the great trees. Through the trees you could look down a hill and see a green bus smoking in the cold air on a busy street.

"I grew up in here," Laura said.

"Did you come here a lot?" Kevin asked. "I came here, you know, a couple of times."

"I always came here," Laura said. "I made my mother give me lunch and I'd come here for the day. Come all alone. I didn't want anybody else. Playing, dreaming. I made-believe I lived here in a house. I'd sit and make-believe and listen. Hear it? Hear the wind going through? I love it here." She bent over and picked up two pine cones. She handed one of them to him. "Present," she said. She held

102

the cone to her nose and sniffed it. Kevin leaned over and nuzzled the side of her neck. Her eyes closed and she craned her neck.

"I have to go to school," she said.

"I didn't say anything," he said.

"You didn't have to," she said. She looked at her watch. It was one-forty-five. She had to hurry home. She had two classes, the first one at two-thirty, and then a paper to do on Chinese history which would take her a good four hours of library work.

She dropped Kevin at an attached brick house a half-block from the tennis stadium in Forest Hills. The stadium ivy rustled in the cold wind.

"Do you want to stop around Dave Peluso's new place tonight?" Kevin said.

"I won't be home from school till nine o'clock," she said.

"So I'll pick you up at your house at nine o'clock."

"Nine-fifteen," she said.

She left the school library at eight-thirty and was home at a quarter to nine. She lived in a three-story attached house on the corner of Union Turnpike and Burns Street in Forest Hills. The entrance was on Burns Street, which is the first street in a private section called Forest Hills Gardens. The side of the house, however, faced Union Turnpike, a service road to a four-lane expressway leading to Brooklyn. She got out of the car, carrying a nine-hundred-page Chinese history textbook. She was dulled from the hours of concentrating in the library. She inhaled the cold air and thought about going out with Kevin. The excitement caused her to run to the front door. She skidded up to the door and then spun around.

Her good tan jumper was at Candy Merritt's house. Candy lived a block up Union Turnpike, right across the street from the entrance to the park. Laura Davidson held the heavy textbook in front of her and began running up the lighted block to Candy Merritt's house. The expressway was depressed at this point, so the street was filled with sound from an unseen source. The brightly-lit sidewalk was empty. She was in the slot between the time when people come home for dinner and the time when they come out to walk the dog. She couldn't wait to get to Candy Merritt's house to hear the squeal of delight that would greet the news that Kevin was back and that he was taking her out. Laura laughed as she thought of this. She laughed as she ran up the block to get her tan jumper. She was

103

young and her eyes gleamed and her pure white teeth showed and she laughed in her happiness. It was the happiest she had ever been. She started to run faster and then her head froze and her feet stopped as she saw him come out in front of her. A black knit cap on his head. A fat face with a silly smile. His hand came out from under his blue zipper jacket and the streetlight showed he had a gun and she closed her eyes and covered her face with her thick textbook and she was about to scream when Bernard Rosenfeld held the gun right against the Chinese history textbook and pulled the trigger. Pulled it once. Rosenfeld jumped up in delight. "I know I got you," he said to the body on the ground. He skipped past Laura Davidson's body. Stuffing the gun in his belt, he ran down Union Turnpike, past Laura Davidson's house, to his car, which was parked on Queens Boulevard.

When Inspector Carillo arrived, he walked directly over to the body, bent down and lifted the blanket from the face. Fresh dark blood gleamed in a small neat hole in the center of the top lip. The front teeth had been blown out. A piece of one of the teeth, a sliver of white covered with dried blood, was entangled in the brown hair alongside her cheek.

"Small entry wound," Carillo said, as if reading from a form. Which he was. He was unsure of himself and almost trembling as he looked at the girl's face. One of the girl's large brown eyes bulged out of the socket. Carillo went to the manual in his mind and recited things they teach in the Police Academy.

"Only one shot fired?" he said.

"That's all, Inspector," Johnny Dwyer's voice said.

"You mean one is all you can vouch for," Carillo said.

"We looked all through the area," Dwyer said. "The people we talked to said they only heard one shot."

"We still don't know how many times he fired," Carillo said. He was becoming ill. His head began to throb. He pulled the blanket back over the toothless alabaster face and pulled away quickly, moving before he straightened up. He walked out to the side of the expressway and stared down at the cars, but what he saw was the face of his eldest daughter.

When a man from the city desk reached him on the phone and told him about the murder, Danny Cahill only half listened to the first sentence or two. Then he heard the address. "Where?" he said. "Where'd you say?"

"Union Turnpike. Near Burns Street. Forest Hills."

"What time is it?" Cahill said.

"Twenty after nine now," the desk man said.

"I won't make the eleven-thirty," Cahill said.

"There's an edition you could make at one a.m."

"That's the one I'll make."

Cahill slammed down the phone and turned to his companion, a famous British actor with whom he had intended to spend a long evening.

"I got to go," Cahill said. "A girl got shot."

"That must happen very often in this city," the actor said. "Why don't you let the youngsters handle these shoot-'em-ups?"

"Then they'll want to handle my paycheck, too," Cahill said.

The British actor laughed. "You realize," he said, "every columnist in New York is trying to find me, and you keep leaving me in pubs. If I get in trouble tonight, you'll be to blame."

"Yeah," Cahill said. He bolted out of the bar and, in the subway, stopped to call home.

"You heard?" his wife said.

"I'm on the way out now. Who is it, do you know?"

"Laura Davidson. My God, six blocks from here, too."

"Do I know her?"

"Oh, you must. She's been here with Moira."

"No, I don't know her," he said.

The train came into the station with a rush of stale wind and a noise that smothered words. "I'll call you when I get out there," he yelled into the phone.

The subway ride to Queens, to the Union Turnpike Station, is the world's cheapest and fastest and best transportation. It eliminates eleven miles of the world's worst traffic. It takes twenty-one minutes and it costs fifty cents. It transports you from a forest of skyscrapers on Manhattan's East Side to a part of Queens where the neighborhoods resemble an Ohio town. The subway stop at Union Turnpike is on Queens Boulevard, only three blocks from the shooting. By the time Cahill arrived, a few minutes before ten, the body of Laura Jean Davidson had been removed. Replacing it was the yellow chalk outline of a body which marks the scene of all homicides. The area was roped off and splashed with the bare light of a Frezzy held by a television technician. When Inspector Carillo saw Cahill, he nodded and walked out across Union Turnpike and looked down at the cars on the expressway again. Cahill stepped over the rope and came up to him. "Hey, I don't mind you coming into my neighborhood socially," Cahill said, "but I don't like seeing you here on business."

Carillo did not smile. He tried to stare at the passing cars.

"Young girl, huh?" Cahill said. "You'll get the rat-bastard."

"I don't know," Carillo said.

"Hey, c'mon," Cahill said. "You been through things like this before."

"This is worse."

"What do you mean, worse?"

"Just that," Carillo said.

For a dozen years, the two men had known each other, and in a dozen years of riots and homicides and coffee and booze, neither had ever lied to the other. Cahill was friendly with a lot of cops, and most of them were, at least part of the time, full of shit. That was what he liked about them, their lies, their exaggerations, their efforts to not only be cops but to play cops. His police friends fed him material every now and then. He would write stories about them, and they would love seeing their names in print, seeing themselves quoted, saying things like, "The alleged perpetrator was seen in the vicinity of the incident." But Carillo was different. Carillo never looked for publicity. What Carillo was looking for was an understanding ear and some reasonably intelligent feedback. Carillo and Cahill did not bullshit each other.

"I think we better have a drink," Cahill said.

"Later," Carillo said. "Later, I could use at least one drink. Give me an hour to make sure everything is going all right." He forced the start of a smile. "It's my burden," Carillo said, "working with all these dumb Irish cops." It was a signal to Cahill, a signal that Carillo's tension was ebbing, just a little.

Carillo got through with his detectives and the forensics faster than he thought he would. By eleven o'clock, he and Cahill were sitting at the bar of an Italian restaurant near the corner of Union Turnpike and Queens Boulevard. Carillo was drinking brandy. Cahill ordered a white wine and a glass of water. He kept sipping the water. He knew he was going to have to write fast to make a one-o'clock edition.

He sat with Carillo for almost an hour, and he did what he could do better than anything else: he listened. He grunted every now and then and shook his head and whistled, gestures to indicate that he was listening and to prod the story along. Carillo told him just about everything he knew. "You remember the Bonventre shooting in Bayside?" Carillo began. "The girl in the car outside the discotheque?"

An envelope marked "Jinni" popped up in the reference room in Cahill's mind. It was automatic; after a quarter of a century in the newspaper business, he had his own personal built-in morgue. "Yeah," he remembered. "I remember that. I know the guy who runs the joint. Billy Lee. Used to be a fighter. Light-heavyweight. Not bad. Yeah?"

"And you remember the two girls who were shot while they were standing on a stoop in the Bronx?" Carillo said. "One got a bullet in the arm, nothing serious, but the other one took a slug in the back. She was hurt pretty bad, paralyzed, maybe permanently. You recall that?"

"Vaguely."

"And then there was a couple sitting in a parked car in Flushing. The guy got shot in the head. He was lucky, just a superficial wound, a scar, some headaches, nothing worse. You remember that?"

"No," Cahill said.

"Well, there's no reason you should," Carillo said. "No reason I should either, except for one thing. The bullets. All three shootings involved forty-four-caliber bullets. That's kind of unusual. Not unheard of, but unusual. I had the bullets checked out. The one that killed the Bonventre girl and one of the bullets that was fired at the boy in the car. I would've tried one of the bullets from that Bronx shooting, too, but they all hit the brick stoop. They were so smashed they couldn't be identified beyond the fact that they definitely were forty-four-caliber slugs. But the Bonventre bullet and the Dugan bullet — Dugan, that's the boy's name — they matched. Perfectly. They came out of the same gun — a forty-four-caliber Bulldog revolver. It's a small gun. Two-inch barrel. Easy to conceal. Follow me?"

"Uh, huh."

"And I can't prove it, of course, but I'm pretty sure the Bronx shooting was the same thing. Same gun. Same guy."

Carillo gulped down his brandy and nodded to the bartender for another. "This one, too. Tonight. I won't know for sure till tomorrow, till Ballistics gets to it, but I know. I know. We got a good slug. It's a forty-four, I know."

The inspector picked up his fresh brandy and rubbed the glass with his fingers. "Counting tonight," he said, "six young people have been shot. Connie Bonventre. Frank Parisi, he was with Bonventre in the parked car. Marie Perrotti. Madeleine Giordano. Jackie Dugan. Laura Jean Davidson. Except for the ones who were together at the time of the shooting, there is absolutely no connection among the victims. None at all. Four of them happen to be Italian. So what? They were shot in Italian neighborhoods. No good motive for any of the shootings. No enemies. Nothing. What do the victims have in common? Well, they're all young, all twenty, twenty-one, right around there, and all the girls have brown hair, long brown hair, I think. We have to think the girls were the targets. Dugan, he's got long brown hair, too. Very long. And he was sitting in the passenger seat. It's very possible he could have been mistaken for a girl. This killer, this person carrying a forty-four, I don't really know anything about him, but whoever he is, he certainly doesn't like young girls."

Carillo paused, drained of words and breath. "You sure it's a guy?" Cahill asked.

Carillo shook his head. "I'm sure of nothing. The ones who've been wounded, the ones who got a glimpse of him, they all say it was a man. Their descriptions aren't very good. You can understand that. One of them, the Giordano girl, who only got nicked on the arm, can't even talk about it. She starts, and her mouth opens and then it closes and she says she feels like she's drowning. She says she wants to help us, but she can't. She says the water scares her."

He drank again, emptying the brandy glass. "A couple of the victims," Carillo resumed, "talk about his eyes, deep eyes, burning eyes, frightening eyes, but, you know, you don't really know whether they're remembering the eyes or the gun. We don't really know anything. We don't know if the guy — if it is a guy — if he comes on foot or by car or what. We figured at least we had a pattern: the guy always struck late at night, between midnight and two a.m., on side streets, dark streets. And then tonight, it isn't even quite nine o'clock, and he goes for a girl all by herself on a main street. It breaks the pattern. It scares the hell out of me. No pattern. No motive. No clues. One of these guys comes along every thirty years. Jack the Ripper type."

"Guy up in Harlem," Cahill said, "mutilated six small boys. Just a year ago."

"Spade crime," Carillo said. "Nobody notices." He looked around at the streets of expensive houses which run off Union Turnpike. "These people will have us up against the wall. And they should. That's my daughter on the ground there."

"Mine, too," Cahill said. He drained the glass of water. "I'm going to write about this," he said.

Carillo looked at him. "I know," the inspector said. "I want you to. Otherwise, I would have had one quiet brandy."

"Why do you want me to?"

"Because I need help. I need all the help I can get. I need somebody to find this killer for me. I don't need a cop to do it. I need a citizen, somebody who can see something no cop can see. I need somebody who knows who the killer is — or thinks he knows."

Cahill used that as the theme of his column, which he wrote in his house, in a garage which had been converted into an office by a local carpenter. He dictated it over the phone to the *Dispatch*. When he finished, he was tired, but excited from the deadline writing, a thousand words in less than an hour. He wasn't used to feeling this way in these surroundings. He wrote columns at home on days when he was throwing a change of pace, a column on an arsonist friend or on an out-of-town whore giving New York a bad name. There was no news writing at home, because there never was any news in Queens. He knew that at this moment, finishing a heavy news story against a deadline, he should be in a city room, with noise and people, and he should be grabbing his coat and heading for the Chinese restaurant to have a drink. He always needed a drink the moment he turned in his column. One high demands another.

Instead, he stepped out of his garage-office and into the silence of the kitchen. He looked in the refrigerator and grabbed a chunk of Swiss cheese. Munching it, he went up to bed. His wife rolled over in irritation when he slumped onto the side of the bed and dialed the office again.

"Goddamn telephone," she muttered.

"If we don't make this call, we don't have the telephone," he said.

"Make the calls downstairs then," she said.

"Hey, what's the matter with you? I just finished working."

"I took a pill and it's got me knocked out," she said.

The nightside guy answered, and Cahill asked if anybody had any last questions on the column. When he was told no, he asked if it was okay, if it read all right. When he was told yes, he hung up and stretched out in bed. But he was too excited to sleep. He stared at the ceiling and thought about his copy going through the news desk, then the horseshoe copy desk, and then on a conveyor belt to the composing room. Always, somebody was looking for it, pointing to it, handling it more quickly than anything else. He watched his story being set in type, hearing the ting-ting-ting of matrixes falling into place on a Linotype machine. Then he watched water pouring over a white-hot semicircular lead plate. The first water turned to hissing steam on the plate and then the steam subsided and the plate, dripping water, came clattering out onto a conveyor belt running through the long pressroom. Finally, in the heat and the noise, and with the smell of ink and paper, here was his story being printed. It was going into great sheets of paper which rose out of the floor and went through rollers up to the ceiling, two stories high, and then dove into the presses, dove and angled and raced upward again and then dove again. Cahill saw his story cross the pressroom ceiling on a conveyor belt, the long white line of Danny Cahill. The thrill of the old technology. He watched his story bouncing through the streets in the back of those black *Dispatch* delivery trucks.

He did not, as he imagined the process, see Bernard Rosenfeld getting out of his car on Broadway in Yonkers at 4:00 a.m. and tugging a *Dispatch* out of the bundle left in the doorway of a candy store.

Rosenfeld drove the car up Broadway. He went past Sam Thornton's old frame house on the corner of Evergreen Street. "You won't even look out at me," Bernard said. Then he turned the corner and went up the hill to Hudson Terrace. When he got into his apartment, he lay on his back on the mattress and held the *Dispatch* up and looked up at the stories on page three. One was a straight news account of the killing. The other was a column by Danny Cahill. When Rosenfeld read the part about all the shootings being done by one person, he started to smile. But when he read the part where

Inspector Carillo called him a woman-hater, he slapped the paper shut.

"I don't hate them," he said to the ceiling. "Don't they know that? I do it because it's my job. Why doesn't Cahill say that? Why doesn't he put down that I just do my job? Why does he let the Inspector say I hate women?"

Carillo got back to his office at 1:30 a.m. The large outer room was filled with detectives talking about the murder. There was nothing for them to do until morning; if you kept knocking on doors and waking people up throughout the night, they either would not cooperate or would be too sleepy to be reliable. As Carillo came through the doorway, the first man in front of him was Luzinski. He was built like a fire hydrant: thick, stubby arms encircled a spiral notebook open on his desk. One of the arms rose and reached out and prevented Carillo from passing the desk.

"Inspector, I got a woman here on the corner of Markwood Road who says she worked for the CIA and all week she says she was watching this man walking around the neighborhood. Says she wants to look at pictures. You think we ought to bring her down now, she's up and everything, or wait for the morning, or what?"

"Morning," Carillo said. "Send somebody up for her. Right now we just have to get organized here." Carillo glanced at Luzinski's notepad. One of the pages was filled with smudgy writing done by a soft pencil. The writing on the page opposite had been done with a ball-point pen.

"Which is which?" Carillo said.

"What's that?" Luzinski said.

Carillo's finger stabbed the pages. "What happened, your pen run out?" he said.

"Oh," Luzinski said. "No. The stuff in pencil is from the suicide in Maspeth yesterday."

"And the ink?"

"Oh, well that's from tonight."

Carillo's face was expressionless. "You're supposed to use a fresh notebook for each case."

Luzinski looked surprised. "Geez, I didn't have time to get near here tonight, you know that, Inspec — "

"I didn't ask you if you had time; I told you to use a fresh notebook on every case."

Luzinski shrugged.

"Take all your notes on this case and put them into a fresh notebook," Carillo said.

"Yes, Inspector."

He was almost going to say it; he was almost going to tell Luzinski to bring in the notebook when it was finished so that it could be inspected. But, instead, Carillo shut his mouth and walked into his own office. Freaking high school, he thought; no matter how many times you tell them, you still have to check on them. When detectives start keeping notes on two and three cases in one notebook, they sometimes become confused: Luzinski could wind up reading names and addresses to you that were from another case.

Carillo sat down at his desk and took out a booklet with the heading, "Instructional Guide for the Investigation of Homicides and Suspicious Deaths." He turned to the first page and tapped it with his finger. The first instructions had to do with the recording of information in a memorandum book. If there was sloppiness at this point, on matters covered on the very first page of the official instructional book, then the margin of error would widen, a brick thrown into a pond, and the effects of the sloppiness could lap up against everybody involved.

Carillo shut the door so that nobody would come in and bother him. He placed a stack of paper on his desk, shuffled through a pile of manila folders until he came to a clean one, and then wrote on the front of the clean one, in big letters, "INSPECTOR CARILLO'S NOTES." He took out a mimeographed sheet of paper with the heading "Major Case Assignment Sheet." No longer were there four separate shootings, two separate murder cases. Now, Carillo was positive, it was all one case. His hand fidgeted as he thought about how he would handle the case from now on. Carillo thought about the gun, the .44. The gun is the guy's trademark, Carillo thought, his label. He doesn't use another gun because he can't get one; he's a square. He winced.

They had just gone through a case with squares. A guy with his face half-gone was in the icebox at the morgue for four months and nobody came to claim him. Then Carillo found out the dead man had nine wives, all of them still living around town. Not one of them came forward. Carillo knew that after all the movies and all the television, after all the detective novels, the business still came down to information: nearly every case he had ever been around was solved on a phone call. Or a witness going off into a corner with a detective and telling everything. Everything else, the forensics, the file-checking, scheming up new angles over whisky at the bar, the crafty questioning, none of it got very much done. Carillo looked at the phone. *Ring, you bastard!* Then he began to write down all the things that everybody should do, all the normal drudgery of detective work, while they all waited for the stool pigeon to appear and solve the case for them.

Carillo went to the map on his wall. With a marking pen, he placed large X's at the places where the shootings had occurred. He sat down and looked at the map. On the Queens side, the X's were all within a couple of miles — one was a matter of blocks — of Creedmoor State Mental Hospital. Carillo leaned back and rubbed his eyes and thought of Creedmoor. Tan buildings surrounded by a wrought-iron fence, parts of which were always missing. Patients who didn't feel like climbing over the fence could merely walk along it until they found one of the openings and slip through it and go onto the street. Then Carillo reminded himself: Why would anybody even bother with the fence when all he has to do is walk out one of the main gates? They are always open and unguarded.

Carillo stopped rubbing his eyes and went back to the map again. The solitary X in the Bronx was perhaps two miles away from the Bronx State Hospital, another mental institution, tan towers rising from the side of a winding, divided highway called the Hutchinson River Parkway. Carillo remembered the hospital had a driveway up to the main building. No gates, no guardhouses. Just a driveway to and from the street. And the street running into a busy parkway which led from the Bronx to a bridge leading to Queens. The guy could come in and out of there, and nobody would ever know. Come in and out of Creedmoor, too. The records could show that he was in the hospital and at the same time he could be out in the street shooting people. Carillo put a finger on the map. With his finger, he ran a direct line from Creedmoor to Bronx State. Including outpatients, he was dealing with maybe ten thousand people there. He kept looking at the map. The two areas with X's in them, the northeast Bronx and a large swatch of Queens, had a population of about a million and a half people. One of them, Carillo figured, liked to hurt young women.

Carillo did not know who the person was, what he looked like, what his name was, where he lived, what he sounded like. He had an unknown shooting people whenever he felt like it in an area of one and a half million people.

"I'm fucked," Carillo said.

He walked away from the map. He went into the crowded outer office and poured a cup of black coffee from a large electric pot, placed the cup on top of a filing cabinet to let it cool, and then said, to himself, as much as to anyone else in the room, "What do we do with this prick?"

Everybody stopped talking and looked at Carillo. He swept his eyes around the room and then began to speak. He repeated everything he had told Cahill, everything about the four shootings all being connected. He had told only a few of his men before, but now they were all going to find out what they were up against. "Do we start sweeping areas looking for the guy or do we investigate the shit out of this?" Carillo said.

"Investigate it all day long," Hanlon, the sergeant, said.

"We got so many things to follow," Dwyer said. He was one of the few who had shared the inspector's discovery that the earlier shootings were related. "The Bonventre girl worked one summer in Alexander's. We just found out yesterday McAuliffe worked there, too. Same place. I mean, we got to check out every fuckin' stock boy Alexander's ever had. We got to do it."

"You know it's going to come from something small," Carillo said. "A traffic ticket maybe. He goes through a red light and somebody looks him over and finds the gun in the glove compartment. We'll be looking for a break. We'll be begging for a break."

"What are we looking for, just one guy or two?" Luzinski asked.

"One," Hanlon said.

"One," Dwyer said. "Got to be."

"Our best information is that it is only one person, one male person," Carillo said. "That's all we know. We've got to figure out where he lives, and what he does, and how he gets to and from the shootings, and how he knows his way around all these different neighborhoods."

"He knows the streets," Dwyer volunteered. "He knows his way around. He must spend a lot of time on the streets."

"Could be a mailman," Luzinski said.

"Could drive a cab," Hanlon said.

"Cabdriver," Carillo said. "Cabdriver." He picked up his coffee and went back into his office. He took a sheet of paper and wrote down a list of possible occupations for the killer: busdriver, United Parcel deliveryman, Con Edison meter man, fuel-oil delivery man, mailman, mental-hospital patient or worker. Then, in capital letters, he put down "CABDRIVER." Investigate the cabdrivers, he told himself. The numbers are better here. Only a couple of thousand of them compared to ten thousand mental patients. The *private* cab companies in both areas, Carillo thought; get at them and you're dealing with a couple of hundred people at most. Then uneasiness flooded into his stomach as he realized again that he didn't know the killer's name or what he looked like or how he dressed or anything. His men could talk to all the cabdrivers alive and it might not make any difference. What could they say to them? Excuse me, but would you tell me if you go around shooting at young women with a forty-four-caliber pistol? He could have one of his detectives talking to the cabdriver who was the killer and the detective wouldn't know it and he'd go right on to the next cabbie and nobody would ever know how close he had been.

Carillo went to the assignment sheet. He drew up a schedule for twenty of his thirty detectives to be on weekend patrol in ten cars. They would cover the two areas around the mental hospitals. Late at night, a single male in a car could be spotted and followed. Cruising on empty streets. Or maybe the guy would run a light. Even a killer drops a dish. Walking, Carillo thought. What if the guy walks? Or rides a bike? That's better, he decided. People are so frightened that a nigger will mug them that only somebody out doing something wrong walks the streets late at night anymore. He decided the patrol should be from 6:00 p.m. to 2:00 a.m. on Friday, Saturday, and Sunday nights.

On the first weekend, he had three cars in the Bronx, driving around the Country Club section, the Tremont Road bars, and the slumbering streets surrounding those bars. The other seven cars covered places in Queens, where the .44-caliber killer seemed likely to strike again. Jinni, for one. Carillo himself drove past the place at two-forty-five on Sunday morning, turning into 218th Street on a whim. In the darkness under the trees, in the same spot where Connie Bonventre had been killed, a boy and a girl sat in the front seat of a gray Ford Elite. Carillo stopped, got out, and walked up to the Ford. The boy and girl were too busy with themselves to notice him. He rapped his knuckles against the car window. The heads jumped and two frightened faces looked out. Carillo held up his badge. The boy rolled down the window.

"Are you a complete imbecile?" Carillo said to him.

"Why?" the boy said.

"Don't you read the papers? Don't you hear anything? Two people got shot in this same spot."

"We know," the boy said.

"Then what are you doing here?"

"Because he already done it here," the boy said.

"Right where you're sitting," Carillo said.

"So?" the boy said.

"What do you mean, 'So?' " Carillo said.

"So two times lightning," the boy said.

9

The rain coming into his face woke him up. The car window was open a little, enough for air but not enough for a hand to come through. The heavy morning rain slanted into the car and struck his face. He lifted his head, closed the window, and then dropped back onto the seat again and tried to go back to sleep. His legs were drawn up, but rather than feeling stiff after four hours of sleeping this way, he felt warm and comfortable. Except that he had to pee. The bottom of his stomach felt the pressure and he wanted to ignore it and fall asleep, but he could not. He sat up and got out of the car and stood in the heavy rain and pissed. Sea gulls moaned directly overhead. He was standing in the big empty parking lot of Orchard Beach, a long curving beach which runs into the flat water of Long Island Sound. Orchard Beach is the last part of the Bronx before you hit suburban Westchester County. In the summer, at Orchard Beach, a crowd of one hundred thousand is normal. On these nights in February that Rosenfeld came to Orchard Beach, the place was too lonely even for love. Rosenfeld came to Orchard Beach and slept because he knew it was the one place were Sam Thornton's dog could not find him. The sand must bother the dog, Bernard decided. The rain on this morning made things even better; all the dogs hid when it rained. So certainly none of them would be out in the rain and wet sand bothering him this morning.

When Rosenfeld closed his fly, he reached back into the car for his jar of water. He filled his mouth with the water. He took his toothbrush and toothpaste off the dashboard and stood in the rain and brushed his teeth. He got back into the car and put his head down. The sound of the rain drumming on the car caused him to doze.

When he woke up, it was nine o'clock. Pretty princess, he said to himself. He wondered why Sam Thornton did not allow him to have sex with Connie Bonventre. Sam had promised him Connie Bonventre. It wouldn't be difficult for Sam to give him Connie Bonventre. She was in the cellar at 22 Evergreen Street, just a few yards up from Sam's house. Bernard knew that all the dead young women are kept in the cellar at 22 Evergreen and the demons come in and rape them and sodomize them night after night, week after week, year after year. Bernard knew that. But if he could have sex with Connie Bonventre, he would be gentle with her. He had not had sex since 1972, because Sam Thornton had not allowed him to. But if he could have Connie Bonventre, all the years would be forgotten. He had been chewing on tablets of ginseng for months while he was waiting for permission from Sam Thornton which never came. He wondered why Sam didn't allow him to take her away, just once, from the demons clawing at her.

At ten o'clock, he drove home to Hudson Terrace. The rain would protect him from the dogs for the rest of the day. He made a ravioli TV dinner and he watched game shows on television. He began thinking of Connie Bonventre again. He wondered why he never had felt anything after he had killed her. Then he thought of the others. He felt nothing about them, either. Well, you just shot them and that's what you did, he told himself. He felt more satisfied than sad. This is what they have done to me, he told himself. They have taken away all my feelings. They have turned me into a soldier. A soldier can't stop after each time he shoots someone. He can't be going around a battlefield and weeping. He shrugged and watched the television.

At two-thirty, he heard Sam Thornton's dog howl. The rain had stopped, Bernard knew. The rain had stopped and the dog was out in the yard. When he walked outside, with his gun and plastic bag of bullets in his pockets, he looked up and saw the sun.

He no longer spent any time thinking of places to go at night. He was going automatically. He would get into his car and turn corners by impulse. Sooner or later, he believed, there would be something waiting for him. It would be all arranged. The demons were working like that now. He didn't have to do anything but kill. His body stiffened against a cold wind. When he got in the car, he put on his black knit cap and pulled it down around his ears. He liked driving with the car windows open. The wool cap, clinging to his oval face, made him seem years younger.

"That was a hell of a picture, wasn't it," Marty Schmidt said to his girl friend, Michele Hudson, as they came out into the light under the marquee of the Cinemart Theatre.

"I really loved it," she said.

"How do you like when they put him on television and he goes, 'Yo, Adrian'?"

"That was funny," she said.

"It was about freaking time they had a movie like this," he said.

"Yeah, it was just a nice love story," she said.

"No, I mean it's time that at least one guy don't back off that big nigger Clay, even if it is in a movie," Marty Schmidt said.

He laughed. "What do you want to do?" he asked.

"Go for coffee," Michele said.

He frowned. "Why don't you go to the car and show me what you have in that box?"

She smiled. "You'll see." She had been carrying the box when he met her in front of Ohrbach's on Queens Boulevard at nine-thirty that night. He had asked her what was in the box and she wouldn't tell him.

They were standing now on Metropolitan Avenue in Forest Hills. About four blocks away, and fifty-one days earlier, Laura Davidson had been shot. The reaction to the Davidson murder could be determined by the small group of people leaving the Cinemart Theatre after the last Saturday-night showing of *Rocky*. The early showing was mobbed, but even for such a made-for-Queens hit, most people did not want to be outside after midnight on a Saturday.

Schmidt, twenty-five, wore a raincoat. His dark hair was unkempt because he had run his hands through it so many times in the excitement of the movie. His girl friend was twenty-three, and she had on a long-sleeved black sweater. A plaid scarf hung from her neck. She shook her head to get long brown hair out of her eyes.

119

"I feel great, let's have a drink," he said.

"I have to get up too early," she said.

"Come on, I got a twenty-dollar raise, the least we can do is have a drink to celebrate," he said.

"We could have done that last night," she said.

"I had to go out with the manager," he said. "You know that."

"Well, I have to get up early to go to my aunt's house," she said. "It's almost one o'clock already."

"So we'll have one drink," he said.

"One drink means you'll be saying one drink at four o'clock," she said.

"Don't be silly," he said.

"Coffee," she said. She said it firmly.

They walked two blocks to the ice-cream parlor, one of the last of the old German places left in New York. They stepped onto a tile floor and sat on backless stools at a marble counter. A partition of dark wood and stained glass separated the counter from the back room, where people could sit at tables.

"Yes?" the owner said. He was irritated. The movie had ended late, only three customers had come in, and he wanted to get finished.

"I'll have coffee," she said.

"Two," Schmidt said.

The owner picked up the coffee cups from a counter and stood motionless. I do not run some cheap diner, his body said.

Schmidt stood up. "Forget the coffee," he said. "Then we'll forget you the next time we come out of the movie early."

The owner turned around. "I said nothing," he said.

"You said enough," Schmidt said. He tapped Michele and they walked out.

"Independent bastard."

"Well, it *is* late," she said.

They walked back past the movie house to the corner of Ascan Avenue. A funeral parlor is on the corner. The street then turns to trees and two-story attached houses. Two blocks up, the attached houses dissolve into the winding blocks of Forest Hills Garden. They walked down the side of the funeral parlor and up to the first house. Schmidt's blue Corvair was parked under the streetlight. Michele slipped into the car and opened the box and took out a blond wig. She glanced in the mirror quickly and then sat back, smiling, as Schmidt climbed into his seat.

He laughed when he finally saw her. "What the hell is that for?" he said.

"The killer," she said. "They say he goes after girls with long brown hair. Everybody's doing something. So instead of getting my hair cut, I decided to look sexy."

He laughed and put the keys into the ignition and then the inside of the car exploded on him and Michele pitched into his lap. Blood poured out of her head onto his thigh. He shouted and tried to get up, but the bleeding head did not go away. Then he fell forward and put his hand on the horn and started to scream.

Rosenfeld, stuffing the gun into his pocket, ran along Ascan Avenue to the first corner. It was like they had it all arranged for me, he said. They picked her out and had her there waiting for me. He shook his head as he thought of the efficiency of the demons. He turned the corner and came onto darkened Manse Street. While he was running, he thought of Halloween in the Bronx, running from the monsters, running from men he had thrown eggs at. While he ran now, Rosenfeld nearly knocked down an old man who was walking his dog.

"Hello, mister," Rosenfeld said. He laughed to himself and kept running. This was the kind of thing he would say back when he was running the streets. He ran down the street in his knit cap until he got to his car.

The old man walking the dog muttered to himself, "Kids, they never watch where they're going."

The old man also wondered why somebody didn't come out and fix the broken horn which was wailing around the corner on Ascan Avenue.

10

Sammy Napolitano, the night boss at the Pearl Cab Company near Co-Op City, walked Benny, one of the drivers, out to the new car at the curb. It was a Dodge Coronet, painted olive, with the company's phone number painted in white on the doors.

"Now this is a brand-new car, just got it today," Sammy said.

"Uh huh," Benny said.

"Now when you drive, you go around potholes," Sammy said.

"Uh huh," Benny said.

"Now if you go through potholes with it on purpose, I'll break your fuckin' fingers," Sammy said.

"Uh huh," Benny said.

Sammy Napolitano handed Benny the keys. Benny slipped into the car and started the engine.

"Let it warm up good," Sammy said.

"Uh huh," Benny said.

"Then pick up at Saint Raymond's Cemetery, front gate. That's three-fifty."

"Uh huh," Benny said.

Napolitano walked back into the office. "I just hadda get a driver out on the road," he said to Bernard Rosenfeld. Rosenfeld, sitting at the desk, shook his head yes.

"You can start right in tonight, right now," Napolitano said. "Just fill in this application so we can have it for the files."

The room was filled with the squeal of an el train pulling into the last stop, the Westchester Avenue stop, which was right above the roof of the office. Co-Op City, which the cab company primarily served, rose out of the swampland and junkyards two miles away. The cabs got a dollar a person to go from the el station to the nearest buildings of Co-Op City and a dollar and a quarter for the buildings farthest away.

As Rosenfeld began filling in the top of the mimeographed form, Sammy stepped on a foot treadle and called into a microphone, "Benny, where are you, Benny?"

A voice coughed over a small loudspeaker on the desk. "Right outside warming up."

Sammy said, "All right, Benny. Let's get going now, Benny. Saint Raymond's Cemetery for three-five-oh."

"Ten-four," Benny's voice said.

Sammy turned to Rosenfeld. "Almost all our night jobs go right to Co-Op City," he said. "We get a few long trips, but most of them are right to Co-Op City and then come right back."

Rosenfeld nodded.

Now the small office was filled with the sound of the loud squealing of one vehicle, then another vehicle, then several vehicles, and the squealing sound rose and rose and then exploded into a crash. Napolitano pushed himself away from the desk and went out into the street. Two blocks down, the early-evening traffic was in disarray: a bus up on the sidewalk, cars in the wrong lane. And against an el pillar, crumpled, the ground around it a bed of glass, was the new taxi.

When it was over, when the cab, totaled, was towed away, and when Benny the driver, front teeth gone, face cut, was taken to the hospital, Sammy Napolitano went into the office to call his partner. The two of them now had no new car, but they did have a full payment book, thirty-six slips, to pay for the new cab they did not have. Cab companies of this sort can get no damage insurance.

Rosenfeld, who had walked down to the accident with Sammy, started to follow him into the office. "What the fuck do you want?" Sammy asked him.

"I'm supposed to fill out the application," he said.

"Fuck the application," Napolitano fumed. "Benny filled out an application. What good did it do me? Here." He threw a set of car keys to Rosenfeld. "Take car four. Try not to kill anybody." As Rosenfeld walked out to the car, Napolitano swept the partially completed application into the trashcan.

When Rosenfeld got home, it was six-fifteen in the morning. He stacked his change and bills on the breakfront. He had $25 and change. He began to pace around the room. How could he live on $25 a day? He had been drifting from job to job since he had finally walked out on Huggy. He looked at the .44, which was loaded and on a chair. Sam would be calling him at any moment. He had done no hunting for Sam last night. Instead, he had worked for a lousy $25. Bernard wondered how he was going to be able to do this. His job was to hunt. But how could he hunt if he had no money for gas? Or money for the rent? Sam was a cruel demon. He never told Bernard the answers. He just kept commanding him to hunt and kill. Bernard was supposed to do it all by himself. He picked up a detective magazine and fell onto the mattress with it.

"You won't kill me?" Mrs. Shires said. "No, just do what I want you to do and you won't get hurt," Pritchard said, forcing her to the floor.

He awoke at noon. A thin shaft of light came through a spot where the edge of one of the bedspreads had fallen away from the window. Rosenfeld found the place where it had ripped away from the nail. He went into his toolbox and took out a nail. Using the butt of the .44 as a hammer, he drove the nail in, and the bedspread again sopped up all the light and kept the room dim, so nobody could see him. He looked out the door, saw the hallway was empty and went down to the mailboxes in the lobby. When he saw the letter from the post office, he became excited. He tore it open and found he had just gotten one of the few breaks in his savaged life: he had passed the examination and was being called to work at the main post office in the Bronx. Now he would only have to work eight hours a day and there would be enough time to satisfy Sam and enough money to pay his bills. And maybe, Bernard thought, maybe Sam would leave him alone someday. No more hunting, no more killing. He held the post-office letter against the side of his face. If he could get this delivered to him on a day when he needed it most and expected it least, then perhaps some greater fortune could come to him from the sky.

"Rosenfeld," the foreman, DiSalvo, said. "Rosenfeld, shut off the machine a minute, I want to talk to you."

Rosenfeld flicked the switch. He looked at the machine. He did not want to look at the foreman.

"Rosenfeld, you're doing all right. I just wanted to tell you that. I want to tell you that you're doing all right here."

"Uh huh," Rosenfeld grunted.

"All right, Rosenfeld, you go back to work now, Rosenfeld."

Rosenfeld flipped the switch to "on." He was the first of twelve people who sat behind each other at small tables which were fastened to the side of a ceiling-high green metal tank, a mail-sorting machine known as a Zip Mail Translator. On the table in front of Rosenfeld was a machine with ten plastic olive-colored keys. At his elbow, on the aisle side of the machine, was a hopper with stacks of mail in it. A small arm would pick up a letter from the hopper and place it in a metal slot directly in front of Rosenfeld's eyes. His job was to glance at the zip code on the letter, then in his mind match the code to one of the 244 slots that were on the other side of the ceiling-high tank, then press the proper keys for that slot. He had to be able to match the zip code with the proper machine slot number instantly. For the letters remained in front of him for only a few seconds each, and then they slipped quickly into the innards of the machine. If no keys were pushed, or if wrong keys were pushed, the letter would automatically be routed back to the starting point. All such mistakes were monitored on a computer in front of the long room. A foreman sat at the computer and, at random throughout the night, pressed code buttons which would give him printouts of any machine operator's work.

On this night, filled with DiSalvo's approval, Rosenfeld began to examine his own ability. Tap 006; that's Philadelphia. Hit 752; Dallas. Here, 070; New Jersey. Memory items, he told himself. I know them all. He felt powerful as he touched the keys. A letter appeared in front of him with big block printing on the envelope. The neatness impressed him. He grabbed the letter out of the machine slot and put it alongside him on the table. He wanted to study it. Rosenfeld looked up at the clock quickly. It was eight o'clock. He had been on the machine for fifteen minutes. Workers stay at the machine for half an hour at a time and no longer. He would be relieved at eight-fifteen and do other work for the next half hour. Another letter flipped in front of him. The bottom line said, "Columbus Avenue, Mount Vernon." Rosenfeld punched out 236. The letter was gone and the arm

125

was bringing another one in front of him. Rosenfeld nearly missed it. He had been glancing down at the hand-printed letter alongside him. At eight-fifteen, Rosenfeld got up, took the hand-printed letter off to the side and copied the letters on the back of a piece of scrap paper. He put the letter into the bin by his machine and went to his other job.

At quitting time that night, he drove to New Rochelle, in Westchester County. He covered the parking lot of a discotheque called Strawberry. Sam wanted nothing. So Rosenfeld drove home. In his apartment, he put on the light and sat on his swivel chair. He placed the scrap paper from the post office on the breakfront. He looked at the printing he had copied from the letter he had seen.

The letter had been sent by a demon, he knew that. As he looked at the large, square printing, it made sounds. A death cart going over a rocky road with thousands of people trailing. A movie scene. The people in the front, the ones right up against the back of the cart, kept jumping up and licking the blood from the open wounds of the bodies in the death cart.

He first wrote in longhand. He began by writing, "I am deeply hurt by your calling me . . ." He stopped and thought. Then the word came to him. "A wemon hater." There. That was good. *Wemon.* He liked that. All right, Bernard said to himself, now tell him. Give it to him. "I am not. But I am a monster." Rosenfeld started a new paragraph. He made it one line. "I am the 'Son of Sam.' I am a little 'brat.' "

He wrote for an hour. Then, when he was finished, he took a pad of white, lined loose-leaf paper and began to copy the letter using the same printing that was on the post-office paper. Ghoul's printing, he told himself. He held his hand above the paper so his fingerprints wouldn't get on it. They had fingerprints at the Forty-fifth Precinct from the time he had joined the auxiliary police. They wouldn't understand that those fingerprints had nothing to do with his new fingerprints. The fingerprints at the police station were taken when he was human.

When he finished printing the letter, he put it in an envelope, addressed it to Inspector Carillo, folded the envelope into a tight packet, and placed it in the breast pocket of his shirt. He would leave it someplace soon. They would find it and they would know. It was time.

On his lunch break a few nights later, Rosenfeld walked to the cafeteria, which was at the rear of the second floor. He had no hesitation about walking into the place, a sepulcher of such dreariness as to make meals a punishment. His obsessive fear of strangers was absent because of his tablemates, people with whom he had gone through training for the job. Two in particular caused Rosenfeld to feel almost comfortable with another person for the first time in several years. One was Hattie Mabry, a twenty-five-year-old black woman with large sad eyes and a soft voice. The other was a pouchy, balding, middle-aged white man, Bob Allen, who held a city job as a clerk during the day. Through a politician, he had been appointed a provisional post-office worker. He needed this extra job to buy a car and pay for furniture; he had split up with his wife.

Rosenfeld brought a plate of chicken and rice to the table. "Hello, how are you; oh, you're fine," he said to Hattie Mabry, answering his own question. She found nothing wrong with this quirk of his; it caused her to smile. Then her face lost expression, and she stared at the color television set which sat atop a coin ice-cream machine.

"You think they leave you alone," she said.

"Come on, now," Bob Allen said. He put his hand on her arm.

"What's the matter?" Rosenfeld said.

"Tryin' sleep this mornin' and they start comin' aroun' and bangin' on my door. Lousy kids tryin' to get me to open it. Then, you know, they come right in on me. They fracture my girl friend's cousin's head with a hatchet last week. So I don't open no door. Then you know what the little bastards do? They start bouncin' a ball up against the door. Playin' handball, like. The noise — pow-pow-pow — kept me awake. Drive me crazy. I couldn't open the door or probably one of them would be there holdin' a gun. They kept it up for an hour."

"Bastards, I get them I kill them," Bob Allen said. "Police don't do a thing."

"No, no, no," Rosenfeld said quickly. "You can't do anything to them. That's the job of the Police Department. An officer should come and arrest those kids and then put them away for a long time. The trouble is, the courts, they're too lenient with these animals. But the police do their job."

"How come the cops don't help her, then?" Allen said.

"Did you call them?" Rosenfeld asked her.

"Woman downstairs got a phone," Hattie said. "No way I was going to go to that phone."

"Open the window and yell," Rosenfeld said.

"My apartment? My windows face a wall. I'd be yellin' into a wall."

"What about the other people in the building?" Rosenfeld said. "They'd hear you and then they'd do something."

She shook her head.

Allen, standing up, said, "You can't get anybody to ever help you. In this world you're on your own." When Allen left, Hattie and Rosenfeld sat in silence.

Finally, Hattie said, "You know what else happen?"

"What?"

"When I leave my house, I go call my brother. He say he pass by the cemetery and he go in and looks at my father's grave, you know, and the whole place is messed up."

Rosenfeld leaned forward eagerly. "Messed up?"

"I haven't seen it, you know, but that's what my brother tell me today. Kids got in the cemetery and they dig it all up and go around markin' up the gravestones."

"Marking them up?"

"That's what he say."

"Well, we're going to do something about that, you can't let that happen, you know?" Rosenfeld said.

"I'll go there this Sunday and see what I can do," she said.

"I'll go with you," Rosenfeld said.

She smiled. "Thanks, but I just get my ass over to the cemetery Sunday mornin'."

"No, I mean it," Rosenfeld said. "I'll go there with you and fix it up."

"No, you have enough to take care of for yourself."

"Not on Sunday morning."

"You a good dude, Rosie."

"You don't understand, I want to help."

"Thanks, Rosie, I can do it all right."

"Well, what's the cemetery?"

"Woodlawn. Can you imagine that? Goddamn kids ruinin' *Woodlawn?*"

"Your father's name Mabry?" Rosenfeld said.

"Uh huh. Michael Mabry."

"Okay, okay," Rosenfeld said quickly. He had it set in his head. Now he wanted the subject changed.

The workweek ended at 1:00 a.m. on Friday night. Rosenfeld rode to Queens, passing discotheques on Grand Avenue in Maspeth and on Fresh Pond Road in Ridgewood. There were no howls or scratchings in his head. He had on 77 WABC, which played rock music. At 4:15 a.m., he had a hamburger and coffee in an all-night stand on the corner of Lefferts Boulevard and Jamaica Avenue. He got home at five o'clock. He took the gun out of the glove compartment and brought it upstairs with him. He sat down on the swivel chair and stared at the covers of his detective magazines and then flipped through one. Every time he became interested in a story and it began to make him hot, he flipped the page. He knew that if he fell on the mattress to play with himself, he would then fall asleep. He had to stay awake.

At seven o'clock he went downstairs, without the gun, and drove to Woodlawn Cemetery, which is only a fifteen-minute drive from Hudson Terrace in Yonkers. The gate was closed, but a worker opened it for him. Rosenfeld said he wanted to go to his cousin's grave, to Michael Mabry's grave, but he didn't know the site. The worker walked into the office by the gate and then came out with the grave number S-932 on a slip of paper. He gave Rosenfeld directions to the site, which was about half a mile away. When Rosenfeld found the grave, there was a large "E" sprayed on the headstone with green paint. The headstone on the left had a "G" on it. The headstone on the other side had an "O." Rosenfeld stood back and saw that a kid had gone down the row of graves and placed a message, a letter at a time, on the headstones. The full message read, "GEORGIE SUCKS." The ground in front of the headstones, bumpy from the winter, also had been dug up. Mud was splattered over many of the headstones.

Rosenfeld became agitated. How could they do this? And where were the police? You'd think the police would cover this place like they're supposed to. Do their jobs. Do their jobs and catch these kids and put them in handcuffs. Put them in leg irons and belly chains. You know? Rosenfeld ran his hands through his hair. They can't even protect a poor girl's father's grave. When he looked at the green paint over the name "Michael Mabry," Rosenfeld thought of somebody doing that to his stepmother's grave. Or to one of the graves near hers, like the one for the child burned in the fire. His eyes filled. "They should be locked up!" he said angrily.

129

He walked back to his car and drove to Kaufman's Hardware Store in Co-Op City. He walked about the store by himself and quickly picked up a scrub brush, a five-gallon watering can, a plastic bucket, a pair of work gloves, and a couple of sponges. He did it all so quickly that the man behind the counter said to him, "You want a job here?"

Rosenfeld paid no attention. He ordered a can of National Alkaline Solution. When he got it, he paid the bill of $7.63, spun around, and left. He drove back toward the cemetery. Two blocks before the entrance, at Marino's Garden World, he pulled in and bought three strips of sod and four tulip plants. The bill was $26.50. At the cemetery, he stopped alongside the workmen's shed and filled the watering can and plastic bucket from a water spigot on the side of the building. Then he drove up the narrow paths to the gravesite. He had the watering can next to him on the floor and the bucket on the front seat. Water splashed over the top of the bucket and ran across the seat under Rosenfeld. He had his mind fixed on the police who did not watch the cemetery. He did not feel the water, which had the entire seat of his pants and top of his pant leg sopping. They were having coffee when they should have been patrolling, Rosenfeld decided.

At the grave, Rosenfeld got on his knees and began scrubbing the green spray-painted letter "E" with the National Alkaline Solution. He tried to lean back and rest his seat on his heels, but his thighs were too fat for that. So he scrubbed the headstone with his rear end hanging in the air and the backs of his thighs burning with the strain. After a while, he changed to one knee, scrubbing the headstone with his right hand, the left hand flat against the headstone for balance. He got up twice and walked around the headstone. At the end of an hour, he had much of the letter "E" gone. The part that remained was faint. With half an hour of steady scrubbing, that, too, was gone. Rosenfeld worked on the stone for another fifteen minutes, in case even the suggestion of paint lingered. He walked back from the stone and looked at it from a couple of angles. He could see no outline. This pleased Rosenfeld. He spilled the bucket of dirty solution water on the ground and walked to his car to get the turf.

He was hungry now. He drove out of the cemetery and went to a stand where he bought a pepper-and-sausage hero and two cans of Diet Pepsi. On the way back into the cemetery, he stopped at the workmen's shed. Nobody was around. He grabbed a pitchfork, felt guilty about taking it without permission, then put it down. He ran his hands through his hair. He saw a stack of mimeograph paper on an old dusty desk. He took a sheet of paper and wrote in pencil on the back of it that he, Bernard Rosenfeld, had borrowed a pitchfork for a little while and that he would be out at the Mabry gravesite and would return the pitchfork before leaving. He took the pitchfork up to the gravesite and began turning up the ground in front and on both sides. When he had the winter ground turned and as many pebbles as possible picked out of it, he brought the tulips and the sod up from the car trunk. He scooped out dirt with his hands and planted the tulips along the base of the front of the headstone. Then he unrolled the strips of sod and placed them in front and on either side. He pounded the sod down with his feet, sometimes stamping with one foot, and then jumping on the sod with both feet. He used the five-gallon watering can and went down to the shack to refill it twice. Finally, when water glistened on the three strips of sod and did not disappear, he stopped. The clean headstone and the bright tulips and the new, neat sod, with water sparkling in its black dirt, caused him to raise his head proudly. When he looked at the headstones on either side of the Mabry grave, he shook his head. The green spray paint was ugly and uneven. The ground around them was dug up and covered with stones. He imagined his stepmother's grave looking like that. His eyes filled. He picked up the pitchfork and dropped it off at the shed on his way out.

It was after one o'clock when he got to his apartment. He took off his clothes, stretched out on the mattress, and pulled the yellow comforter over him. He thought about how quickly the next morning, Sunday morning, would come. He wanted to see Hattie's face when she arrived at the grave. He imagined her approaching it slowly, a hand coming up to her mouth. Then, as she got to the grave, she covered her face with both hands and cried. She turned her face to him. Then his imagination retreated. He knew he would pass up the cemetery and wait until Monday night at work. See if she would come to him. He pulled the comforter up around his face and wiggled his legs in delight.

He woke up at ten-thirty at night. He went into the shower and washed his hair, but the minute he came out and had it dried, he could feel the demons dousing oil on it. He took his .44 and his bag of bullets and left. He drove down to upper Manhattan, to Washington Heights, where he stopped at a McDonald's and ordered two hamburgers, a Coke, and two orders of French fries. He drove the car with one hand, eating with the other, across the George Washington Bridge and out Route 4 in New Jersey. He went past the Teterboro Airport and then pulled to the side of the road at a spot between a gas station and a white building with a sign on it saying, "Little Angels Disco Dancing." He munched French fries and stared at the building. Then he drove up to it, his wheels running up on the dirt embankment on the side of the road. He turned into the parking lot behind the nightclub. It was nearly full. He drove through it and then came out on the other side of the building. Out of the car, into the car and go, he said to himself. There would be no place to leave the car and run to it. He pulled out onto Route 4, which was eight lanes of buses, trucks, and speeding Jersey auto traffic. He made a turn and drove back to a parkway, the Garden State, which he rode for an hour into South Jersey. He went into the town of Red Bank, drove past a place called Faces on the edge of the Monmouth County Community College and then drove back on the parkway and back up to Route 4. It was close to three o'clock when he was back on the side of the road by the Little Angels. People came out the front door, skirts flashing in the light, hair swinging, but he felt nothing. Sam did not call to him. No command. Not even a hint. He started the car and drove home.

On the way home, he put his hand into his shirt pocket and brought out the folded letter. The creases of the envelope were dirty. Fingermarks were all over the thing. He put it back. When he got into his apartment, he ripped up the envelope and sat and slowly printed out another one: "For Inspector Carillo." That was better, he thought. He hated things that were dirty. He did not think he would be carrying this new envelope long enough for it to become dirty.

At lunch on Monday night, Rosenfeld brought his tray to the table, slipping into the chair with his head down so he wouldn't look at Hattie.

Bob Allen was talking about the last days of his marriage. He had lived in Levittown, on Long Island, and both he and his wife, Margaret, drank too much. "The night that did it," he said, "was back in February. We had all this snow and she went outside in her nightgown and she was mowing the front lawn. Except it was under a foot of snow. Somebody in the house next door said something and Margaret started a fight."

"Where were you?" Hattie said to him.

"Inside the house. I was too drunk to get out of the chair."

Everybody laughed, including Rosenfeld, whose head raised. His eyes met Hattie's and a feeling went through him that was almost as good as what he had been anticipating.

At twelve-twenty that night, as he was sitting down for his last shift on the sorting machine, Rosenfeld looked behind him. Hattie was just getting up from a half hour on the machine. She nodded to him and then pointed with her finger toward the back door. She smiled and walked away to work on the bins. Rosenfeld, secure that he would not miss her, that she would meet him at the back door after work, flicked on his machine and his stubby fingers hit the olive keys as the first letter popped up. Zero seven zero. New Jersey.

At one o'clock, she stood by the door and watched Rosenfeld punch out. Then they walked out into the cool spring darkness. The street behind the post office, Anthony Griffith Place, has no lights. Hattie put her arm through Rosenfeld's as they walked onto the street.

"I went down to the cemetery yesterday," she said.

"Uh huh," he grunted.

"And it wasn't like my brother told me at all."

"Uh huh."

"Why did you go to all that trouble for me?"

"What trouble?"

"All that trouble, Bernard."

He said nothing.

"Bernard."

"Because nobody dead should be dishonored. We should remember all the dead." He blurted it out quickly, without looking at her.

She leaned over and kissed him on the cheek. "Thank you," she whispered.

She let go of his arm and walked out into the street. Her friend from Prospect Avenue pulled up in an old Ford, the muffler pounding, and Hattie waved and got into the car.

Rosenfeld watched her go off. He was glad, he told himself, that Sam didn't want her dead.

Gene Doyle lived in the Bronx, in the Parkchester Apartments, a series of tall buildings set back from winding streets and inhabited by the last of the Irish living in the borough. He had Monday and Tuesday off after patrolling and Carillo told him to start checking the cab companies in the Bronx rather than drive to the precinct on Wednesday. At noon, Doyle walked into the Pearl taxi office. The owner, Gus Giovanelli, looked at him warily.

"Can I help you?"

"I'd like to check your drivers," Doyle said.

"What are you looking for?" Giovanelli said.

"I don't know yet," Doyle said.

Giovanelli turned his palms up. "What can I tell you? Should you have a warrant or something?" Giovanelli was trying to be careful. If he cooperated blindly, it would not only be against his nature, but it would cause him trouble getting drivers. Most of them had had trouble with the law at least once, and if they thought their boss was a stool pigeon, they would disappear on him and warn others. At the same time, the cops could shower traffic violations on his cabs and put him out of business.

Doyle smiled. "I don't care if you got guys wanted for a hundred heists. I'm only interested in homicide. I'm looking for the guy with the forty-four."

"That's all?" Giovanelli said.

"Absolutely."

"What about a guy they want for rape? If you come across him while you're lookin' for the killer, what happens? I'm just axtin' you."

"He goes out tonight and rapes somebody else," Doyle said. "My only business is with the wack with the forty-four."

Giovanelli reached behind him and pulled open a file. "We got applications for everybody hired here since we started," he said. "There's a lot. Some of these guys was with us for only two, three nights. What particular type of guy are you lookin' for?"

"I'll know when I see it," Doyle said. He did not want to tell Giovanelli the truth; he did not have the slightest idea what he was after.

He copied names and addresses and license numbers for two hours. When he was finished, he said to Giovanelli, "Is there any one guy in this pile, if you had to make a pick, that you'd tell me to look at specially close?"

Giovanelli smiled. "All of them are capable of any fuckin' thing," he said.

Doyle laughed and got up to leave.

"We get the real nuts at night," Giovanelli said. "I'm not here to see them. I got a night man might know something. His name is Fritzie. He's only been here a couple of weeks, though."

"Who was there before him?"

"A guy named Sammy. Sammy Napolitano. He was my partner, but he couldn't take this business no more. He went to California."

Doyle got to the precinct at four o'clock that afternoon. He sat at his desk and ran down the lists of drivers he had taken from three private cab companies in the upper Bronx.

"What you got?" Carillo said to him.

"You got to hand it to the Jews," Doyle said. "Out of all these names I collected today, not one of them is a Jew. They're too smart to get their asses stuck in a job like this."

"You bet they are," Carillo said.

"I hate to tell you who does take the jobs," Doyle said.

Carillo pointed a finger at him. "You're a bigot," he said.

Doyle began to read from his list: "Bonafede, Colucci, Russo . . ."

Carillo walked into his office. Then he called out to Doyle, "I'll take him, even if he is a guinea."

Doyle laughed. He went back to looking at his lists of names and wondering how he could start looking each of them over.

11

The order sheet said he was to get one hundred cases of Sprite. Edward Nodari rode the Hi-Lo back through the aisles, reading the signs on the posts, looking for the sign that said 2200. The Sprite was at 2296. He was heading for a corner of the big warehouse where nobody else was working at the moment, and he welcomed the chance to be alone. Ten minutes before, when he'd gone to the desk for the order slip, they had started up with him.

"We're working till three tonight, all right, Nodari?" Flatbush, the foreman, said to him.

"Not tonight," Nodari said. Fuck this, he said to himself. It was Friday night and he was leaving at his regular time, 1:00 a.m., and meeting his girl friend, Linda Tomasello, at Casa Lou on Tremont Road, which is in the Bronx.

"What are you telling me?" Flatbush said.

"I'm telling you that I'm going home at one o'clock."

"That right?"

"That's right."

"Not for nothing, but why won't you stay?"

"Because I won't."

"Then why don't you check out now?"

Nodari shrugged.

"Better yet, I'll check out for you now." Flatbush picked Nodari's timecard out of the rack. He held it over the slot in the clock. Nodari looked straight at him. He needed his job, as lousy as it was; he had no idea what he would do if Flatbush put the card in the clock. For if the foreman clocked him out tonight, Nodari knew that when he came back to work after the weekend, he would find that he had been permanently clocked out. But he could not back down. He would wind up losing the job and punching the hell out of Flatbush, maybe getting beat up in return, or even arrested. But he would not ask Flatbush not to put the card in the slot.

"Not for nothin', but you won't even tell me why you won't stay?" Flatbush said again.

Nodari said nothing.

"Ah, ya fuck," Flatbush said. He put the card back in the rack and handed Nodari the order sheet with the soda on it.

"He don't have to stay?" another worker said.

Flatbush grunted.

"He don't have to stay and we have to. What kind of shit is this?"

"Go to work," Flatbush said.

Now, circling about the corner of the warehouse, Nodari found the 2200 row, the Sprite row. He stood at the foot of a sheer cliff of cardboard cases that rose into the fluorescent lights hanging from steel rafters. At one end, he found an indent in the mountain and he began pulling cases from it and placing them on a pallet. It was five minutes after midnight. Nodari thought about his girl friend, Linda. She was at her girl friend Ann Marie's house. In a few minutes, Linda would say that it was time she went home and this would start the usual litigation between Linda and Ann Marie's family. The family would tell her, Oh, come on and stay over. Linda would say, No, she had to go home. Ann Marie's father would sigh and say that he would get dressed and drive her. Oh, no, Linda would protest. She would go to the phone to call a cab. If the father gave up at this point, Linda would get in the cab, say good night, and head straight for the Casa Lou. If the father prevailed and drove her home, Linda would run up to her front door, press on the wood above the bell, as if she were ringing for her parents to open the door, then wave to Ann Marie's father. The moment he would drive away, she would run down to the corner and get a Throgs Neck cab for the Casa Lou. Either way, she would be at the bar at the Casa Lou, watching the door hopefully, when Nodari arrived.

It took him fifty minutes to load the soda. As he drove it out to the loading platform, he checked his sheet. This gave him eleven

137

hundred cases loaded for the night, one hundred more than Flatbush demanded of a worker. At three minutes past one, Nodari clocked out and walked past Flatbush. He was the only one on the night crew leaving. "Thanks," Flatbush said.

Rosenfeld heard his name being called. Standing out in the street, his hands on his hips, was Larry Wozniak, who worked on the first floor.

"Bernie, how'm I going to get my car out? You got me blocked."

"Oh, oh, okay," Rosenfeld said. He walked toward his car, his hand pulling out the keys.

"Hey, Bernie, next time you do that, I'll put four bullets into your tires. You know that, Bernie? Better watch out. I'll put four bullets into your tires."

"Okay, okay," Rosenfeld said. He jumped into his car and pulled out and drove off. At the corner, he stopped and opened the glove compartment. He patted the .44 and the plastic bag of bullets. He felt his breast pocket for the letter. It was there. Tonight, he said to himself, tonight they all will know about Sam. He drove up the Grand Concourse past the gray apartment houses. As Rosenfeld went past, he could see the ceilings of the apartments, where unshaded light bulbs were shining harshly on the cracked walls, once white and now yellow with grease. The fronts of the houses were lined with garbage cans, many of them spilled. Blacks would be in front of one house, Puerto Ricans the next. He turned right on Tremont Road and started the long drive through the black and Puerto Rican area on his way to where he was going.

Rosenfeld drove to Westchester Avenue, then went under the el for a couple of blocks. He made a right and drove down several blocks. He pulled into a vacant spot in front of a two-story attached brick house. He walked to the farthest corner. He was right on the mark. His car was on Mayflower Avenue. The street it ran into was Waterbury Avenue. He looked down Waterbury Avenue. Two blocks down was Tremont. On the left-hand side was the Casa Lou. Rosenfeld had driven past the place thirty times in the last couple of months.

When he came up to the Casa Lou, Edward Nodari turned up Waterbury Avenue. He flinched. It was packed solid with cars. Then the taillights glowed on a car parked at the corner of the first cross street, Puritan Avenue. The car started to pull away from a spot in front of the Puritan Electric Shop. Nodari grabbed it. He was in luck, he told himself.

Linda Tomasello smiled when Nodari came through the door into the Casa Lou. She saw him push through the crowd standing by the jukebox. Her head was rocking and her jaw worked steadily on gum.

"Here long?" he asked her.

"Ann Marie's father took me all the way home. I'm only here a half hour."

He started to talk, but she held up a hand. From the jukebox came Hall and Oates's "Rich Girl."

"This is one of them," she said.

"One of what?"

"The songs I went out and bought today. 'Rich Girl,' 'Sara Smile,' 'Right Time of the Night.' "

She began to hum with the jukebox. "You're a rich girl. . . ."

He reached out and pretended to twist her nose. "You're a bitch girl. . . ."

"That's in the record," she said. "You listen to it, you'll hear them say 'bitch girl.' "

"Then I was right," he said.

"You're always right," she said.

They had a couple of beers and then Nodari scooped up a handful of quarters. He dropped them into her cupped hands. "Play something," he said.

She walked to the jukebox and he stood behind her, his hands on his hips and his chin resting on the shoulder of her black velvet jacket. The little foyer where they had the jukebox was alongside the door and was a fluorescent blue color. The jukebox was up against a picture window which was a blue glow. They stood there for a long time, nuzzling and selecting records and never looking up, never looking out the blue window in which their heads were framed.

Her long hair turned Bernard Rosenfeld's head into a bonfire. As he stood across the street, in front of an auto-insurance storefront, the more he stared at the picture in the blue window, the more agitated he became. The black dog paced around the walls of his head, stopped pacing, raised its head, the throat cords standing out like taut reins, and emitted a howl which caused Bernard to slap a hand onto the top of his head. Now he looked at Nodari, too. Then he drew his eyes back and took in both heads. The fire inside intensified. A German shepherd joined the black dog. The two raised their heads and howled in unison. Two, Bernard told himself. Two, two, two, two. The blood of these two people put in bowls could satisfy the demons. It was spring. Children ran the streets. The blood of these two in the window could keep a thousand demons from running over a thousand children on the spring streets of the world.

An hour later, Nodari was walking back to the bar from the men's room. He was feeling warm from the beer, and pleased with himself, and then he glanced at the clock. It was three-thirty. He trotted to the bar. He had only a half hour before closing. "Give us another beer," he called to the barmaid.

Linda looked at the clock. "I'll get killed," she said.

"One or two more," he said.

"My father'll kill me."

"What's the difference, you're this late already," Nodari said.

In the last hour of the night, from 3:00 to 4:00 a.m., as the Casa Lou emptied, Rosenfeld alternately froze as a couple came out the door, then sulked when he saw it wasn't Nodari and Linda. At four o'clock, a knot of people came out laughing. Rosenfeld's eyes darted over the group. Wrong ones. An old man, the porter, stepped out, put a chair in the doorway to keep it open. He began carrying out garbage cans. Rosenfeld panicked: he was sure they had gotten out on him. How could they do that to him? They were going to save a thousand children. How did they get out? Bernard asked himself. They took the back way, he decided. Back way, back way. I should've looked. I should've looked. Twin howls rose from the dogs inside his head. And then they were there, in the blue window, and now they were out onto the street. They walked to the corner of Waterbury Avenue.

Rosenfeld bolted out of the doorway of the auto-insurance store. He ran across Tremont and then ran along the opposite side of Waterbury Avenue from Nodari and Linda. Nodari was romantic. He held Linda tightly around the waist and he had his face buried in the side of her neck. He did not notice or hear this bulky guy in sneakers padding quickly on the opposite side of the street. At his car, Nodari opened the passenger door first and then dove in ahead of Linda and

140

sat there with his arms out and she slipped into them.

"Please, let me close the door," she said.

Rosenfeld jumped. He was on the other side of the cross street, Mayflower Avenue, and now he came running back across the cross street, then past the corner house and past one, two, three more houses and now he was running into the street, behind the car, and he took the gun out of his pocket and he did not stop. He came onto the sidewalk and ran up to the car and fell into his crouch and he was standing up to the car, with the Puritan Electric Store at his back, and he brought the gun down with his right hand and slapped it into the palm of his left. The left thumb gripped metal and he fired. The windshield exploded. The gun jumped. But it did not jump as much as it used to. It works, Rosenfeld told himself. He pulled the trigger again. The two in the front of the car were down now. Down on the seat, on the floor, he couldn't tell. Just forms that were down. Fire down at them, he said to himself. Fire down, fire down. He kept pulling the trigger and the gun jumped, but he could bring it back down again. Finally, when he started to fire again, he realized the gun was empty. He shoved it into his pocket. He reached into his breast pocket and took out the letter and threw it on the ground alongside the car. Then Rosenfeld was running. He raced across Puritan Avenue, ran down the next block, then cut across to the far side of the street and careened onto Mayflower Avenue. He was running toward his car on a street that was like all the other streets on which he had run in the night: sleeping one-family houses. But something told him this night was different. The two hands on the gun made it different. He was pretty sure as he ran that, on this night, Sam would be pleased.

It was 4:00 a.m., and Carillo didn't want anything strong to drink. He stood alone in his kitchen and poured himself a glass of milk. He reached into a box and his hand crackled through cellophane while he pulled out three Oreo cookies. He nibbled on a cookie and sipped the milk and looked at the bills his wife had left on the kitchen table. The moment the phone rang, he knew what it was.

"I only stopped working twenty minutes ago," he said. "What kind of luck — "

141

He picked up the phone. "Yeah?"

Sergeant Hanlon's voice was low. "The Bronx."

"Bronx?"

"Two."

"Two this time," Carillo said mechanically.

"The guy left a note for you," Hanlon said.

"A note? Where?"

"Everything is up at the Four-seven."

"I'll go up there now."

Carillo hung up. He swallowed the rest of the milk and flipped over one of the window envelopes on the kitchen table and scrawled on the back of it, "Had to go back to work."

At a quarter to five, Carillo sat alone in an office on the third floor of the Forty-seventh Precinct in the Bronx. Outside, cars and tractor trailers hissed by on the elevated Cross-Bronx Expressway. The outer office was filled with detectives who were waiting for morning to come so they could go out and canvass witnesses. On the desk in front of Carillo was a bunch of plastic folders. Inside each folder was one page of the strangely printed letter. Carillo looked at the envelope first, with his name in big printing. Then he picked up the folders and began to read:

I am deeply hurt by your calling me a wemon hater. I am not. But I am a monster.

I am the "Son of Sam." I am a little "brat."

When father Sam gets drunk he gets mean. He beats his family. Sometimes he ties me up to the back of the house. Other times he locks me in the garage. Sam loves to drink blood.

"Go out and kill," commands father Sam.

Behind our house some rest. Mostly young — raped and slaughtered — their blood drained — just bones now.

Papa Sam keeps me locked in the attic, too. I can't get out but I look out the attic window and watch the world go by.

I feel like an outsider. I am on a different wavelength than everybody else — programmed too kill.

However, to stop me you must kill me. Attention all police: Shoot me first or else keep out of my way or you will die!

"Why, this lousy bastard," Carillo said. "How do you like this lousy

142

bastard." His fist thumped on the table. Now it was all personal. He began reading again:

> Papa Sam is old now. He needs some blood to preserve his youth. He has had too many heart attacks. "Ugh, me hoot it hurts sonny boy."
>
> I miss my pretty princess most of all. She's resting in our ladies' house. But I'll see her soon.

Carillo stopped. "Some Catholic," he said. "He doesn't even know how to spell Our Lady."

He went to the next folder:

> I am the "Monster" — "Beelzebub" — the Chubby Behemouth.
>
> I love to hunt. Prowling the streets looking for fair game — tasty meat. The wemon of Queens are prettyiest of all. I must be the water they drink. I live for the hunt — my life. Blood for papa.
>
> Mr. Carillo, sir, I don't want to kill anymore. No sir, no more but I must "honour thy father."
>
> I want to make love to the world. I love people. I don't belong on earth. Return me to yahoos.
>
> To the people of Queens, I love you. And I want to wish all of you a happy Easter. May God bless you in this life and in the next. And for now I say goodbye and good night.
>
> POLICE: Let me haunt you with these words:
>
> I'll be back!
>
> I'll be back!
>
> To be interpreted as — bang, bang, bang, bank — ugh!!
>
> Yours in murder,
Mr. Monster

Carillo went back to the first page and began reading it again. For three hours, he sat in the office and read the letter from the killer. Each time he started it, he had to restrain himself so that he did not race through a sentence so he could get to the next one. He forced himself to study it, to look for a word that would say something to him. At a quarter of eight, he rubbed his eyes and called outside, "You got a Xerox of this for me?"

"We had a couple of them made, Inspector," a Bronx detective said.

"Well, give me one. I want to go home and study this thing."

He came out of the office and took the sheets of paper from the detective, folded them, and stuck them into his jacket pocket. Now he noticed that everybody in the room was looking at him and saying nothing. Sergeant Hanlon had come up from Queens and was standing in front of him.

"Well?" Carillo said.

"We made a phone call about this," Hanlon said.

"What do you mean, 'We made a phone call'?"

Hanlon said, "Well, this sonuvabitch gets personal with you."

"Forget it," Carillo said. "What about this phone call?"

Detective Dwyer said, "Chief Maloney said that —"

"Maloney! Who called Maloney?"

Dwyer did not back off. He didn't understand what he had done by making the call, so he thought he could argue with Carillo about it. "Chief Maloney said he thought he ought to have somebody with you so this guy don't just pop up on you."

"Bullshit!" Carillo said. Now they had done it, he snarled to himself. They had called in Maloney.

"Wait a minute, Inspector, with all respect, it isn't bullshit. This guy could —"

"I'm not going to have any detail near me and that's it. Now I'm going home for a couple of hours' sleep. I'll be back at the office in Queens by two, three o'clock."

As he walked out, he waved his hand. "I don't want to see anybody following me."

He was in a trance as he drove home. The letter from the killer infested his brain. He was in Queens, on the Cross Island Parkway, when he saw the car, a brown Fury. It was three cars behind him, tucked in behind a bread truck. But he could see it.

"I told them!" Carillo said.

His lips compressed and he stepped on the gas and raced off the parkway at the Fourteenth Avenue exit in Whitestone. Then he made a right turn on a side street, rode on it to the first cross street, made a right turn on that, made another right turn on the next corner. This brought him back to the place from which he started, the Fourteenth Avenue ramp. He stopped his car. Nobody came. No brown Fury. He had taken the textbook step to see if he was being followed: three turns in the same direction. There was nobody.

He told himself that this was good. He'd handle anything that came up by himself. Then he thought of his son, James, and his

144

daughters. A chill ran through his arms. Through the rest of the trip home, he became more troubled. The sonuvabitch *had* made it personal. Who the hell knew who he was?

When he got to the house, nobody was outside yet. He reached on top of the dashboard and clicked the beeper that would open the garage door. He drove the car out of the morning light and into the dimness of the garage. As he stopped the car, there was a rush from the dark right-hand corner of the garage. Something hit the top of the hood with a thump. The inside of the car tumbled as Carillo grabbed his gun and threw himself down on the seat. He kept the windshield fixed. Everything else was tumbling, but he kept the windshield straight. He aimed the gun at it.

Then he heard his wife's voice. "What is it?"

He did not move. He stayed there, half sprawled on the seat, gun pointing at the windshield.

"Oh, you!" his wife said. "Sensation, get out of here. He almost ran you over."

Carillo's eyes closed. *The fuckin' cat.*

12

"Why the fuck didn't the desk call me?" Danny Cahill was screaming into the telephone.

At seven-thirty in the morning, the alarm on his clock radio had gone off, automatically clicking on WCBS, one of New York's all-news stations, and before his eyes had even opened, Cahill had heard the report about the double killing in the Bronx.

Now it was after nine o'clock, and the managing editor of the *Dispatch* had walked into his office just in time to pick up Cahill's angry call. "The desk has standing orders to call me any time that cocksucker hits," Cahill shouted. "Now I'm five, six hours behind everybody else."

"I don't know what happened, Danny," the managing editor said. "I'll find out."

"I want the prick shot," Cahill said. "Who the fuck does he think he is — not calling *me*?" He slipped into his I-am-the-greatest routine, sort of an overweight Irish Muhammad Ali. Finally, Cahill paused, then said, "I'm going to see Carillo now."

"Ask him about the letter."

"What letter?"

"We got a tip from a guy at Police Headquarters that the killer left a letter at the scene. We hear the letter was addressed to Carillo by name, that the guy threatened to kill him next, something like that."

Cahill hung up without saying a word, which was typical of him, and went to his desk in the garage and took out a battered notebook and found Inspector Carillo's home phone number. On the first ring, Carillo's wife answered the phone. "He's not home," she told Cahill. "He came home a little while ago and had a cup of coffee and went back to work. He hasn't slept all night."

Cahill called the inspector's office. "Can I talk to you for a minute?" he asked Carillo. "I don't want to get in your way, but just for a minute."

Carillo tried a hollow laugh. "Talk to me now," he said. "Might be the last chance for a while. The Commissioner's coming out here, and he told me the Mayor'll be coming out in a few days. I guess they're all coming out to tell me how much they like Italian cops and to wish me luck."

"What about the letter?" Cahill said.

"I've gotten nicer," Carillo said.

"What's in it? What's he say?"

"Come on, Danny, you know I'm not going to tell you."

"Ain't you going to release it?"

"No."

"How come?"

"Unless the Commissioner overrules me, and I don't think he will on this," Carillo said, "I'm holding the letter for two reasons. First, right now, nobody knows what's in that letter except me and a couple of detectives and the guy who wrote it, and when we catch that guy, he's going to tell me what's in the letter. That's one of the ways I'll have of knowing it's him. And, second, there are parts of the letter where he just goes crazy, where he writes about crazy, terrible things. People are scared enough now, I don't want to panic them."

"What kind of crazy things?"

"Blood, monsters, bones — it's all sick and frightening."

"God bless," Cahill said. He hung up the phone and walked to his kitchen to get a glass of orange juice. His son Patrick was sitting at the kitchen table, sipping a cup of tea. "What's he doing here?" Cahill asked his wife. "Why ain't he in school where he belongs?"

"He's sick," the wife said. "He was up all night with a stomachache. I found him in the den this morning sitting on the couch, moaning."

"All night?" Cahill said. "You up all night?"

"Yeah," Patrick said. "I couldn't sleep at all, it hurt so much. I stayed in the den. I didn't bother nobody. I even answered the phone for you in the middle of the night."

"You what?"

"I answered the phone. It was some guy wanting to talk to you, and I did like you told me to do if I didn't recognize the voice. I told him you weren't home."

"You told him I wasn't home? At, about, four o'clock this morning?"

"Yeah," Patrick said, brightening. He was proud of himself. "I told him you went swimming and you'd be home in a couple of hours."

Inspector George Ryan, the head of the police laboratory, reached into the pocket of his red-plaid vest for a lighter. As he lit his pipe, he looked through the flame at Phil Lenahan, one of his technicians, who held the first page of the letter in one hand and a spray can in the other. Lenahan stood at a glass screen which had an opening at the bottom. The spray can contained a chemical spray known as Ninhydrin. It reacts on the sweat and amino acid left by fingers on any surface they touch. The spray is highly toxic, which is why the lab had the glass screens set up. Lenahan sprayed the first page of the letter for a few seconds. He brought the paper out and walked it across the hall to a darkroom, where he put the page on a shelf. Then he returned to the screen and sprayed the next page of the letter. When he had the entire letter sprayed and on the shelf in the darkroom, Lenahan looked at Inspector Ryan.

"I still say I'm going to need seventy-two hours," he said.

"Oh, you'll get the time," Ryan said. "But can we just get a little look at part of it now? I'd like to tell them something."

"We're liable to lose anything we've got," Lenahan said. "That's if we got anything at all. So with all due respect, Inspec —"

"You're in charge," Ryan said. He was an administrator, not a technician. He could figure out staff and equipment purchases and record systems, but chemistry eluded him. He knew certain basic facts of each of the forensic sciences: when dealing with documents, it was best to let them sit for three full days after spraying before applying heat which would cause anything on the paper to show up. From that point on, it could be a day, a week, or even a month of careful chemical treating to build up the fingerprints to a point where they could be turned over to a team that would examine them and try to match them. When Lenahan warned him that any quickening of the process could cost them the entire evidence, or hope of evidence, Ryan reacted properly. He was not going to order such a gamble. But, at the same time, Ryan knew that throughout the city, from the mayor to the men working the case, they were waiting for some report on the fingerprints, if any, left on the letter from the .44 killer. When the chief of detectives had called him at six o'clock this morning, Saturday morning, he had asked the chief if it would be all right to call in his best lab man, Lenahan, on overtime, and the chief had said, "He'll be on undertime, no time at all, if he isn't in there pretty damn quick."

Now, late on Saturday afternoon, Ryan went into his office at the lab and called Carillo. He was told to try him at the 109th Precinct in Queens. When he got Carillo on the phone and told him they couldn't even look for prints for at least three days, he could hear the deadness in Carillo's voice.

"Why so long?" Carillo said.

"It's the business," Ryan said. "If it's on paper, you've generally got a long haul in front of you. Any other surface is fine. But paper, that's always a problem."

When Carillo hung up the phone, he shook his head. "Science," he said. "When you need it, you find the fuckin' thing doesn't even exist."

The mayor fidgeted with the sheet of paper lying in front of him. On the opposite side of the table, Carillo, out of habit, lifted his chin so that his eyes could make out, upside down, the words on the paper. When Carillo caught the phrase, "I have every confidence . . ." he thought immediately of his father. If there was one lesson Dominick Carillo, Sr., had taught his son, it was to believe the exact opposite of anything a politician said.

"And we have a special police number they can call?" the mayor said.

"Right there, at the end of your statement, Mr. Mayor," a voice said. It came from the doorway, where two men stood. One, with dark hair and glasses, the one who'd answered, was Abe Wise, the mayor's press man. The other was Larry McDermott, a light-haired man with a square jaw and slightly protruding teeth. He was the deputy police commissioner for public affairs, which is a police title for press agent.

The mayor glanced at a Xerox of the killer's letter, and then again read the typewritten speech in his hand. "Now tell me this once more," he said. "Why are we not releasing the letter to the public?"

Timothy Bracken, the police commissioner, sitting next to the mayor, said nothing. Down at the end of the table, John Maloney, the chief of detectives, coughed.

"Will somebody tell me why?" the mayor said.

Bracken looked over at Carillo. "Inspector, why don't you explain?"

"Yes," the mayor said. "I'm interested." Suspicious blue eyes looked at Carillo, who found he could not think. He was surprised and humiliated to find the mayor had intimidated him and made his mind go blank. *You* always keep things secret, he wanted to tell the mayor. Instead, he fumbled for words which refused to come. He forgot his theory about having some facts that only the real killer would know. He forgot his fear that the blood-lust in the letter would spread panic. He tried hard to remember why it was he wanted the letter held back.

Finally, Carillo managed to say, "We need to keep the public from seeing the letter so that if we hear from him again, we can compare the letters and know whether we're dealing with the real guy or with a phony who copied his style of printing."

The mayor grunted. In the doorway, his public-relations man said, "That doesn't seem like such a good rea—" The mayor waved his hand to stop Wise. Then he said to Carillo, "It's your investigation; do what you think you have to do." It was clear the mayor was not impressed.

"All right," the mayor said. "Now let me get this straight: I'm promising to assign another fifty men to this investigation?"

"Fifty top detectives, not just men," McDermott said.

"All right, then," the mayor said. "I'll make my presentation and then I'll turn the meeting over to you." He faced the police commissioner. Bracken's gray-wire eyebrows rose in assent. "And then," the mayor went on, "you can tell them as little as you want about this, ah, this, this . . ." His right hand began waving as he searched for a name.

"Yes, Inspector Carillo," Commissioner Bracken said, "what are you calling this perpetrator?"

It took Carillo by surprise. "Well, ah, I had been calling him *him* — we didn't really have a name for him."

"We got to have a name for him," McDermott said.

"Let's see now," Maloney said. He picked up the Xerox of the killer's letter and read it. He studied the very precise printing. Then he put the letter down. "I think . . ." he said. He stopped to clear his throat. The mayor turned to look at him. The two press agents standing in the doorway looked at him. Maloney now spoke in a low voice. "I think we'll call him 'Son of Sam.' "

"Very good," the mayor said.

In the doorway, McDermott said, "What's that? I couldn't hear you?"

Maloney's voice rose, "I said, 'Son of Sam.' "

"How do you get that?" Wise, the mayor's press secretary said.

"Well," Maloney said, "I'm just noticing as I read this, in one part here, he tells us that he is 'a monster,' he is the 'Son of Sam.' We can't just call him 'Mr. Monster.' I think we ought to use 'Son of Sam.' "

"I like it," Wise said.

"More important, I'll bet the killer likes it," Commissioner Bracken said.

"It's like calling him 'Lepke,' " the mayor said. "The man's real name was Louis Buchalter, but once they called him 'Lepke,' it stuck. He liked it, too. He never told anybody not to call him 'Lepke.' "

The mayor looked at Maloney. "You just came up with 'Son of Sam' right here?" the mayor said.

"Well, I just happened to be looking at the letter, you know," Maloney said.

The fuck, Carillo said to himself. The fuck stayed up half the night to pick out the name. Carillo became even more angry with himself for having blanked out.

The sound of chairs scraping filled the room as the mayor stood up and everybody else followed him. As the group of men started downstairs, they could hear the noise made by the reporters in the lobby. Hot-white television lighting reflected on the wall along the staircase.

Wise held out his hand to Carillo. "We're counting on you. You've got a big job."

"Thanks," Carillo said. He rolled his eyes toward the growing noise. "It'll be a lot easier for me when we can get these press people the hell out of here and keep them out. Geez, there's no way to work with them all over us."

Wise smiled. "I know what you mean, I know what you mean. But you've got to live with it this time."

"What do you mean?" Carillo said.

"We think two things," Wise said. "One, it's the only way you can keep the public alerted to this guy and maybe turn him in. And, two, whether you like the reason or not, it's still important: the man here has got an election this year."

"But I got an investigation," Carillo said.

"And we're going to have it with you," Wise said.

"I don't like doing my business in public," Carillo said.

Wise shook his head. "Why don't you cut it out? You think you got war secrets? You got a letter there you want to keep secret. Secret from whom? The killer knows what he wrote to you and how he wrote it to you. And you know what the killer wrote and how he wrote it. So from whom are you keeping it a secret?"

"We're going to let out a little of what's in it," Carillo said. His head was clearer now. "We don't want to scare the people by telling them everything."

"Sometimes I think the public can take it better than we can," Wise said. "What makes us so smart we should determine what they see and what they don't see?"

Carillo wanted to spit at him. He had never met Wise before, but he knew that the man had a reputation for hiding as much bad news as possible from the press at City Hall.

"I don't want to have to have an investigation jammed with a hundred letters all printed like the one we got," Carillo said. "That's why I don't want any copies passed out. I don't want anybody to see the printing."

"But suppose you let the public see the letter and somebody says, 'Hey, I know that printing, that's the guy lives right over the candy store,'" Wise said. "Suppose that happens?"

Carillo kept his face straight while his mind groped again.

At the bottom of the staircase, the mayor called, "Abe!"

Wise mumbled to himself. Carillo simmered the anger growing against Wise and against himself. Inside Carillo, the thought arose that the press secretary could be right: What if somebody does recognize the printing? Carillo's resentment of Wise smothered the thought. The inspector was fuming as he came into the big ground-floor room. He stepped into bright lights which made him squint at first. Then something told him to relax his eyes and open them properly. The clicking of newspaper cameras, still cameras, filled the room. Blocked by a gray barricade, the television crews aimed their cameras at the mayor, who took a seat at a desk along with Bracken and Maloney. Carillo stayed out on the edge, avoiding everybody's attention. But as the mayor cleared his throat and began to talk, Carillo unconsciously began to push toward the center, trying to place himself as close to the desk as possible, so that if his name were called out, he would not be way out on the edge where nobody could find him.

They were on the ground floor of the 109th Precinct in the Flushing section of Queens, only a mile or two east of the site of the 1964-65 World's Fair. The 109th is one of those newer police buildings whose antiseptic quality removes some of the fear station houses generate, and all of the glamour. The building is on Union Street and Forty-fifth Avenue, a dull street on the fringe of a shopping area which spreads from the last stop of a subway line to Manhattan. The investigation was to be run out of this building from now on.

Commissioner Bracken had come to Carillo's old office in the Fifteenth Homicide Division late Saturday morning, about eight hours after the double shooting, and had told Carillo that he was going to be getting extra men, that the mayor would be holding a news conference on Monday to announce the formation of a Special Homicide Task Force and that he, Carillo, should look around Queens to find a good place to house the operation he would be commanding.

Carillo had picked the 109th Precinct for a few reasons. In the first place, he liked the location. It was midway between Jinni, the discotheque where Connie Bonventre was killed, and the area in Forest Hills where Laura Davidson and Michele Hudson were killed. And the precinct was only a couple of minutes from a highway which served as the approach road for the Whitestone Bridge. The other bridge to the Bronx, the Throgs Neck, could be reached by using the same highway for two or three minutes longer. In the second place, the 109th had space available that was large enough, and private enough, for all the people who would be working only on the case of the .44-caliber killer.

The offices Carillo took over were on the second floor of the precinct. The central office for the investigation, he decided, would be the place which until then had been used by the precinct's youth division. There was one large room, big enough for at least a dozen desks, and a couple of small rooms in the back. Then, in the front, off the large room, was a squad commander's office. It looked out on a municipal parking lot across the street. Across the hallway from this set of offices was a large, bare room. He would use this for conferences and meetings.

At 2:00 p.m., when the mayor and all the police bosses were gone, Carillo walked upstairs and looked at his base. The floor was littered with cigarette butts and gum wrappers. The green metal municipal desks were smeared. And the walls were covered with a film of dirt. Carillo shuddered. He believed that when there was sloppiness at any point in an investigation, starting with something as small as a dirty ashtray, the sloppiness spread, and soon the sloppy ashtray was turning into a confusing notebook, a notebook with two cases in it, and then the sloppiness went on and affected the questioning of witnesses and soon your case was in the sewer. Carillo had a killer out on the streets and Carillo knew he was not going to get the killer unless he had clean floors under his feet.

The investigation, he believed, was neither going to be short nor easy. When he had first gone to the 109th to look it over, late on Saturday afternoon, his eyes burning from no sleep, the call from the police laboratory had furthered this perception. And now, on Monday afternoon, he went downstairs, to the area of the regular precinct cops, and located the two janitors. Two great Afros framed faces which were, at the least, insolent. Carillo liked this. The two blacks were, like all the police department janitors, out of a drug-rehabilitation project. Federal funds paid the salaries. The blacks took the jobs gladly, but the strong ones, like these two, did not at the same time genuflect to their new surroundings. A cop fuck is a cop fuck forever. Carillo asked the two janitors to come upstairs with him. He showed them the main office and the meeting room across the hall. He said he wanted the walls scrubbed and the desks cleaned and the floors cleaned and waxed.

"We're going to have a big investigation and you're the key to it right now," Carillo said.

The janitors' eyes narrowed.

"Unless you do this for me," Carillo said, "we can't do anything else."

He went outside and walked up to a diner on the corner of Forty-seventh Avenue. The food was an act of war on the part of Greece. Iodine coffee and an indifferent omelette left Carillo muttering to himself.

When he returned to the second floor of the precinct, he found the two janitors scrubbing the walls. He walked up to a desk, bent down, and looked under it. The bottom of the wall, below the desk, was black. Carillo pointed this out. One janitor bent over, reached under the desk and scrubbed the bottom of the wall. Carillo moved the desk away from the wall. This part of the wall, too, was filthy. Carillo went around pulling all the desks from the walls. The janitors then, for the third time, scrubbed the same wall area.

"If you'd done it right the first time, you'd only be doing it once," Carillo told them.

One of them muttered.

"What's that?" Carillo said.

The one black stared at him. "I said, you sound like a motherfuckin' housewife." Now both blacks faced him.

Carillo beat them with a laugh.

And at five o'clock, Carillo paced the polished, shining floors, ran his hands over the scrubbed desks and walls and watched as more desks were being lugged into the room. Telephone-company installers walked about while they set up the phones with the special numbers. One of the installers stopped working with his screwdriver, bent over, and dropped a cigarette butt on the floor. He ground it out with a workboot.

"Come on!" Carillo said.

"We're working as fast as we can," the installer said.

"The floor!" Carillo said.

He walked over, bent down, and picked up the butt from the floor. He dropped it into a wastebasket and walked into the small office which was immediately off the front of the large room. He had left his briefcase sitting in there, on top of the desk. He sat down, opened the case, took out his folder which said, "INSPECTOR CARILLO'S NOTES" and then called for Sergeant Hanlon, who was sitting at a desk near the front of the room. Hanlon walked into Carillo's office.

"The first order we post is to keep all cigar and cigarette butts off the floor," Carillo said. "We're liable to be living here a long time with a lot of people."

Hanlon nodded and went out to make up the order. Carillo started

155

going through his assignment sheets. He would have, it turned out now, sixty detectives to fit into seven days, or a total of twenty-four hundred man-hours to spread over 168 hours. He could have fifteen detectives working at all times, or he could concentrate more men on the days and hours when the killer was more likely to strike. He knew he would choose the second system. He took a blank sheet of note paper and wrote on it:

1. Fingerprints
2. Gun
3. Single white male roaming around at night

He knew these were his avenues to catch this killer. All three of them required manpower and tedious work. All three required luck. The last point, catching the dirty bastard on the street one night, was his song, his mist, his dream. He turned back to the assignment sheet and started to fill it in. He didn't have the names of the new detectives yet, but he was playing with numbers to see how many men he could have investigating, or on days off, and how many he could throw out onto patrol at night, particularly on Friday and Saturday nights. When he thought of patrol, he went to another sheet of paper. He had to order up cars. He would need twenty of them. No, he would need twenty-five. Right away, he saw a problem and he wrote it down. The detectives using the cars would be parking them across the street in the municipal lot. At the end of a shift, they would try to leave the keys in the patrol cars, then go directly to their own cars and go home. The patrol cars could get stolen, or the detectives waiting upstairs to go out on a shift wouldn't know which patrol cars to go to. "Very important!" Carillo wrote. "Detectives must turn in car keys to the office at the conclusion of a shift." He wanted a sense of order for the men coming to work: Here's your keys, your car is there, your patrol sector will be here, look at it on the map. Now go catch the bastard for us.

In the big room, at his desk, Hanlon was testing his transmitter to make sure he could speak to the patrol cars that were going out under the old schedule. The new, heavier schedule would start tomorrow night. Carillo kept making notes to himself.

At 11:00 p.m., somebody brought in the *Dispatch*. The name "Son of Sam" in a black headline was better than acid etching into metal, Carillo knew. At 1:00 a.m., tired, he went out of the building, walking the opposite way from the diner. This took him to Northern Boulevard. He turned right and walked up a few doorways to Lum's, which was probably the largest and best Chinese restaurant in, at least, Queens. Carillo sat at the bar and ordered a Rémy Martin.

The bartender was reading the *Dispatch*. Carillo said aloud, "Son of Sam." The bartender put down the paper. "You police?" he asked.

"Yes," Carillo said.

"How come you not on television tonight? I see all the police around the corner on television tonight."

Carillo was on his second brandy when he began thinking about the bartender's question. He asked himself why he had not pushed himself forward and answered one of the reporters' questions. After all, was it not he who had to run this investigation, who would take all the criticism if it did not lead to the killer? Of course, there was a chance that this killer would simply stop killing and disappear, or commit suicide, or be thrown in jail on another charge and wither away in jail while he, Carillo, searched for him on the night streets. So was it not his career that could be ended here? Why not, therefore, allow the one doing the job to do the talking, too?

Carillo reached for a bar napkin. He wanted to write down something of brilliance. He also wanted another drink. Something told him that the brandy had him at the foothills of that plateau from which all things are possible and all thoughts are dipped in wisdom. Carillo stood up. He waved his hand to stop the bartender from refilling his glass. Should have had dinner, Carillo told himself. He knew that one more drink would have him at the bar till he closed it down. He looked at the clock. It was 2:30 a.m. already. He had a meeting coming at eight o'clock with the personnel man from the detective division to go over the new bodies promised to him for this investigation.

"Good night," Carillo said to the bartender.

"My name Harry," the bartender said. "I see you again soon. Good night."

13

At three o'clock on Tuesday afternoon, Phil Lenahan, the lab technician, went into the darkroom, took the pages of the killer's letter and held the pages, one at a time, over a bottle which was placed atop a burner. All documents must be kept in fifty percent humidity, and the boiling water in the bottle helped keep the room at that point. As the steam heat warmed the page in Lenahan's hands, purple splotches began to show on the paper. They were parts of fingerprints. Lenahan held the paper and waited for more to show. The purple became clearer in some spots, but remained the same in others. Lenahan looked at the page through a jeweler's glass. Faint, partial fingerprints were on the paper, all right. And a larger smudge at the bottom seemed to be part of a palm. It was this way on each page of the letter. There was not one full clear print.

Lenahan went out to talk to Inspector Ryan. "We got partials," Lenahan said.

"That's not bad, right?" Ryan said.

"Nope. But I don't know how good it is, either. We're going to have to work for some time to bring up what we have."

"How long?"

"Inspector."

"I know," Ryan said.

He called Carillo. Carillo was silent as Ryan gave him the report.

Then Carillo said, "I don't care what he's got. We'll work with the partials if we have to. Let's get the Identification Section ready to give this a real look."

Ryan held the phone, and said to Lenahan, "He'll work with the partials you got."

Lenahan shook his head. "He can't."

Ryan said into the phone, "He says you can't."

Carillo shouted back, "Why not?"

Ryan looked up at Lenahan. "He wants to know why not."

Lenahan grimaced. "Because we don't even know what fingers we got on this letter."

Ryan's eyebrows went up. "You can't tell?"

Lenahan shook his head. "I don't think anybody can. You get a print, you're guessing what finger it is."

Ryan duplicated Lenahan's gesture. He shook his head, then he said into the phone to Carillo, "You can't do it because they can't even tell what fingers the prints are from."

"When will they know?"

"They won't," Ryan said. "That's the problem. You can't tell one finger from the other."

"Well, why do we bother with this shit?" Carillo yelled.

"Inspector, just relax and give us time; we'll get you something," Ryan said.

"Get me what?" Carillo shouted.

Ryan could not answer. When he hung up, he looked at Lenahan. Then, rather than talk, Ryan picked up his pipe. This job gets confusing, he told himself.

In Flushing, Carillo walked out of his commander's office and into the large office. Two of the men originally working on the case, Seibert and Swanson, sat with computer printouts of owners of registered .44-caliber Bulldog revolvers who were living in New York, New Jersey, Connecticut, and Pennsylvania. Carillo could see by checkmarks made by the detectives that there were still over a hundred registered owners to be checked.

"Are you fellas looking to retire?" Carillo asked.

"Not me," Seibert said.

"Me, either," Swanson said.

"Oh, I was just wondering," Carilo said. "Somebody told me that one of you, or both of you, I forgot which it was, but anyway that somebody was going to retire."

"We been up to our asses in this thing," Seibert said. He had received the communication and was attempting to answer it. "See,

Inspector? We got a guy here in Malone, New York. We ask the Sheriff up there to go to the guy and have him fire his weapon and send us the slug so we can test it, and you know what the Sheriff in Malone says? He says, 'I got no way to do that.' We tell him, 'Just get a pipe and shoot down the pipe into a tub of water.' The Sheriff says to me, 'Send me the pipe.' "

"What did you do with the guy?" Carillo asked.

"Nothing, Inspector," Seibert said. "That's what we're sitting here talking about."

A hand began to scour Carillo's insides with sandpaper.

"This is tough going, Inspector," Swanson said. "Maybe here and there only we get a break. Like this one here in Hamden, up in Connecticut. Guy died. So we can go past him now. Otherwise, we'd have to stop at the name and go all through what we're going through with this quiff in Malone."

"What do you do so different if the owner is dead?" Carillo said.

"We scratch him out," Swanson said. "Guy can't be the killer if he's dead."

Carillo screamed inside. His face became very straight and his words came out slowly. "The guy could be dead, but his gun is still alive. Whoever has the gun could be the killer. Find me the gun."

Swanson thought. "You're right," he said finally. "I guess we'll have to check out the dead guy just like he's alive."

Back in his office, Carillo looked through his folder. His eyes fell on the sheet of paper with the three main points of the investigation listed. He looked at them.

Fingerprints. He shook his head. He had nothing, he thought. He just had to sit and wait while they played with chemicals. Who knows what they're going to come up with? He looked at the second item.

Gun. He thought of Seibert and Swanson outside. And he knew that there was no central place in the country to check the destination of a gun. For years he had been reading about the FBI and the Treasury Department's Alcohol, Tobacco, and Firearms Division having a great computerized system for locating guns. Carillo had found with two phone calls that there was no such computer, that the FBI and the Treasury Department had been lying to people for years. The search for the .44 Bulldog that was killing his people was going to be done by detectives on the telephone, Carillo knew. He felt tired and confused. He looked at his third point.

The killer wandering the streets at night. An excited feeling suddenly ran through him. Tonight, we could sweep him up on a street corner, he told himself. That reminded him. He looked out the door and called to Hanlon. "I want you to get a memo up to all these new men about them returning the car keys to this office upon the conclusion of their shift. We're going to have a lot of new men coming in here tonight and I don't want to tell it to them more than once. We'll give them a memo on it, so they'll always be reminded."

Danny Cahill sat in the bar opposite the Queens County Courthouse. He had five sheets of paper in his left hand and a cup of Sanka in his right. He never drank coffee anymore because his nerves were shot. He had sweated out too many deadlines. When he was younger, and the pressure got bad, he imagined he was having a heart attack. He had sat up in bed in the middle of the night and listened to the pains pounding through his chest. Then, when the false heart attacks went away, he fought great bouts with what he took to be emphysema, or, on very bad days, cancer of the lung. He gave up cigarettes in his thirties and coffee in his early forties, and now, in his middle forties, he drank Sanka and smoked foreign cigars, and his hands shook and his rumbling cough still caused tremors in newsrooms. He was actually quite healthy.

His left hand was holding a column he had just written for the *Dispatch*. He was attempting to hold it steady enough to read it over once more, trying to sense where it was weak, where he could make a few changes, a word maybe, or a construction — something to improve it before the next edition. He had never written a column that he did not think could be improved. A phrase yes. Even a sentence. On rare occasion, a whole paragraph. But never a column. Not from top to bottom. That was too much to expect.

In my neighborhood, the people are always thinking about important things, like where they should go for dinner Sunday night, and why it is getting so difficult to find good help, and which college should their child attend. These are big matters and deserve a great deal of thought. But now the people in my neighborhood are being forced to think about something else. They are thinking about death. Not the death of a relative who might leave them a few dollars. Sudden, violent, senseless death. The kind of death people in the ghettos live with every day of their lives.

Shelly Cohen, the owner of the bar, was reading over Cahill's shoulder. When he was not running a saloon or putting up cash as a bail bondsman, Shelly Cohen was a literary critic. He read the first paragraph of the column and made his judgment. "You know, you're a fuckin' anti-*Semit*," Shelly Cohen said.

"No, I hate everybody," Danny Cahill said. "Without regard to race, religion, or national origin."

Cahill sipped at his Sanka and concentrated again on the column:

Somewhere out in the night-empty neighborhoods of the city is a guy with frenzy in his eyes and a .44-Bulldog in his pocket. He shoots at young girls with brown hair. In doing so, he has killed five people and wounded four others in the last eleven months.

He shot two girls within six blocks of my house, and the streets where I live are totally deserted at dusk. I know one secretary who now wears a blond wig over her brown hair. She says a lot of girls are doing the same thing. . . .

His eyes moved quickly down the column, searching for flaws, listening for a false note in the rhythm of the piece. Four paragraphs down, the story began describing a walk through Cahill's neighborhood with a detective assigned to the case of the .44 killer, a detective who had spent most of his police career working in ghetto neighborhoods. The detective was Irish, but by now he often slipped, without affectation, into the *patois* of the areas he worked.

"These murders never would happen in a black neighborhood. Too many people out on the streets. Everybody would see who did it. Man we after is only workin' white streets. Nobody comes out at night and he can prowl around and catch him a stray girl and do what he has to do.

"We got us a Jack the Ripper case and everybody thinks they're better off hidin' inside the house. All they doing is makin' it easier for this guy to go around killin' people. Black people are the only ones who know what to do about crime. The more people you have out on the sidewalk outside the house, the less can happen to you."

Cahill read to the end and spotted a few things he wanted to change. He reached across the bar to Shelly Cohen's private telephone, lifted it up, and put it next to his cup of Sanka, then dialed the

Dispatch. He got an assistant city editor and told him the changes he wanted. "Next edition, Danny," the editor said.

"God bless," Cahill said.

He crumpled up the pages of his column, rolled them into a tight ball, and tossed the wad at a large wastebasket behind the bar. He missed. A customer, one of the regulars at the bar, made an elaborate show of picking up the ball of paper and flipping it, behind his back, into the basket.

"Fuck you," Cahill said. "You used to get paid for *missing* baskets." The man had played basketball during the years of the point-shaving scandal, the years when dozens of young men ruined their careers and their lives by getting caught fixing the results of games. The man had never been implicated in the scandal. In fact, his coach had pointed to him as a shining example of integrity and high moral character. His coach was full of shit, and they both knew it.

"Hey, come on, Danny," the man said.

"Hey, I'm only kiddin'," Cahill said. He lifted the cup of Sanka, and, even though it was now barely half-full, still managed to shake a few drops over the edge. "I can't help it. I am fuckin' scared. I don't like my wife going to the store. I don't like my daughter going to school." He turned to Shelly Cohen. "I move in here with all you Jews," he said, "and this is what happens. Serves me right for social-climbing."

Cahill tried to laugh, tried to shrug it off, but he could not. All his adult life, he had built a career as a literate tough guy, a guy who could write out of the corner of his mouth, a guy who knew bookmakers and murderers, con men and hookers, loan sharks and cat burglers, a street guy, a hit man who happened to use an Olivetti instead of a Smith & Wesson. And now the tough guy was frightened, frightened of someone without a name, without a face, frightened of someone who shot young girls who very much resembled his own nineteen-year-old brown-haired daughter who was coming home from college on her spring vacation. "I am sending Moira and her mother to Florida for two weeks," he told Shelly. "I don't want them around here."

The phone rang on the bar and Shelly picked it up. "For you," he said to Cahill. "Your office."

Cahill grabbed the phone in a meaty hand. "Yeah?" he said.

"Danny, you better come in here."

163

"What for? I'm written. What are *you* doing there? You write for tomorrow?"

"No, no," Mike Malamud said. "I just came in to pick up my mail and some copy paper, and Joanne said she wanted to show me something." Malamud was another columnist for the *Dispatch*. He shared an office with Cahill, and a secretary named Joanne Salerno.

"What'd she want to show you?" Cahill said.

"A letter," Malamud said. "A letter came for you today. She said she didn't like the way it sounded, and she wanted you to look at it. She's been trying to find you all afternoon, but the line was busy at home and then there was no answer."

"I took it off the hook. Two bill collectors called this morning. They murder concentration. What was the letter?"

"You better come take a look. I think it's on the level. I don't know for sure, but you look at it, see what you think. It's signed 'Son of Sam.' "

"Signed what?"

"Son of Sam."

"Bullshit," Cahill said. "It's another cuckoo. They call all day long. They're driving Joanne crazy."

"No, this is different."

"Sure. It'll wait till morning. I'll be in tomorrow."

Cahill did not wait for an answer. He hung up the phone as he said "tomorrow." He was going swimming at the Y. He could glide through the pool for an hour and not think about anything except the water. He did not have to use up any emotion on the water. Swimming was the only thing he could do without emotion. He loved swimming.

At the office, Mike Malamud and Joanne Salerno turned the letter over to Stan Richards, the city editor. Richards read the letter, then picked up a telephone, and called Larry McDermott, the deputy police commissioner for public affairs. The deputy police commissioner used to be a reporter for the *Dispatch*. "We'll have a man there to pick up the letter in twenty minutes," McDermott said.

Richards quickly found a staff photographer to make a picture of each of the four pages of the letter signed Son of Sam. Then he put the four pages back into the envelope addressed to Danny Cahill — he noticed the Englewood, New Jersey, postmark — remembered to have a picture taken of the envelope, and waited for the detective.

When the detective arrived, he took the envelope from Richards and did not open it and took it to police headquarters. Half an hour later, the deputy police commissioner for public affairs called Richards, who used to be his boss. "It's a match," McDermott said. "Same printing as the letter we found by the bodies. Nobody's seen that letter but half a dozen people in the Department. They got to be written by the same guy."

"You mean it's legit?" Stan Richards said.

"Uh huh," McDermott said.

"We may want to print it then," Richards said. "Any problem?" Richards had already decided he was going to print the letter. He was simply being polite.

"We want you to print it," the deputy commissioner said.

"You do? Why?"

"We want to set up a chain of communication to the killer. We'll go through Cahill if we have to. We'll feed him things to pass on to the killer."

"He works for a newspaper, not the police," Richards said.

"I'll admit," McDermott said, "we're not exactly overjoyed with the setup."

"Why not?"

"Cahill. Who knows what he's going to write? You can get more reliable messengers from Fleet Service."

When Danny Cahill got home from his swim, his wife told him that Stan Richards had called every ten minutes for the past hour. "I think you oughta call him back," she said.

Cahill called the office. "The letter is legitimate," Stan Richards told him. "We've turned it over to the cops and they say it matches the letter they found by the bodies. It's from the killer and it's for you, and you're never going to see the original. But we made copies."

"Read me it," Cahill said.

"Dear Mr. Cahill," Richards began. "Hello from the gutters of NYC which are filled with dog manure, vomit, stale wine, urine, and blood. Hello from the sewers of NYC which swallow up these delicacies when they are washed away by the sweeper trucks. Hello from the cracks in the sidewalks of NYC and from the ants that dwell in these cracks and feed on the dried blood of the dead that has seeped into these cracks."

165

"Sonuvabitch writes good," Cahill interrupted. "Read me that last sentence again."

"Hello from the cracks in the sidewalks of NYC and from the ants that dwell in these cracks and feed on the dried blood of the dead that has seeped into these cracks."

"That's so good it's scary," Cahill said.

"D.C.," Richards continued, "I'm just dropping a line to let you know that I appreciate your interest in those recent and horrendous forty-four-caliber killings. I also want to tell you that I read your column daily and I find it quite informative.

"Tell me, Dan, what will you have for May thirtieth? You can forget about me if you like because I don't care for publicity. However, you must not forget Connie Bonventre and you cannot let the people forget her either. She was a very, very sweet girl but Sam's a thirsty lad and he won't let me stop killing until he gets his fill of blood.

"Mr. Cahill, sir, don't think that because you haven't heard from for a while that I went to sleep. No — "

"What's that — 'heard from for a while'?"

"He left out a word," Richards said. "He left out a 'me.' I'll read on.

"No, rather, I am still here. Like a spirit roaming the night. Thirsty, hungry, seldom stopping to rest; anxious to please Sam. I love my work. Now, the void has been filled.

"Perhaps we shall meet face to face someday or perhaps I will be blown away by cops with smoking thirty-eights. Whatever, if I shall be fortunate enough to meet you I will tell you all about Sam if you like and I will introduce you to him. His name is 'Sam the Terrible.'

"Not knowing what the future holds I shall say farewell and I will see you at my next job. Or, should I say you will see my handiwork at the next job? Remember Ms. Bonventre. Thank you.

"In their blood and from the gutter, 'Sam's Creation' Forty-four."

Richards paused. "That's not all," he said. Then he read on. "Here are some names to help you along. Forward them to the Inspector for use by NCIC:

"The Duke of Death

"The Evil King Evergreen

"The Twenty-Two Disciples of Hell

"John 'Wheaties' — Rapist and Suffocator of Young Girls.

"P.S.: D.C., please inform all the detectives working the slayings to remain —

"He stopped the sentence right there," Richards said, "and started it over again:

"P.S.: D.C., please inform all the detectives working the case that I wish them the best of luck. Keep 'em digging, drive on, think positive, get off your butts, knock on coffins, et cetera.

"Upon my capture, I promise to buy all the guys working on the case a new pair of shoes if I can get up the money.

"Son of Sam."

Richards coughed, clearing his throat. "That's the end of the letter," he said, "but underneath the name there's a little drawing. It shows the biological signs for male and female next to each other with an X across them. On top of the X there's a cross, and under the X there's an S. You won't believe the printing. It's like an artist did it. Maybe a cartoonist. It's easier to read than if he'd typed it, it's that good."

"It don't read too bad, either," Cahill said. "You ain't got six guys working who can write that good."

"We're gonna print it," Richards said.

"Terrific," Cahill said. "Make the 'Dear Mr. Cahill' part very big."

"We want you to write a column to go with it."

"Yeah? What kind of column?"

"Shit, you know. Open up communications with the killer. Tell him you know what he's going through. Maybe suggest he turn himself in to you. Tell him you'll meet him someplace safe."

"You go and fuck yourself," Cahill said. "Safe? Safe for who? You go and meet him. He's carrying a forty-four. You know what a forty-four does? It makes meetings very unpleasant. It ruins conversation."

"We've already talked it over with the police," Richards said. "You'll have protection twenty-four hours a day. They'll have a plainclothes guy close to you every minute."

"Bullshit," Cahill said. "I don't need that." He looked up at his wife who had been listening to the whole conversation. "You just tell 'em," Cahill continued, "to put two cops outside my house. That's all. I don't want that cocksucker coming around here. But I don't want no cops with me personal."

Cahill stopped to light a cigar. He was starting to feel a little better. "Hey," he said to Stan Richards, "get a copyboy on the phone to read me the letter again. I like that 'Mr. Cahill, sir' part."

14

Mitchell Block held up the *Dispatch* so that all the people in the crowded and untidy room could see the banner headline on the front page: KILLER WRITES TO CAHILL: I LOVE MY WORK. There were fourteen people in the room, two on a piano bench, one in an armchair, three on rickety wooden chairs, one on a hassock, the rest sprawled on the floor, seven women and seven men, none younger than twenty-three and none older than thirty-two, except for Lionel Silver, who was fifty-four and bearded and sitting in the armchair. Lionel was the leader. He and his followers called themselves The Moment of Truth, and their headquarters was The Moment of Truth Gallery, a storefront on Waverly Place in Greenwich Village. The members of The Moment of Truth were all writers or painters, and although none of them was ready yet to earn a living with his or her writing or painting, most of them seemed bright and very earnest. One wall of the storefront was covered with the work of the painting branch of The Moment of Truth. Some of the paintings were fairly accurate copies of the covers of science-fiction comic books. Some seemed to be sort of impressionistic genitalia. Others were quite realistic.

"It's obvious he's possessed," Mitchell Block said.

"Of course," Selma Sagerman said.

"He is in the hands of the demons," Mitchell Block said.

"Of course," Selma Sagerman said.

"They are evil," Mitchell Block said. "We were right to free ourselves from them."

Lionel Silver coughed, indicating that he desired to speak. "The great world conflict of the future," he said, "will be not between nations, but between ideologies. Science versus spiritualism, I'm certain of it."

"Of course," Selma Sagerman said.

Silver turned to a small table next to his armchair and leaned over and picked up a copy of a new paperback book. The title of the book was *Hostage to the Devil,* Dr. Malachi Martin's account of five exorcisms that had freed Americans possessed by Satan. "It takes tremendous strength of character to break away from the demons," Silver told his followers.

To the members of The Moment of Truth, *Hostage to the Devil* had become almost a Bible. It was, surely, *their* good book, their constant support in their struggle against the demons. Not too many months earlier, however, before they turned to *Hostage to the Devil,* The Moment of Truth, as a group, had put its faith in a very different collection of writings known as the "Seth Books," written or compiled by a woman named Jane Roberts. Seth was a spirit guide, a discarnate, a nonphysical entity, and Jane Roberts was his medium, his conduit, his means of getting his views across to the incarnate of the world. The Moment of Truth people had accepted the Seth Books so completely that each of them had, through great concentration and belief, established direct contact with his or her own spirit guide, own discarnate, and this contact had developed into lively — one would almost say "spirited" — dialogues between the physical and nonphysical entities. "What Arthur was to me," said Mitchell Block, referring to his own now-discarded spiritual guide, "Sam is to the forty-four-caliber killer."

The MOTs, as they sometimes called themselves in a little inside joke, an allusion to the Jewish background (members of the tribe) of most of The Moment of Truth people, had run into trouble with their spirit guides. The guides had stirred up jealousy within the close-knit family of writers and artists. Arthur, for instance, told Mitchell, after their conversations had grown quite intimate, that it wasn't right that only Lionel should be allowed to sleep with all the women in the group.

"You have as much right to sleep with Selma as Lionel has," Arthur advised Mitchell, "and, besides, you are younger and stronger and more handsome, and for Selma's good, you should sleep with her, too."

169

As part of his commitment to total truth, Mitchell had reported this conversation with Arthur to all the other members of The Moment of Truth, and it was not long afterward that Lionel, not without some misgivings, because he was rather fond of quoting his own spirit guide to reinforce each new idea and plan he brought to his followers, had informed the group that he feared the spirit guides were leading them astray, preaching not pure truth but evil distortions. Under Lionel's direction, the writing branch of The Moment of Truth assembled and distributed a mimeographed pamphlet entitled, "Beware of Ghosts Bearing Gifts — A Critical View of Seth."

"If you read the whole letter from the killer to Cahill," Mitchell Block said, "it confirms what we've suspected all along. The forty-four-caliber killer is possessed. Look at this." He pointed to the text of the letter on page three of the *Dispatch*. "'Sam's a thirsty lad, and he won't let me stop killing till he's had his fill of blood.' Obviously, Sam is a demon."

"The spirit guides lie," Lionel Silver said. "They flatter, they entice, they want to control all of us in mind, body and spirit."

"They are the fallen angels," Aaron Castle said.

"Of course," Selma Sagerman said.

All around the City of New York, on April 28, 1977, people were reading in the *Dispatch* the letter from the killer to Cahill, and Cahill's response, a suggestion that the killer give himself up, or, at least, give Cahill a call on the telephone. "I accept calls from everybody except collection agencies," Cahill wrote. Besides the letter — the full text set in type next to a photostat of the first page — and Cahill's column, the *Dispatch* ran a short editorial, on page three, decrying the atmosphere of terror created by the unknown killer and offering a $10,000 reward for information leading directly to his arrest and conviction.

At the lower tip of Manhattan, in a carpeted and wood-paneled office — two floors above an ancient newsroom where ratty desks stood on faded linoleum — the publisher of the city's afternoon newspaper, the *Express*, looked out his window toward the Borough of Brooklyn and fumed about the coverage in the *Dispatch*. The publisher of the *Express*, Malcolm Bromwich, was an Englishman who considered himself the most powerful press lord in the world, and the most clever.

"What kind of bloody assholes am I paying?" he demanded of his managing editor, who was standing in front of him, holding an unlit pipe in his left hand. "Why didn't we come up with this first instead of that drunken Irishman at the *Dispatch*? Why didn't we have a letter from the killer?"

"I'm afraid it's a legitimate letter," Geoffrey Miles, the Canadian-born managing editor of the *Express*, said. "The police have confirmed its authen — "

"I want results, not excuses," Bromwich said, interrupting as he always did. "I'd give ten thousand pounds — I mean dollars — for one of our columnists to get a letter from the killer. A good letter. Gory, but not too gory. Menacing. And be careful about the phrasing. You better let one of our Yanks write it — at least the first draft."

Miles tapped his pipe against his right palm. "I'm not certain we can trust them," he said. "They're always carrying on about integ — "

"If they have so damned much integrity," Bromwich said, "why do they keep accepting my paychecks? But, perhaps you're right. Give it to Henry. Henry Glenville. He's lived here so many years now he sounds like a Yank, but, thank God, he doesn't think like one. He'd bash his grandmother for a story."

"The man is a machine," Miles said. "He'll have it ready for the next edition."

"No, no, no," Bronwich said. "Too obvious. And no real impact. We must wait awhile. Ten days should be about right, don't you think?"

Bromwich did not wait for a reply. He did not really care what Miles thought, or what anyone else thought. He made all the important decisions about the *Express*, and Miles's job, in essence, was to transmit those decisions to the staff. "Geoff," Bromwich said, "I want to see at least two stories in the *Express* every day about the killer. I want people to have to read the *Express* if they want to stay abreast of the case. What does the chap call himself? Son of Sam? We will be the Son of Sam newspaper in this city. This is important. For us and, of course, for our city."

Bromwich turned, dismissing Miles, and looked out his window again at Brooklyn. He wondered what it was like over there, across the river. He made a mental note that someday he ought to go over and take a look at Brooklyn.

171

Inside the offices of the national newsmagazines, *Time* and *Newsweek,* and inside the offices of the television networks, ABC and CBS and NBC — all five of those firms jammed in the heart of Manhattan, in an area only two blocks wide, from Madison Avenue on the east to Avenue of the Americas on the west, and only five blocks long, from Forty-ninth Street on the south to Fifty-fourth Street on the north, a sophisticated one-sixteenth of a square mile, a total of forty acres of concrete and steel and confusion and indecision — inside this tiny cluster of communications giants that determines what most Americans will either know or not know about what is going on in the entire world — dozens of editors and producers were looking at the *Dispatch* and coming to a decision that the case of the .44-caliber killer had become a story whose appeal transcended the five boroughs of New York. *Time* and *Newsweek* started putting major stories, potential cover stories, into the works; Telexed queries went to bureaus across the country seeking local reaction to the mad killer loose in New York. The networks began assembling reports for their nightly news shows; requests went to their film warehouses in New Jersey and Connecticut for archival footage of the Speck murders in Chicago and the Whitman shootings in Texas, for all available footage relating to mass murderers. Son of Sam, faceless or not, was about to become a national celebrity.

The case was irresistible to the news media for many reasons: the residents of the largest city in the country were now beset not by their vague everyday fears but by an enormous and specific fear, a fear that was ruining the sex lives of young couples who did not have access to apartments or hotel rooms, a fear that was stimulating business for beauty parlors, catering to young women with long brown hair who wanted the hair cut short or dyed blond.

Every aspect of the case fascinated: the victims were young and attractive women. There was no warning, no discernible motive. The killer had shown great cleverness in eluding the police on six separate occasions and now, in his letters to Carillo and Cahill, he was toying with the police, offering them hints to his identity and threats that he would strike again. The killer seemed a man of unusual intelligence; his letter to Cahill was strikingly well written, rich in its images and precise in its grammar. "This is the first killer I ever heard of who understands the use of the semicolon," Cahill told a television reporter who came to interview him in his office at the *Dispatch*. And the killer's choice of a name for himself was pure genius: Son of Sam. It fit so easily into headlines. It sounded so good. It came off the tongue trippingly, as Vladimir Nabokov had once written of the name Lolita. Three syllables. Perfect. Lo-li-ta. The perfect name for a prepubescent temptress. Son of Sam. The perfect name for a shadowy killer. It was, in its own way — SOS, look out, beware — every bit as good as the four-syllable classic, Jack the Ripper.

In the century before the emergence of Son of Sam, there had been dozens of mass murderers who, like him and like Jack the Ripper, had killed strangers and had killed repeatedly. There was the Frenchman, Vacher, and the German Peter Kurtens, the Monster of Dusseldorf, and in the United States alone, there was the Torso Killer of Cleveland, the Moonlight Murderer of Texarkana, the Zodiac Killer of San Francisco, and even in Queens, within a few miles of Son of Sam's exploits, there was the Lipstick Murderer of the 1930s. None of these American murderers was ever apprehended, and each had his own colorful nickname, yet none's fame, or infamy, endured quite like Jack the Ripper's. Jack the Ripper was the superstar of his game. His name became a synonym for horror, for sudden, violent death, but now most people who invoke his name do not realize that Jack in his career claimed only five victims, all prostitutes, all in the Whitechapel district of London, that his reign of terror lasted for only three months in the fall of 1888 and that, although half a dozen leading suspects have emerged over the years, the Ripper was never caught and never absolutely identified. Shrouded in mystery, Jack the Ripper had star quality; he had charisma; he inspired plays and movies and television specials long after his crimes. He wrote to the police, too. The first letter attributed to him began, "Dear Boss," and continued:

> I keep on hearing the police have caught me, but they won't fix me just yet. I have laughed when they look so clever and talk about being on the right track. . . . I am down on whores and I shan't quit ripping them till I do get buckled. Grand work the last job was. I gave the lady no time to squeal. I love my work. . . .

The Ripper's handwriting was remarkable: a precise, almost artistic script. *I love my work.* Eighty-nine years later, the .44-caliber killer used the same words exactly.

" 'I am still here,' " Mitchell Block read to his fellow members of The Moment of Truth. " 'Like a spirit roaming the night. Thirsty, hungry, seldom stopping to rest; anxious to please Sam. I love my work . . . . ' "

Mitchell Block paused, and Lionel Silver coughed. "We are all agreed that the man who calls himself 'Son of Sam' and 'Sam's Creation' is possessed, are we not?" said Silver. "The next question, logically, is what shall we do about this? We could draft a letter to the *Dispatch*."

"No," Aaron Castle said, "that won't do any good. They'll just think we're crazy. Like everyone who writes letters to the *Dispatch*."

"Well," Lionel Silver said, "we could seek the assistance of Jane Roberts."

"What do you mean?" Block said. "I thought that was over, we were finished with her and Seth."

"We do not trust Seth, we do not revere him," Silver said, "but we do know that he exists, that Jane Roberts is in contact with him and that he can see into the past, present, and future, that all human affairs are known to him."

"Of course," Selma Sagerman said.

"So," Silver continued, "we can call upon Jane Roberts to ask Seth to identify the forty-four-caliber killer, to give us the man's name, to tell us where he lives, what he does, what he looks like. If Seth does this, through Jane Roberts, we can then seek out the man who is possessed by Sam and we can conduct an exorcism. We can drive Sam from his body. If Seth refuses, then Jane Roberts will realize, as we already do, that Seth is not pure, is not compassionate, that he is evil and unwilling to do anything to reduce human suffering. Jane Roberts may then be freed of her demon, her spirit guide."

"And suppose Jane Roberts refuses to help us?"

"Then," Silver said, shaking his head sadly, "I'm afraid that she is completely possessed by Seth."

"But don't we already believe that?" Aaron Castle said.

"Of course," Lionel Silver said.

"In the meantime," Mitchell Block said, "why don't we skip the intermediaries — the *Dispatch,* Jane Roberts, and Seth — and just write directly to Son of Sam?"

"A brilliant suggestion," Lionel Silver said, and by acclamation, The Moment of Truth decided, as its part of the drive to rid New York of the .44-caliber killer, to write him a letter. The group of writers and artists spent the next several days drafting and redrafting the letter, crossing out words and phrases and sentences, trying to incorporate everyone's ideas precisely. Finally, the letter was ready:

Dear Son of Sam:

We're writing to let you know that you are not as alone as you think you are. We know about Sam. We, too, have been involved with inner voices. We have found that these voices lie to us and revel in the confusion and misery they cause. Sam wants to own you, body and soul, and to use you as his agent to cause as much pain as possible to others. Sam knows that you are lonely, and he takes advantage of this by pretending that he is your friend in order to get you to do whatever he wants. You will not want to give Sam up because you fear you will have nothing to replace him with. But soon you will have nothing at all—Sam will have everything. He wants things because he wants to destroy them. He is evil and hates humanity. Remember: Sam is a big liar and will tell you anything to get you to hurt others. Hurting others might get you big headlines for a while, but it won't get you the love you need.

"Okay," Mitchell Block said when the letter was finished, "now where do we send it?"

"Let's just send it to the post office," Aaron Castle said. "Let them figure out where it goes."

"Of course," Selma Sagerman said.

15

If he had read one, he had read a couple of hundred of them. "Look for a man whose last name is Samson," the letter began. He threw it away and reached for the next one. There were no more. Earlier, at 3:30 a.m., at the end of the night patrol, he had decided to stay for a few more minutes and read through all the mail that had been forwarded to the Special Task Force. Even if one of his detectives had already read and checked a letter, Carillo decided he wanted to see it: always give a lottery ticket one last look before throwing it away.

Now, finished with his reading, which hadn't given him a single clue, Carillo stared out the window at the early daylight. In the municipal parking lot across the street, there were enough people getting out of cars and walking toward the subway to let Carillo know that it had to be around seven o'clock. He winced. He had an eight-thirty meeting at the laboratory with the fingerprint people, and the drive to Manhattan would have to be made in the vortex of the rush hour.

His face felt dirty and his mouth was hot. He knocked his pipe clean and stuck it into his desk. He wouldn't be able to smoke again until he got some sleep. The newspaper pictures, identifying him as the man in charge of the Special Task Force, had made him look like a pipe-smoking detective from the annals of literature. In reality, if somebody taking the photos had bothered to ask him how things were going, he would have told him that his tongue felt like a dog had chewed on it.

At the foot of the staircase, before Carillo opened the door to the lobby of the precinct, he stopped and checked his gun. He stuffed it back into his belt, clipping it onto the top of his pants, and then came out into the lobby. At the doorway, he paused and his eyes swept the people walking by. He scratched his ear while pretending he was trying to remember if he had forgotten anything. On a plane takeoff, Carillo always made the sign of the cross by acting as if his forehead itched, then running his hand across his chest as if he were smoothing his jacket.

As he stepped onto the sidewalk, Carillo's eyes were everywhere. A man in a warm-up jacket came walking down the block from the diner. Right away, Carillo went to the hands. The man's two hands were swinging naturally as he walked. Keep them out where I can see them, Carillo thought. A black man came out of the parking lot. Carillo gave him only a casual glance; suddenly, a black was a positive in Carillo's life. As Carillo came up to his car in the lot, he tensed. The guy could come out from behind any car on me, he thought. A sense of absurdity finally came over him. "Grow up," he said. He walked directly to his car, got in, and drove out of the lot.

He still was berating himself as he drove to the corner of Northern Boulevard, where he stopped for a light. During the wait, he kept watching the hands of any men crossing the street in front of him. Two hands, he kept thinking, let me see both hands, mister.

At the laboratory, Inspector Ryan and the technician, Lenahan, were waiting for him. "It's been twelve days," Carillo said. "I thought you fellas had forgot about me."

"You can't tell a chemical to react," Lenahan said. "It takes its own sweet time."

The letter Lenahan was working on was the first one sent by the killer, the one that had been left by the bodies of Edward Nodari and Linda Tomasello. Lenahan had hoped the second letter, the one to Cahill, would yield better prints, but he had been disappointed. The only good prints on the Cahill letter belonged to Joanne Salerno, his secretary. The killer's prints were there, too, but they had been exceedingly faint to start with and now they were blurred beyond use.

Lenahan had the original letter out on a table. In places there were purple smudges, which were from the fingerprint spray, he explained. In other places there were brown smudges. This was the result of treating the paper with heated iodine crystals. The crystals react to the fats left on the paper and cause the fats to become brown. Lenahan gave Carillo a magnifying lens. Through it Carillo saw fingerprint lines in several places, not full fingerprints, but the beginnings of them. Sometimes the lines were almost completed. But these formed smaller circles than the prints Carillo was used to working with.

"Whoever he is, he's got tiny fingers," Carillo said.

"That's the tips of his fingers you're looking at," Lenahan said. "You're used to working with fingerprints you get by holding a guy's hand flat on a pad. This guy was writing, so he had the tips of the fingers touching the paper. Actually, the tips are better to work with, they're clearer. Providing the guy gives us a whole print. As you can see, this man does not give us very much."

"All partials," Inspector Ryan said.

At the bottom of the second page, there was a series of longer, more rolling lines. Obviously the palm. "Will the palm do us any good?" Carillo said.

"Yeah, if we catch a guy with the same palm," Inspector Ryan said.

Carillo put down the magnifying lens. "Well, what am I looking at?" he said.

"You've got one shot, Inspector," Lenahan said. "This one here is the best." He moved the magnifying lens over a smudge on the right side of the second sheet of the killer's letter.

"See the bull's-eye whorl?" Lenahan said.

Carillo was looking at a swirl of black dots. He knew a whorl was circular, a loop appears to be thread doubled over, and arches look like a series of small waves. He was dealing here with a whorl. At the end, at the bottom of the funnel, there was a tiny horseshoe with a black dot in the exact center of it. The fingerprint ended there, at the black dot.

"The dot is the bull's-eye?" Carillo said.

"Absolutely," Lenahan said. "Doesn't it look just like one?"

"Is this unusual?" Carillo said.

"Sure it is, Inspector. You figure, seventy percent of fingers are loops, twenty percent are whorls. I got to say one out of a thousand whorls have a core like this."

Carillo could feel file cards and folders in his hands. The file cards being slapped over, making it sound like men playing cards. And mug shots falling out of the folders and hands reaching for them.

Hundreds of hands doing this at the same time and then a shout, a loud shout from somebody. Then lights and horns blaring, he liked the horn ahead of the siren, and the killer in handcuffs in the back of the car.

"What finger is this?" Carillo said as he looked at the bull's-eye. Anxiety squeezed his throat.

"You can't tell what finger," Lenahan said.

"You've got to do better than this for me," Carillo said. He stopped himself from saying anything more. He was embarrassed that he had made such an immature plea. Lenahan had done all that he could do; he had done his job.

"We tried to bring up more, but this is as far as we could go," Lenahan said. Carillo listened gloomily. "We used silver nitrates; they react to the body salts. Then we used the iodine. Trouble is we got to deal with a piece of paper. You got to be careful of paper, you got to watch out for how much it can absorb. You put too much on paper and you lose everything."

"That's the business, I guess," Carillo said.

"It all depends on how a man secretes," Lenahan said. "A good secretor gives you enough to go on. This guy is a bad secretor. He could have paper fibers in the pores of his fingers. That would keep them dry. Guy could be a mailman handling envelopes all day. You ought to think about a mailman, Inspector. Mailman knows the city, particularly the neighborhoods this guy's been going into. Nobody knows where half those neighborhoods are, except somebody like a mailman."

Carillo turned his face away to make Lenahan stop talking. A mailman, yes, he could be a mailman, Carillo thought, but he could also be a cop. Bet your ass he could be a cop. I hope to hell he isn't an Italian cop.

"It's better to work off these," Lenahan said. He held a sheaf of enlarged photographs of the prints.

"I already sent a set down to the Identification Section," Inspector Ryan said.

"So that's it?" Carillo said, getting up to leave.

Lenahan said, "He's a bad secretor, Inspector. I only wish the guy had put his fingers onto some paper that had been wrapped around butter. Then we would've had no trouble."

Going down in the elevator, Carillo felt like he had just made a visit to the doctor's office, and the doctor had said he certainly could fix the knee, except that it had been so banged up.

Carillo got back in his car and drove downtown from the Police Academy, which housed the lab, to police headquarters. The drive took him ten minutes. He parked in a section reserved for police officers and then took the elevator to the third floor, to the offices of the Fingerprint Identification Section.

The windows of the Identification Section looked out onto the Municipal Building. Through the archway of the Municipal Building, Carillo could see the sidewalks crowded with the people who feed off the government: the lawyers and assistants to the commissioners, the clerks and drivers and department heads and courtroom attendants and judges. Carillo felt superior to them. We got an emergency and none of you are worth anything, he said to himself. His arrogance faded as he glanced at the fingerprint photographs he held. I may not be worth much either, he told himself.

A few feet away, a civilian aide sat at a computer and tapped keys which caused a list of names and addresses to appear in green print on the computer's screen.

"What do you have there?" Carillo asked.

"People called for jury duty in Brooklyn," the aide said. "Just checking to see how many of 'em have been arrested. Not *if* there's been any arrests, but *how many* of 'em have been busted."

On the screen four names appeared, along with B numbers, the file number given to a person arrested in New York.

"See?" the aide said happily. "Give me all day here and they'll have *no* juries in the whole of Brooklyn."

"Good for you," Carillo said. "How does this work for me?"

The operator looked up at him. "If you give me a name and address, I can put it in here and we'll find out if the man has any prints. We'll come up with the prints. But you got no name and address. This computer can't retrieve anything for you, because you can't tell it what to retrieve."

Carillo became uneasy standing there. If there is anything that laboratory people and those working with them are supposed to do for the cops out working a case, it is to give them hope, even false hope. Investigations live on it. Tell me anything, Carillo said to himself, but don't tell me I've got nothing.

The head of the Identification Section, a captain, came out to see

180

Carillo. He waved a hand disdainfully at the computer. "That's no good unless you already got a suspect," he said. He took Carillo up two flights to a room in which a $250,000 McDonnell Douglas fingerprint-checking machine sat in its gray splendor.

At the end of the 1960s, when the fear of blacks and antiwar activists was at its height, many millions of federal dollars were made available to police departments across the country. Immediately, defense contractors moved in like metal sharks. They put together and sold the most sophisticated of machinery. Police departments whose problem was street crime were equipped to trace lunar trajectories. The McDonnell Douglas company, which makes military jets to sell to countries which do not have roads, became one of the sellers. The New York Police Department, using federal funds, bought the massive fingerprint-checking machine. The machine shoots a laser beam through a latent fingerprint and registers the amount of light passing through the print. This is recorded on film which, when developed, is placed into the machine again. Stacks of IBM cards are fed to the machine. Another laser beam tries to match the amount of light in each fingerprint with the amount of light which went through the latent print. The cards flip out of the machine and into hoppers which are marked first best, second best, third best, and no good. The machine can cut down the amount of files to be checked. How close it comes to being correct is a question. Neither the manufacturer, who wants the sales, nor the policemen assigned to the machine, who want the power of running their own operation, will admit that the machine is anything but perfect.

"You need a lot more here than what you're giving us," the captain told Carillo.

"What can you do for me?" Carillo asked.

"We can start you off. Get you into the ball park. There's seventy thousand cards for recidivists. We'll start running them through and see what happens."

Carillo thought of his friend, Vincent McNamara, who once was assigned to a machine which took a victim's verbal description of a robber and then snaked across thousands of mug shots in search of the villain. One day, McNamara admitted, "The only way my machine works is if you give the size of the mole on the guy's ass."

As Carillo left, he said to the captain, "I wish I could give you more."

"Yeah, something that would help us," the captain said.

"The mole on his ass," Carillo said.

As Carillo left the building, he tried to guess how much work was ahead. At its best, he decided, the $250,000 machine would leave him with the task of checking fifty thousand sets of fingerprints. Fifty thousand, at ten prints a card, comes to a half million fingers, Carillo thought. And if the killer never had been arrested in New York, or had been arrested only once, all the work would be for nothing. Carillo was glad that he was too tired to let the shock fully reach him.

He drove out to the 112th Precinct in Queens, where another machine, Miraquic, was in operation. This was a $38,000 machine put together by Eastman Kodak and given to the New York Police Department as a sales promotion. As Carillo came in, Lacey, the lieutenant in charge of the section, came toward him like a salesman.

"If he ever got arrested in Queens County, we'll have him for you in an hour," Lacey said to Carillo, his hand out for the fingerprint photos Carillo held in a manila envelope. "You remember the case at Saint John's University? Where the retired Fire Lieutenant working in the bookstore got killed? Remember that? We had the one print off of a magazine the bum picked up. Well, we run it through the machine here and we come up with him right away. He'd once robbed the Queens College bookstore. Got caught and we filed his prints. We got the guy the same night he shot the Fire Lieutenant, Inspector. Remember that? Well, let me see what you got. Maybe we'll do the same for you."

His voice fell and his smile needed help as he glanced at the prints Carillo was carrying. Lacey sat down and began to examine them. "This one here," Carillo said, leaning over Lacey's shoulder and tapping the bull's-eye whorl.

Lacey looked at it. "Well, let's try it," he said. He took a magnifying glass and examined the bull's-eye. On a slip of paper he wrote a 5, for a whorl, a 2, for a whorl with a visible core, and then the numbers 001 for a white male. He walked inside to a computer, punched out the 5 − 2 − 001, then hit another key, and pointed to a small dial.

"That can tell us right away how many people got arrested in Queens with these characteristics," Lacey said. "It's a start." The dial began to buzz and red numbers appeared. First a single digit and then double figures, up through the twenties and thirties and forties. It slowed and stopped at fifty-one.

182

"We got only fifty-one guys who are white and have a whorl like this on any one finger," Lacey said.

"Fifty-one out of all your arrest records for the whole borough?" Carillo asked.

Lacey's smile grew weaker. "Well, no, not exactly the whole borough," he said. "We've only had this system in for a couple of years."

Carillo's eyes closed. "How many prints can you check for me?" he asked.

"You know, to get this machine originally set up, we had to go to Kodak and get them to put all our arrest rec —"

"How many can you check for me?" Carillo asked again.

"About twenty-five thousand," Lacey said.

"Out of how many?" Carillo said.

"Seventy-six thousand fingerprint cards are not yet set up for this machine," Lacey said.

"Those I do by hand?" Carillo said.

Lacey nodded. "If we just knew which finger," he said.

Carillo walked out. When he got into his car, it was after four. He had to go over to the 109th Precinct and get ready to turn out the night patrols. It was only a half-hour drive to the 109th, but he had to shake his head to remain awake in the car.

When Carillo got home late that night, he began thinking of a master cop, a man who could sit at one desk in the office and control all the filing and examination of records and the tracing of fingerprints. He was a large, open man, the master cop, who greeted each question with a smile that became a laugh as he answered. "Cabdrivers? Of course, Inspector, here's your list of every cabdriver who's worked in the city in the last two years. Medallion cabs are first and then come private car services. Every driver's name, address, phone number." After handing over the thick, neat file, the master cop picked up his phone and called the police lab and spoke to the technicians in their own language. As Carillo dipped into sleep, the vision of the master cop enlarged and now Carillo saw dozens of them, one desk after the other, like an insurance company with guns, and the hands of each master cop ceaselessly went through the folders. Digging, digging, digging, while Carillo sat in the front of the room and smoked his pipe and waited for one of the master cops' faces to explode into excitement as he discovered the sheet of paper which carried the name and home address of the killer.

Carillo awoke at 7:00 a.m., irritated from too many nights of too little sleep. Over coffee, his wife asked him about the case and he did not answer.

"I said," she repeated, "how do you think it's going?"

"I don't know," he said.

"What do you mean, you don't know? You must know something."

"I'm too tired to talk," Carillo said. He got up to leave.

As he approached his car, the woman next door, Mrs. Carlson, stepped across her small lawn and came up to him. "Well, what about this killer?" she said.

"I don't know what to tell you," he said.

"It's certainly not like the television, is it?" she said.

Carillo grunted. "Fingerprints," he said. "On 'Hawaii Five-0,' the prints check out in fifteen minutes. You know what I got? The guy left a set of partial prints on the letter to me. We'll be going through files for three weeks checking on them and probably we won't come up with a damn thing." He shook his head. "Kojak hears from the lab before the next commercial."

She clucked her tongue. "And what about this woman who saw the shooting?"

"What woman?" he said.

"I heard it on Channel Five."

Carillo stared at her.

"They're making it up again?" she said.

"You know it," he said. He got into the car.

He was in his office at the 109th for about fifteen minutes when his wife called. "You wouldn't talk to me," she said, "and then you go right outside and tell Ruth Carlson that you have fingerprints? Why don't you talk to me? Why don't you tell me? I want to know all about the fingerprints."

Carillo froze. How the hell could I have told that woman about fingerprints?

"I never told her a thing about fingerprints," he said.

"She says you did."

"She confused me with what she hears on television," he said.

He thought that this might stop neighborhood gossip about fingerprints. His wife would go to Mrs. Carlson immediately and tell her that she had it wrong. Also, it would prevent his wife from being angry about him speaking to a neighbor and not to her: You sang at everybody's party but mine. That he made Mrs. Carlson a liar was a separate subject.

One of the new detectives put on the case, a six-foot-three, 250-pound man named Daley, came in. "My first day, I just want to say hello," Daley said.

"Where are you from, Daley?" Carillo said.

"Thirteenth Homicide. Brooklyn. I work out of the Seven-seven on Utica Avenue."

"How are you at checking guns?" Carillo asked Daley.

"I've done it," Daley said.

"You're going to do it again," Carillo said. His dream from the previous night was in his mind again. "I want to get the name of every guy in this country who owns a forty-four-caliber Bulldog revolver. I want the names on a computer and I want them gone through with a magnifying glass. I want to know where every forty-four Bulldog that's ever been made has gone. Try every law-enforcement agency in the country. If you can't get cooperation, come and see me. What's the matter?"

Daley was shifting on his feet. Pain sprayed from the corners of his eyes. "Inspector," he said, "if I run into this man out on the street, this man with his big fuckin' gun, I'll put him on the hood of my car like a deer and drive him down here to you. I'll call you up on the radio and say, 'If Son of Sam is married, tell his wife she's a widow.' That's what I want to do for you."

Carillo paused. He wanted to get his point about master cops over to Daley. "The easiest part of this investigation," he began, "is to sit here and say, 'I think so-and-so did it,' and then go running out and follow some guy around. That's the easy part of this one. You know what I'm doing? I'm putting all the quiffs onto that type of work. They can go out and play detective and stay out of my way. I'm putting the top men on the major job. The hard part, the only part of the case that might give us a chance, is going through records. Digging through files, looking for a name on an application blank, on a license, anywhere. He had to print his name somewhere, some time. That's the only way we're going to get him. Some uniformed guy may bump into him, you know, give him a traffic ticket, and then have the balls to ask the guy to get out of the car and shake him down and find the gun. That's the way it could go. But till then we can only go one way: checking the files until some of us go blind. I'm only using my best men on that. My best."

Daley's large head nodded, but Carillo knew it was only perfunctory. "I'd still like to meet up with him on the street, him and his big fuckin' gun," Daley said again.

As Daley left, Carillo thought, I got to get a few Jews around here. They're the only ones at home around paperwork.

The first one he thought of was Levine, who was in the Personnel Department in headquarters. Carillo remembered meeting him once. Carillo had Levine assigned to him by lunchtime and had him reporting the next morning. With a flourish, Carillo shoved a desk for him almost up to his own doorway. It was to be the central monitoring desk for his master detectives. Levine appeared surprised to find that he was suddenly so prominent a member of such a large and highly publicized investigation. Carillo ordered Levine to have ten to twelve top file men at work in the fingerprint rooms at both police headquarters and the 112th, going through the file cards with prints of recidivists on them. Levine also was to oversee the combing of records for the owners of Bulldog .44s. Carillo watched with approval as Levine began to arrange neat stacks of paper, marked wire baskets with "Incoming" and "Special Handling," and got on the phone with a fine display of energy. He could use his contacts in personnel to ferret out the best file men and folder men in the department.

Carillo went into his office and began to look over the list of phone messages. The chief of detectives had called twice, he saw. He returned the call and then went over assignment sheets. He came outside to ask Levine a question. The desk was empty.

"Where is he?" Carillo asked.

Daley and Sergeant Hanlon both held up their hands. Carillo went back inside. He came out fifteen minutes later, in time to see Levine coming in the door. Carillo did not like the look on Levine's face.

"Where were you?" Carillo asked mildly.

Something moved in Levine's eyes. Moved once, then moved again. "I was just downstairs looking over the switchboard operation," Levine said.

Two days later, Carillo went into police headquarters in Manhattan to start the day. He arrived at the 109th in mid-morning. As Carillo entered the room, Levine's eyes were on him, as if he had been sitting there and watching the door. Carillo nodded and walked past Levine. "I'm going to be tied up in here for quite a while," Carillo called out. He stepped into his office and shut the door. He stood behind it and counted slowly to ten. Then he opened the door. Levine was gone.

"Where does he go?" Carillo asked Sergeant Hanlon.

"Anywhere he can," Hanlon said.

"Why the hell can't he stay put?" Carillo asked.

"Because he doesn't like to work," Hanlon said.

"I'm fucked," Carillo said.

They're as bad as the Irish, he thought.

16

The hunt for the .44-caliber killer turned quickly into a full-fledged media event, like the death of a rock star or the emergence of a transsexual tennis player. Television crews, lugging their $50,000 minicameras, bumped into each other in the crowded squad room on the second floor of the 109th Precinct. Tucked in his corner office, a color photo of a .44-caliber Charter Arms Bulldog revolver tacked to the bulletin board behind him, snapshots of the killer's victims tacked to another bulletin board at his side, Deputy Inspector Carillo occasionally allowed the cameras to capture him at work, to show him sifting endless stacks of reports, but he turned down all requests for personal interviews.

"That's all I need," Carillo said. "People keep seeing my face on the TV, and they'll say, 'Why doesn't he spend some time trying to catch that guy instead of getting his own face on the television?' "

Carillo parried requests for interviews with him by suggesting that the interviewers talk, instead, to working detectives, to the men who were out on the street on the case. Carillo then selected the detectives he felt should talk to the press. He selected them very carefully. He picked the ones who were smart enough to sound articulate — and to say nothing.

The reporters had no choice. They had to talk to somebody. They had to keep the story going. They had to keep up the pretense of news. Gabe Pressman of WNEW-TV worked one end of the squad room, his microphone pressed persistently into the face of Detective Richie

Paul, while Milton Lewis of WABC-TV worked the opposite end, firing questions in his best Cagney style at Detective Bill Clark. Pressman and Lewis had been covering murders in New York when Detectives Paul and Clark were in grammar school, but their questions still did not elicit very exciting answers. Yes, the Task Force was following up all leads. No, they did not have a prime suspect. Yes, they thought they'd catch the killer eventually. No, they would not predict an imminent arrest. Yes, Gabe, it certainly was very frustrating, chasing a shadow without a face or name or even a discernible motive.

The detectives operating out of the 109th worked nine-, ten-, twelve-hour shifts, and if their shifts ended at ten or at midnight or even at two in the morning, they would adjourn to George Lum's restaurant around the corner from the 109th, and while they sat at the small, dark bar and talked about the killer and what they would do to him if they ever got their hands on the bastard, they fell victim to Harry, the Chinese bartender, a man who abhorred an empty glass. By the second time anyone came to Lum's, Harry knew his preferred drink, and a filled glass would land in front of his hands just as his rear end settled onto the barstool. Most of the guys from the 109th were beer drinkers, which made it easy for Harry, but the inspector liked brandy, Rémy Martin, and his newspaper friend, Danny Cahill, who was in almost every night, got a glass of white wine, unless he asked for something different. Something different generally meant a scotch on the rocks when Cahill didn't feel like working, or water on the rocks when he did. Detective Johnny Dwyer got a beer automatically.

Late one night, a few weeks after the sixth shooting, Dwyer was sitting in Lum's, nursing a beer, eating spare ribs, thinking about the phone calls he had taken that afternoon and evening. The calls were coming in by the hundreds now, the phones ringing every minute with tips and suggestions and questions and demands, most of them surprisingly rational, most of them genuinely trying to be helpful. The most common suggestion was that Son of Sam meant Son of *Uncle* Sam, which was a way that GIs in Vietnam had referred to themselves; the killer, therefore, had to be someone who fought in the war in Vietnam. A logical enough thought — but not very limiting. One guy who got through to Dwyer said, "I've figured the whole thing out by numerology, and based on the killings, and the hours, and the street numbers, I'm sure the killer has got to be the fifth son of a fifth son."

"You're sure?" Dwyer said.

"Positive," said the caller.

Dwyer said thank you and good-bye, hung up the phone, and looked at the clock on the wall. The center of the clock, the place where the two hands lock together, was covered with a square piece of cardboard bearing the printed number "44." The last retirement dinner Dwyer had gone to, he had been seated at table 44. He had taken the cardboard number off the table and brought it to the office and put it up on the clock as a symbol of the .44-caliber killer.

"I think he's more likely to be the fourth son of a fourth son," Dwyer said to himself.

He got other tips based on biorhythms and on astrology — four callers, one right after another, had insisted that the killer was, in order, a Scorpio, a Gemini, a Virgo, and a Pisces — and several suggestions that Son of Sam was a biblical reference, probably pointing to Samson; conceivably, the killer was trying to revenge himself upon long-haired Philistines who had shorn his locks, literally or symbolically. "That's just fascinating," Dwyer said, pleasing the caller immensely.

Ten minutes later, a very earnest man — he said he was a certified public accountant — told Dwyer that he had been unable to sleep for days; that thoughts of the killer kept racing through his head; that he had finally spent a full day in the public library, studying volumes of Greek mythology, and had deduced that Son of Sam really meant Son of Zeus because Zeus, the Greek god, lived on Samothrace and, naturally, his offspring, having been raised on Samothrace, would be likely to refer to themselves as Sons of Sam. "No shit?" Dwyer said. He promised the accountant that the Task Force would check out all sons of Zeus living within fifty miles of Queens.

Several persons called to report hearing a rumor that Son of Sam backwards — *masfonos* — meant mass murderer in Greek, an indication, these callers presumed, that the killer was trying to reveal his Greek heritage. Actually, *masfonos* meant nothing in Greek or in any other language, so far as any linguist knew. Literally, hundreds of phone calls came in from young women who had broken up with their boy friends during the six months prior to the murder of Connie Bonventre; each of the young women said that her ex-boy friend had reacted bitterly to the breakup, that he had shown himself, in moments of anger, to be capable of violence and that, yes, she herself did happen to have long brown hair. The number of jilted boy friends in the metropolitan area may have been exceeded only by the number of men who, according to informants, liked to refer to themselves in casual conversation as "Son of Sam." No one had ever met anyone called "Son of Joe" or "Son of Hank," but there must have been thousands of New Yorkers who called themselves "Son of Sam." And most of them, it seemed, had access to an arsenal of handguns.

Most of the phone calls led nowhere, which was only to be expected. Ultimately, Dwyer hoped, one phone call would point in the right direction, would lead to the killer, but until that special call came in — and was recognized — all the other calls, however well intentioned, would provide only false leads.

Yet there was one call Dwyer had taken that day, only an hour before he adjourned to Lum's, that sounded good, that rang true, partly because the call named a suspect who lived in Kew Gardens, an area adjacent to Forest Hills, the site of two shootings. Dwyer had developed a theory that the shooting of Laura Davidson, the one shooting that did not fit the killer's pattern, the shooting that took place at the wrong time, on the wrong street, with the wrong target, was strictly an impulse-shooting. Dwyer believed that whatever it was that drove the killer to kill had built up inside him to the point where he simply had to run out on the street and strike immediately, without regard to his own safety, without regard to his own pattern. That belief led Dwyer to reason that the killer would have to live in the vicinity of the Davidson killing — in Forest Hills itself or in a neighboring community, such as Kew Gardens.

The man who called the 109th that evening told Dwyer that he was worried about a Howard Goodman, who lived at 177 – 09 Crescent Avenue in Kew Gardens, had a history of psychological disturbances, and had served in combat in Vietnam. "The guy," the caller said, "is always talking about blood, about needing blood, wanting blood, loving blood. I mean, I hope I'm wrong, I hope it ain't him, I know the family and everything, but he sure fits the bill."

"What's he look like?" Dwyer said.

"He's got long hair, mod, you know," the caller said, "and he's average height, maybe five-nine, a little thin, probably just under thirty. He don't look special, or anything, except for his eyes. He's got real cuckoo eyes."

Before he left Lum's, Dwyer decided that the next day he and his new partner, Herbie Klein, would make their first stop at 177–09 Crescent Avenue, to pay a visit to Howard Goodman.

Late the following afternoon, Dwyer and Klein parked in front of the upper-middle-class house on Crescent Avenue, in the best section of Kew Gardens. Dwyer, the senior member of the team, knocked on the door, and a woman, somewhere between fifty and sixty, answered the door. She was wearing a great deal of makeup, but she still looked very tired.

"I'm Detective Dwyer, ma'am," Johnny Dwyer said, showing his badge, "and this is Detective Klein, who works with me, and we'd like to talk to you about your son."

"I know," she said.

"You know?" Dwyer said.

"Yes. It's all done."

"Done? What's done?"

"We had him committed last Friday," Mrs. Goodman said.

"I'm sorry," Dwyer said. He bobbed his head to show that he was really sorry. "I'm really sorry to hear that. Would it be all right if I asked you some questions anyway?"

"Certainly," Mrs. Goodman said. "Certainly. He was such a brilliant boy. He played the violin so beautifully. Did you know that when he was in his teens we sent him to Los Angeles to study with Heifetz? Did you know that?"

Dwyer wasn't even sure who Heifetz was. "No, ma'am," he said, "I didn't know that." He paused a moment, then, without thinking about it, without trying to set up the question, said, "Mrs. Goodman, is your husband's name Sam?"

Mrs. Goodman looked startled. "No," she said. "I mean, yes. But how did you know that? He hasn't used that name for more than thirty years. He hated the name, and when we got married, he dropped his first name and began using, at first, S. David Goodman, and then, eventually, just Dave Goodman. Nobody knows his name is Sam."

"Nobody?" Dwyer said.

"Nobody outside the family," said Mrs. Goodman.

Dwyer could feel the juices flowing, the suspicion emerging that he might have stumbled upon the killer, the same sort of feeling he got when he looked at a guy on the street and he knew the guy was dirty, knew the guy was carrying something he shouldn't be carrying, grass or smack or a switchblade or something stolen.

A violinist? Why not? "Mrs. Goodman," Dwyer said, "would you mind showing me your son's room?"

"Not at all," the mother said, "as long as you don't mind climbing up a narrow set of stairs. His room used to be the attic."

Now Dwyer's eyes expanded, and he turned and looked at his partner, and he could see Herbie Klein tensing, too, listening a little harder than usual, looking at everything, almost like a hunting dog on point. The letter the killer had left for Inspector Carillo had said, "Papa Sam keeps me locked in the attic, too. I can't get out but I look out the attic window and watch the world go by."

Mrs. Goodman led the detectives from the top of the narrow stairway to her son's attic room. The room was lit, dimly, by one overhead bulb that could not have been more than forty watts. There was a single bed, stripped of sheets and blankets, a straight chair, and a desk with nothing on top. Dwyer looked for a poster, a picture of a girl, a dirty magazine, a newspaper clipping, for anything that might indicate a killer had lived in the room. He saw nothing. He walked over to the room's one small window and looked out at the backyard.

"In the last few weeks," Mrs. Goodman said, "he just wasn't my son anymore. He frightened me." She shook her head. "You know what he did?"

"What?" Klein said.

"He accused me of burying bodies in the backyard," Mrs. Goodman said. Her voice cracked, and tears washed the corners of her eyes.

"Behind our house some rest," Son of Sam had written in his letter. "Mostly young — raped and slaughtered — their blood drained — just bones now."

"He what?" Dwyer said.

"I know," Mrs. Goodman said. "I know it sounds crazy. But Howard accused me of burying bodies in the backyard."

Dwyer looked at Klein, and the two detectives nodded at each other. "Mrs. Goodman," Dwyer said, "I think I ought to tell you something. The reason we're here is we got a telephone call from some guy saying he thought that Howard, your son, could be the forty-four-caliber killer, the Son of Sam. Of course, we get a lot of phone calls like that, and most of them don't mean nothing, but we have to check them out."

"I understand," Mrs. Goodman said, slowly.

"We'd like to come back tomorrow," Dwyer said, "and talk to you some more. The odds are there's nothing to it, but, you know, just in case. That be all right if we come back tomorrow?"

"Of course," Mrs. Goodman said, and now the makeup hid none of her years.

Dwyer and Klein stopped at the 109th, checked in, then went over to Lum's. Dwyer called his wife and told her he had a suspect who looked very good. He said he would be home in about an hour and tell her all about it. Klein called his wife and told her that he and his new partner, Johnny Dwyer, were just going out to follow up a fresh lead. Klein said that he probably would be out working very late. "This is some helluva case," he said.

The next day, back in Kew Gardens, Dwyer and Klein followed Mrs. Goodman into the living room. Only Dwyer looked as if he had gotten any sleep all night. "It would help us a lot," he said to Mrs. Goodman, "if we could get a sample of Howard's handwriting, or his printing. Do you have any papers of his? Anything like that?"

Mrs. Goodman got up and went to the master bedroom. When she came back, she had a small tray in her hands. "Howard burned all his papers last week," she said. "All I have are these few personal things that the institution took from Howard on Friday."

She handed the tray to Dwyer, and he picked out a wallet and leafed through it. He stopped at one folded piece of paper and opened it up. It was a receipt from a motel in Butte, Montana. The dates on the receipt were December 12 through December 17, 1976. Dwyer felt as if he had just been kicked in the gut. The killing of Laura Davidson took place on December 15 in Forest Hills.

"Was Howard out in Montana in December?" Dwyer asked.

"I don't know," said Mrs. Goodman. "I really don't know. I know he went out to the West Coast, but he didn't keep in touch with us while he was away. He just reappeared here one afternoon and went upstairs to his room as if he had never been away. He played the violin beautifully that night."

"Do you mind if I borrow these papers?" Dwyer said. "I'll get them back to you tomorrow or the next day."

"It's quite all right," said Mrs. Goodman.

Back at the precinct, Dwyer placed a phone call to the Butte Police Department. He explained that he was calling in reference to the

194

case of the .44-caliber killer — by now, national publicity had made the case known in every police department in the country — and that he wanted to get some information about a young man named Howard Goodman.

"What you want to know?" the chief of the Butte police asked.

"Well," Dwyer said, "I've got a receipt saying that Goodman was staying at the Big Sky Motel in Butte from December twelfth through December seventeenth. Can you check that out for me?"

"I can do better than that. I can tell you that your Mr. Goodman did not spend the nights of December fourteenth, fifteenth, and sixteenth in that motel. He did not spend those nights in the motel because we had him in the lockup. We got him causing a public disturbance, screaming and carrying on in the street, saying that the blood of Vietnam was on everyone's hands and that nobody could wash it off. He kept pointing at his own hands and saying, 'See the blood,' and his hands were as clean as could be. Real crazy fellow. Remember him well. We kept him locked up till he calmed down, then released him and — hope you don't mind — told him to get his ass home to New York. We figured you people know how to handle that kind better than us. That help you?"

"Yeah," Dwyer said. "That helps. It wipes him out as a suspect. Just to be sure, I'm going to send you a picture of Goodman, make sure it's the same fellow you locked up. If it's not, let me know. And, anyway, thanks."

"Any time," said the chief of police of Butte, Montana.

Dwyer sat at his desk, frustrated once more. He was used to being frustrated; it was the nature of his job. At least this time he was only losing an innocent suspect; he knew the frustration, infinitely worse, of losing a guilty suspect. Three years earlier, he had been involved in the investigation of a case where a Rastafarian had killed a fellow West Indian in Brooklyn. The Rastafarians originated in Jamaica; back in the islands, they were a religious-philosophical sect, disciples of the Ethiopian emperor, Haile Selassie (*Ras* means prince in Ethiopian), and disciples, too, of *ganja,* a West Indian brand of marijuana that the Rastas devour in quantities that defy imagination. They believe that Haile Selassie was a direct descendant of King Solomon and the Queen of Sheba, and they believe, with equal fervor, that *ganja* is good for men, women, and children. The Rastas are easily recognizable by the way they keep, or fail to keep, their hair: dread locks — long, kinky, uncut ringlets, Medusa-like snakes sticking out of their heads. For religious, or philosophical, reasons, the Rastas do not believe in haircuts.

The Rastafarians living in New York had brought with them some of the group's religious and philosophical practices, but that was not what distinguished them in their new setting. The New York Rastas virtually controlled the marijuana market among West Indians. And some of them were terrorists, terrorizing their own people, not attracting much publicity, not so long as they killed only their own.

The murder which had involved Dwyer took place at a West Indian apartment party in Brooklyn. Three Rastas showed up at the party, uninvited, and one of them sat down next to a man and his wife. The Rasta asked the wife to dance with him; she said no. "I want you to dance," the Rastafarian said. "No, thank you," the wife said. The husband then interrupted. "My wife said she does not want to dance with you," he told the Rasta. The Rasta pulled out a gun and, from two feet away, fired three shots into the husband's stomach. The husband pulled himself to his feet and staggered toward the door. He never made it. Three more bullets finished him off. There was a pool of blood where the West Indians had been dancing only a few minutes earlier.

The three Rastafarians fled, and the people holding the party immediately called the police. When Dwyer and three other homicide detectives showed up, a boy at the party, a fourteen-year-old nephew of the murdered man, said that he had recognized the man who pulled the trigger, that he knew where the killer and his companions hung out. The cops staked out the place, and barely six hours after the shooting, the three Rastafarians pulled up in a gypsy cab. Dwyer himself captured the accused murderer and one of his associates.

For a variety of reasons, the case did not come to trial until almost three years later, until after Dwyer began working on the .44-caliber killer. Then Dwyer got a phone call, telling him to take a couple of days off from the Task Force and pick up the original witness, the nephew of the murdered man, and take him to court to point out the killer. Dwyer got the witness's address, went to his apartment, and rang the bell. When the door opened, Dwyer knew the case was dead. The kid, seventeen years old now, was standing at the door with his hair in dread locks. He had become a Rastafarian.

"I don't remember a thing," he told Dwyer.

196

"You motherfuckin' sonuvabitch," Dwyer said. "You stood there at your uncle's grave—your own mother's brother—and you cried 'cause he was dead, and now you tell me you don't know nothin'. I don't know how the fuck you can live with that. Do yourself a favor—and me, too—and die quick."

That was the most frustrating experience Dwyer had had on the force. Losing Howard Goodman hurt, too, but not quite so much as that one.

Son of Sam stood in the lobby of the Bronx Post Office and looked at the poster of himself which they had hanging on the wall by the registered mail window. The drawing wasn't that good and it wasn't that bad, he decided. Then Son of Sam went over to a glass-topped table and took the letter he was going to mail out of his pocket and began reading it:

Sam Thornton,

I have asked you kindly to stop that dog from howling all day long, yet he continues to do so. I pleaded with you. I told you how it is destroying my family—we have no peace, no rest.

Now I know what kind of person you are, and what kind of family you are. You are cruel and inconsiderate. You have no love for any other human beings. Your selfish, Mr. Thornton.

My life is destroyed now. I have nothing to lose anymore. I can see that there shall be no peace in my life or my families life until I end yours.

You wicked evil man—child of the devil. I curse you and your family forever. I pray to God that he takes your whole family off the face of this earth. People like you should not be allowed to live on this planet.

A Citizen

That the letter was to Thornton, who was his master, did not unsettle Bernard. Now and then, he attempted to struggle against the demons, to clutch a throat and rip it open as if it were a Kleenex. Had he not tried to kill Sam, to kill the dog, in the cemetery? Now, as he read the letter he had been working on all night, he knew again that he had to challenge Sam Thornton. Two nights before, the dogs had been howling all night long and he, Son of Sam, had given them no blood to swell their insides and still their tongues. And then, on the radio in his car that next afternoon, Son of Sam heard about an earthquake that had taken place in Turkey. Many hundreds died. Sam Thornton had caused the earthquake, Son of Sam believed. If Sam Thornton didn't get blood, they could happen with greater frequency, these mass killings. Either he got the blood or he somehow was stopped completely, these were the only ways to prevent more mass killings, Son of Sam believed.

He stood in the post office, with his "Wanted" drawing staring out at him, and he sealed the letter to Sam Thornton and mailed it.

17

Gil Rodgers' beeper began to buzz while he was sitting on a couch in the Blue Room at City Hall, holding a microphone, asking questions of the empty air, then sticking out the mike and reacting as if he were actually hearing answers to his questions. He nodded. He smiled. He looked thoughtful. He looked doubtful. Rodgers was doing "reverses," which is what television people call the process of repeating while facing the camera the questions they have already asked with their backs to the camera. The reverses are needed by the editor who will cut the interview for airing; without them, he cannot move smoothly from one "sound bite" — one section of the interview — to another. The process is neither so complicated as it sounds nor so silly; it is just a necessary part of electronic journalism, like $15-haircuts and $300-suits.

When Rodgers' beeper buzzed, he responded predictably and swiftly. He finished his reverses, went to Room Nine, the pressroom at City Hall, and phoned the assignment desk at his office. "What's up?" he asked.

"You knock off the Mayor?" the assignment editor said.

"Wrapping up now," Rodgers said.

"Good," the assignment editor said. "Break the crew for lunch — they've been on since eight; they've got to eat now — then take them out to Flushing to the One-oh-ninth Precinct. See if there's anything new on the Son of Sam thing — any leads, any new strategy, anything at all. Okay?"

"Sure," Rodgers said. "Sure."

Rodgers passed the word along to the crew, which elected to take lunch in Manhattan, at an Italian restaurant not far from City Hall, before driving out to Queens. Rodgers promptly borrowed $10 from a soundman who was earning half what he was; the night before, Rodgers had been at Studio 54, the newest "in" disco, and now, after impressing his latest stewardess, he was broke. "I'll cash a check later," Rodgers said to the soundman, a promise that, if kept, would have stunned both the soundman and Rodgers' bank.

The conversation over the veal parmigiana and ziti was not the camera crew's usual the-niggers-and-the-broads-are-taking-over-our-business, probably because the cameraman happened to be black, and the electrician a woman. During lunch, while the crew concentrated upon their food, Rodgers insisted upon bringing them all up to date on his life story; he expected them to be as fascinated by the subject as he was. He kept talking because he knew that the more he talked, the less he would eat, and it was important for him, professionally and socially, to keep himself trim. He also kept talking because, like many people in his profession, he loved the sound of his own voice. Actually, he sounded slightly effeminate, or like a more masculine version of Barbara Walters, depending on your point of view. But his delivery was slick and self-confident, and if occasional flaws slipped through — "We'll keep you appraised of all future developments," he said more than once — his arrogant good looks and glib manner, as is usual on television, overcame both semantic lapses and a total failure to understand what reporting is all about. His idea of digging deep into a story was to read the clips from both morning papers, and then interview one or two of the principals. Like many television reporters, he had a gift for stating the obvious as if it were a revelation. "When the news of the fire that burned to death six children spread through their neighborhood," he would say in a dramatic tone, before pausing, as though building to a climax, and adding, "everyone was deeply saddened."

Rodgers was very highly regarded by many people in the business; he was the ideal complement to the superficial nature of the medium. But like most of his rivals on his own station, and on competing stations, he dreamed of moving up to better things, to being an anchorman, to reaching a position where he would not have to go out on the street and write his own stories and do demeaning things like that.

All he needed was a break — some gimmick that would turn him into a true star. "Suppose I talk Son of Sam into giving himself up to me?" Rodgers said to his crew. "Would that be the greatest thing that ever happened on local TV?"

"Yeah," the camerman said, sarcastically. "Why not have him do it live — you know, come into the studio in the middle of a broadcast, hand you the forty-four, then turn to the camera and explain how you had made him see the error of his ways. He could throw himself on the mercy of the Director."

"Fuck off," Rodgers said. "I mean it. I'm going to make an appeal to the killer tonight. We'll shoot it right in the One-oh-ninth Precinct, right outside Inspector Carlino's — is that his name? — or whatever it is — right outside the Inspector's office. Let me stop along the way and pick up a copy of this afternoon's *Express* so I can be up to date on the story. Okay?"

Rodgers and his crew finished lunch, divvied up the bill, then went out to the company Chevrolet and started toward Queens. Rodgers picked up an *Express* at a newsstand only two blocks from the restaurant. The paper had a banner headline: MAYBE IT'S *DAUGHTER* OF SAM. The headline was backed up by a quote from one of Carillo's detectives saying, "We're not ruling out anything," and by an interview with a psychiatrist who had the feeling that the killer was, as he put it, "a bull dyke" — "there's no sense in using complicated medical terms that would only confuse your readers," the psychiatrist explained — who hated to see young women lowering themselves to the companionship of young men. Why, then, had the killer shot at the two young women standing on the stoop in the Bronx? "In that instance," the psychiatrist replied earnestly, "her mind might not have been functioning normally."

The afternoon *Express* also had an accompanying editorial written by Henry Glenville, a passionate plea for the killer to give *him*self up to the *Express*, which would, after offering *him* an exclusive opportunity to give *his* side of the story to the world and after posing *him* for exclusive pictures, turn *him* over to the proper authorities. In addition, the *Express* would provide the killer with the sort of medical help *he* so obviously needed, including, presumably, a session with the psychiatrist who was convinced that he was a she. Glenville's plea was maudlin, self-serving, and badly written, and his publisher, Malcolm Bromwich, loved it. Bromwich told his managing editor, Geoffrey Miles, that if the killer should contact the *Express*, he — Bromwich — was to be notified first; then, after he gave his approval, the police.

Half the journalists in New York were praying that Son of Sam would turn himself in to them, and the other half were praying that he would not turn himself in to Cahill. The jealousy directed at Cahill, because he had heard directly from a demented killer, was so widespread, so intense, it was almost impossible to understand. Cahill understood it. If the letter had been sent to someone else, he would have been just as jealous. He was absolutely delighted that he had received the letter, although he did feel some real fear for himself and for his family, and he affected even greater fear. "The cocksucker has got very good literary taste," Cahill said.

Ever since the publication of the letter from the killer, Cahill and his office had been flooded with telephone calls and letters from people offering and seeking information. Three men had called so far to turn themselves in as the Son of Sam, but two of the three were slurring their words drastically, and the third was actually hiccupping. One woman called and asked Cahill if he would put her in touch with Son of Sam, she wanted to ask him to do her a favor. Cahill explained very patiently that Son of Sam knew exactly how to reach him, but he did not know how to reciprocate. The woman said she was surprised; she thought the two of them talked regularly. Most of the letters to Cahill offered suspects:

> It is with great reluctance that I write this, but some of the specifics in the "Son of Sam" case leave me no choice. Please have the police keep a constant eye on a young man named Ari Lebetkin. Only the obligation to prevent further murders compels me to name him. He comes of a good family. . . .

> There is a teacher at Franklin D. Roosevelt High School in Brooklyn who fits the description of the .44 Killer. He has been turned down by several women. He has a crazy stare in his eyes. . . .

> I just have a feeling that the killer is a detective or a cop. . . .

> Owen Coyne murdered his mother several years ago, was declared mentally insane, escaped from the institution to which he was com-

mitted and subsequently collected the teacher's pension of his murdered mother. I believe at this time he is out there walking the streets. It's just a thought. . . .

P.S. His father's name was Sam.

The worst letter came on lined notebook paper and was very neatly printed:

Mr. Cahill and pigs,

If Son of Sam isn't so bright, then how come you haven't caught him yet? You want him to give himself up because you know you won't catch him. He's to smart for you. But I hope you never catch him.

Mr. Cahill, Son of Sam is watching you and he's going to get you.

From the gutters
    of NYC
Fans of Sam's

Next to the signature was an exact copy of the symbol the killer had used at the end of the letter to Cahill.

Cahill did not put any more credence in the threats than he did in the tips. But, just to be safe, he changed his habits, he began varying his pattern. In other words, he started going to different saloons at different hours. And everywhere he went, strangers who recognized him from his television appearances would walk up to him and say, "You hear from Sam lately?"

He'd just shake his head and try to look humble.

Gil Rodgers did not bother to try. He stormed into the 109th Precinct, his camera crew trailing him, as if he owned the place. He led the crew upstairs to the squad room, walked inside, and asked a sergeant where the inspector's office was.

"Over there," the sergeant said, nodding toward the small office just off the front of the squad room.

"Thanks," Rodgers said. "Thanks a lot. Just one other thing. What's his name again, the Inspector?"

"Queeg," the sergeant said.

"Queeg?" said Rodgers. "That doesn't sound right."

"Just kidding," Sergeant Hanlon said. "It's Carillo. Deputy Inspector Dominick Carillo."

Rodgers turned and marched up to the door of the small office and looked in on Carillo, who was going through a mountain of mail. "Inspector," Rodgers said, "I'm Gil Rodgers."

"Yes?"

"Er, uh, I'm going to be doing a stand-upper — that's where I just talk straight into the camera — about the forty-four-caliber killer, and, uh, you don't mind, do you, if I do it right here, standing in your doorway, with you in the background?"

"I do," Carillo said.

"Excuse me?" Rodgers said.

"I said I do," Carillo said. "I do mind being used as a prop."

"Well, you see, Inspector, having you in the background gives it, you know, a look of authenticity. Believe me, it's a good touch."

Carillo gave Rodgers the dark look he used to give opposing pitchers, hoping to stare them down. "You go downstairs," Carillo said, "and you do your — what do you call it, your stand-up? — you do it downstairs by the desk and you'll have authentic cops in the background wearing real uniforms." Carillo paused. "It'll be a good touch," he added.

"But, Inspector," Rodgers said, "this is where it's all happening, this is where the investigation's taking place."

"Exactly," Carillo said. "And we have a great deal of work to do. I'm sure you can understand." Carillo motioned to Hanlon. "Sergeant, would you show Mr. Rodgers where he can put his cameras downstairs?" Carillo turned back to his mail, concentrating once more, ending the conversation.

Rodgers led the crew downstairs with a little less bounce to his step. While the electrician set up lights, and the cameraman tried to figure out the best camera position, Rodgers sat in a nearby room, at a combination chair-desk, the kind usually seen in classrooms, and jotted down a few notes for his stand-upper. He rehearsed the speech in his mind a few times, then walked into position in front of the camera, looked straight into the lens, and began to smile. He was careful not to smile too broadly. He didn't want to appear to be amused. He only wanted to appear to be sincere.

"Rolling," the cameraman said.

"We have sound," the soundman said.

"What the fuck's going on?" said a patrolman, as he came through the front door and cut past Rodgers.

"We *were* filming a news report," the cameraman said.

The cameraman and the soundman got ready once more; Rodgers revived his smile, waited four seconds, then began. "This is the One hundred and ninth Precinct in Flushing, Queens," he said, "the headquarters for the greatest manhunt in the history of this great metropolis — the massive manhunt for Son of Sam, the forty-four-caliber killer. Fifty of the city's finest detectives — hand-picked men who know the streets and know the criminal mind — are based here in this precinct, working around the clock, sparing no effort, hoping to catch the killer before he kills again. The forty-four killer must feel right now like a hunted animal. He must feel the ring closing in on him, his time growing shorter."

Rodgers paused, then held his sincere smile for two full seconds. "I think I know how the killer feels," Rodgers continued. "In my lifetime, I have known what it's like to be the underdog, to be up against overwhelming odds." Another pause — while his black cameraman wondered when in his life Rodgers had ever been an underdog — and now the smile was gone, replaced by a look of complete concern, one of the looks Rodgers had been practicing on the couch in the Blue Room at City Hall. "Son of Sam," he said, "your time is growing short. The sands are running out. The clock is winding down. You could be shot down on the street at any moment. You need help. You *want* help. I can sense that you, in your own way, are crying out for help. And I want to help you — and help this great city. I want to help you turn yourself in to the proper authorities. I will go with you. I will escort you. I will see that you are treated fairly. Call me, or write to me, and I will meet you anywhere you say. You have created an atmosphere of fear that is crippling a great city, but I am not afraid." Big smile. "No, I am not afraid."

Rodgers stopped, looked down, then up, then said, "Gil Rodgers, 'On-Scene News,' in Flushing, Queens." He smiled through the whole signoff and held it for five more seconds. Then the cameraman clicked off the camera, and Rodgers said, "That ought to teach that Inspector a lesson, kicking me out of his office. I got even. I didn't mention his name."

Gil Rodgers' plea to the killer played on the "On-Scene News" show at six o'clock, right after a live five-minute interview with the psychiatrist who had told the *Express* that the killer might be a woman. On the air, the psychiatrist said that the killer could very well be a man; that, if so, he was obviously a schizophrenic; that the revolver was a symbolic extension of his penis; and that each killing was, for the killer, an incomplete orgasm. The more the psychiatrist talked, the more excited he became. It was understandable; for many years, even when he was back in medical school, he had had almost erotic fantasies about appearing live on television.

The psychiatrist had been interviewed by a black TV reporter, Meredith Tompkins, and when Tompkins walked into his office the next morning, his phone was ringing. He picked it up. "Stop fuckin' over Sam, nigger," said the caller. "Worry about your own kind."

The next call was not so threatening. "This is Mitchell Block," the caller said, "and I'm from The Moment of Truth Gallery."

"Uh, huh," Tompkins said.

"We are a group of artists and writers dedicated to the total truth, and we saw your report last night on Son of Sam."

"Uh, huh."

"We believe that the killer is possessed, that he is under the control of a demon — we think that's who Sam is — and since we ourselves have been in touch with spirit guides, you know, discarnates, we're thinking of holding a séance, perhaps re-establishing contact with our spirit guides to see if they can provide a clue to the killer's identity or to his whereabouts."

"You're kidding."

"No, we're quite serious, and we would like to know if you might perhaps care to cover our séance, possibly even film it for your news show."

"You're inviting me to film a séance at which some ghost is going to announce who Son of Sam is?" Tompkins said.

"Well, yes," Block said.

"Listen," Tompkins said, "I have spent the last ten years of my life trying to give myself an image of dignity, of intelligence, and you want me to go put some voodoo, some black magic on the air? Forget it. No way. Thanks, but no thanks." Tompkins hung up the phone.

In the next office, Gil Rodgers leaned back in his chair, looked up toward the ceiling and began to formulate in his mind the words he would say when, and if, Son of Sam decided to turn himself in to him. Rodgers also began calculating which sincere look he should have on his face at the most dramatic moment.

206

18

The tip came, first, from a cop in Queens, nobody Johnny Dwyer had ever met, just a patrolman calling in on the Task Force hot line. "Hey, listen," the cop said, "I know you guys are working on the forty-four thing, and I seen that letter the guy wrote to Cahill, the newspaper guy. I got it here in front of me. You know the part near the end where he says, 'Here are some names to help you along. Forward them to the Inspector for use by the NCIC. . . .' Well, that rang a bell with me. I locked up some guy four, five years ago who mentioned the NCIC to me."

"Yeah?" said Dwyer.

"What happened was, he was wanted for robbing a bank, and some guy turned him in for the reward. When I asked him, you know, the perpetrator, what his name was, he said, 'Alexis Count Cadaverous,' and I said, 'Cut the shit, what's your name?' And he just looked at me and said, 'Run it through NCIC, you'll get my real name.'"

The cop paused. "The reason I'll never forget him saying that is that I didn't know what the hell he was talking about. I didn't know what the NCIC was. I thought he was making it up."

"I hate to tell you this," Dwyer said, "but I still don't know what the NCIC is. What is it? National Crime Investigating Commission?"

"No. It's the National Crime Index Code. Some computer some-place."

"Anyway," Dwyer said, "what was the guy's real name?"

"That's the funny part. I remember the NCIC perfectly, and I remember that Alexis Count Cadaverous, but I don't remember the real name. It was a strange name, I know that. I'll check it out. I'll get it for you in a couple of hours if you think it's worth it."

"Sure," Dwyer said. "Let me know."

An hour later, the cop from Queens called back. "His name is Pablo Birani," he told Dwyer. "He's Mexican, I think, but he's lived here since he was a little kid. He'd be twenty-six years old now. We turned the case over to the FBI."

"Thanks," Dwyer said.

Then he called the Federal Bureau of Investigation in Manhattan, explained who he was and what he was looking for. He got a call back from the FBI within thirty minutes. Birani, they said, had served thirty months in federal prison in Lewisburg for bank robbery. He was still on parole. "We'll get you copies of all the files," the agent said.

"Has he got to check in with a parole officer every month?" Dwyer asked.

"Yeah."

"Could you tell me the Parole Officer's name? And his phone number?"

"Sure. Dowling. Stanley Dowling. Six-six-four – one-one-four-six."

Dwyer dialed the number. "I want to talk to Mr. Dowling," he said.

"Mr. Dowling is gone for the day," a woman who answered the phone said.

"How about his supervisor?" Dwyer said.

"I'll connect you with Mr. Reynolds."

Dwyer heard the phone buzz once and then a voice say, "Reynolds."

"Mr. Reynolds," Dwyer said, "this is Detective Dwyer. I'm with the Special Task Force investigating the forty-four-caliber killings."

"Oh," said Reynolds. "What's this about? Birani?"

Dwyer almost dropped the phone. "Yeah," he said. "Yeah, it's about Birani. How'd you know?"

"We just got a feeling here," Reynolds said, "right after that letter appeared in Cahill's column in the *Dispatch*. It sounded like something Birani would write. And the printing, too, that strange printing. Birani prints like that. We were going to give you people a call."

"Yeah?"

"I could tell you some other things," Reynolds said, "but Birani's

208

Parole Officer, Stanley Dowling, really knows a lot more of the details than I do. I think you ought to talk to him. He's home now. I'll give you his home number."

Dwyer called the parole officer at home and told him about his conversation with Reynolds. "I've got samples of his handwriting," Dowling said. "Letters he wrote from prison. You'll see what we mean about his printing. It's not the same, but it's close."

"Where's Birani live?" Dwyer asked.

"He lives in Rego Park, right off of Queens Boulevard."

Rego Park was, at most, a fifteen-minute walk from the site of the Forest Hills murders.

"But he knows the whole city," Dowling went on. "He loves to walk. He walks constantly. Through the streets. Queens. Manhattan. The Bronx. He walks everywhere. He says he knows every street in the city. In fact, it's his walking made us suspicious."

"What do you mean?"

"Well, that letter, the one in the paper, to Danny Cahill."

"Yeah?"

"It was postmarked Englewood, New Jersey, right?"

"Right."

"Well, Birani always used to brag that he would violate his parole, he would go out of New York State, which he wasn't supposed to do, by walking across the George Washington Bridge to New Jersey. He told us he'd walk to Englewood and then turn around and walk back to Manhattan."

"What else? Anything else?"

"Birani's a nut on numbers. He robbed the bank on Thirtieth Street because he said thirty was one of his lucky numbers. And that first murder, the Bonventre murder, that took place on May thirtieth, didn't it?"

"Yeah."

"Well, right before that, just the day before that, I think — I checked it in my diary — Birani was in to see me and he said, I remember it exactly, he said, 'I'm a new man now. I'm a different person. My life has direction now.' And ever since that day, he's been hard to talk to. Right up till then, he told me everything, I couldn't shut him up, but since then he's been, like I say, almost uncommunicative, like he's got things he doesn't want to talk about."

The parole officer paused, thinking. "One other thing," he said.

"Birani's going to school nights."

"Where?" Dwyer said.

"John Jay," Dowling said. "John Jay College of Criminal Justice. Birani's studying criminology."

Dwyer thanked Dowling, said he would get back to him soon, then made a note to himself to check with the John Jay College of Criminal Justice.

But the next day, before he had a chance to call the school, he received a phone call from one of the professors there, a former police captain named Leonard Oniskey. "I'm at John Jay College," Oniskey said, "and I teach a course in Sex Crimes Investigations — back to Jack the Ripper and all that stuff — and I've got a student I think may have something to do with the forty-four-caliber killings."

"His name Birani?" Dwyer couldn't resist saying.

"Yes," said Oniskey. "Yes, it is. How did you know that?"

"I'm hearing a lot about Mr. Birani these days," Dwyer said. "But I want to hear more. Tell me more. Tell me about him."

"He's a murder buff," Professor Oniskey said. "He shows great insight into the psychodynamics of murder."

"I think we better get together," Dwyer said.

Dwyer stopped working on anything else and concentrated on learning everything he could about Pablo Birani. Dwyer went to the FBI offices and read all of their files. He went to John Jay College and had lunch with Professor Oniskey. He went to the parole board and had a couple of beers with Stanley Dowling. Nights, he took home the Birani material and read it over and over, and the next day he would tell his partner, Herbie Klein, everything he had learned. Klein, in turn, told all the stories to the girl he was seeing after work. She said they were fascinating. "They sure are," Klein said. "I hope we've got the right sonuvabitch."

Everything Dwyer learned reinforced his suspicions about Birani — even the way Birani had been arrested for bank robbery. Birani, a few months after the robbery, had become emotionally involved with a girl who was a junkie. Emotionally involved is accurate. He worshiped her. She never spoke to him. He followed her around. She never looked at him. One night, in a Greenwich Village coffee shop, she OD'd, passed out cold, and when nobody else paid any attention to her, Birani picked her up, got her address out of her purse, and took her to her East Village apartment, on Fourth Street, between First and Second avenues, in a taxi. He found the keys in the purse, took her inside, talked to her, and splashed her with water till she became conscious, then walked her around the room for a couple of hours till he was convinced she was going to be all right. Then he let her go to bed. He turned around and faced the wall while she pulled off her dress and fell onto the stained sheets. He kept his head turned to the side while he pulled a blanket over her. She had gotten sick on his trousers, so he pulled them off, washed them in her bathroom sink, then sat in his shorts next to her while she slept. About four o'clock in the morning, her brother came into the apartment, saw his sister in bed naked, and saw some guy sitting in his shorts next to her. The brother announced he was going to beat the shit out of Birani. "You screwin' her?" the brother said. "You rape her?"

"No, no, no," Birani said. "I can't. I'm impotent. I can't screw anybody." He started to cry.

"I think you're bullshittin' me," the brother said. He pulled Birani out of the chair.

"Wait," Birani said. "Don't hit me. Don't hit me, and I'll make you ten thousand dollars."

"You're full of shit," the brother said.

"No," Birani said. "I'm wanted for bank robbery. There's a ten-thousand-dollar reward for me. You take me down and turn me in, and you'll get the reward. Then you can get your sister a better apartment. She deserves to live in a nicer place than this."

The brother was skeptical, but he decided to gamble that Birani was telling the truth. He turned Birani in and, six months later, collected the $10,000 reward. It didn't do his sister much good because by then she was dead. Hepatitis. Dirty needle.

She had had long brown hair, the brother later told Dwyer.

In his classes at John Jay, Dwyer learned, Birani was unusually lucid and incisive in discussing famous sex murderers. "It was almost as though he could imagine himself inside the head of Albert De Salvo," Professor Oniskey said, in reference to the man accused of being the Boston Strangler. But when other subjects came up, the professor added, Birani was very shy. He never used profanity in class, and he seemed unable to relate to his female classmates. He was very critical of the police, Oniskey said, and was always pointing out their shortcomings, their blunders that allowed sex murderers to continue killing.

"The subject of the forty-four-caliber killer came up in class several times," Oniskey told Dwyer, "and, strangely, Birani had nothing to say about that, nothing at all. He obviously didn't like the subject."

After their long lunch, Oniskey asked Dwyer for a favor. "Please," the professor said, "don't let Pablo know that I gave you all this information. If he is not involved in the shootings, I would regret the loss of his friendship."

When he repeated the professor's request to Herbie Klein, Dwyer said, "Everybody in this city is crazy."

Dwyer got copies of half a dozen letters Birani had written from prison. They were all printed, in two distinctly different styles, and while neither style was quite the same as Son of Sam's, handwriting experts told Dwyer that the man who printed the prison letters could well have printed the Son of Sam letters, too. Birani's letters showed that he could think — and he could write. "There simply is no magic and mystique left," he wrote one day. "We're all forced to march in lock-step instead of being permitted to stroll about. The convertible car is nearly extinct. People no longer dine; they eat. The dirigible is an aerial anachronism. The great interstate trains will never be restored to their former glory. We no longer light streets to enable us to see! We use sodium high-intensity lights to reduce incidents of crime."

Another time, Birani wrote: "I have led a very active life out there in the urban broth. People accuse me of being unhappy. Not true! To each his own. I do what I do because I am compelled to."

And: "Confinement is a truly liberating experience."

One of Birani's letters was addressed to the president of the bank he had robbed and was signed, "Your Friendly Neighborhood Bank Robber." Another, to the judge who sentenced him, was signed, "Alexis Count Cadaverous, Member, Ancient Order of Pharaohs."

A psychiatric report on Birani, prepared by a resident psychologist at the federal penitentiary, said that he was schizophrenic and definitely capable of sudden violence. "His dream," the report said, "is to become a murderer someday."

When Dwyer was satisfied that he had done all the research he could do, he went to Inspector Carillo. He told Carillo everything he knew about Birani. "Italian?" said Carillo, when he heard the name.

"No, no, Mexican," Dwyer said.

Carillo smiled. "You absolutely positive he's not Irish?" the inspector said.

Dwyer said he was sure. He said Birani was too smart to be Irish.

Carillo liked that. He loosened up. He listened carefully. When Dwyer finished, Carillo nodded and said, "It's about time you did some real work around here. I want you to follow this guy. I want you to find out where he goes and who he knows and what he does. I especially want you to follow him on weekends when our friend usually strikes. Got it?"

"Okay," Dwyer said.

"One more thing," Carillo said. "I want a set of his fingerprints. Ask the FBI for them."

"I already did," Dwyer said.

"And?"

"They're lost."

"They're what?" Carillo said.

"They're missing from his file," Dwyer said. "The FBI guys say they don't know where they went. I don't know. Maybe they're holding them back. Maybe they're looking to make the collar themselves. I don't know. They told me they're going to keep searching for them."

Carillo mumbled something.

"What did you say?" Dwyer said.

"I said, 'Fuck Efrem Zimbalist.' "

Bernard Rosenfeld lay back on his bed and held up the *Express* so that he could look at it. He bought the *Express* every afternoon to see what new stories it had made up about the .44-caliber killer and the killings. He never knew before that newspapers made up so many stories. When he was growing up in the Bronx, his father used to get the *Dispatch* in the morning and the *Express* in the afternoon, and sometimes, as a child, he would take the two papers into his room and read them and believe every word he read. Now he did not believe any of the papers anymore. He had given up on expecting the papers to understand what he was doing, but he thought that at least they would not print lies about him. If they make up their stories about me, he said to himself, they must make up even bigger stories about the President and the Pope and all the kings and queens of the world. They would lie about Sam Thornton, too, if they knew about him.

It was late in the afternoon, the brink of twilight, the last rays of sunshine beating against the blue bedspreads and the gold tablecloth guarding Bernard from the world. The *Express* had a big headline on its front page.

IS SON OF SAM
A VOLKSWAGEN MAN?

The story on page two quoted an anonymous witness who had seen a man in a yellow Volkswagen leaving the scene of the most recent shooting. The witness said he was pretty certain he had spotted a "2" and a "5" in the license number. The *Express* said the police were checking out the owners of all yellow Volkswagens in the metropolitan area. Rosenfeld tried to remember if he had seen a yellow Volkswagen as he was leaving the area of the shooting in the Bronx. He couldn't remember one.

Rosenfeld turned over the paper and on page three he saw a story about the police artist who had drawn a pair of sketches of the .44-caliber killer, based on the recollections of witnesses. The two sketches were reproduced at the bottom of the page. The two sketches looked very much like each other, except that in one sketch the subject's hair came down over the left side of his forehead, and in the other the subject's hair came down over the right side of his forehead. Neither of the sketches looked anything like Bernard Rosenfeld.

The artist's name was Peter Bertucci. When he was in the fourth grade, the newspaper story said, he could draw so much better than anyone else in his class, his teacher said that he was certain to grow up to be a Michelangelo or a Picasso or at least an excellent commercial artist. But although he loved to draw and paint, neither his technique nor his perception improved much after the fourth grade. He did not become a commercial artist. He became a cop. After he had been on the force for seven years, he heard that the department was looking for artists. He volunteered, and was accepted, and in the six years since then, he had drawn hundreds of sketches of suspects. The process, he explained, was a very frustrating one, largely because most people are not very good at description: they cannot give you much detail about a stranger they have glimpsed for only a few seconds. Once in a while, he would get an exceptional witness, someone who had gotten a good look at a suspect and could retain most of what he had seen. "For instance," Bertucci told his interviewer, "I've had a guy say to me, 'The guy I saw was very tall, like a basketball player, maybe six foot five or six, and he had a nose that looked like it had been broken a few times, and he had a scar on his right cheek. His hair was blond, he was wearing a bright-red sweater and he limped.' Now, that's a hanger. That's one you can do, and when they catch the perpetrator, and he looks just like the sketch, or a lot like it, anyway, then you feel terrific, like you've really done your job, like you've helped make an arrest. But that don't happen very often."

Bertucci went on to say that, almost always, he had to jog the memories of witnesses by showing them drawings and photographs of other people. Did the suspect have a head shaped like this? Did he have eyes like this? Was his nose like this one? Or this one? Was his mouth shaped this way? Or this way? What about his hair? Curly, like this? Or straight? Or crew cut? Or what? Show me somebody here who looks a lot like the suspect. Go ahead: go right through the pile.

On his worktable, Bertucci kept more than five hundred mug shots that he could show to witnesses in the hope that they would then match a known face with an unknown face. Then he would start to draw, and once he had sketched a recognizable face, he would start over again questioning the witness. Does this look like the subject? Are the eyes too far apart? Is the nose too large? Are the ears too conspicuous? Is the hair too long? What else should I change? How?

"We haven't had much luck with this Son of Sam," Bertucci said. "All we keep getting is, you know, average eyes, average nose, average mouth, average size, mod hair, brooding kind of look, no visible scars, no limp, no nothing special. What we got here describes maybe a million guys in New York. And look, I'll admit it, if you look at our earlier sketches, the ones after the first two or three shootings — I didn't work on them, another guy did — they don't look too much like my sketches. I don't know, I hope this stuff helps get the guy, but I don't know. I'm doing my best, that's all."

Bernard Rosenfeld looked at the sketches again. Sam was right. As long as he did what he was told, they could not catch him. They could not hurt him. He smiled. The demons were pleased by his latest performance. The howling had subsided. The dogs knew that now he was going out hunting every night, and that now he was not going to miss anymore. He had learned his job well.

He turned onto his side so that he could rest the *Express* on the bed and flip the pages comfortably. He went quickly through the paper, ignoring the gossip columns and grocery ads, until, deep into the paper, he came across a column written by Roger Lofting. The headline on Lofting's column said:

VILLAGE SECT SAYS
A DEMON'S BEHIND
THE .44 KILLINGS

"They live in an insulated world," Lofting's column began, "in the heart of Greenwich Village, but this group of writers and artists who call themselves The Moment of Truth think that they have the key to the fear that grips all of New York today. The Moment of Truth people insist that the .44-caliber killer, the so-called Son of Sam, is possessed, possessed by a demon whose name is Sam."

They understand, Bernard said to himself. They understand. He read the story, and a few paragraphs down he came to the letter addressed to Son of Sam: "We're writing to let you know that you are not as alone as you think you are. We know about Sam. . . . " Bernard began to cry, he was so happy. They know. They know. They know. They can tell the world that he is just doing his job, he is just following orders. The Moment of Truth. He would talk to them, explain everything to them. He went to his table and sat down and began to write. "No one but a few people like you would dare choose to believe that one such as Sam exists. . ." he began. No delicate printing now. He was excited, writing fast, scrawling, and now, inside his temple, Sam Thornton's dog started up with a whimper, then a bark, then a series of short barks, followed by a long baying bark, almost as if he were sounding a warning, telling his master that danger approached. Rosenfeld got up and walked to the window. He peeked through a blue bedspread. It was early spring and the trees had not yet turned totally green, and he could see into Sam Thornton's backyard. He could see the dog standing there, black and brassy. The dog would not be quiet. He could not write. He could not concentrate.

He grabbed the piece of paper off the breakfront and rolled it into a ball and threw it into a corner of the room. It landed on top of one of his magazines, obscuring the face and most of the body of the girl on the cover. Only her jackboots peeked out from behind the wad of paper; only the tip of her whip flicked out toward her cowering target.

Rosenfeld rushed out of his apartment, pulling the door shut behind him. He did not wait for the elevator this time. He went down the staircase, taking two steps at a time, going out the front door, and then trotting to his cream-colored Ford Galaxie, parked in front of the apartment house.

He drove down into the Bronx, then across the Throgs Neck Bridge into Queens. He curled around onto the Cross Island Parkway, took the Cross Island to the Long Island Expressway, the LIE to Northern State Parkway, Northern into the Meadowbrook. He went only a few miles on the Meadowbrook, exited, turned right and cruised three or four blocks to the entrance to the campus of Nassau Community College. The school stood on ground that had been, during World War II and earlier, an air force base. A handful of reasonably new brick buildings mingled with quonset huts and barracks. Students roamed among the mismatched buildings, the boys carrying their books at their sides, the girls pressing theirs against their chests. Rosenfeld pulled into a parking lot near the student center.

He got out of his car and walked to the front of the center. Then he saw the sign that said: TONIGHT! NCC POLITICAL UNION PRESENTS: A LECTURE BY DANNY CAHILL, NOTED COLUMNIST OF THE NEW YORK DISPATCH. The lecture was supposed to start at eight o'clock. It was now eight-thirty. As Rosenfeld stared at the sign, a chubby man in his mid-forties swept past him, muttering under his breath. "I'm late," Danny Cahill was saying. "Why the fuck do I agree to do these things?"

Rosenfeld followed Cahill into the auditorium in the student center. The room was filled, overflowing, not an empty seat. Rosenfeld joined a group of students who were standing in the back. When the audience spotted Cahill making his way to the podium, they began to applaud. Cahill looked at them with a sheepish smile, ran a hand through his curly hair, and said, "Things really gotta be dull around here you got nothing better to do than wait for me." He talked for about twenty minutes, telling the students how he had wasted his own educational opportunities and how he had regretted it ever since; then he said he would be happy to take questions. The first question was about the letter from Son of Sam, and most of the questions that followed were about the killer. Rosenfeld listened to the first answer — "I wish I could write a letter that good," he heard Cahill say — and then he went outside, to suck in the spring air.

He was still standing outside when the lecture ended, and hundreds of students flowed past him. Finally, Cahill came out, a small squadron of students still buzzing about him, asking him questions. Rosenfeld came up on the outer edge of the circle surrounding Cahill. "I read your column daily," Rosenfeld managed to say.

"Yeah, yeah," Cahill said. "That's good. God bless. I need all the readers I can get."

"I find it quite informative," Rosenfeld said.

"Terrific," Cahill said.

The columnist moved away, heading toward a hired car. *I read your column daily and I find it quite informative.* Jesus Christ. People were always saying things like that to him. He never tired of hearing it.

When Cahill's car pulled away from the campus, turning right toward the Meadowbrook Parkway, a cream-colored Ford Galaxie was right behind it. Danny Cahill was going home to try to think of what he would do for a column the next day. He was tired of writing about Son of Sam. He needed a change of pace. Something light.

Bernard Rosenfeld was going to Queens, too. He was going hunting.

19

Eugene O'Hara snapped his scissors theatrically over a customer's head, waved his comb as if it were a baton, turned, and smiled at the camera. Son of Sam was the best thing that had ever happened to him. For one thing, he had more business than he could handle — girls and women from fifteen to twenty-five who wanted long brown hair cut short or dyed blond — and for another, he was getting publicity that was helpful to his business and essential to his psyche. His real name was Mario Colucci, and from the time he was ten years old he had dreamed of becoming an actor. He had selected the name he would use — Eugene O'Hara — when he was only fifteen. Back then, he could see the name in lights. But his career as an actor had never quite materialized; he had become a hairdresser instead, and now he could see his name in black letters on the door to the shop he owned, The Hair Apparent, a beauty parlor situated on Queens Boulevard that, with rock music and psychedelic décor, catered to the young.

O'Hara was about to be interviewed by Gil Rodgers for a series Rodgers was preparing on the wave of fear generated by the .44-caliber killer. The fear reached into every corner of the city, but it was most intense in Queens, especially among the sort of young women who patronized The Hair Apparent. "Now when the camera rolls," Rodgers said to O'Hara, "I'm going to ask you if your customers are afraid. Okay?"

"Okay," O'Hara said.

"Roll," Rodgers said.

"We have speed," the cameraman said.

"Your customers," Rodgers said to the hairdresser, "do you find that most of them are frightened?"

O'Hara smiled straight into the camera. "They're simply terrified," he said. "This madman who's out walking the streets is just driving them all crazy. They're all coming here to have their hair cut or dyed. And we've sold more blond wigs in the past month than in the previous two years. It's scary."

"That's perfect," Rodgers said, pulling the microphone back from O'Hara. "That's all I need." The newsman leaned forward and placed the microphone in front of the young woman who was sitting in O'Hara's chair. "And you, miss," Rodgers said, "are you frightened?"

"Oh am I!" she said. "I hate to be out after dark. And I really hate to stop at traffic lights. Every time I do, I keep thinking he's going to pull up next to me. I try to time it so I don't ever have to stop at a light."

"Thank you," Rodgers said, turning to another customer. "What about you? Are you worried about the forty-four-caliber killer?"

She nodded. "I don't go out with my boy friend anymore," she said. "He comes to my house and we go downstairs, we have a finished basement, you know, and we watch television or listen to music, but we don't go out. We used to go to a disco almost every Friday and Saturday night, but not anymore. I told my boy friend he ought to buy me a nice present with all the money he's been saving not going out."

The boy friend of the girl at The Hair Apparent was a typical "casualty" of the fear created by the killer: he was horny — he hadn't parked with his girl in months, and her folks refused to go out while the young couple was in the basement — but at least he was saving some money. The disco business in Queens was taking a terrible beating. The girls who normally frequented the spots were staying home, frightened away by the Son of Sam, and with no girls on the scene, there was no good reason for young men to go to the discos. Frank Parisi, Connie Bonventre's companion in the first attack attributed to the .44-caliber killer, had recovered completely from his wounds, and he was back on the disco scene, but he didn't find much fun in it anymore. Frank himself was understandably nervous, and his hangout, Jinni, was no longer vibrant, no longer exciting. Jinni used to draw four to five hundred people on a Saturday night, and now sixty or seventy showed up. There was plenty of room on the dance floor for the dancers to show their moves, but there was hardly anyone to watch. The waitresses, who had been earning between $150 and $200 on tips each weekend, were now going home with $25 or $30. They were so angry they were ready to take on the killer themselves — with their bare hands. Frank Parisi was not willing to take that chance — unarmed. He carried a gun now, a .38. "Sure, it's illegal," he told his friends, "but who's going to take it away from me? Who's going to tell me I can't carry this? You know what it's like to be looking into a gun and not have nothing of your own? It's never going to happen to me again."

If Parisi was willing to take the law into his own hands, so were others whose lives had been touched by the .44-caliber killer. A cousin of Marie Perotti, the girl who had been shot while standing on her own stoop, had organized a vigilante group in the Bronx. The group was supposed to protect the Country Club neighborhood, to patrol the streets and report anything that seemed suspicious to the police. But the real purpose of the Country Club Civic Association was to chase away blacks and to catch the Son of Sam and punish him. Marie Perrotti was paralyzed from the .44-caliber bullet that tore into her back; she was confined to a wheelchair. Her cousin walked around with the wheelchair rolling through his mind. "We find that guy before the cops do," Matty Perrotti said, "I feel sorry for him, what we're gonna do to him."

Michele Hudson's boy friend, Marty Schmidt, was another survivor. Of all the people connected with the killer's victims, he was the most accessible. Every newspaper, every magazine, every television station pursued him. Three different times, when he went to the cemetery where Michele Hudson's body lay, he was persuaded to pose placing roses on her grave. By the third time he did it, when the photographer shouted, "Hey, look at the tombstone, that's good, you know, with that same sad look on your face," he realized that he was being used, he was being made to appear foolish. But by then there were so many photos in circulation — the Associated Press had sent out one of them — that they could be used over and over again. People who saw the amount of publicity he received and were appalled by it called him a professional mourner. Schmidt wished he could fight all the bastards who didn't realize how much it hurt him, the death of Michele Hudson.

Schmidt had turned down Gil Rodgers' request for an interview. Rodgers was disappointed by the rejection. He had wanted a shot of himself consoling the boy friend. He had even worked up a speech in which he would promise the boy friend that he, Gil Rodgers, a reporter with a conscience, would not rest until Michele Hudson's killer was apprehended. But you can't win 'em all, Rodgers told himself, and without Schmidt, he was perfectly willing to do his closer — the last shot of his three-part series — standing in The Hair Apparent, with hairdressers and dryers and customers clustered in the background.

The shot worked very well on the air: "Son of Sam," Rodgers said, staring deep into the lens, establishing perfect eye contact, "you have done what you set out to do. You have terrified half the population of this great city. You have created fear and havoc. You have left a bloody trail behind you. Now it is time to stop. Now it is time to spare the people — and to spare yourself. Now it is time for you to give yourself up. Call me. Let me help you. My number is six-six-five . . . three-two-one-one. That's six-six-five . . . three-two-one-one." The phone number flashed on the screen, across Rodgers' chest, and then the camera panned up onto the clock on the wall in The Hair Apparent. "Hurry," Rodgers said. "Hurry before time runs out." Pause. "This is Gil Rodgers, 'On-Scene News,' at The Hair Apparent in Queens."

Rodgers' series had two immediate effects. First, one of the competitive stations decided to assign a woman reporter to the case, an attractive young woman with long brown hair. She was exceptionally sweet-looking, the central-casting version of a human sacrifice, and she, too, was going to appeal to Son of Sam to turn himself in — to her. "If he does it," she told a makeup artist, as he was brushing out her hair, "I'll be a fuckin' star."

Second, one of the other competitive stations decided that most of the media were mishandling the case, that it alone would cover the case with dignity and with perspective. The news director sent a memo to his staff: "There will be no further on-air references to either 'Son of Sam' or the 'Forty-four-Caliber Killer.' Those phrases glamorize the killer and sensationalize the case and will no longer be used on our broadcasts."

"What do we call him then?" one of the station's reporters asked. "The man who is allegedly shooting at young women with a forty-four-caliber revolver?"

"That sounds okay," the news director said.

"I got a better idea," the assistant news director said, after his boss was out of earshot, "We'll just call the guy, 'That cocksucker.' "

Johnny Dwyer hung up the phone and ran into Inspector Carillo's office. "They found 'em," he said. "They found 'em."

"Who found what?" Carillo said.

"The FBI," Dwyer said. "They found Birani's prints. They had fallen into the back of some filing cabinet. Somebody happened to pull out the bottom drawer this morning and noticed an envelope in the back and pulled it out. And that was where Birani's prints were. They'll have them in New York tomorrow."

The next day, Dwyer went to the FBI office in Manhattan, picked up the envelope containing Birani's prints, and delivered the envelope to the Fingerprint Identification Section at police headquarters. Then Dwyer went back out to the 109th and sat at his desk and took phone calls and pretended to work.

He had to wait only half an hour. Then Carillo came to the door and called out his name and waved for him to come into the front office. Dwyer went in, and as he sat down, Carillo said, "No match. No bull's-eye whorl on any of Birani's ten fingers."

"Shit," Dwyer said. "He looked so good, I can't believe it. That wipes him out, huh?"

"No, it doesn't," Carillo said.

"Why not? What do you mean?"

"You know all we got that's any good at all is that one partial fingerprint, right?" Carillo said.

"Yeah. So?"

"So, I hate to even say this, but we don't know that that print belongs to the killer. No way we can know that. It could be anybody's print, anybody who had a chance to touch the letter. We fingerprinted every cop working in the Bronx that night and we checked every set of prints we got out of that against the bull's-eye whorl and we didn't get a match. We didn't get anything close. But who knows if we missed somebody or if one set of prints, for some reason, didn't get checked? Who knows who might have touched the letter before the killer dropped it off? Who knows if anybody touched it before we got there? We don't know. We just don't know."

"You mean," Dwyer said, "we've gone through tens of thousands of fingerprints looking for a match with that letter, and we don't even know if the print on the letter belongs to the guy we want?"

"That's right."

"Then I should keep following Birani?"

"Hell yes," Carillo said. "He's still the best thing we've got. Nothing else is even close."

He looked up at the streetlight and tried to imagine the face. He saw opaque eyes now, not centered properly, their dullness speaking of more danger than all the visions he had had of pop-eyed, furnace-eyed gunmen. The car moved and the streetlight was gone, and Carillo was looking at the night sky.

He picked up the microphone clipped to the dashboard. "Flushing One to Base," he said.

"Flushing Base," the dispatcher, Sergeant Hanlon, answered.

"We're on East Tremont in the Bronx heading to the Whitestone Bridge. We'll be in Queens in a couple of minutes. Anything doing?"

"Flushing One, it's all very quiet."

"How are we doing on the radio?" Carillo said. "Keep checking the cars?"

"Yes, sir."

"All right then. I'll be on the bridge in a minute. Ten-four."

"Ten-four," Hanlon said.

Daley, the detective who was driving, started to say something, but Carillo held up a hand. He wanted to listen to the radio.

"Flushing Base to Flushing Nineteen," the radio said. Carillo listened. A beat. Another beat. A drop of annoyance fell on an exposed nerve. Then he heard Hanlon say, "All right, that's Ten-four, Car Nineteen."

Carillo exhaled. On his radio he could not hear the other cars speaking, but it was obvious that car nineteen had jumped right in on the radio to Hanlon. He turned to Daley. "What were you saying?" Daley began to talk again and Carillo turned to the window. He did not listen. He was thinking of his radio system. All night, it had been working perfectly: call a car and the car responds immediately. Carillo had sat at the desk, right alongside Hanlon, for the first five hours of the night. Maybe this would be the way to catch the bastard, he told himself. The moment the base calls, the cars must pop right back on the radio. It was 2:30 a.m. now, and he had all twenty-five cars out, driving along parkways, running up and down side streets, patrolling the avenues, looking, looking, looking for a white male, age twenty to thirty-five, riding alone in a car.

The Task Force cars were on a special radio band giving them direct contact with the second floor of the 109th Precinct. If the 109th received a call from headquarters in Manhattan, or from a blue-and-white patrol car, neither of which were on the special Flushing band, the information was only as good as the speed with which it was disseminated, and the speed with which the detectives in the cars responded on radio. If the killer struck, then only the unit nearest the scene was to make the run. All others were to fan out, block parkway intersections, halt traffic on the Whitestone, Throgs Neck, and Triborough bridges and then inspect every car for that white male, age twenty to thirty-five, riding alone. And keep responding to the radio. The only way the system could work, the only way they would ever stop the guy from getting away, was if all the detectives in the cars were on the radio the instant they were needed: pop-pop-pop. No buying cigarettes or having coffee in a diner, Carillo kept telling them. Just get the call, let the base know right away that you received it, and then go to work. You have maybe three minutes to trap the man, he insisted.

Each night, Carillo had Sergeant Hanlon calling out to the cars to check their reaction time. And all through this night it had been three beats, maybe four beats, but never more, before Hanlon's voice indicated the car was in touch. They were on the job, Carillo told himself. They wanted the guy so badly that they had started to talk about nothing else. Have a drink with any of them and say, "What do you think he does for a living?" Then the next thing would be a suggestion to forget the drink and take one last look around the streets.

". . . and then he could be hidin' his ass in one of these buildings right here, while we're drivin' our asses around. . . ." Daley was rattling on, talking about the killer. Carillo nodded, as if he were listening.

Men never perform well against the unknown, and the attempt this time was tiring Carillo. Every time he thought of the fingerprints, his mind began to ooze and then stop. He had a bull's-eye whorl that was as useless as tits on a bull. If they caught the killer and took his print and he had a bull's-eye whorl, then they would know that this was the same guy who sent in the letter. Terrific, Carillo said to himself. That'll really help some girl on the street, won't it? The ballistics identification was also wonderful. They knew that the same gun had done all the .44 shootings. Now all they had to do was go out and find that gun.

When he had first learned that all the shootings were the work of one gun, Carillo made the logical opening move. He found out everything he could about the weapon. Some of the information was easy to get. He found out that the Charter Arms Corporation of Stratford, Connecticut, had only started making the .44-caliber Bulldog revolver in 1972, and that since then a total of twenty-eight thousand had been manufactured. The number did not frighten him. "Only twenty-eight thousand of them in the whole world," he said. "That's not bad. I know blocks in Harlem where they have twenty-eight thousand guns." He found out that one model of the gun had just a two-inch barrel, and weighed twenty ounces — easy to carry and easy to conceal — and that the suggested retail price was $149. He found out that it was a fairly low-velocity weapon, which meant increased accuracy and decreased damage. He found out that the gun was popular with hunters, to finish off wounded prey, and with air marshalls because the bullet was likely to stop a man and stay in him, rather than ricochet all around an airplane. Carillo found out that until Charter Arms began selling the Bulldog revolver, .44-caliber bullets were scarce in the United States; they had become more easily available as the use of the Bulldog had increased. The killer, ballistics people said, was using Winchester Western .44 Specials for his gun.

Carillo wanted to know more. For instance, he wanted to know how many .44-caliber Bulldog revolvers were registered in the United States. That was when he went to the Alcohol, Tobacco, and Firearms office in Washington.

"I want to know how many forty-four-caliber Bulldog revolvers are registered in the United States," Carillo said.

"You know how many were manufactured?" the T-man said.

"Twenty-eight thousand," Carillo said.

"Then that's how many there are," the agent said. "It's a new gun. They don't wear out."

"I already know how many there are," Carillo said. "I want to know how many are *registered,* and then I want to get the names of the owners and their addresses."

"Oh," the T-man said. "In the whole country?"

"Uh huh."

"Well, we can't help you with that," the agent said. "You better check out the FBI."

The special agent in charge of the Manhattan office of the FBI told Carillo, "Our computer system for tracing guns is such a mess that, to be truthful, we can't help you on this case."

Carillo felt like he was getting an education. He called the Charter Arms Corporation and he asked if they kept any records of who owned their guns — warranty records or something like that.

"We know where each gun gets sent to from here," a spokesman for Charter Arms said, "but that's as far as we go. Like we know if we send fifty guns to a distributor in Tulsa. But we don't know who buys them in Tulsa. The gun goes from the distributor to a dealer and then he sells it. Some of the dealers keep records."

Carillo next found out that there were 166,000 gun dealers in the United States. He also found out that 641 Bulldog revolvers had been stolen in shipment from the manufacturer to one distributor. Nobody could say how many had been stolen from distributors or dealers or individuals, or even from the property departments of police departments that had confiscated them.

Carillo was given the names of fifty-six people in New York City itself who were licensed to carry .44-caliber Bulldogs. Those fifty-six people were checked out first: they all came up clean. Carillo knew that fifty-six names only scratched the surface of all the .44-caliber Bulldogs in New York City. The Task Force took phone calls tipping them off to dozens of owners of unregistered Bulldogs. None of those tips had led to the killer, but at least there were now a few more registered gun owners. Carillo never did find an exact number on the registered Bulldogs in the United States, but he guessed that no more than fifteen percent of all the guns made were traceable through registration. He asked police departments throughout the country to check the registered .44s in their areas, and a surprisingly large number did. Or said they did. They all came up empty. Carillo couldn't believe how bad the figures were in the field of gun distribution and registration. He also couldn't believe the reaction he got from one gun distributor he talked to on the telephone. "This is getting me upset, I got to admit it," the distributor said.

"Why?" Carillo said.

"Hell, this Son of Sam shoots a man in the head with a forty-four and the man don't die. This means all we got here is just a big horse pistol with no power."

"I see," Carillo said.

As Daley drove the car up to the toll plaza at the Whitestone Bridge, Carillo's eyes began to go over the cars around him. He counted the heads in each car. Two, no good; three, no good; two, no good; one black, no good; two blacks, no good; a white alone, too old, no good; another white, too old; a white alone, a white alone, a white alone. . .

"Police Department," he called to the change clerks. "Don't let those cars through."

He was out of his car, trotting between other cars, and coming up to the tollgates where the cars with the lone whites were. Two of the cars were at the gate closest to Carillo. The third car was waiting at a gate on the other side of the two cars. Carillo skipped past the two cars and stood in the middle of the lanes, so he could watch all three cars at once. He had his badge out and had his hand on his gun. He motioned with his hand for them to roll down their windows.

"Police," he said. "Would you three gentlemen kindly get out of your cars?"

"What for?" a voice called.

"Because I'm asking you to," Carillo said. Daley was at his side now. The guy in the first car, a maroon LTD, got out. He was a dark-haired guy in a yellow sports jacket. When he moved, the guy behind him, a chubby guy in a T-shirt, also got out. The guy in the last car, a yellow Firebird, did not move. Carillo motioned to him.

"Got a warrant?" the guy said.

"I got a warrant," Daley said. He walked toward the car. The exhaust from other cars billowed Daley's shirt, which was hanging outside his pants. Daley walked directly at the yellow Firebird. The face in the car, tanned and young, under light hair, watched Daley's huge form approach. The light hair dipped, the door opened and the guy stepped out.

"Excuse me," Daley said. He patted the guy down and then stepped over to the next one. When he was finished doing that, Daley and a tollgate man, a Bridge and Tunnel officer, checked the insides of each car. Daley had the drivers open the trunks. Carillo took the three licenses and registrations, walked back to the unmarked patrol car, and called in the numbers to the base in Flushing. He sat in the car while Sergeant Hanlon had the records checked with the Motor Vehicle Section of police headquarters. This is the one police computer system which works as well as or better than the pamphlets say it does. Our technological systems may be weak in the protection of lives, but they are ferocious in the preservation of personal property. Hanlon called back on the radio that all three records were in order, the cars were not stolen, and Carillo got out of the car. This time he was carrying a black case. He walked over to the first car, the maroon LTD, and placed the case on the hood and opened it. "Come over here, would you?" he said to the three drivers. As they came up to him, Carillo was arranging the fingerprint cards and the pad.

"Which one is Carnevale?" he said, reading from the license.

The black-haired guy nodded. "Here's your license and registration," Carillo said. "Now if you'll just put your hand here for a moment."

"What's this about?" Carnevale said.

"You're helping us find a killer," Carillo said.

Carnevale stepped back. "Hey, I ain't no fuckin' Son of Sam!"

"I want to prove that you're not," Carillo said.

Carnevale took another step back. "I want a lawyer."

Daley's big hand spread across the shoulder of Carnevale's yellow sports jacket. He pushed Carnevale up against the car and Carillo took the hand and brought it over the inking pad.

"I want you to hold your fingers down, so I get the tips of them," Carillo told Carnevale. "No, not straight out. Have the fingers pointing down. I need the fingertips. There's a reason for it. We need the tips."

Carillo glanced up for a moment. At the last tollbooth, a blue Granada rolled up, paused, a lone white male, age twenty-five or so, then was gone. Another car came right up after it. A single white guy driving. Carillo's hand came out to wave at it, and the car was gone. Now there were more cars moving rapidly through the gate. Carillo realized it was the exact-change lane. There was a string of headlights approaching it. The next car to come into the bright lights of the plaza had a lone white male, age thirty maybe, and Carillo called to the car and waved at it, but the car was gone. As Carillo stood at the hood of the maroon car with his fingerprint pad, he saw all the cars going past him and through the last tollgate, his blood dripping out a back door.

Carillo grabbed Carnevale's thumb. "Now give me the tip, just the tip," he said. He pressed Carnevale's thumb onto the ink pad and then onto the fingerprint card while the other two detained drivers watched. And down at the end, car after car with a lone white driver ran through the tollgates and sped off into the night.

20

Pablo Birani was working in the Time-Life Building at Fiftieth Street and Avenue of the Americas. He was working partly as a researcher and partly as a messenger for an enlightened lawyer who believed in hiring ex-cons as long as they were willing to work for the minimum wage. The first time Johnny Dwyer and Herbie Klein went to the Time-Life Building to tail Birani, they used his parole officer, Stanley Dowling, as a guide. At a quarter to five, fifteen minutes before the end of Birani's workday, Dowling went up to his office and said that he just happened to be in the neighborhood and wanted to say hello. He hung around until Birani was ready to leave. Then the two men went down in the elevator together. When Dwyer and Klein saw Dowling step out of an elevator in the Floors 22–34 bank, with a thin, almost gaunt young man walking at his side, the two detectives knew they had found their target. Previously, they had seen only outdated photographs of Birani, from his bank-robbing days, showing him with a pencil-thin mustache. Birani, now clean-shaven, and Dowling shook hands in the Time-Life lobby, and the parole officer went one way, the ex-con the other. Dwyer and Klein followed Birani. The thing that struck Dwyer right away was Birani's eyes, almond-shaped and dark, almost black, set deep in his swarthy face. They were either very sad or very threatening.

Tailing Birani, Dwyer and Klein discovered, was not easy. In the first place, there were more than half a dozen different ways to leave the Time-Life Building. There were two exits to Fiftieth Street, one to

Fifty-first Street, plus entrances from the lobby into a variety of shops — a candy store, a steak house, and a custom-shirtmaker's, for instance — which then emptied out to the street. There were also a stairway and an escalator leading from the main lobby to a lower level that in turn led to the Rockefeller Center subway station.

Birani never seemed to use the same route twice in a row. Often, but not always, he would take the escalator to the lower level, walk by a branch office of the Manufacturers Hanover Trust Company, turn right past Dawson's Pub and Joe Cione's Barbershop, turn left past the Photomat and La Petite Brasserie, then go through a set of glass doors. Then, instead of going straight ahead to the Exxon Building, the McGraw-Hill Building, or the Celanese Building, he would turn left, go down eleven steps, ignore the exit on the left to Radio City Music Hall, and go past a grocery, a Little Nick Pizza Stand and a Nedick's toward the Independent subway stop. He might then take the subway uptown, to Harlem or the Bronx, or downtown, or out to Queens. Sometimes, he skipped or postponed the subway and just wandered underground, ranging from Forty-eighth Street to Fifty-second Street, from Fifth Avenue almost to Seventh Avenue, perhaps pausing in the RCA Building or the Associated Press Building or the Uniroyal Building or the International Building. It was a city down there, beneath Rockefeller Center, a city offering every conceivable service, with a post office and banks and fast-food stands and elegant restaurants. A man could live there for a long time, without ever surfacing for fresh air or even the air of Manhattan. Birani seemed to know every shop, every phone booth, every tunnel, every turn, every inch of this underground world, and he walked through it at a remarkably brisk pace.

To make pursuit even more difficult, Birani always acted as if he were being followed. Dwyer and Klein were positive that he never made them, never picked them out, yet Birani quite often would suddenly reverse direction or make a series of sharp, quick turns. He had another little trick. He would stand on the subway platform until a subway came in, then make no move to get on it — until the door was about to slide shut. Then he would dart in, occasionally leaving both Dwyer and Klein standing on the platform, feeling foolish. Eventually, the two detectives worked out a system: if Birani was poised in front of a train, one of them would get on, and the other would remain on the platform. That way, one of them usually managed to stick with Birani, and the other one got the night off. When Dwyer was the one left on the platform, he generally went back to the 109th Precinct and put in a few hours on the telephones.

One of the eeriest things was following Birani past a newsstand and watching him stop to pick up a copy of the *Express*, the after-noon paper, with its latest bold headline: MORE THAN ONE SON OF SAM MAY ROAM THE STREETS, for instance. The story sup-porting that headline pointed out the disparity between the early police sketches and the more recent ones. The story quoted an anonymous police source as saying, "The killer could have an ac-complice, a man driving a getaway car. That would help to explain his quick disappearing act." The story added its own theory: "The two-man team might well be a pair of thrill-killers like Loeb and Leopold." To further bolster the case for *Sons* of Sam, the *Express* revealed that there were obvious qualitative differences between the rambling, almost incoherent letter sent to Inspector Carillo and the very literate letter "allegedly sent to a columnist for a morning news-paper." Most days, Birani turned immediately to the Son of Sam cov-erage in the *Express*. So did everyone around him. Dwyer would watch Birani on the subway reading about the .44-caliber killer, perhaps sitting between two young women, each with long brown hair, each reading the same paper, same story, each growing a little more fearful day by day, each sharing the panic spreading through the city, afflicting particularly the boroughs of Queens and the Bronx. The fear twisted through the city like the subway system itself, a stench, a growl, a roar vibrating just beneath the surface. Dwyer could read the fear on the women's faces. And then he would try to read Birani's deep, dark eyes.

One Saturday morning, the first one in May 1977, a crisp and clear day, Dwyer, working by himself, picked up Birani outside his Rego Park apartment house and, at a discreet distance, followed him to his office. Birani went up in the elevator. On weekdays, Dwyer enjoyed waiting in the lobby of the Time-Life Building; the scenery — especially the secretaries and researchers who worked on *Time* and *Fortune* and *Money* and *Sports Illustrated* — made the hours pass quickly. But on Saturdays, only *Sports Illustrated* had a full staff in, and waiting in the deserted lobby would have been too obvious. Be-sides, on Saturdays, the passage from the lower level of the Time-Life

Building to the subway was closed. Dwyer stayed outside, cruising the Avenue of the Americas, back and forth between Fiftieth and Fifty-first streets, hoping that he would not miss Birani's departure.

Not long after noon, Birani came down, went out the farther west of the two doors leading to Fiftieth Street, turned right and walked to Eighth Avenue. Dwyer spotted him and followed him. Birani turned right again on Eighth Avenue and walked uptown to a Howard Johnson's motor lodge and went inside, through the lobby, to the coffee shop. He sat down and ordered a cup of coffee. Within five minutes, a woman joined him. She was wearing an ultra-short skirt, a desperately tight sweater, and black stockings. She was heavily made up, a circle of green around her eyes, her lips a bright, almost incandescent red. She looked like a typical Eighth Avenue hooker, except for one thing: unless she was incredibly dissipated, she had to be at least fifty years old. Not even the grubbiest of the massage parlors and conversation pits and art studios — LIVE NUDE MODELS!!! — used fifty-year-olds, certainly not ones that looked fifty.

Birani and the grotesquerie — the mother-hooker figure — sat in the coffee shop for almost an hour. Dwyer watched from a stool at the counter, studying the couple in a mirror, fascinated and repulsed. He could not hear what they were saying, but Birani was doing most of the talking. Birani paid the check, grandly kissed the woman's hand and left, alone.

Dwyer followed him to the subway and then, on the subway, up to Washington Heights, not too far from the George Washington Bridge. There, on a corner on Broadway, Birani ducked into a plain brick building bearing a sign saying: United States Public Health Service. Dwyer had to go up close to read the smaller lettering on the sign. It said: Center for the Treatment of Venereal Disease.

Dwyer waited across the street, more convinced than ever that he was following the right man. He had been talking and thinking about Birani for more than a month now, and he had showed his material to half a dozen detectives of varying backgrounds and all had agreed that the odds were good — maybe as good as three to one — that Birani was, in fact, the .44-caliber killer. "He's a sick prick," Herbie Klein said.

"He's our number-one suspect," Inspector Carillo said. "Don't let him out of your sight."

Dwyer couldn't quite figure out the significance of the woman in the coffee shop, but the VD center fit in perfectly with a theory, widely held, that the killer was seeking revenge, that he had been badly hurt by a woman, emotionally or, perhaps, physically. He might well have caught a venereal disease from a girl with long brown hair.

Birani spent more than an hour in the clinic, came out and took the subway to Times Square. He emerged from the underground and walked quickly to a Broadway movie theater playing a double feature, *Deep Throat* and *The Devil in Miss Jones*. Halfway through the second film, just as Miss Jones was about to go down on a snake, Dwyer had to go to the men's room. When he came out and walked back into the orchestra, Birani was gone. Dwyer dashed out into the street and looked around. It was early evening, and Broadway was starting to swell with sightseers and sights, with pimps and homosexuals and plainclothes cops, the whole melting pot of New York. Birani had melted in. He was nowhere to be seen.

"Sonuvabitch," Dwyer said. "How the fuck could he walk out on that scene?"

That night, in the Bronx, Son of Sam struck again.

The interns and nurses had drawn the curtain around the bed so that you couldn't see anything from the doorway to the trauma room. At the bottom of the curtains, green canvas shoes, splattered with dried blood the color of pale roses, shifted about. Carillo walked around the bed to the side where the curtain was not drawn. His face was drained of expression. His eyes allowed nothing to show.

One intern was adjusting a bottle of pale-yellow fluid which dripped through a tube into a thin, alabaster arm. Carillo's eyes went from the tube to a clear plastic nozzle. He followed the coils up to where they came into a plastic mask which covered a face. Directly above the nozzle, the forehead bulged out, as if it had a rock inside it. Dark, matted hair had streaks of blood in it.

"Well, we'll see," the intern mumbled to Carillo.

Carillo's face did not move.

"Actually, she's better than she looks," a second intern said.

"All right, let's just get her up there," an older doctor said.

Carillo backed out into the hallway. He stood against the wall as they wheeled the girl past him. He made himself look at the bulging forehead. Then she was gone through the double doors. He stepped past a cluster of his detectives and went into a small men's room. He spread his right hand over a sink faucet. When it hit him, when the rage screamed against the inside of his ears, he tried to pull the faucet out of the sink.

When he came out to the lobby, the television people jumped off chairs. He ducked back inside.

"I'm going for a cup of coffee, but I'm not going to have it here," he said.

"You want us to bring something back?" Daley said.

"No, I tell you what. Go out there and tell Cahill that I'm walking over to that big candy store on the corner. On Gun Hill Road. They should be open by now. Tell him I'll be in there. But tell him to come alone, will you? I can't have those other bastards all over me."

"It's done," Daley said.

Carillo went down the corridor and went out an entrance on the other side of the hospital. He walked down the Bronx street in the Sunday-morning quiet, crossed Gun Hill Road, and went into the candy store. It was just six-fifteen. He looked back at the hospital, Montefiore Hospital in the Bronx. The street with the emergency-room entrance on it was clogged with police cars and brown Plymouth Furys, detective cars. He counted the police cars. There were seven of them. He didn't want that many. These fellows ought to be home sleeping, he said to himself. We're going to need them again tonight. It was, he decided, typical of anything in life: for the first shooting, nobody went to the hospital in time. This time, there were too many people.

He was halfway through his coffee when Cahill came in.

"I don't know what to tell you," Cahill said.

"Neither do I," Carillo said.

"The boy is all right, huh?" Cahill said.

"The boy is all right."

"The girl?"

"We'll see," Carillo said.

"He hit her twice, right?" Cahill said.

"The boy got one in the wrist that went into the shoulder. The girl got two in the head."

"Two?" Cahill said, his voice rising.

"Two," Carillo whispered.

"How the fuck can she live?"

"We'll see."

"And you got nothin'?" Cahill said.

"Nothing," Carillo said.

"Geez, isn't that somethin'," Cahill said. "He's that smart."

"This is a shrewd guy. Mean bastard, too. He must time these jobs. He must spend a month going up and down a place until he has just what he wants. He comes up, does it, and gets away and gives us nothing."

"What about the blue Mustang they saw on Fieldston Road?" Cahill said.

"Forget about that," Carillo said.

"What do you mean?" Cahill said.

"You can't use that," Carillo said.

"What do you mean, I can't use it?"

"I can't let you print that," Carillo said. "We have to do a lot of checking."

"Hey, I work for a paper, not the Police Department," Cahill said.

"You want to catch a killer, don't you?" Carillo said.

"Of course."

"You don't want to be responsible for this guy getting away and then coming back next week and killing some other girl, do you?"

"Of course not, but what you're saying is a lot of bullsh —"

"It's what?"

"Bullshit," Cahill said.

"What are you talking about? You're telling me catching a killer and saving a life is bullshit?"

"Nobody wants it more," Cahill said. "And I think we'll do a lot better if we start putting everything out in public. Let the people start to get into this and save their own asses."

"If you put the blue Mustang into the papers, you're warning the guy," Carillo said.

"No, I'm not. I'm telling his neighbors to turn him in."

"Let me be the policeman," Carillo said.

"You are," Cahill said. "And I'm the newspaperman. You do your job and I'll do mine."

Carillo stared straight ahead, finished the coffee, and held out his cup. "I'll have another," he said to the counterman. He sat in silence, and motionless, while he waited for the coffee. His hand fell over the sugar bowl. He lifted it, just an inch off the red formica counter. He held it there, while he thought about lifting the sugar bowl over his head and then smashing it on the counter. He exhaled and put the sugar bowl back on the counter.

"I'm telling you I'm right," Cahill was saying.

"You're wrong," Carillo said.

"What do you mean, I'm wrong?"

"You got one letter from the guy and you think you own the case," Carillo said. Instantly, he heard Cahill's voice rise, higher and thinner and less certain, as Cahill denied this.

"One letter turned you upside down," Carillo said evenly.

"It still bothers you that I got it," Cahill said. Suddenly, his voice was lower and firmer. He put a couple of dollars on the counter and got up and left.

It took Carillo long minutes of sitting alone at the counter to get over the remark. He did it by telling himself that Cahill was clinging to his letter — and the status it gave him — so tenaciously that Cahill would say anything, even make up a lie about Carillo, to retain his position.

When he got back to the hospital, it was seven o'clock. He went up to the operating-room floor. Daley was walking around with a box of doughnuts he had bought somewhere. He was handing them out to the nurses. Con the nurses, the number-one rule, Carillo thought.

"Isn't this something?" Richie Paul said. He was a blond-haired guy from Manhattan Homicide.

"He was in the blue Mustang," somebody said.

"Never," Daley called back.

"How do we know what he was in?" Paul said. "We're fighting a ghost. We don't know what he looks like, what he sounds like, where he comes from, what he —"

"I'll be in the office," Carillo said. "If you need me, call me."

In Flushing, he went up to Saint Andrew's Church on Northern Boulevard and slipped into a back row for the eight-o'clock mass. The sound of the priest's voice saying the prayers in English irritated Carillo. He never understood why the Church gave up its mass in Latin. There was an order in Latin. It kept everything the same. You could depend on it. He closed his eyes and started to say a prayer for Lisa Sharry, the girl who was in the operating room. But his mind skipped away from the prayer and settled on Cahill's attitude. Why, that prick thinks his newspaper column is more important than my job, Carillo said to himself. He tried to concentrate on praying for the girl, but he was too distracted and he blessed himself and left.

Back at the precinct, he went into a small office in the rear and stretched out on an old leather couch. His face stuck to the leather when he turned on his side to get some sleep. He looked out the dusty window at the hot sky. "You fuck," he said aloud, thinking about Cahill. Then he thought of the bulging forehead and the dark matted hair with the blood streaks and his mind said his daughter's name. He froze inside. He closed his eyes against the thought and, troubled, on the far outskirts of shock, as he had been from the moment the call came into the base at 4:10 a.m., he fell asleep. It was nine o'clock.

At one o'clock, Daley came in the doorway.

"Inspector?"

"Huh?"

"Inspector."

Carillo's face was wet with sweat. He lifted it from the hot leather couch.

"I just fell asleep," Carillo said.

"The girl is all right," Daley said.

"Thank Christ," Carillo said, sitting up.

"They took two slugs out, and the doctor says she'll have nothing but a headache. One stuck in the back of the neck and the other was under the skin in the forehead. Windshield deflected them."

"You say she's all right?" Carillo said.

"Thrashing around and complaining like a bitch already," Daley said. "You never saw anything like it. I left her. We'll get all we need from her tomorrow."

"Thank Christ," Carillo said.

"Young girls, they're made out of wire cable," Daley said.

Carillo stood up and walked to the window. "We're going to get this sonuvabitch," he said.

"You know it," Daley said.

"We're going to get him and stick it right up his ass," Carillo said. A little sleep, and now he could hope again. He didn't even think about Cahill.

21

The phone was ringing on Danny Cahill's desk, but he kept typing. "Hey, Joanne," he yelled on the third ring. "Answer it, will ya?" The phone rang again. "Joanne? Joanne? Where the fuck is she?"

"She's getting you the Sanka you sent her for," Mike Malamud, the columnist in the adjacent office, called out.

"Oh," Cahill said. He picked up the phone himself. "Yeah?" he said.

"Is Mr. Cahill there?" a voice said.

"Yeah. This is he."

"Mr. Cahill, I never expected to get you directly. My name is Sam Thornton, and I live in Yonkers, and I think I know who this Son of Sam person might be."

"Yeah?" Cahill said. "Who?"

"I don't know his name," Sam Thornton said, "but someone has been writing me very strange letters, threatening me and my family. Whoever writes these letters says he's going to destroy me because my dog's barking is destroying him. I got the first letter —"

"Yeah, well, listen," Cahill said. "I'm on a deadline right now. I got to get a column done in five minutes. Now you call the Special Homicide Task Force out at the One-oh-nine and —"

"I keep trying to call them," Sam Thornton said, "but all I ever get is a busy signal. And I already talked to the cops up here and —"

"Look, they just added another number," Cahill said. "It's nine-six-one – nine-six-one-three. You ought to be able to get through on that one without no trouble."

"Somebody shot my dog," Sam Thornton said. "Shot him in the leg. I think it may be the same guy who wrote me the letter."

"Just tell the Task Force," Cahill said. "Tell them the whole story. They'll follow it up. I got to get this thing written or I'll blow the whole first edition."

"Sure," Sam Thornton said. "I understand. Sure." He hung up.

"Who was that?" Malamud yelled. "Sam?"

Cahill coughed a laugh. "Yeah," he said. "The *wrong* Sam. Some guy whose dog got shot. Thinks the guy who shot his dog is the forty-four-caliber killer."

"Dog have long brown hair?" Malamud asked.

Cahill didn't answer. He resumed his typing. I wish they would catch this guy so I could stop writing about him, he thought. I don't need this motherfucker to give me things to write about. I'd trade him in tomorrow for a good thief. Somebody with a sense of humor. Trouble with this cocksucker is that there ain't nothing funny about him. Never is with murder. I remember, I don't know, ten, fifteen years ago, the Star of India case. Big jewel robbery. Murf the Surf. Alan Dale. Some other guy. Three hustlers out of Miami. A terrific case, a real-life *Topkapi*, a sensational story till one day Murf's girl friend showed up floating in a river. Dead. Then the story stopped being fun. Murder. Son of Sam. Hell, I'd rather write about Willie Sutton. At least he can make you smile once in a while.

Cahill shook his head. He was tired of Son of Sam. He wished it would go away. But it was now Thursday, May 26, 1977, and Cahill was working on a column for Friday's paper, and it had to be another column about the .44-caliber killer. Cahill had no choice: The killer's anniversary was approaching. He had struck for the first time shortly after midnight on the morning of Sunday, May 30, 1976, and in the year starting with that initial attack, he had killed five young people and wounded six, and he had not left even a hint to his own identity. He had fired his revolver on seven separate occasions. The most recent incident had come on another Sunday morning, after 3:00 a.m., on May 8, 1977, only twenty-nine days after the previous shooting. That was the shortest interval in his murderous career; the longest was almost three months. There was no discernible pattern to his madness, no easy link with the phases of the moon, but there was a burgeoning fear that he would hit again during the coming holiday weekend, sometime between Friday night, May 27, and Monday night, May 30, a hit to celebrate his anniversary, to celebrate — as one newspaper headline put it — his first *deathday*.

The killer's letter to Cahill had indicated that he might mark his anniversary with a shooting. "Tell me, Dan," the killer had written, "what will you have for May thirtieth?"

Cahill took the cup of Sanka from Joanne Salerno, took off the plastic top, sipped off a quarter of an inch, then put the cup down next to his typewriter. "Is this weekend so significant to him that he must go out and walk the night streets and find a victim?" Cahill began. "Or will he sit alone, and look out his attic window and be thrilled by his power, this power that will have him in the newspapers and on television and in the thoughts and conversations of most of the young people in this city?"

The phone rang. Joanne answered it this time. "Mr. Cahill is not in," she said. "Can I take a message?" She listened for a while. "And when did you have this vision?" she said.

Cahill grunted approvingly. He reached over to the left-hand side of the desk and picked up the memorandum that Carillo had sent out to every police precinct in the city and in surrounding areas. Cahill was groping for inspiration. Usually, the deadline of the presses was inspiration enough, but now Cahill was running way ahead of the real deadline, four hours ahead. He wanted to get his column finished early so that he could get out to the 109th and see Carillo before the weekend began. After one very bad week between them, they were talking again.

Cahill looked at the one-page memorandum, the latest in a series of directives put out over Carillo's signature: "Please acquaint all members of your command with the following information concerning the person responsible for five homicides and six felonious assaults (gun) committed between May 1976 and May 1977 in the Bronx and Queens."

Then came the information:

.44-CALIBER KILLER

Description

The ".44-CALIBER KILLER," who calls himself "SON OF SAM," is described as follows:

A Male, White, 20 to 35 years old, medium to tall in height, medium build, dark hair (mod style, well groomed), clear skin, pale complexion, clean shaven, dark piercing eyes. During cold weather he has worn a tan, form-fitting, ¾-length coat; during chilly weather, a knee-length beige raincoat; in warm weather, dark pants and a blue polo shirt with white stripes.

He is probably right handed. He shoots combat style: two handed and from a crouch. He carries a .44-caliber "Bulldog" revolver manufactured by the Charter Arms Corp. The gun may be carried concealed in a plastic or paper bag or on his person.

Modus Operandi

He travels from one area to another probably by vehicle. He then prowls a selected area on foot in search of victims. He has chosen attractive white females aged 17 to 25, in a public area, on foot or in a vehicle, alone or with a male or female companion. If the intended victim is in an auto, he approaches from behind and shoots through the passenger-side window. If the intended victim is on foot, he approaches as if to ask directions and then shoots the victim at close range. All his attacks have been during hours of darkness, and all, except one, after midnight.

Psychology

Psychiatrists and psychologists disagree —

Joanne interrupted his reading. "There's a messenger here with an envelope for you," she said. Cahill looked up. He had asked his literary agent to send him a $1000 advance. By messenger. His daughter's college tuition was overdue by one semester. "Send him in," Cahill said.

The messenger walked in, and Cahill looked at him very carefully. He was thirty, maybe, medium height, medium build, dark hair, pale complexion. His hair was light, not dark, but he did have kind of strange eyes, shifty eyes. "Some fuckin' job you got," Cahill said.

"Uh huh," the messenger said. "Sign this over here, please."

"You must spend a lot of time movin' around the city, huh?" Cahill said.

"Oh, sure," the messenger said. "Right here. Anywhere below that line."

"You get out to Queens much?" Cahill said.

"Queens?" the messenger said. "Nobody sends nothin' out there. Just Manhattan and sometimes the airports, that's all."

Cahill reached into his pocket to give the messenger a tip and then remembered he had given his last dollar to Joanne for his Sanka and her coffee. "God bless," he said to the messenger with a wave.

"Uh huh," said the messenger with the shifty eyes.

Cahill had spotted the killer that morning on the subway coming in from Queens. Then he had seen him walking through Grand Central Station toward the shuttle. And he had seen him at least twice on Forty-second Street as he was walking to the *Dispatch* building. He was seeing the killer everywhere now, and so was everybody else. Cahill could see everybody doing it on the subways. He could see New Yorkers, people who never looked at anybody else before, looking at all the other passengers. Their eyes, trained to be blank, came to life. He could see them thinking. He could taste their suspicions. Look at the eyes. See that weird expression. Hey, that guy could be him. Sure. He could be the Son of Sam. And look at the guy sitting two seats over from him. He could be, too. Cahill saw the fear, too. Young women who rode the subways in New York City were used to guys being crushed up against them, one guy copping a feel with his elbow, another pressing his leg against a soft ass. Most of the women tolerated it, and some even enjoyed it. But not now. Now the young women recoiled at a stranger's touch, especially if the stranger looked even remotely like the police descriptions of the .44-caliber killer. Blacks were the only ones who got off easy. For the first time in the lives of some of them, they were above suspicion. They had, in the context of this terrible fear that swept through the city, turned white. They could sit or stand on a subway and not catch a suspicious or a hateful glance.

Cahill turned back to the memorandum.

Psychology

Psychiatrists and psychologists disagree on his motivation but diagnose him as a neurotic, schizophrenic, and paranoid, with religious aspects to his thinking process, as well as hinting of demonic possession and compulsion. He is probably shy and odd, a loner inept in establishing personal relationships, especially with young women.

Religion

There is a strong likelihood that he is a Christian and probability that he has had Catholic or Episcopalian schooling.

Education

Educators estimate that he is at least a high-school graduate and that he may have had some college training.

Caution

This man is armed and dangerous. He may shoot at police who attempt to stop or arrest him.

Notification

Any information concerning this case should be telephoned to the Special Homicide Task Force at the 109th Precinct:

Telephone# 961 – 9613
961 – 9600
Dominick Carillo
Deputy Inspector

Cahill pushed the memorandum back toward the corner of his desk. He put his hands on the sides of his typewriter and he forced himself to think. He knew what he wanted to say. He wanted to say that an army of three hundred policemen was gathering this weekend to try to make sure the killer's first anniversary was his last.

Terrible things happened on the weekend that marked the anniversary of the first .44-caliber shooting. Gil Rodgers, the television reporter, thought the worst thing that happened was that he had to give up a super dinner party Friday to do a spot for the eleven-o'clock news live from the lobby of the 109th Precinct. He wouldn't have minded so much if something newsworthy had happened, like a double shooting, or if he could have gotten someone important to come on the air with him, but he lost on both counts. Inspector Carillo, the only major police official around, was always hunched over the radio with Sergeant Hanlon, checking with his cars and checking with headquarters, and the only moment of real excitement came just before midnight, right after Rodgers went off the air. Gunshots were reported only two blocks off Northern Boulevard in Flushing. It turned out to be a dispute over a drug buy, but within five minutes after the first shot was heard, twelve cars from the Task Force had the block sealed off. When the gunman was found, hiding under a parked car, he couldn't believe the number of detectives he found surrounding him. "Who you motherfuckers 'spectin'?" he said. "John Dillinger?"

It was a terrible weekend for Frank Parisi. On Saturday, a few minutes after midnight, he was standing at the bar in Jinni when he saw a guy with a familiar face walk in the front door and pay the entrance fee. I've seen that guy somewhere, Parisi said to himself. Now where the hell was it? Then he remembered. It was the guy who kissed Connie Bonventre on the cheek in Jinni the night she was murdered. Parisi was certain of it. He was also certain that the guy looked exactly like the latest police artist's sketch of the killer. As soon as Parisi figured out who the guy was, he reached inside his sports jacket and made certain he hadn't forgotten to carry his gun.

Parisi walked over to his friend, Jess DeStefano, at the front door. "That's the guy," Parisi said.

"What guy?" the bouncer said.

"The one who was hitting on Connie that night."

"Which one?"

"The older guy with the wavy hair. The soft lips. Don't he look just like the drawing that was on the front page of the *Express* yesterday?"

"Oh, yeah," Jess said. "Sure, he does. I guess. What are you going to do?"

"I don't know."

The guy was looking around the room. There wasn't much to see. This was the worst weekend in the history of Jinni. Even the girls who couldn't stand their parents and hated the houses they lived in were staying home this night. The dance floor belonged to Sam.

The guy walked to the bar, ordered a shot of rye, drank it, reached into his pocket, pulled out a dollar and put it next to his empty glass for a tip. Then he turned toward the door. Parisi intercepted him. "Where you think you're going?" Parisi said.

"Out," the guy said.

"You ain't going nowhere," Parisi said.

The guy looked very scared. "Why not?" he said.

"Because," Parisi said. "Because I seen you in here once before. You were in here a year ago, right?"

"No, I never came in here before," the guy said.

"You full of shit," Parisi said.

The guy turned to walk out, and Parisi reached out and tugged at his arm, and the guy pulled away and started to run, and Parisi went to his inside pocket and pulled out the .38. "Stop!" he shouted. "You stop, you cocksucker, or I'll kill you." He fired one shot and missed the guy and missed everything else. The bullet whizzed through the discotheque without hitting anybody. On a typical Saturday night a year earlier, the shot probably would have cut down a dozen customers.

The guy stopped cold. He fell on the floor out of fright. At the same moment, two plainclothes detectives spun away from the bar and dove at Parisi from his back. One smacked him in the mouth with a tight fist. The other grabbed the .38. Then they both recognized him. "Jesus Christ, it's the kid from the first shooting," the detective with the gun said. "What the fuck are you doing with this thing?"

"Protecting myself," Parisi said, wiping blood off his face.

"Yeah? And who's the guy?"

"I think he's the guy who shot Connie," Parisi said.

Now both detectives went for the guy on the floor. He was literally shaking. One detective patted him all over to make sure he was clean. "You got identification?" the detective said.

"Y-y-y-yes," the guy said. He pulled a driver's license and an American Express card from his wallet.

"We're taking both of you in," the detective said.

They went through the back entrance at the 109th and then up the stairs to the squad room. The guy checked out. He was an English teacher from a Brooklyn high school who admitted that he went to discotheques because he liked to watch teenaged girls dancing. He said he had never been to Jinni before, but he figured that with all the publicity about Son of Sam, and with all the warnings to young people from Brooklyn to stay out of Queens and the Bronx, he wouldn't bump into any of his own students there.

The two detectives from Jinni talked with Inspector Carillo and then told the teacher to go home to Brooklyn and forget what had happened. He was more than willing. Then the detectives told Parisi to go home, too. They kept his gun, but they did not book him.

"Okay, kid," one of the detectives said. "You been through enough. Just don't play with no more guns, please."

The next disturbing incident took place on Sunday. Late in the afternoon, a rumor started going around the Country Club section of the Bronx that a guy had been seen in Saint Raymond's Cemetery dancing on Connie Bonventre's grave. The rumor reached the Country Club Civic Association.

In five minutes a posse of ten had gathered. The men were carrying three baseball bats, two shotguns, one Colt .45 and a historical necessity for such a group: an overwhelming belief in the rightness of their cause. They drove into Saint Raymond's in two cars and went all the way to the back, where the cemetery brushed up against one of those rare wooded areas left in the City of New York. They parked their cars and got out and looked around. It was turning dark now. It was almost one year to the hour from the time Connie Bonventre started getting dressed to go out for the last night of her life. One of the members of the Country Club Civic Association thought he saw something in the distance. "What's that?" he said, pointing down a long row of headstones.

"What's what?" somebody else said.

"Down there. All the way down. You see the guy down there? What's he doing there, all alone?"

The men started running toward one man in the distance. He was a young serviceman, just into his twenties, and he was visiting the fresh grave of his mother. She was his last blood relative. He heard them first. Then he saw them. He saw a pack of men coming at him, and he turned to run. He didn't know what they wanted, but he wasn't going to wait and find out. He could have outrun them easily except, as he pivoted toward the front gate, he sideswept a tombstone and stumbled and fell, twisting his ankle. He tried to get up and the ankle gave way. He tried again, and all he could do was hop. From even a short distance, it looked as if he were dancing.

Two of the men with baseball bats got there first, both of them swinging at once. He took three glancing blows, on his arms and shoulders, before the first solid one caught him in the forehead and sent him tumbling down a deep black hole. He didn't even feel it when the other men pounded him with their fists and kicked him with their feet. When he woke up, bandaged and sedated, he was in

Montefiore Hospital. He was scared. He had been given a four-day emergency leave to arrange his mother's funeral and burial, but now he was due back at the base in North Carolina the next day. He wanted to make a call and tell his commanding officer why he was going to be late getting back, but the supervising nurse told him that the base had already been notified. When the police, responding to an anonymous phone call, had come and picked him up and brought him to the hospital, they had found his travel orders lying on the ground next to him.

At about the same time the young soldier was lying in the cemetery, tried and convicted and punished for a crime he knew nothing of, the members of The Moment of Truth were beginning a special séance. For the benefit of a television crew and two newspapermen, Mitchell Block of The Moment of Truth was attempting to re-establish contact with Arthur, the spiritual guide whose teachings he had rejected the previous year. The idea was that if contact could be made, Arthur might be prevailed upon to reveal to Mitchell, and through him to both the print and electronic media, exactly who Son of Sam was. It took more than an hour, and two four-hundred-foot rolls of film, before Block announced he had made contact. It took another half an hour before he said he could hear Arthur clearly. Then, mixing his own questions with questions suggested by Lionel Silver, Block entered into a dialogue with Arthur. Of course, no one else could hear Arthur's replies, so periodically Block had to repeat them for the benefit of his fellow members of The Moment of Truth and for the reporters present. Unfortunately, Arthur was being unusually elusive. He was hurt, he said, by the way Block had treated him, and Block had to spend almost the entire period of contact salving Arthur's feelings. Both of them agreed, at the end, that perhaps in the near future Arthur would be in the proper mood to discuss more substantive matters.

"That's it?" the field producer for the television crew said.

"I'm afraid so," Block said. "I'm sorry Arthur wasn't better, but, you know, you can't push him."

"I'll tell you what," the field producer said. "I won't tell anybody Arthur wasn't cooperative if you don't tell anybody I spent four hours here and two thousand feet of film."

It was a bad weekend for the people who believed in discarnates and for Gil Rodgers and for Frank Parisi and for the army private whose mother had died. It was a bad weekend for all the detectives who patrolled all night each night through the Bronx and Queens and came up with nothing. It was a bad weekend for the newspapermen and television people and magazine writers who had never dreamed they would spend most of four days sitting in a Chinese restaurant called Lum's eating and drinking and waiting and waiting and waiting.

The only good thing that happened all weekend was that nothing happened. When the sun came up Tuesday morning, 366 days after the death of Connie Bonventre, the people of the City of New York considered themselves fortunate. Son of Sam had not claimed a single new victim.

22

He stiffened when he saw the name on the doorbell. It was in the slot directly over his name. It was the nameplate for apartment 8M, which had been empty for weeks. Suddenly, here was this new name, "Mort Cole." Right under it, in the slot for apartment 9M, was "B. Rosenfeld."

Rosenfeld was alone in the vestibule of his apartment house. He said aloud, "Now they're in the same building with me." He was certain that Mort Cole was a demon. "Mort is Mort and Mort is death," he said. When he went upstairs, he placed a water glass on the floor and put his left ear against the glass. He was on the floor in an uncomfortable position, his ear to the glass and his body on the mattress. He complicated this by pulling the .44 out of his pocket with his right hand and pressing the muzzle against the floor and holding his finger on the trigger. He had to keep his right arm in a tiring position to do this. Move, he said to himself. Move and I'll Mort you, Mort.

His ear began to hurt. He turned over onto his other side and pressed his right ear to the glass. This meant the .44 had to be held with his left hand. This bothered Rosenfeld. The arm quickly became numb. He wanted to make sure he fired through the floor at Mort with a firm hand.

He remained in this position all through the night, changing from one side to the other, but he could detect no movement in the apartment below. Finally, he pushed the glass out of the way, put the safety on the .44, dropped it on the floor, and fell back on the mattress to get some sleep. And then Mort's hand came out of the wall. Mort had climbed inside the wall, and now his hand was inside Bernard's apartment. But it was not reaching for Bernard. The hand was guiding a tan, round-faced dog which hopped out of the wall and trotted over to Bernard, who immediately twisted onto his stomach and started to get up. Bernard held out one hand to hold off the dog while he tried to roll off the mattress and get the gun, but the dog ducked under his hand and jumped inside Bernard's head, jumped as if it were clearing a fence. The moment the dog got inside Bernard's head, he began to howl for death. Not one death or two deaths. This dog demanded many deaths.

"Mort is Mort," Bernard moaned. He began to hit himself on the head to silence the dog, but the dog would not be quiet.

At the post office that night, Charley Weppler, who worked on the ZMT machine with Rosenfeld, Hattie Mabry, and Bob Allen, came over to their lunch table and pulled out a color photograph of himself with a young woman.

"I got engaged," he said.

"You did?" Hattie said.

"See, here's her picture," Weppler said.

"She's cute," Hattie said.

"Here, you see?" Weppler said. He held out the picture to Rosenfeld. "How do you like her?"

Mort howled, and Rosenfeld grew angry as he looked at the picture of the young girl, who was wearing a low-cut white blouse. He threw it back at Weppler.

"Get it out of here," Rosenfeld said.

"What?" Weppler said.

"I said, get it out of here," Rosenfeld said again.

"What the hell is the matter with you, man?" Weppler said.

"Shit!" Rosenfeld said. He got up from the table and walked out of the room. Why is he doing this to me? Rosenfeld asked himself. Why is he showing me the picture of the girl when he knows that Mort wants me to kill her?

Two nights later, Rosenfeld came up to Weppler in the lunchroom as if nothing had happened.

252

"Where do you go on weekends?" he asked Weppler.

"I go out with my girl, but we can't go around the Bronx because of this Son of Sam. So we go out on Long Island."

"Where on the Island?" Rosenfeld said.

"Now that it's getting close to summer," Weppler said, "we're going to be going far out. We go to the Hamptons."

"Discotheques and all out there?" Rosenfeld said.

"Oh, they got some terrific ones," Weppler said. "It's early now, but next month, in July, the places really get busy."

Rosenfeld became eager. "They do? Where? Which ones do you go to?"

"Well, there's this place The Cave and —"

"Do you go there?" Rosenfeld cut in.

"Yeah," Weppler said.

"Where is it?" Rosenfeld snapped.

"Hampton Bays, right on the Montauk Highway there."

"You going to be there this weekend?" Rosenfeld asked. "What night do you go there?"

Something made Weppler hesitate. "Well, it's not really summer yet," he said. "I'm not sure what I'm doing this weekend." Weppler didn't know why he said that, but he knew that for some reason he did not want to tell Rosenfeld where he would be. Before he could think about this, the lunch hour ended, and Weppler had to go to work on the ZMT; it was his shift on the machine.

On Friday night, right after Rosenfeld finished at the post office, he drove across the Throgs Neck Bridge, followed the Cross Island Parkway to a sign for the Long Island Expressway and went onto the expressway and headed east. It was one-thirty in the morning, and the traffic, still fairly heavy, was moving well. The forecast had been for a sunny and unusually warm mid-June weekend. Rosenfeld drove in the right lane so that he could watch the cars whipping past him. He drove for many exits past the New York City line, deep into Nassau County, wondering whether Weppler was in front of him or behind him. Probably behind. Weppler had probably stopped to pick up his girl.

Bernard could see Weppler's girl. He could see her on the beach. She was in the middle of a stack of young girls, and blood was running from all of them, splashing from one to the other, like water falling on rocks.

The red taillights of the car in front of him caught Rosenfeld's eye. The taillights grew larger and larger, and as he got closer to them, Bernard could see that the lights were really eyes, dog eyes, and then as he took in all the cars in front of him and around him, their taillights became the eyes of a great pack of dogs, and the dogs tried to nip at him and force him faster along the road.

"Wait, wait, I'm not ready yet," Bernard told the dogs. "I don't have it yet."

The dogs howled.

"I need it so I can do my job in the Hamptons better," he said.

The steering wheel felt like fur standing on end.

"I have to do it right," Bernard said.

He pulled off the road and into a gas station and watched the traffic to the Hamptons go by. He would be joining them soon.

Two weeks earlier, right after the anniversary of the first shooting, a weekend when Rosenfeld stayed in his room and read every word in the *Dispatch* and the *Times* and the *Express* and a handful of periodicals, he had spotted the advertisement in the gun magazine, *Straight Shooting*. The ad said: "Big New Action, Big New Power: You've Got to Feel It to Know It!" The name of the weapon was the Ranger Strike IV, a .45-caliber semiautomatic rifle made by a small company, Jayhawk Enterprises, in Kansas City, Kansas. Rosenfeld was glad that he had bought the gun magazine; it had been on the rack next to the rows of *True Detective* and *Inside Detective*. He looked at the picture of the rifle in the ad. A big, handsome weapon. A real man's weapon, the ad suggested. Rosenfeld got up and wrote a letter, in script, to the company, asking where in New York would he be able to buy the weapon. He was surprised that the manufacturer was so sloppy as to leave the zip code out of the address. Rosenfeld took his letter with him to work the next day, looked up the zip code for Kansas City, Kansas, 66110, bought a stamp at the first-floor counter, and dropped his letter in with the out-of-town mail.

Rosenfeld pulled out of the gas station in Nassau County and turned around and drove back to Yonkers. He stopped at an all-night diner for a hot dog and French fries. When he got home, he went straight to his mailbox. The letter he was waiting for was there, from

Jayhawk, telling him that the weapon he wanted was on sale at All-American Sports on Seventh Avenue in Brooklyn. He could feel the demons pushing him, leaning against the backs of his knees and making him move. They wanted him to get this new gun.

He was in Brooklyn by ten o'clock Monday morning. The gun store shared a street with two dry-cleaning stores, a candy store, a grocery, and several empty stores, all on the ground floors of three-story brick buildings. Puerto Ricans and wary whites lived in the apartments over the stores. Seventh Avenue was already heavy with traffic, but the sidewalks, Rosenfeld noticed, were empty of pedestrians. The whites were afraid to walk out in front of the Puerto Ricans, even in daylight, and the Puerto Ricans stayed inside because of the blacks, who were not visible but who, the Puerto Ricans felt, could pounce on them at any moment.

Rosenfeld found a parking space directly in front of the store. He put a quarter in the parking meter. The front of the store had two show windows filled with antique rifles and black Nazi helmets fitted atop plastic skulls. Rosenfeld looked at the antique weapons for a few minutes. He was standing there to make sure that he felt at ease. It was a wondrous thing to him how the demons sometimes allowed him to be with other people. When he walked into the store, a bell rang. The counter had a .357 magnum display in it. Along the right wall were telescopic rifles and World War I hand grenades. Dolls were placed between the rifles.

A woman came out of the back of the store. She was tall and amply built, and had a long nose with a sharp ridge in it. When Rosenfeld told her what he wanted, she said she did not have the gun in stock. She would have to order one for him, she said. She did have a used Ranger Strike IV, which he could look at if he wanted to. But the gun was promised to someone. She took the weapon off a wall rack and handed it to Rosenfeld. The moment he hefted it, he knew he had to have it. The rifle made him feel warm and at ease. The demons commanded him to buy it.

"What do you think?" the woman said.

"I have to have it," Rosenfeld said.

"It's a beauty," she said.

"I have to have it," he said.

She laughed. "You sound as if you're gonna die if you don't get it."

"That could be, too," Rosenfeld said.

She giggled. Rosenfeld looked at her. "I mean it," he said. She laughed louder.

"I'll tell you," she said, "this is some popular gun. Every ding-a-ling that comes in here wants to play with it."

Rosenfeld gave her a $50 deposit and left his name and home address. The woman told him that he had to get a permit from the New York City Firearms Control Board. She said it would take him a few weeks to get the permit. By then, she said, she would have the weapon from Kansas. She gave him the name of a woman on the control board. Rosenfeld couldn't waste any time. He left the gun shop and drove straight to Manhattan. He put his car into the municipal parking lot alongside the new police headquarters building. Then he walked outside, wandered up to Park Row, bought a hot dog from a wagon man, and ambled through the archway of the municipal building and along the brick walkway to the entrance to police headquarters. As he walked, he glanced up at the police building. In the windows on the third floor, there were the backs of several men who stood in shirtsleeves and smoked cigarettes. They were taking a break. One of them, stretching, held his hand to his back as if it hurt, as if he had been bending over files looking for a bull's-eye whorl.

At a desk on the first floor, a patrolman told Rosenfeld that the Firearms Control Board was at 42 Broadway, in the center of the financial district. Rosenfeld walked the several blocks down Broadway and went up to the office. The woman at the control board gave Rosenfeld forms to fill out. He needed the signatures of two people who knew him on one form, and he needed to have another form notarized. This one asked if he had a police record, was a fugitive, was a mental defective, or was planning to use the weapon to commit a crime. Rosenfeld took the forms with him.

That night, at the post office, he got two guys in the washroom to sign the one form for him. He told them he was buying a gun to go hunting.

The next day, he went to a notary public who was in a stationery store a block from the Firearms Control Board. He answered no to all the questions, showed his driver's license for identification, and got the form notarized. Then he brought all the papers back to the woman, who took them, smiled, and said, "Now I need three more things. Ten dollars for the city registration fee, ten dollars for a state fee, and I also need your fingerprints."

"Sure," Rosenfeld said. He gave her $20, allowed the woman to take his hand, put it on the inkpad and then roll the fingers on a white fingerprint card. She got all ten prints, fine flat prints. Without a magnifying glass, she could not see the exquisite bull's-eye whorl on the seventh finger, the index finger of the left hand.

"We'll mail the permit to you," the woman said.

Rosenfeld went home. His fingerprint card was placed in an envelope and mailed to the New York office of the Federal Bureau of Investigation, which either checked Rosenfeld's prints on the computer and found that he was not known to be wanted for any crime or, more likely, merely let the card remain in a basket for a week and then mailed it back to the control board with the word "Nothing" scrawled across the card. Upon getting the card back from the FBI, the woman at the control board typed out a slip of paper which said that Bernard Rosenfeld was authorized to own a .45 semiautomatic rifle in the City of New York. She mailed the slip to him, and he received it two days later. The whole process had taken only a month, from the time Rosenfeld spotted the ad in *Straight Shooting* to the time he got the license from the control board.

It was a month during which the hunt for the .44-caliber killer intensified (seven different suspects were arrested and released within hours), the climate of fear worsened to the brink of hysteria (the *Express* bragged at one point that, in its coverage of the Son of Sam case, it had published more words about sexual deviants than Krafft-Ebing), and among the men on the Special Homicide Task Force a suspicion grew that, because not a sign of the killer had been seen for two full months, perhaps he had been killed or had committed suicide or, through some strange set of circumstances, had been cured of the sickness that drove him to shoot young women, one and two at a time.

As soon as Rosenfeld got the permit for the semiautomatic rifle, he called All-American Sports. The woman in the shop said she had the weapon for him. Rosenfeld drove to Brooklyn again, put another quarter in the meter outside the store, and went inside to get his weapon. The weapon had been delivered from Kansas by United Parcel Service. It was inside a white Styrofoam box. Rosenfeld did not open the container to check the piece. He paid the balance for the weapon, $152. Then he bought two fifty-round boxes of .45-caliber military ammunition. Each box cost $9.50. When Rosenfeld took the last $20 bill out of his wallet, he was down to his last $16. There were three days to get through before payday. How can I pay for all the gas I use every night, he asked the demons in his head. They did not answer. They make me do everything, Bernard fretted. They don't give me any help.

"Gonna be doin' some plinkin'?" the woman asked him. This meant target shooting.

Rosenfeld did not answer. The woman smiled at him. "See this pellet gun here?" she said, pointing to a black pistol in the show window alongside the magnum .357. "I gave this to my nine-year-old last year. He went upstate to the country with it. By the end of the first weekend we was ass-deep in chipmunks. My son shot every chipmunk that they had in the whole upstate in the country. Just nine years old."

While she talked, Rosenfeld smiled and looked at the drawers where she kept the boxes of ammunition. He wondered how many boxes of .44 bullets she had in there. Under the rules of his firearms license, he could buy ammunition only for the weapon he had. But he was pretty sure, listening to her talk, that he could ask her for a box of almost any kind of bullets and she would not be too upset. He didn't need any right now. He had plenty of .44s at home.

When Rosenfeld woke up on his day off, Saturday, he took the rifle out of the Styrofoam box, loaded it with a clip of twenty-five bullets, hefted it, aimed it at the wall, then slipped the gun back into the box. He picked up the .44, loaded it, too, put it into his pants pocket and, with the Styrofoam box under his arm, went downstairs and got in his car. He drove to Queens and got on the Long Island Expressway again, heading east. He spread a road map on the seat alongside him and drove on the sunbaked road for an hour. On both sides of him, the Long Island suburbs ran up to the edges of the road: split-levels and colonials on rolling, wooded land. Then the land flattened and scrub pines and cheaper ranch houses covered the sandy ground. The expressway ended and he followed a road to the right, toward the ocean, and then made a left on another highway. This one took him out of the scrub pines and into the weathered wood and blazing glass of the Hamptons. Main Street in Westhampton was crowded with people in jeans threading their way through fields of Mercedes cars.

Dune Road, in Hampton Bays, became a drive through India: thousands of tanned, almost bare bodies forced Rosenfeld to creep along. He wondered what the places they were coming out of were like at night: Cat Ballou, Hot Dog Beach, Hermosa Beach, Castaways. But he had no impulse. Sam and his dogs didn't like the beach. Hadn't he been able to get away from them by going to Orchard Beach to sleep?

He turned away from the beach and onto a road that led to the highway. The first thing he came upon was a tower sticking out of a flat lot. The sign on it said, "The Cave." He pulled up to it. A thin, light-haired guy of about twenty-one was at the door.

"Help you?" the guy said.

"What is this, a disco?" Rosenfeld asked.

"Downstairs, opens at eight o'clock," the light-haired kid said.

"You get a big crowd here?" Rosenfeld asked.

"Shit, we don't get less than five hundred people."

"That's a lot, that's a lot," Rosenfeld said.

"I'm warnin' you, if you come, bring oxygen," the kid said. "Everybody down there has to fight for air. They keep me sittin' out here all night, so it don't bother me none. But you could die downstairs."

"What do you do, park the cars?" Rosenfeld said.

"Shit no, I'm the lookout for Son of Sam," the kid said. "They want me to look for parkin'-lot freaks."

Rosenfeld nodded.

"Everybody says Son of Sam is comin' out here," the kid said. "Two years ago, with *Jaws*, they said it was sharks. Now it's him. Shit, I'll bet he's been here already. I tell you, boy, I watch like a bastard all night."

"He could be anywhere, huh?" Rosenfeld said.

"Anywhere," the kid said.

"Maybe I'll see you tonight," Rosenfeld said.

"Yeah, well I'll be right around here somewhere, lookin' for some goofy bastard."

Rosenfeld began to drive narrow side roads which twisted around bays and inlets, past potato fields and shacks where field-workers lived. At dusk, he was again on Main Street in Westhampton Beach. A strong wind blew along the street and the sky did not grow dark gracefully; murky clouds smothered the end of the day. He noticed a small bar on the left-hand side of the street and alongside the bar was a yard with people sitting at tables with candles on them. There was a metal picket fence between the tables and the sidewalk. As he passed by, the car barely moving, Rosenfeld saw the long hair of the young women spilling onto their tanned shoulders.

A hot coil, red at the ends, turning to white in the middle, dropped into the bed of straw inside Rosenfeld's head. As the straw ignited, the black dog stood in the flames with his tongue flopping out of the side of his mouth.

The car jerked. Rosenfeld drove it to the corner, made a right, and drove away from the ocean, onto a road that went to nowhere, ending along the railroad tracks. His hands were sweaty. He put them to his head. He could feel the grease and he took his hands away. He wiped them on his pants legs. Then he took out his .44 and checked it. He reached into the back seat and pulled the Styrofoam box into the front with him. He pulled the Ranger Strike IV out, held it in his hands, his fingers curling into the notches of the front grip, flipped the safety off and placed the weapon on the seat alongside him. He turned the car around, then started driving back toward Main Street. He would stop the car in front of the bar, step up to the metal picket fence, and fire the semiautomatic at the young people sitting at the tables. His head bucked against the dog pacing around inside. The black dog had been standing in a fire, but the pads of his feet still were cold to the touch, causing Bernard to cringe.

He was still on the empty road leading from the railroad tracks when it started to rain. Big drops splashed onto the windshield. Wind blew dead leaves through the dust. There was a crash of thunder and more raindrops. Suddenly, it was pouring. The sound of rain filled the car, and as Rosenfeld came onto Main Street he could feel the dog running from the rain, head down, coat dripping, the rain concentrating on one part of his coat and causing the black hair to part and leave ugly gray-blue skin standing out, giving the dog the appearance of being an enormous rat. The black dog whimpered and ran up to the house and went under the shed, out of the rain. Rosenfeld drove past the bar. The yard was empty except for two people, a boy and a girl, sitting on a table, drinking from tall glasses, watching the rain pour off a big beach umbrella over the table.

Rosenfeld turned right at the corner and headed back for Queens. It was a long drive in the heavy rain, and when he got there the streets were empty. He went home to his apartment early, at 2:30

a.m. As he was getting comfortable, another dog, not the black one, raised his head and began to howl. This dog had a big round face and was kept inside a doghouse. The dog did not allow the rain to fall on even the tip of his nose. At the same time, the dog made himself heard. He berated Bernard. This was Mort doing it to him, Bernard thought. Mort was in the walls, he decided. Mort had climbed up through the ceiling of the apartment downstairs and now was in the walls of Bernard's apartment.

"Can't you leave me alone?" Bernard called out.

In the doghouse, Mort Cole's dog brought his head up again and began to howl.

Mort made drums sound a few nights later. Drums and screams of people. Bernard paced the room and listened. He thought of the souls of all his victims. They had been snatched by the demons as they left the bodies, and the demons had chained them and raped them and molested them. The drums got going and then a dog began to howl. "Little brat, little brat," the drums were pounding.

Bernard sat down, with the noise crashing inside him, and he started to write. He had tried to kill Mort. He had tried to destroy Sam Thornton, too, by shooting his dog, but in both instances, his bullets had failed him. Words, he thought, may be the only weapon. He had threatened Sam Thornton by mail, and he knew that the threat had lessened Sam Thornton's thirst for blood. In the week after he wrote to Sam, Rosenfeld did not find a single earthquake story in the newspapers. He would try to stop Mort Cole with a letter.

To Mort, he knew, he was not Son of Sam. His name in this relationship was Demi-Schmutz. That's what Mort thinks of me, Bernard said to himself, I'm Schmutz. Schmutzicker, dirt that's dirty. That's what he thinks of me.

Through the drums and the howling, Bernard wrote for the first time to Mort Cole. Again, as in the letter to Sam Thornton, Bernard scrawled his thoughts:

"You will be punished. How dare you force me out into the night to do your bidding? True, I am the killer, but Mort, the killer kills on your command. The streets have been filled with blood at the request of Mort."

When Mort Cole came home from work the next evening and read the letter, he went directly to the Yonkers police, to a satellite station house on Warburton Avenue. The station house was in a storefront, and two patrolmen were on duty. When Cole arrived, Officers Juliano and Charles were sitting at desks behind a long counter. Cole showed them the letter he had received.

Charles read the letter and shook his head. "You know," he said, "this is the second one of these wacky things. Guy lives right near you, Thornton, his name is, got a letter as crazy as this one. His daughter lives right in your building. She works over at police head-quarters. She brought us the letter her old man got. Screwy letter. We gave it to the psychiatrist. He said it was a real nut case that wrote it."

The next day, Cole returned to the satellite police station and met with the two patrolmen and Sam Thornton's daughter, Micki.

"You know, with all this Son of Sam business around, it makes you think," Cole said.

"You said it," Juliano said. "You never know."

"I think I know who wrote the letters," Micki Thornton said. "I'd swear it."

"Who?"

"Fellow who lives in nine-M. I looked it up, his name is Bernard Rosenfeld. He lives by himself. I heard people say they think he's weird. Makes noises at crazy hours. Mumbles. I never met him, but I've seen him. He looks strange to me."

"Why don't you guys talk to him?" Cole suggested.

"We'll start keeping an eye on him," Charles said. "We've got to be careful here. Warrants and all that. Only the detectives are supposed to do that. We're in charge of street crime. If we get into their terri-tory, they get a little nervous. So we got to be careful."

"But, don't worry," Juliano said, "we'll keep an eye out for this guy, what's his name, Rosenfeld?"

"Bernard Rosenfeld," Micki Thornton said.

Rosenfeld picked up the Ranger Strike IV and aimed it at the wall of his alcove. That was where it was coming from, he told himself.

"Fuck you, Mort! Die!"

In the apartment, the shot going off sounded like a bomb exploding. The .45 slug dug deep into the wall and caused a section of the plasterboard to cave in. Bernard saw Mort Cole standing inside the wall. Cole opened his mouth. His big long yellow teeth grinned at Bernard. Then the .45 bullet rolled off Cole's chest and dropped onto the floor.

23

Mike Fazo held his arm across the doorway. "Don't go out there for a minute," he said. The man and woman nodded and stepped back. Fazo held the door open with his foot and looked out at the cream-colored car parked on the opposite side of the street. Look at this fuck, Fazo said to himself. He kept staring at the guy sitting at the wheel of the Galaxie.

Fazo, the headwaiter at the Canal House in Howard Beach, in Queens, was built like a tow truck. Since the Son of Sam shootings had infected Queens, his job was to stand in the doorway and watch for anybody suspicious. The problem was that the Canal House was next to a motel which did heavy turnover and many times an aggrieved man parked on Cross Bay Boulevard, hoping to catch a wife or a girl friend leaving the motel with another man. Therefore, Fazo never could be sure of anything. Lately, he had started to escort people to their cars in the restaurant parking lot. This prevented the Canal House's night business from disappearing completely in the fear-ridden summer, but it also placed Fazo under considerable tension. His habit of standing at the door and running his fierce dark eyes up and down each white male walking into the restaurant caused many of them to change their minds and return to their cars. And now Fazo had a particularly dangerous scowl on his face as he watched this guy sitting in the car on the opposite side of the boulevard.

A white guy alone in a car. Fazo felt a little excited. Then he smiled. Isn't it a pisser, he said to himself, here all year you only get worried when you see a nigger outside in a car? Now you're hopin' you see a nigger instead of a white guy. Fazo told himself it was ridiculous to think that this was the Son of Sam. The killer wouldn't be this obvious; the guy across the street had to be some broad's husband or boy friend, Fazo thought. I hope he's engaged to some broad who's inside blowin' the United Parcel driver. Fazo opened the door and stepped out on the front steps so that the guy in the car would see him and would know that Fazo was looking at him. When the cream-colored car did not move, Fazo said aloud, "Come on, you miserable fuck. What are you doing here?" His voice did not reach the car, and the car did not move. Fazo became uncomfortable in the spotlights that played from the top of the building onto the restaurant entrance. If this degenerate across the street was Son of Sam, Fazo thought, he was giving the bum a beautiful shot. "Fuck this," he said. He stepped back into the restaurant, letting the door close.

"Call the police," he said to the bartender.

There was a sound outside. Fazo peered out just in time to see the cream-colored car speeding by the restaurant. In the few moments that Fazo had the restaurant door closed, the car had made a U-turn around the traffic island in the center of Cross Bay Boulevard and had come back past the Canal House.

"Let me get this fuck's number," Fazo said. He ran down the steps and onto the sidewalk, but it was too late. He was looking at red taillights.

"Sonuvabitch," Fazo muttered. He called up to the couple in the doorway. "All right, you can come on down now." After he saw the couple to their car, Fazo went back into the bar. "You call the police?" he said to the bartender.

"No, I was waiting for you to come back in," the bartender said.

"Well, it's too late now. The bum is gone."

"You think it could've been the guy?" the bartender said.

"How the hell do I know who he is?" Fazo said. "I know one thing. He was sittin' on us."

"Shit, I'm bringing a shotgun in with me tomorrow night," the bartender said.

As he drove away, Bernard whimpered. Why had Sam done this to him? Sam was in charge of tonight, he knew that. Mort was the one who was going to make him go out to the Hamptons and make the blood come up like tide. Sam Thornton, who wanted only one and two at a time, was his master tonight, and Sam was tormenting him. Why had Sam made him drive all the way down to this restaurant and then have this big guy come outside and scare him away? Here he had been sitting in the car, ready to get Sam some blood, with Sam howling and tearing at him, and at the same time Sam made the big guy come out of the restaurant.

Sam had been doing things like this all night, Bernard reminded himself. Rosenfeld had started the evening way out on Long Island, an hour's drive from the city. The road going into a town called Huntington was lined with bars, with cars parked in dark lots behind the bars. But each time Rosenfeld would slow down, or would drive into a parking lot, something would happen. A face would look at him. Car headlights suddenly would sweep over him like accusing fingers. He drove back into Queens, and nothing was right there, either. In front of the bar called Pep's Place on Hillside Avenue, there were only two cars. And through the window of the bar, he could see the bartender staring out at the street. Rosenfeld drove past, and out of the corner of his eye he could see the bartender watching the car. Not doing anything —just staring at the car. Bernard knew he had to keep going. He went onto the Belt Parkway until he came to the Aqueduct Race Track barns, which stood like military barracks. He came off the parkway at this point and into Howard Beach. He was sure he would get something at Howard Beach. He had been there so many times and there had been so many opportunities, but Sam never told him to take advantage of them. On this night, however, he was sure he would get the command.

But now, here he was, at 11:45 p.m., Saturday, July 16, 1977, driving out of Howard Beach, chased by somebody Sam caused to be present. Rosenfeld got back on the Belt Parkway and drove toward Brooklyn. The hunting had to be better in Brooklyn, he thought. Insides wrenched, ears dulled by the dogs, he could not face going back to his apartment and being tortured by demons who had not been fed their blood.

The parkway, going to Brooklyn, ran along the edge of Jamaica Bay. Across the water, a string of lights stood out. This was the Rockaway peninsula. The darkness beyond the lights was the ocean. He followed the amber lights of the parkway as it took him past marshlands, over creeks and then along the edge of Brooklyn, the part where the enormous borough, the fourth largest city in the United States, puts its shoulder into the Atlantic to form the entrance to New York Harbor. At an area called Sheepshead Bay, the parkway became an overpass, and as Rosenfeld looked down he saw the familiar light-blue fishing boat, the *Blue Marlin*, sitting in its slip, awaiting the early morning bluefish crowd. Now, on his right, was the white-brick Coney Island Hospital. He cruised on and reached the point where the Belt runs almost level with the water of the mouth of the harbor. On the right side of the road were the attached brick houses and apartment houses of Brooklyn. On the left side was the walkway along the seawall and the water and, in the water, just yards off the parkway, were the long, low, dark shapes of oil tankers riding at anchor.

He went under a footbridge going from the houses on the right side of the road to the walkway and benches along the seawall. Benches where people had been sitting for years, watching the great ships of the sea enter and leave. Bernard's head turned in panic as he went under the overpass. Was this the place? Had he gone past it? No, he told himself, the place he wanted was farther down. He could not be sure, however. He was so busy with this, looking around and questioning himself, that he was not ready when the next footbridge came up. He looked up in time to see "George THC" painted on it in big white letters, and then he was under it, past the spot, going along the road as it curved around and began heading for the great gray span leaping over to Staten Island, the Verrazano Bridge. Claws dug at the inside of his temples, reminding him that he had missed the turnoff. A sign said, "Bay Eighth Street."

He swung off the Belt and made an immediate right onto a street called Fifteenth Avenue and now he was in familiar territory, tree-lined streets and silent houses. He made a right on the first corner, Cropsey Avenue, and drove past houses, past a Texaco gas station. On a street called Bay Eighteenth, he made another right. This street was one-way. He went down to the end and made a right. This put him on Shore Road, which runs parallel to the Belt Parkway. An eight-foot-high chain link fence separated Shore Road from the Belt. Ahead, two short blocks ahead, was the footbridge he wanted: the footbridge and the cars parked along Shore Road, right up against the chain-link fence. He had been watching them for months, these couples who parked by the footbridge, walked over the footbridge to

267

look at the water, and then came back to their cars parked by the fence.

He made a right at the next corner, Bay Seventeenth Street, and drove slowly up the block looking for a parking space. On both sides of the street were three-story garden apartments. Halfway up the block, in front of the apartment-house entrance at 290 Bay Seventeenth Street, there was a space. A fire hydrant, painted black, with a silver top, stood at the curb. Many of the fire hydrants in the area still carried the red, white, and blue stripes of the 1976 bicentennial celebration. The striped ones mainly were on streets where people owned houses. This hydrant was on an apartment-house block and thus was unpainted. Rosenfeld pulled into the spot. He was disturbed that he had to break the law and park in front of a hydrant. He reminded himself that when he was a volunteer fireman in Co-Op City, he had maintained that any person caught parking in front of a fire hydrant should be fined $100. While he thought about this, he finished parking the car, got out, held the door for a moment, then shrugged and swung it shut and started walking. He had a job to do, and his job was more important than his beliefs. If he had to break the law to do his job, then that was the way it had to be. He was sorry that he had to block a fire hydrant, but he couldn't help it, he had to go out and kill somebody. Sam wanted him to.

He walked to Shore Road, turned right, and went to the next corner, Bay Sixteenth Street. He came to a small park, which was on his right. On his left was the eight-foot fence between the street and the Belt Parkway. Rosenfeld walked in the middle of the street, Shore Road, until he came to the footbridge. On his right was the entrance to the park. He looked around. Parked along the eight-foot fence, sitting under a brilliant sodium streetlight, was an empty tan Volaré. Across the parkway, along the seawall, were the dark forms of two couples watching the lights of the tankers and of the great bridge splash across the dark water like fiery diamonds. Bernard thought there were too many people on the walk along the seawall. He decided to go into the park. He went across to the entrance and went along the walk between sycamore trees which shielded the walk from streetlights. He went as far as a red-brick attendant's house which had been vandalized and gutted by fire and then he heard a squeak. Then another squeak. And another. The squeaking fell into a steady pattern. It was coming from the recesses of a play area behind the gutted house.

Rosenfeld looked into the darkness and made out the outline of a girl, sitting on an aluminum swing, riding back and forth, the swing squeaking gently in the night. His eyes adjusted to the darkness, and the hazy outline of the girl became clearer, and then he was able to see her face, and the brick walk under Bernard Rosenfeld's feet turned into a fire whose flames enveloped him.

As she swung forward, she came out of the shadow of the sycamore tree and the moonlight hit her, and the tiny droplets of spray in her platinum-blond hair glistened as if they were glass. Then she touched the apogee of her swing and fell back, gently, into the darkness, until she felt Vinny Masone's fingers press against the small of her back and send her forward again. She was completely relaxed, perched on an aluminum swing in a small playground within a dimly-lit park on the edge of the harbor where it washes up against the Bath Beach section of Brooklyn.

It had been a lovely night, Mitzi Levinson decided, this first date with Vinny Masone. They had gone to the Midwood Theater on Flatbush Avenue in Brooklyn to see *New York, New York*, the film with Liza Minnelli and Robert DeNiro, and as they came out, she noticed that a few people nodded at Vinny and said, "Doesn't he look a lot like Robert DeNiro?"

"To tell you the truth," she overheard someone else say, "I think he looks more like Al Pacino."

From the movie, they had walked to Aquarius, a disco only a couple of blocks away. The place had been filled, wall-to-wall people — the same fear that had destroyed the discos in Queens had kept the Brooklyn crowd in its home borough — and even though Mitzi loved the way Vinny moved on the dance floor, she was happy when after half an hour and one drink apiece, a rye and ginger for him and a grasshopper for her, he had suggested that they take a drive around, that they get a little air.

They walked to the garage in which he had parked his father's car, a tan Volaré, only eight months old, and after a black cowboy wheeled the car off a ramp, they climbed in and he drove to the Belt Parkway. He followed the parkway to Bath Beach, his own neighborhood, then exited onto Shore Road. At the corner of Bay Sixteenth Street, just past the small footbridge that arched over the highway,

Vinny found a parking place. He pulled in, in between an Impala and a Toyota, right under a streetlight, the brightest place on the block. The couples who had arrived earlier had taken all the good dark spots.

Vinny and Mitzi got out of the car and walked to the footbridge, then crossed over to the water. They leaned against the seawall, and he put his arm around her waist. With a summer breeze coming off the bay, his arm felt comfortable and reassuring.

"Look at all those stars," Vinny said. "You can see a million of them tonight. And that moon — full! It's really beautiful."

"And look at the water," Mitzi said. "It's like, you know, like a mystery."

They stood silently for several minutes, his hand on her waist moving just slightly, so that she could feel his presence.

They had met only three days earlier, on Wednesday, in the offices of a small trade magazine, based in Manhattan, which employed both of them. The magazine was devoted to the plumbing business, featuring everything from the latest in therapeutic shower sprays to the newest imported decorative faucet. Neither Vinny nor Mitzi had anything to do, directly, with the stories that ran in the magazine. Vinny was the assistant to the production manager, which meant mostly that he made certain that both editorial copy and advertising copy were carried promptly to the hands of the courier who would deliver it to the composing room of the printer in Philadelphia. For extra income, Vinny did odd jobs around the office. He painted walls. He repaired typewriters. He moved furniture.

Mitzi had just started work on Monday as secretary to the advertising director. He was the most important person on the magazine, because the advertising content was not only the major part of the magazine, it was the best. The ads, in fact, tended to be more literate than the few articles that ran in between them. The advertising director had asked Vinny to paint his office after work Wednesday and had also asked Mitzi to stay late to finish sending out invoices to the advertisers. In between her typing and his painting, they found out that they were both twenty-one and from Brooklyn. She lived in Flatbush. He lived in Bath Beach. They made a date for Saturday night. She gave him her address, and he said he would pick her up at eight-thirty. He showed up precisely at eight-thirty, which impressed her, and they were able to make the nine-o'clock show.

They spent almost half an hour looking at the water. Mitzi said she wanted to know everything about Vinny, what his dreams were, what his fears were, everything that would help her to understand him as a person. Her questions were longer than his answers, which were more controlled than she would have liked. She told him that she was an only child, and spoiled, and that her parents had urged her to go to college, but she had wanted to be a model. She had tried modeling for a year, she said, and the only paying job she got was posing as the victim of a mugging for the cover of a detective magazine. "I'll show you the magazine," she said. "I keep a copy of it at home. Only I'm lying in the street and you can't see my face. You wouldn't know it was me if I didn't tell you."

Vinny laughed. "I believe it's you," he said.

"Then I went to secretarial school, just for six months," Mitzi said. "I don't really want to be a secretary, not for long anyway. I want some kind of an administrative position, like maybe in personnel, but this is a good way to get started, and those skills, you know, will always come in handy."

"I want to go into some kind of electronics," Vinny said. "I'd like to be a television cameraman, something like that. There's a school for that, a couple of my brother's friends went there, and they got good jobs out of it. One of 'em works on the football games on Sunday, he gets to go all around the country, you know, Baltimore, Pittsburgh, Cincinnati, Miami, too, I think. I'd like to do that."

Vinny shook his head and smiled. "We got lots of time to make up our minds, I guess," he said. He brushed back his black hair with his hand, then reached for Mitzi's hand. She held his tightly. "C'mon," he said. "Let's go back across. I'll show you the swings in the park. I used to play on them when I was a kid."

And now she was sitting on one of the three swings, and he was pushing her, and they both were relaxed. They could see other people wandering through the park, even at this hour. There was a couple pausing to embrace. There were two guys together, one of them whistling. And there was one guy, all by himself, standing by the attendant's house. The guy alone, Vinny thought, almost looked as if he were smiling. But it was hard to tell in the dark.

Mitzi let her feet drag along the ground until she brought the swing to a halt. Vinny's hands rested on her shoulders. "I hate to go home," she said, "it's such a pretty night, but it is getting kind of late."

"Yeah, I know," Vinny said.

271

"Before you picked me up," she said, "my father said to me, 'I don't want you to stay out late, and I don't want you to go to Queens, understand?' "

"Your father said that?" Vinny said. "That's funny. My mother said the same thing. I mean, about Queens. I think my mother's more scared of that Son of Sam than anybody I know."

"I'm scared of him, too," Mitzi said. "I guess just about everybody is. I'm glad we stayed in Brooklyn, and I'm glad I decided five years ago I wanted my hair blond. It makes me feel safer these days."

"Yeah," Vinny Masone said. "I know what you mean." He massaged her shoulders. "Hey," he said, "it's such a bright night, it's so peaceful here, let's think about something else. I don't even want to think about that creep."

"Here we go," Chris McPartland said. He pulled the car over, picked up his ticket book and got out alongside a red LTD, which blocked the corner of Cropsey Avenue and Bay Seventeenth Street. McPartland stood in the glow of a streetlight, wrote out traffic ticket number 732932-1, and stuck it under the windshield wiper of the LTD.

"One more," he said to his partner, George Rizzo. McPartland liked to write a couple of tickets each night, so he wouldn't be caught trying to fill his quota at the end of the month. It's no fun trying to fill it on a day tour, he reminded himself, with people screaming at you while you write the things out.

The idea of a quota for tickets is neither scandalous nor arbitrary. The temper of the area, the Bath Beach part of Bensonhurst, demanded the issuance of a certain amount of tickets: it is a place which does not react too kindly to blocked driveways. If the police are visibly after such cars, particularly if each squad car in a sector is expected by the precinct commander to produce eight tickets for each five days of patrol, then residents, sensing official justice, retain their serenity.

It was a few minutes after midnight. McPartland drove along Cropsey Avenue looking for another violation. "Look at those fucks," he said, nodding toward all the cars parked legally, "not one of them giving me a good shot at him."

"You ought to give any of them a ticket so we can go someplace and relax," Rizzo said.

They drove down to Shore Road, turned onto Bay Seventeenth and then they both saw the cream-colored Galaxie parked in front of the fire hydrant outside the three-story garden apartment at 290 Bay Seventeenth Street.

The summons was number 732933-1, and as McPartland filled it in, he printed the license number 773-YTD in large block letters on the ticket, which is thin cardboard. The cardboard is torn and placed on the offending vehicle, while the carbon, which looks like an American Express receipt, is turned into the precinct at the end of a tour. It is recorded in a ledger and then tossed into a bin. The bin then is emptied and taken to the Parking Violations Bureau in Manhattan, which is in charge of collections.

McPartland put the ticket on the windshield of the Galaxie, got back into the squad car, and started off. "That takes care of that," he said. He slapped the ticket book onto the dashboard. A few minutes later, they were on Shore Road, passing the park and the steps going up to the footbridge over the Belt Parkway. They turned right on the first corner, went up three blocks, made another turn, and pulled into a space in front of a large frame house. McPartland parked the car in the deep shadows in front of the house and lit a cigarette.

He and Rizzo sat and smoked cigarettes and listened for the radio. Rizzo thought about what he would do on his days off. He'd better get at the boat, he told himself. If he didn't do it now, he might as well leave it in the garage all summer.

Johnny Dwyer and Herbie Klein were sitting in the back of a van parked outside Pablo Birani's apartment house. They had tailed him all evening, and, at eleven o'clock, they had seen him enter the building. Now it was well after midnight. "Quiet night," Klein said.

"I'd like to go home and get some sleep," Dwyer said.

"I got better things to do," Klein said.

Dwyer laughed. "Your wife really believe you're putting in sixteen-hour shifts three nights a week?"

"Sure. She don't like it, but she believes it. You know how many guys on the Task Force are telling their wives the same thing? Shit, got to be half the guys. My wife's going around telling all the neighbors I'm a hero, I'm going to catch Son of Sam all by myself."

Dwyer looked out through the side of the van, through the special two-way glass. He could see clearly, but no one could see in. The sidewalk in front of the apartment house was empty. Dwyer moved to the back of the van and looked out. He could see a small park a block away, a park with a fountain and benches and dozens of shade trees. A year earlier, there would have been a minimum of ten cars parked by the trees, with couples inside them in positions ranging from affection to lust. Now, the street was empty, and so was the park. No one sitting in a car. No one sitting on a bench. No one daring to tempt a friend — or the killer.

"I'm just asking," Dwyer said, "but who's the broad you been seeing?"

"The volunteer in the office. The social worker. The one who's answering phone calls. You know, the brunette with the big tits."

Dwyer whistled. "No kidding?" he said. "You fucking her?"

Klein suddenly looked sheepish. "You want to know the truth?" he said.

"Sure," Dwyer said.

"I ain't touched her," Klein said. "Don't tell none of the other guys. They all think I'm putting her away."

"You ain't touched her?"

"No," Klein said. "I mean, I think about it a lot. The way you Irish think about drinking, my people think about fucking. But all I do is have a cup of coffee with her and sit and talk with her and help her kill time till she meets her boy friend. He's a bartender. He don't get off work till three, sometimes four in the morning. She picks him up."

"And you keep her company till then?"

"Yeah."

Dwyer shook his head. "What about the dyed blonde in the office? The one who thinks she's Angie Dickinson?"

"She's a volunteer, too," Klein said. "She's a supervisor with the phone company."

"Who's knocking her off?" Dwyer said.

"Beats me," Klein said. "She acts like her shit don't smell."

"I'd like a piece of that," Dwyer said.

"It's better than beer," Klein said.

"Hey, look." Dwyer pointed up to the sixth floor, to the apartment Birani shared with his mother, a registered nurse. "He's looking out the window. Maybe he wants to wave good night to us."

"Sleep tight, Pablo," Klein said.

"Let's wait around a while," Dwyer said. "Let's give it another hour or so."

"You fucked half the state of California," Arthur Marchese said. He was talking to Errol Flynn, who was in the late movie on Channel 5. The movie was called *Dive Bomber*, but Marchese, sitting in his pajamas, in his darkened living room, was thinking about sex, not war. He remembered standing outside New Utrecht High School in the morning, waiting with everybody for the doors to open, and every face would be buried in the *Dispatch*, which was running all the testimony from the big statutory rape trial Flynn had to go through when two underage girls said that he had molested them. Marchese laughed as he remembered it. He waved his cigar at the set. "You ought to get the Congressional Medal of Honor for screwing all those young broads," Marchese said.

He sat alone in the living room of his apartment on the first floor of the building on the corner of Shore Road and Bay Seventeenth Street. Directly across the street from his building was the edge of the park, and from his bedroom window, open to the soft night, Marchese could see Shore Road clearly, including the spot under the sodium light, the one right near the steps to the footbridge, where a tan Volaré was parked.

Now Marchese cheered a Flynn dive-bombing run. "Go get —"

The sound of the four shots came through the open window. It was no car backfiring, Marchese knew that. On the television screen, Errol Flynn dove into noisy machine guns. Marchese did not hear them. His ears were filled with the sound of the four shots out on the street. He got up and went to his bedroom. A horn was blaring on Shore Road, up by the steps to the footbridge. Then he saw somebody leaning against the lamppost and shouting. Screaming actually.

Son of Sam, Marchese said to himself. Then he said it again, Son of Sam.

"It's that bastard!" he yelled.

His wife picked her head up from the bed. "What is it?" she said, frightened.

275

"A murder," Marchese said. He ran into the kitchen and dialed 911.

The phone rang four times at police headquarters.

"Police. Five-four-oh. What is the emergency?"

"Somebody just was shooting. I think it's Son of Sam. The shooting is on Shore Road between Bay Fifteenth and Sixteenth streets."

When Marchese got off the line, Alberto Torres, the police phone clerk, tapped out on his computer, "S2 10B4 X. On Bay 15, 16 streets, Shore Road. Report of shots fired at that location. I/2:13." Simultaneously, the green letters appeared on the terminals of Clint Brown, who was a glass partition away from Torres, and who was in charge of the radio for the Tenth Division in Brooklyn. Brown had on a headset and he was giving a cardiac call to the Sixtieth Precinct in Coney Island. Immediately after that, he would read off the Shore Road report. Tucked into a corner of the ninth floor of police headquarters was Eddie Ryan, a patrolman, who was handling the detective band. When he saw the "shots fired" come up on his terminal, he read it off immediately: "In the Six-two Precinct in Brooklyn. Location, Bay Fifteen, Bay Sixteen streets and Shore Road, report of shots fired that location. Units to respond."

Dominick Carillo, sitting at the radio table in the big squad room at the 109th Precinct, stiffened as he heard the report.

In the patrol car parked in the shadows in front of a large frame house, George Rizzo jumped as he heard the radio report. McPartland's head automatically came up. He had the car moving as Rizzo picked up the radio microphone, held it for a moment, then said, "Six-two-Charlie, on the way." Rizzo fell backward as the car lurched into a burst of speed.

In Bensonhurst, Bernard Rosenfeld, still huffing from his run of almost two blocks, drove straight up Bay Seventeenth. He went across Cropsey Avenue and kept going. Across Eighty-sixth Street, and then he began turning. He had no reason, he just began turning. He found himself on Eighteenth Avenue, leading into the center of Brooklyn. He decided to stay on this street. He neither saw nor heard police cars. He put on the radio to an all-news station, 1010, WINS, and he waited for news about himself. "I got him, too," Rosenfeld said aloud. "He tried to duck, but I got him, too. Oh, I know I got him."

24

When McPartland got out of the car, he saw a young guy in a brown sports jacket stretched out on a blanket somebody had put on the sidewalk. A towel was under his head. The towel, saturated with blood, caused the people trying to assist the victim to turn their faces away.

"Shot," somebody said.

"Son of Sam."

"Christ!"

McPartland looked down at the young guy on the sidewalk. "You're going to be all right," he said.

Rizzo came trotting over. "The girl in the car doesn't even know she's hit," Rizzo said.

"Where is she hit?" McPartland said.

"Right in the back of the head."

"Shit," McPartland said. He dove into the squad car and grabbed the phone. "Six-two-Charlie to Central K," he said.

"Go ahead, Charlie."

"Put a rush on an ambulance to Bay Sixteenth and Shore Road. We have two people shot, one male, one female. Young people. In a parked car. Have the Homicide Squad and the Boss respond."

Just as Dwyer and Klein were getting ready to pack up and move out, the radio connecting them to the 109th Precinct crackled to life. "Flushing Base to all cars," they heard Sergeant Hanlon say. "We have a report from the Tenth Division Dispatcher of a couple shot in a parked car in the Six-two. Shore Road and Bay Sixteenth."

Then a pause, no more than ten seconds. "Sergeant Coffey is responding," Hanlon said.

"That's in Brooklyn," Klein said.

"Bath Beach," Dwyer said. "Got to be some wise guy caught his wife."

He looked up at the sixth floor. Still dark. No lights in Birani's apartment. "Just in case," Dwyer said, "why don't you go wait by the elevator?"

Klein got out of the back of the van, went to the door of Birani's apartment house, rang the bell for the night porter, and showed his police identification. Then, for the first time since they had placed Birani under surveillance several months earlier, he went inside the apartment house.

Dwyer waited in the van. In ten minutes, the next message came from Sergeant Hanlon. "Coffey says it appears to be Flushing-related," Dwyer heard. *Flushing-related. Flushing-related!* "Motherfuckin' sonuvabitch cocksucker," Dwyer said. "Our guy."

In the 109th Precinct, Carillo carefully picked up his pipe. His hand started to go for the tobacco pouch, but his fingers fumbled with it. He put the pipe down. He pressed his hands against his hair. His eyes remained on the radio, as if he could see the words before hearing them. And inside him, he tried to fight the elation. This is the only way, a voice was saying inside him; it's a shame that somebody had to get hurt, but that's the way it goes. But now we got him out in the open. He screwed us; he's in Brooklyn. But he's out there somewhere, driving around in his car. We got a real shot at him. Goddamnit, maybe we can get him tonight.

Carillo shook his head when he thought of all the rest of it, the prints and the records. What the hell good were they? Here was how you get this guy. Yeah, it's a shame somebody had to get hurt, but — Carillo's chin began to shake with excitement — we have him where we want him, out on the streets.

The bridges, Carillo reminded himself. Get ready to shut the bridges down. Then Carillo's face became pain, and he closed his eyes. The guy hit in Brooklyn. That meant he could take bridges and tunnels that never figured in Carillo's planning, bridges without tollgates, some of them. The thrill of the chase submerged Carillo's doubts. We'll figure some way to nail the bastard, he told himself.

Now, at this moment, Carillo told himself that the killer lived in the Bronx and that the killer would be trying to get there and that he, Carillo, would have men waiting for him. The thought sent a sudden thrill rippling through him. He hated the sensation: two people were hurt somewhere in order for him to have this feeling. It was the work of the devil. Then he forgot the two people, and another thrill went through him as his imagination told him what the capture was going to be like.

The voice on the radio interrupted his thoughts.

"Inspector? This is Dwyer. We're outside Birani's apartment. Should we go up? Should we wait? What?"

There was silence for about five seconds that seemed to Dwyer like a thousand. "Hit it," Carillo said, finally. "Go on up."

Dwyer flew out of the van, raced to the building, flashed his identification, and grabbed Klein. "Let's go." They pressed for the elevator, waited for the door to open, got inside, pressed six, and waited forever for the door to close. The elevator crawled up five flights to the sixth floor.

Dwyer and Klein jumped out and ran to Apartment 6A. Klein leaned on the bell. Dwyer rapped on the door with his fist. In fifteen seconds, the door opened up a crack, the safety latch still on it. A woman in a nightgown peeked out under the metal chain. "What is it?" she said.

"Police," Dwyer said. He held out his badge. "Open up."

Birani's mother was too tired to argue. She opened the door.

"Where's your son?" Dwyer said.

"Sleeping," the mother said.

"Where?"

"In his room. Back there." She pointed to a room off the living room.

"Get him."

The mother disappeared into the back room, and in a minute, the door opened wide and Pablo Birani, in pajamas, came into the living room, his deep eyes blinking out the sleep.

Dwyer wanted to cry.

"Yes?" Birani said.

"Pablo Birani?" Dwyer said.

"Yes?"

"I'm Detective Dwyer. This is Detective Klein. We're investigating a bank robbery in Forest Hills yesterday and —"

Dwyer and Klein wasted five minutes on their false interrogation.

Then they fled from Birani's apartment, jumped into the van, and raced to Brooklyn, from the Van Wyck Expressway to the Belt Parkway, breaking all speed limits, the legal and the logical. When he saw the flashing red lights of patrol cars and the crowd gathered at Shore and Bay Sixteenth, Dwyer jammed on the brakes, spun into a U-turn, and pulled off the highway onto the grass. He ran from the van to the tan Volaré lit by television lights. He could see the bloodstains on the sidewalk.

"Yeah?" Dwyer said to Sergeant Coffey.

"Our guy," Joe Coffey said. "No ballistics yet, but I'd swear it. Two kids. Boy and a girl. Shot them both in the head."

"Cocksucker," Dwyer said.

"Tough," a reporter said, sympathetically.

Dwyer shook his head. "Worse than tough," he said. "There goes our number-one suspect out the window. And number two and number three and number four." He paused. "There go all our good suspects out the window. We had 'em all under surveillance tonight."

Dwyer walked up to the car and stared at the pool of blood on the front seat. He could almost see his own reflection in it. "We know less now than we knew yesterday," Dwyer said. He kicked at the ground. "We don't know a lousy fucking thing."

McPartland and Rizzo, in the patrol car, siren wailing, led the ambulance carrying the boy and the girl right up to Coney Island Hospital. Doors swinging, aluminum clicking, wheels grinding on the floor, the victims were wheeled into the emergency room. In a couple of minutes, the ambulance driver came out and yelled, "Kings County, we gotta get out there." There was a click of aluminum, and the first stretcher came rolling back out of the emergency room.

McPartland's siren screamed at late-night drivers in his path as he led the ambulance up Ocean Parkway and then off to the right, off into the heart of Brooklyn. Ahead, the towering gloom of Kings County Hospital Center, one of the largest physical plants in the nation, was outlined against the night sky.

Doctors in green smocks waited in the lights of the emergency-room entrance. McPartland jumped out, looking for something to put his hands on, the side of a stretcher, the door, anything, but attendants were everywhere and, as he stood there, the girl was carried past him, still and pale, and then the young guy, a new towel soaking up some of the blood on his face. The two victims were through the doors and now they were not McPartland's business anymore. But he was caught up in it. By being there, by the simple act of driving a car, he had become a part of it. McPartland walked through the emergency-room doors and stood in the entranceway to the trauma rooms. A man in a gray business suit was standing there.

"You with the hospital?" McPartland said.

"I'm the night administrator in charge."

"All right, then," McPartland said. "You can go in."

When the two were taken upstairs to the X-ray rooms, McPartland rode up in the elevator with them. He was there for ten minutes. Then he saw the gold badges of detectives walking down the hallway and he decided to leave. He and Rizzo drove back to Shore Road. The street was white with floodlights from both a free-lance television crew and the forensics unit.

McPartland called in that he was back at the scene of the crime. When he received only a ten-four, he and Rizzo got out of the car, ducked under the ropes, and began to pace up and down, looking for evidence. There were too many doing that, he decided, so he walked over to the car, got a flashlight, and then went into the park and began inspecting the path. Halfway along it, the light fell on a new silver cufflink. He picked it up with a handkerchief and, balancing it lightly on his palm, walked back to the roped-off area. He found Gene Laughlin, a homicide detective he knew well from the Sixty-second Precinct. He handed it to Laughlin, who gave it to a forensics man. Laughlin was signing a voucher for the evidence when a voice called out, "What's that for?"

Laughlin turned to see Inspector Carillo, who had just arrived. "For the evidence the patrolman found and turned in to me," Laughlin said.

"Well, thank you," Carillo said, "but this is the Homicide Task Force's job."

"Inspector, I got a shooting right under my nose," Laughlin said. "I mean, this is my territory."

"Yes, I know. But we are handling this case."

"Inspector, are you telling me I shouldn't work on a homicide in my own backyard?"

"Of course not. But too many people in here will get us mixed up."

"Inspector, my boss, Lieutenant Fitzsimmons, told me that I caught this case. If it's my ass, then it's my ass. And if it's my ass, then I'm protecting my ass."

Sergeant Coffey came up. "Hey, who told you to —"

Carillo held a hand out. "That's it," he said to Coffey. Then, turning to Laughlin, he said, "You're right to worry about it if the Lieutenant said you caught the case. You just keep working on it, and if anything is going to change, you'll hear it from superior officers. All right?"

"Right," Laughlin said. Laughlin gave McPartland a pat on the stomach. "Brooklyn can handle this one, right, Mac?"

McPartland nodded. "I'm going in now," he said.

"All right, Mac," Laughlin said. "We'll see you."

"The guy looked a lot worse than the girl," one of the reporters, a guy from the *Dispatch*, was saying. "You see the blood on him?"

"Yeah," the one from the *Times* said. "She looked like she'll be all right. Probably just grazed her skull. I didn't even see any blood. But the guy, I mean I don't see how he can make it."

"Yeah."

They talked softly as they stood in the corridor next to the emergency entrance to Kings County Hospital Center. They talked softly because they were in a hospital, and because they were standing right outside a small alcove that had been turned into a waiting room. Mitzi Levinson's mother and father were sitting in the alcove, along with an aunt, a cousin, and Henry Glenville, the reporter from the *Express*. Glenville had his arm around the mother, Leah Levinson. He was calling her "Mom," and offering her Kleenex to dry her tears.

The two reporters in the hallway were guys on the lobster shift, working from midnight till 8:00 a.m. Often, on that shift, they had nothing to do, or nothing meaningful, but now, at five o'clock in the morning, they were at the heart of a major story, a double shooting that appeared to be the work of Son of Sam. What made the story even bigger was that it was his first strike outside the Bronx or Queens, his first attack upon a blonde.

The two newspapermen had been sent straight from their office to the hospital. (Another pair of reporters, also representing the two morning papers, had gone to Shore Road and Bay Sixteenth, and photographers had been dispatched to both places.) They had been the first two reporters to reach the hospital. They had gotten there, remarkably, just as the victims were being brought in, fully an hour before the girl's parents arrived. The two of them had been stunned to see that when Mr. and Mrs. Levinson got out of their car and walked to the emergency entrance, Henry Glenville was with them. It was obvious from his flaming eyes and his whisky breath that he had not been roused from sleep, that he had somehow made it from a saloon to the home of one of the victims in an incredibly short time. And now, not even an hour later, he had clearly ingratiated himself with the family. Glenville's performance — he hovered around the family as if he were half lapdog and half watchdog — was distasteful to observe, but, journalistically, it was useful to him.

Now, other reporters began gathering in the hospital, one from the Associated Press, another from United Press International, and then a couple of radio men clutching their Sony recorders. The television crews were conspicuously absent. They would be the last to arrive for several reasons, many of them economic. To begin with, at most of the stations, the man on the assignment desk was the only person in the local news office in the middle of the night. He was usually a person with little experience and less authority. He could not order out a full crew at overtime rates without consulting with his news director. His news director, upon being awakened, had to stop and think about whether he should order in an overtime crew. He knew the freelancers, out roaming the streets and monitoring the police frequencies, would already be at the scene, shooting the mandatory shots of the blood-stained car and the investigating officers and the bystanders. He also knew that by the time he could get one of his own crews notified, equipped, and on the road to the scene of the shooting, all the traces of the shooting — the victims, the car, the bullets, the blood — would either have been carried away or cleaned up.

Besides, the man on the assignment desk said there was no official word from ballistics as to whether the shooting was actually the work of the .44-caliber killer. The site of the shooting was certainly out of his usual area, and if it turned out to be just another double shooting, why then it really wasn't worth it to call in an extra crew. No point in calling in a crew early, either. That would mean premium payments. All three networks were eager to put up $75 million or more for the privilege of covering the Olympic Games in Moscow, but nobody could come up with a few hundred in premium payments for an early crew. The news director told the man on the assignment desk to be sure to send the first regularly scheduled crew that came in right to Kings County Hospital Center. By then, they might know whether the double shooting was the work of the alleged .44-caliber killer, and it would be easier to decide what to do with the later crews.

There was also one other reason the television crews would show up last. A television reporter couldn't just grab a ball-point and a notebook and dash out the door and rush to the scene of a crime. He had to shave and wash his hair and blow-dry it — for a woman reporter, there would be even more work — or otherwise all the information he might gather wouldn't do him any good: if he looked bad on camera, he might as well not do the story.

The newspapermen and the radio reporters at Kings County Hospital Center looked terrible, grubby, unshaven. They could afford to. The television reporters would show up eventually, looking as if they were attending a wedding.

A doctor came walking down the hall, and the reporter from the Associated Press got to him first. "Any word yet on the bullet?" the AP man asked. "Is it a forty-four?"

The doctor was an intern who happened to be on duty in the emergency room when the victims were brought in. "I heard some of the police talking," he said. "I think I heard one of them say it is not a forty-four-caliber bullet. I think I heard one of them say it is a thirty-eight."

"You sure, Doc?" the reporter said.

"I'm pretty sure," the intern said.

"Thanks, Doc."

The AP man did not go back into the hallway where the other reporters were waiting. He went straight to a pay phone in the lobby, called his office, and began dictating aloud: "A doctor at Kings County Hospital Center indicated this morning that a double shooting in the Bath Beach section of Brooklyn was not the work of Son of Sam. The doctor said that he had been told by police officers that the bullet found in one of the victims was not a forty-four-caliber bullet, Son of Sam's trademark. The bullet is believed to be a thirty-eight. . . ."

The wire service moved the story as a bulletin, and when it came into the offices of the daily newspapers, deskmen frantically radioed and telephoned their men at Kings County to have the AP report verified. It took about ten minutes for the intern's story to be knocked down. The doctor who had taken charge of the victims told a hasty and informal press conference that no one knew for certain the caliber of the bullet; that no bullet had yet been removed from either of the victims. He said that based on the size of the entry wound — and at Kings County he had seen plenty of gunshot wounds — he believed it was a large-caliber bullet, quite possibly a .44.

By six o'clock, the parents of Vinny Masone were at the hospital. They came walking down the corridor toward the Levinsons, and Marty Levinson, Mitzi's father, a husky man, got up and walked toward the Masones, and he and Lou Masone, who had never met before, threw their arms around each other. Leah Levinson greeted the Masones, too. "What a handsome boy your son is," she said, "and so polite. A lovely boy."

Henry Glenville quickly shepherded the Levinsons back into the alcove where they had been waiting, and he guided the Masones in, too, cutting between them and a cluster of reporters waiting to ask them questions. "Give them a break, mates, will you?" Glenville said. "It's a terrible ordeal. They really can't talk now." And he went back to sit with the families and listen to their sadness and share their vigil, which, he thought, would give him an exclusive story in Monday afternoon's *Express*.

Soon, the more adventurous reporters from other publications began invading the alcove, seeking to establish basic biographical facts about the victims, correct spellings of their names, ages, schooling, jobs, simple necessities of the journalist's trade. As Glenville shooed one rival out, two came in, and as he realized he was losing the battle, he ducked out of the alcove, went into a hospital administrator's office, and emerged five minutes later with a small, but smug smile on his face. The smile vanished when he saw Marty Levinson about to hand a snapshot of his daughter, Mitzi, to the reporter from the *Dispatch*. Glenville whisked the photo out of Levinson's extended hand and turned to him and said, "You really don't want to do that, mate, it isn't a good idea," and Marty Levinson nodded and took back the picture and replaced it in his billfold and permitted Glenville to lead him away from the man from the *Dispatch*.

A few minutes later, the hospital administrator came to the alcove and invited the Levinsons and Masones and their relatives to use a small conference room, where they could have some privacy during their wait. At Mrs. Levinson's insistence, Henry Glenville joined the Levinsons and the Masones in the conference room. "He's like family," she said.

A short time later, both families emerged, but just briefly. The two victims were being taken to surgery, Mitzi Levinson right there in the main building of Kings County Hospital Center, Vinny Masone to an ophthalmological building close by. Mitzi did not look bad as she was wheeled past her family on a stretcher. That was because she was lying on her back. One bullet had merely grazed her scalp, but a second had gone into the base of her skull, in the back, shattered a bone, and lodged in the cerebellum. If the bullet were not removed swiftly, and skillfully, if the bone fragments were not also removed, she would not live out the day. The doctors knew that even if she did live, the odds were that she would be severely damaged mentally. They did not tell all of this to the Levinsons.

"My beautiful baby," Leah Levinson said, as she watched the stretcher go by. "She's so still."

Vinny looked much worse, but actually, he was better. His blood was visible, but his vital signs, unlike Mitzi's, were strong. The bullet that had struck him went in through the left temple, shattered the left eye, ripped across the nose and exited above the right eyebrow. The left eye was destroyed, the right one devastated. Without immediate surgery, a doctor paused to tell the Masones, Vinny would surely be blind. With immediate surgery, Vinny would probably still be blind. Lou Masone, when he heard this, let out a short, low half-scream, as if he were being strangled, and he spun and slammed a clenched fist against a cement wall. Then he pounded the wall with both fists until a pair of uniformed policemen grabbed him and held him and forced him to stop punishing himself.

"Why, why, why, why?" he moaned, and he turned back to see his son on a stretcher, being lifted into the ambulance that would take him a few hundred feet to the building for ophthalmological surgery.

"Daddy, Daddy," Vinny Masone said softly and clearly.

Then the two stretchers were gone, in opposite directions, and Henry Glenville secluded the families once more.

When Patrolman McPartland arrived at the Sixty-second Precinct, there was a swarm of people both behind and in front of the desk. Somewhere in the middle of the crowd, the desk lieutenant's head bobbed around like a quarterback in a huddle. The lieutenant didn't even acknowledge McPartland and Rizzo; he was barely able to handle inspectors.

McPartland and Rizzo went downstairs to their lockers. McPartland unbuckled his belt which, with gun, handcuffs, bullets, and summons book, felt as if bricks were hanging from it. He removed the gun, put the belt on the locker shelf, put the gun on the belt on his civilian slacks, and changed clothes. Son of Sam, he told himself in wonder. The biggest case maybe the department ever had. He slammed the locker door, but it would not shut. The thick end of the black summons book was in the way. He pushed the book and the belt farther in on the shelf, then slammed the locker door, made sure it was locked, and, pulling his shirt down over the gun so that it would not show, walked up the stairs and slipped through the crowded main room of the precinct. Deer Park, the place on Long Island where he lived, normally was an hour's drive. In the empty Sunday-morning traffic, he figured he could be home in fifty minutes.

"I'm beat," he said to Rizzo. He slipped into his car, and Rizzo walked over to his.

Half an hour later, Inspector Carillo and Sergeant Hanlon walked into the noise and smoke of the Sixty-second Precinct. Behind the desk, a captain and a lieutenant looked up.

"Anybody give out any tickets last night?" Carillo said.

The lieutenant looked through a ledger book, shook his head no, and then leaned over and went through a batch of tickets in a bin. He looked up. "Nothing from that sector at all," he said. " 'Course, once the shots were fired, nobody looked to give out tickets."

Sergeant Hanlon slapped the rail in front of the desk. "Doesn't this guy make any mistakes?"

Carillo said quietly, "Come on now, you know he made mistakes tonight. We got a good eyewitness."

"But you'd think a fingerprint, a traffic ticket . . ." Hanlon said.

"Let's get coffee," Carillo said.

Across the street from the Kings County Hospital Center, in a bakery shop operated by and for Black Muslims, Danny Cahill stood with Johnny Dwyer. "I just got to wait," Dwyer said. "The Inspector told me to stay here till they get a bullet out and then get the bullet to ballistics, so that's what I'm doing."

Cahill leaned against a poster of the late Elijah Muhammad and sipped at a cup of black coffee. The Black Muslim bakery did not serve Sanka. Cahill stared at a photo of Muhammad Ali behind the counter. This was the only place open in the neighborhood on a Sunday morning.

"There ain't no chance, is there?" Cahill said. "I mean, it's got to be your guy, right, nobody else?"

"Sure," Dwyer said. "The one bullet they found in the car was too banged up for ballistics, but I make it a hundred to one it's the fuck."

"Anybody see anything?" Cahill said.

"You didn't get this from me, you know," Dwyer said.

Cahill nodded.

"They got a witness," Dwyer said. "A couple of witnesses, anyway, but one real good one, a young girl. They all say that a guy came out of the park, walked slowly up to the car, went into that combat shooter's crouch — you know, like you see on the TV, two hands on the gun — and fired. Then he went back into the park. One guy says he ran. The girl says he walked. The girl, she says she swears she can identify the guy if she ever sees him again. She says she'll never forget it. She sure as hell shouldn't. Now get this, let me tell you how she happened to see him. She's parked in a car, maybe two cars or three, in front of Masone. She's with her boy friend in the front seat, and the way I get it, she had just finished blowing him, and now he's going to go down on her. She sits on his lap facing him, and he sort of slides down, halfway to the floor, and she arches herself up so her pussy is in his face. The boy friend must be some kind of contortionist. But, anyway, she's enjoying it, and she's looking out the back window, not really thinking about anything except what's between her legs, and she sees this guy come out of the park and go for the two kids. I mean, she sees every step, and at the same time, she's got this guy's tongue in her. She lets out a scream, and she's not even sure now whether it was from coming or from seeing the shooting. That's the story. You tell me how you're going to get that in your newspaper."

Dwyer was telling the story in full voice. The proprietor of the bakery heard the whole thing and looked at the two white men and

288

shook his head. Elijah Muhammad was right, he thought. Blue-eyed devils.

"What does she say the guy looks like?" Cahill said.

"I don't know," Dwyer said. "Three different guys told me that story, but nobody bothered to tell me what she said the guy looked like." Dwyer turned to the owner of the bakery. "Give me five dollars' worth of rolls and pastry and cookies," he said. "Mix it all up." He turned back to Cahill. "Got to take care of the nurses so I can stay up there by the OR and wait for the bullet. They got plenty of coffee up there."

"What kind of shape are the kids in?"

"The girl's bad," Dwyer said. "She may not make it. The boy, there's only one chance in a thousand he'll ever see again."

"That motherfucker," Cahill said. He went across to the hospital, and just as he was walking in the emergency entrance, Marty Levinson, the girl's father, was going outside for a smoke. Somebody pointed out the father to Cahill, and he went up and introduced himself and said it was a terrible thing that happened. "I always wanted to meet you," Marty Levinson said. "I like your writing."

"Thanks," Cahill said.

"My wife, I'm sure she'd like to meet you, too," Levinson said. "She went home for a while to get herself straightened up. The doctor said there's nothing we can do for the next few hours. We can just wait."

"It's a goddamn shame," Cahill said.

"Why don't you come in and wait with us?" Marty Levinson said. "The hospital's been real good. They gave us our own room to wait in. Come on in."

When Henry Glenville saw Danny Cahill coming into the conference room, to share the families with him, his face fell as if it had been he who was shot.

At eleven-fifteen on Sunday night, when Patrolman McPartland came back to work, there was a relief captain just walking out. "We had a day here," he said, shaking his head. McPartland went downstairs and got dressed. He put on his belt, attached the gun to it, pushed the summons book back into place, and went up to turn out. He spent the night patrolling the few blocks around the scene of the shooting. Keep letting the people see you, the sergeant ordered. Maybe somebody will offer you something we can use.

The car came through the Battery Tunnel, the underwater connection between the Brooklyn end of Long Island and the lower end of Manhattan Island. When he emerged from the Manhattan end of the tunnel, the driver maneuvered onto the strip of highway that curls around the bottom of Manhattan, and, at some mysterious point, changes from the West Side Highway to the East River Drive or, as it is officially known, the Franklin D. Roosevelt Drive. The car headed up the FDR Drive. Below Fourteenth Street the drive separates a massive housing development from a series of small parks on the edge of the East River. "A perfect place for Sam," the driver said.

"There's a million perfect places now," Danny Cahill said.

It was Monday morning, the day after the shooting, and he was on his way up to the *Dispatch*. He had gotten a friend of Shelly Cohen's, the saloonkeeper, to drive him to Brooklyn so that he could walk around by Shore Road and Bay Sixteenth Street. There were still a few dark stains on the sidewalk where Vinny Masone had fallen out of the car, screaming for somebody to help. Otherwise, there were no signs left of the shootings.

Cahill had been out in the Hamptons, where he had a summer house, when the killer struck. He had been planning to take a week off from his column. "You won't see me till a week from Monday," he had told the city editor on Friday. He reached the Hamptons by 2:00 a.m. Saturday and then he had gotten the phone call at 2:45 a.m. Sunday. By eight-thirty in the morning, he was at Kings County Hospital Center, and he had worked right through till midnight. Then he had gone out and gotten drunk. He had had five hours of sleep Friday night, two Saturday and four Sunday, and now he was dragging.

He had written about the families, about the agony of their wait for word about their children, and the point he had made was that these were not special people, that it could have been any family. Now his column was on the newsstands, and every newspaper, every radio station, every television station was spreading the same message: No one is safe; there are no longer geographical limits as to where the killer will strike. Now that he has strayed into Brooklyn, no one can say that Manhattan will not be next, or Staten Island, or Jersey, or Connecticut, or even the Hamptons. Forget the blond wigs and the close-cropped hair, Son of Sam is not looking for scalps, he is looking for blood. With one terrible strike, the killer had cut across so many mythical boundaries: a different borough, a different hair color, even a different religion. Jews, Catholics, Protestants all shared the same fear. White killing white, it was a switch.

"Now it could be panic," Cahill said to the guy who was driving. "Now everybody's a vigilante."

At the 109th Precinct, there were two dozen telephone lines in operation, and every line was in use every minute. "I got a boarder," one caller was telling an auxiliary cop, "and just for one thing, he keeps changing the color of his car every six weeks. It's a Volkswagen, and in the past four months, it's been red, yellow, and now black. He used to be a perfect boarder, you know, neat, polite, paid his rent on time. Then, about a year ago, he broke up with his girl friend. Or, actually, she broke up with him."

"Uh huh," the auxiliary cop said.

"He hasn't been the same since," the caller went on. "He snaps at my wife. He says all women are whores. He's angry, too, because he says he's a writer and he can't get anybody to publish his writing. And, oh, yeah, I know he's got a gun. I don't know what kind, but he's got a gun, I saw him cleaning it once. Looked to me like the pictures in the paper of the forty-four."

"Anything else?"

"He goes out late at night, very late, and sometimes he comes home at four and five in the morning, and sometimes he don't come home at all."

The tips, the suggestions poured in in incredible numbers — and incredible detail. If one out of every ten calls could be believed — and nine out of ten rang true — then the City of New York contained dozens or hundreds, perhaps thousands, of potential mass murderers. That was the scary part. Only one bomb had gone off in one head, and already five young people were dead because of it, but anybody working on the case knew that there were dozens of similar bombs, ticking inside similar heads, each one capable of exploding momentarily or never. Pablo Birani was not the .44-caliber killer, but he could have been. Pablo Birani could kill. He could kill without motive, without reason. He had a good mind; he was an intelligent man. It was just that his wires were crossed.

Sergeant Hanlon took a break from the phones to smoke a cigarette. "You hear what happened last night?" he said to Detective Dwyer. "We get a phone call from a bartender in Bayside who says he's got a crazy in his place, a mental patient, and he says the guy's talking about the shootings like he did it. So we send Cami and Reid over there to check it out, and just as they're walking in the door of the bar, they bump into a guy hurrying out. They stop him and he's wearing a little wristband identifying him as a patient at some nuthouse upstate. So they grab him and walk inside, and the bartender says, 'No, that's not the guy, the guy in the blue shirt.' They look down the end of the bar and see a guy in a blue shirt and grab him and he turns out to be an outpatient at Bronx State. The bartender shakes his head again and says, 'No, the one in the *dark* blue shirt.' They end up grabbing three guys, and all three of them turn out to be mental patients — all in one bar at one time. And those were three guys who didn't do anything. This time."

"We don't get this guy soon," Dwyer said, "we're all going to be in the loony bin. I can't take much more of this shit. Three different people told me today the guy has got to be a cop, that's the only way he could get away with all this. Have we checked out every guy on the force?"

"Sure," Hanlon said, "but we could have missed somebody. Who the fuck knows? I ain't eliminating anybody."

An older detective walked into the room. "Just one thing," he said. "It ain't a Jew."

"How do you figure that?" Hanlon said.

"No Jew's going to go around shooting people like this," the older detective said. "There ain't no money in it."

On the streets, in offices, in schools, in homes, no one was talking about anything except Son of Sam and the shootings. The Yankees were in a pennant race, the Mets were not, and nobody in New York gave a damn. There was a killer on the loose. If you read the *Dispatch* and the *Express*, you would think that nothing else was happening in the whole world. They didn't even give Sadat a mention for talking about the prospects for peace in the Middle East. The *Times*, despite its editors' knowledge that even *its* audience cared about nothing except the shootings, stuck to tradition and refused to devote more than thirty percent of its front page to Son of Sam. Sadat got almost a whole column on the *Times*'s front page; nobody on the subways or the commuter trains even noticed him. The *Express* outdid itself. The bottom half of the front page was a picture of the bodies being lifted out of the car. The top half was just four words:

YOU
COULD
BE NEXT

Malcolm Bromwich, the publisher, was very proud of the front-page headline. He had written it himself.

Inside the *Express*, two full pages were devoted to Henry Glenville's "EXCLUSIVE!!! Death Watch with the Families." The story contained three facts and four hundred adjectives. Glenville paid tribute mostly to the families' courage and to his own compassion. His heart went out to these brave people twice in three paragraphs; an editor should have caught that.

293

The television coverage was less hysterical, mostly because the television stations were handicapped by a lack of pictures. They had all purchased the same basic footage from the one free-lance camera crew that had covered the site of the shootings, but that footage showed neither of the victims, showed only the bloody car and the moon overhead and the neighboring parkway and a handful of policemen examining the car. No camera crew—only still photographers—had gotten to the hospital before the two victims were moved to surgery, so there was no footage at all of Mitzi Levinson or of Vinny Masone, just some long shots of the families and some artistic exteriors of Kings County Hospital Center.

The only way the television stations could beat the newspapers was with timeliness. Gil Rodgers went on the air, live, at two-forty-five Monday afternoon. He cut right into the middle of an adult soap opera. It was an adult soap opera because it dealt not with standard soap opera pap, but with "real" crises: Gladys had just found that Damon was being unfaithful—with another man. "We interrupt this program to bring you a special news bulletin," a voice said, and the picture of the soap opera faded from the screen and was replaced by a slide saying: "Instant News."

Then the slide gave way to a shot of Gil Rodgers sitting behind a typewriter in the newsroom. Other reporters, at their desks, were in the background. Rodgers had heard the countdown, "Five . . . four . . . three . . . two . . ."—the "one" was never spoken because, if the count was slightly off, the "one" might be heard on the air—and then, as he had been taught, he kept his head lowered for two more seconds, creating an air of drama, then brought his head up, bearing an appropriately somber look. "Mitzi Levinson," Rodgers began, "the young Brooklyn woman who was shot early yesterday by the so-called forty-four-caliber killer, died in Kings County Hospital Center just a few minutes ago. She was twenty-one years old. Miss Levinson underwent a six-hour operation this morning in an attempt to alleviate swelling of the brain stem. The brain damage was irreversible and caused a series of heart stoppages which culminated in death. Vincent Masone, Miss Levinson's companion Saturday night, is in serious condition, but he is expected to survive. Doctors say it will be weeks, perhaps even months, before they will know whether or not young Masone may regain part of his vision."

The same words came over the AP machine at the *Dispatch*. A copyboy ripped them off and ran one of the five copies to Danny Cahill's desk. Cahill read the words and folded his fist around the sheet of paper and squeezed it into a small ball. "Six dead, seven hurt," he said, "and nobody knows what the bastard looks like except, maybe, a broad who was getting eaten."

On Tuesday morning, after two nights of patrolling the vicinity of the crime, Patrolman McPartland went off duty at 8:00 a.m. He had the next three days free, and instead of going right to sleep when he got home to Deer Park, he walked into the kitchen and took a twelve-ounce can of beer out of the refrigerator. He walked out the back door and stood in the sun on the stoop and drank the cold beer. The first swallow filled his mouth with mildly bitter, pungent malt. The second mouthful was colder and sweeter. He needed a couple of beers. Right now, he was missing the excitement of patrolling the murder scene, the thrill of imagining that he could find the killer walking down one of the streets.

His wife came into the kitchen with the two kids. "Ready?" she said.

"Yep," McPartland said. He threw the empty cans into the garbage and followed his wife and kids out to the car. They drove to her mother's summer cottage out at the end of Long Island, at a place called Wading River. They were going to stay for three days.

In Queens, Carillo sat in his kitchen and dawdled over coffee. He got up and carried a chair outside to his small backyard. He put the coffee on a birdbath and took out a small notebook and pen and began to think. He went over the last murder night and the following morning. He went all the way to the point where Sergeant Hanlon drove him back to the 109th. That was at about noon. As he recalled each step, nothing bothered Carillo. Then for some reason he began to think about the lieutenant going through the bin for the traffic tickets. Now why does this bother me, Carillo thought. He told himself that he was starting to fantasize, that he was trying to make tickets appear that were not there. Then he remembered: he never had interviewed the two patrolmen who had been first on the scene of the crime. It made him feel better that this was the reason his mind had become cranky; he was not coming apart. He made a note to himself on the pad.

By the time he arrived at the precinct, the phones had become enemies. Twenty detectives were nailed to desks answering calls. There was no way for a man to walk to the men's room. Carillo picked up his own phone while he was still standing. The echo of a long-distance call was on the line. The man on the other end was calling from Hilo, Hawaii. "Do you see some connection in his name, Son of Sam, to Samson?" the man said. On his desk, in the piles of new mail, Carillo noticed a letter from a woman which began, "I am not a kook. I have never written a letter like this in my life. I am afraid to say this, but I think my husband could be Son of Sam. . . ." Somewhere during the afternoon, Carillo told Sergeant Hanlon to get in touch with the two officers from the Sixty-second who were the first on the scene.

"How the hell did we miss them?" Carillo said. "I never heard of a homicide where somebody didn't interview the first officers on the scene."

At six o'clock, Hanlon walked into Carillo's office. "We located one of them. McPartland. He's off until Friday at eight a.m."

"Where is he?"

"At his mother-in-law's at Wading River."

"Where's his partner?" Carillo said.

"I just worked on finding McPartland."

Carillo nodded. "All right. What I'll do is ask Chief Maloney to bring them in for us."

Hanlon said, "One other thing. What are we supposed to do with the eight-o'clock patrol? Since Brooklyn wants to keep the case, do we let them do their own patrolling?"

"No, no, no, come on now," Carillo said. "You know they can't do that."

"Well, why do they want to hang on to the rest of the case then?" Hanlon said.

"I'm going to get that straightened out when I talk to the Chief tomorrow," Carillo said. "Don't worry about it."

On the next morning, a Wednesday, John Maloney, the chief of detectives, asked Carillo to keep the Task Force functioning on every part of the case except the Bensonhurst shootings. Maloney wanted to let Brooklyn detectives handle that for a few more days. "Give them a chance to work out their enthusiasm," Maloney said. "If it gets bogged down, we'll just shift it back to you. Give it till the end of the week. We need those guys all year, you know."

"Well, tell them they better interview the officers first on the scene," Carillo said.

"I'll remind them," Maloney said.

On Wednesday night, when he got home with his wife from a movie in Wading River, McPartland found a note from his mother-in-law on the kitchen table. A captain named Finan from the Tenth Homicide Division had called. McPartland froze: the locker door slammed shut on the locker with the thick black traffic ticket book on the shelf; it had gone completely out of his mind. He picked up the phone and held it in his hand and tried to think. He held the phone so long that the automatic whine began in the earpiece. He hung it up, picked it up again and called Homicide Division and asked for Detective Laughlin. "He'll be in at eight in the morning," the voice on the other end said.

At 8:05 a.m. Thursday, McPartland was on the phone.

"Laughlin."

"Yeah, this is McPartland from the Six-two."

"Hey, what do you say?"

"I want to see you," McPartland said.

"What the hell's so tough about that?" Laughlin said.

They made a date for three o'clock in Gargulio's, the best restaurant in Coney Island. The detectives, of course, hung out there. McPartland left Wading River at 12:30 p.m. and was in Gargulio's twenty-five minutes early. He sat at the bar and had a beer. The place was between-meals empty. He watched the busboys setting the tables. He had a second beer. Laughlin came in at three-thirty.

"What's up?" he said.

"Have a beer," McPartland said.

"No, I've got a guy waiting outside in the car. I got to be back in the office at four. Tell me, what's your problem?"

McPartland told him about the traffic tickets.

"Well, give 'em to the clerical man tonight," Laughlin said.

"I could, but now I got a call home from a captain in your office."

"Finan?"

297

"Uh huh."

"Did he ask about the ticket?"

"I don't know what he wanted."

Laughlin walked to a phone booth and pushed himself in. When he came back, he was smiling. "Forget about the call," he said. "That Inspector at the Task Force is so pissed off that he doesn't have this case too that he's trying to run it remote control. He calls the Chief of Detectives and reminds him to do this, do that. Your name got into it somehow. You and your partner. Rizzo your partner? Right? You and your partner weren't properly interviewed the night of the shooting. Some shit like that."

"So what does the Captain want from me?"

"Nothing. I'll go in now and tell them I saw you and interviewed you and that will end it."

"It will?"

"Certainly. But you have to give me the traffic tickets. I ought to check them myself. You never know. Thousand-to-one shot. But maybe we could find somebody who saw something. So I tell you what. You get the traffic tickets and bring them to me. I'll handle them for you from then on."

"Where do I bring them to?" McPartland asked.

"Bring them up to me in the office."

"It'll take me about twenty minutes," McPartland said.

"Not today. I'll be in eight o'clock tomorrow morning."

"I'm working an eight-to-four, too," McPartland said.

"Perfect," Laughlin said. "See how all good things come to you because you're Irish. If you was a guinea on the Task Force, you'd be nowhere."

McPartland was in heavy traffic for a good part of the way back to Wading River, but he didn't mind it. Nor did he mind, the moment he got there, putting his family into the car and driving back to Deer Park.

The next morning, a Friday, McPartland and Rizzo got into a patrol car and drove over to the Tenth Homicide. McPartland went upstairs and found Laughlin sitting at the desk and fighting morning cough. "Just leave them here," Laughlin said. "They're mine now." His eyes were watery. As McPartland walked out of the Tenth Homicide, he began singing a wordless song. He was out of trouble.

An hour later, Laughlin looked at the tickets. He called the Bureau of Motor Vehicles Identification Office, read the two license plates, and waited for a couple of minutes. The clerk came back on the line and read him two addresses. One was in Bensonhurst and the other, for the cream-colored Ford Galaxie, was for a Bernard Rosenfeld, 743 Hudson Terrace, Yonkers.

Laughlin called the Bensonhurst address first. The guy was sore about the ticket. "You was so busy giving me a ticket that you let a whole killing go on," he said. He didn't see or hear anything Saturday night, he told Laughlin.

"Laughlin?" The captain, Finan, was standing in his office door.

"Yes, sir," Laughlin said.

"Let's all of us get together in here and see where we stand with this mess," the captain said.

A dozen Brooklyn detectives sat in Finan's office and discussed the case for two hours. They all spoke about the same things because nobody had discovered anything new. During the meeting, Laughlin told the captain that he could forget about interviewing the two patrolmen who had been first on the scene. He, Laughlin, had taken care of that himself.

"I don't have it on paper," the captain said.

"You will," Laughlin said.

At three-thirty, finished with his typing, Laughlin picked up the Rosenfeld ticket. He called Westchester County information. There was a Bernard Rosenfeld on Hudson Terrace in Yonkers, phone number 914-793-9066. Probably down here with some wop broad, Laughlin said to himself. Fuckin' Jews and wops get along. Look at the two that got shot, wop and a Jew. And here's another Jew coming all the way down from Yonkers for wop pussy. He dialed the number and let it ring several times. There was no answer. Laughlin reminded himself to try the guy later. You never know, he said to himself, the guy just might have seen something and doesn't even know it himself till you talk it out of him. Gene Laughlin left for the day.

At lunchtime in the Bronx Post Office that night, Charley Weppler came up to Rosenfeld's table.

"You all through with that shit?" Weppler said.

"He's all right," Hattie Mabry said. "Leave him alone now. Sometimes things get to all of us."

"Well, I got next week off," Weppler said, "so I thought I'd say good-bye to all of you."

"Where are you going?" Hattie said.

"Out to the Hamptons. Me and my girl."

"Sounds great," Hattie said.

"I'll be at that place I was telling you about," Weppler said to Rosenfeld. "If you want me, I'll be at The Cave. They got a big thing every night now. Even Monday night." Charley Weppler felt loose. He forgot that the last time he had had that strange feeling about telling Rosenfeld about the Hamptons.

As Weppler talked, Rosenfeld ate and said nothing. The Cave, Bernard said to himself. Mort wants that. He knew that by the time he got home, Mort would be screaming about The Cave. How could he not? Sam Thornton would tell him to do it.

At the end of work that night, Rosenfeld walked out into a heavy rain. He got in the car and started to drive to Queens, but the rain was coming so hard against his windshield he knew that Sam was hiding in his own house. Rosenfeld turned around and drove home. In the apartment, he put a Kiss record on the stereo. He wanted a lot of noise to keep the dog sounds out of the apartment. The number was called "Parasite." For the next two hours, Bernard walked around the room and growled out his own lyrics to the number, whose electronic thunder rolled out of the speakers.

> *Parasite Lady,*
> *Going to Die!*
> *Parasite Guy,*
> *Going to Die!*

Still, the dogs scratched to be heard over the noise. He sat down at his breakfront and tore at a piece of paper with his pen. "Won't they ever leave me alone?" he scrawled. He walked around the apartment a few times, then went downstairs and took a five-gallon can of gasoline out of the trunk of his car. Up in the apartment, he looked around and finally found a king-size Coke bottle. He put gasoline and soapsuds into the Coke bottle and twisted a rag wick in. He crumpled individual newspaper pages, then filled one of his pants pockets with the .45 ammunition. With the bottle in one hand and the crumpled newspaper pages cradled in his other arm, he walked downstairs. It was four o'clock in the morning. His chest thumped as he crept along the hall to 8M, Mort Cole's apartment. He put the newspapers on the floor up against the door to the apartment. Then he dropped perhaps a dozen bullets onto the papers. He lit the wick, stepped back and threw the bottle at the door. It exploded into flame and Rosenfeld flung himself through the door to the staircase, so the bullets would not zip into him. Then he tore upstairs and, on tiptoes, sprinted along the hallway to his apartment. He fell on the mattress, chest heaving, and listened to the shouting from the apartment underneath him.

He began chanting to himself, "Parasite guy, going to die, parasite guy, going to die." He heard many people talking downstairs; when it became silent he fell asleep.

After the firemen left, Mort Cole walked out of his apartment, with its front entrance blackened and blistered from the firebomb, and drove down to the police station house on Warburton Avenue. Juliano and Charles were sitting at their desks when he came in.

"Again?" Juliano said.

"I just had to have the Fire Department," Cole said. "I know he did it. The guy is a wack."

The three of them drove to Yonkers Police Headquarters. Upstairs in the Detective Division, a beefy man, Lieutenant Joe Campion, took notes as he listened to the story. "We'll get on this guy," he said.

"When?" Cole said.

"We'll go to court on Monday and get a search warrant on the joint he's living in and we'll see what's what."

"We been watching this thing," Juliano said.

"Well, you better be watching more than just this," Campion said. "You're patrolmen and you got to take care of your sector. This here is the work of the Detective Division. When you get to be detectives, you can sit on a guy like this. Until then, just go do your job and leave my job to me."

Juliano and Charles and Cole went out to the street. "I don't know what I'm going to do," Cole said.

"Do what you want," Juliano said. "We can't play with this thing anymore."

When Cole parked his car in front of the apartment house at 743 Hudson Terrace, he saw Micki Thornton coming out.

"Did you hear what happened?" Cole said.

"I looked out and saw the firemen leaving," she said. "I was so tired I went back to bed. Then when I got up, the super told me. I came up to see you, but you were gone."

"I went to the police," he said.

"And?"

"Same thing. I told them who it is, the things he's doing. They say they're going to get a warrant on Monday to search his place. Lot of good that's going to do me all weekend."

"I tell everyone I see," Micki Thornton said. "Even when I just say hello to someone in the parking lot, I tell them, 'I think we have a serious nut living in the building.' And what happens? Nothing."

Cole shrugged and went inside. Micki Thornton drove off to her job at the headquarters of the Yonkers Police Department.

26

On Sunday morning, the day after the fire outside Mort Cole's apartment, Detective Laughlin was at his desk at the Tenth Homicide at
eight o'clock. He looked over a list of people he had to recanvass. All
of them lived on Bay Sixteenth Court and Bay Sixteenth Street, and
he knew he would be jeopardizing his life if he bothered them before
it was time for them to get up and go to mass. Laughlin made the
ten-o'clock mass at Regina Patias Church in Bensonhurst, then
began canvassing people at eleven-fifteen. He came back to his office
at three-thirty. He was about to type up his reports of the canvassing
when he remembered the Rosenfeld ticket. He flipped through his
notebook for the Yonkers number and dialed it. There was no answer
again. Laughlin was irritated. When is this guy home, he said to himself. He wanted to include Rosenfeld in the report to show how
thorough it was: he had checked out people as far away as Yonkers.
Laughlin called the Yonkers Police Department.

"Hello," he said to the female operator, "this is Detective Laughlin,
New York City Police Department, Tenth Homicide Division. We're
trying to get in touch with a Bernard Rosenfeld, Seven-forty-three
Hudson Terrace, Yonkers, but so far our efforts have not succeeded.
I'm wondering if you could connect me to the precinct nearest his
home so I could ask one of the officers to contact Rosenfeld for us."

"What do you want Rosenfeld for?" the operator asked.

"Come on, it's police business," Laughlin said. "We had a homicide
down here, and Mr. Rosenfeld's car received a ticket on the same

303

night. He was in the area. We just want him to call us and tell us if he saw anything."

"Was that the Son of Sam murder?" Micki Thornton said.

"Certainly was."

"Well, if I were you, I'd talk to Rosenfeld myself," she said. "There's something seriously the matter with him. He shot my father's dog a few months ago. He writes crazy letters to my father. And yesterday, I'm pretty sure, he tried to set fire to the apartment underneath him."

"And who are you?" Laughlin said.

"My name is Micki Thornton, and I live at Seven-forty-three Hudson Terrace, too. My father is Sam Thornton, and he lives about a block away. He was down to see your Son of Sam Task Force last month. He told them about Rosenfeld."

"He's one of a thousand," Laughlin said.

"Well, we really think Rosenfeld is crazy," Micki Thornton said. "Dangerous crazy."

"You know what you do, give me the precinct nearest his house anyway," Laughlin said.

"It's a neighborhood precinct, right on Warburton Avenue," Micki Thornton said. "The two fellas in there who know about Rosenfeld, they aren't on today. They come on tomorrow."

Laughlin took their names, Juliano and Charles. Then he hung up and started typing, two fingers, the cigarette on the edge of his desk alongside his left hand, the dirty typewriter keys forming a lot of black circles where the O's were supposed to be. The E's, too. Laughlin reported on his canvass and then on the call to Micki Thornton. He placed the report in Captain Finan's box and then left.

Laughlin was back in early the next morning, Monday, July 25, 1977. He glanced into the captain's office, saw that he had not come in yet, picked up the report from the basket, and began reading it over. As he came to the part about Rosenfeld, he walked to his desk with it and sat down. He shook his head.

"What's that?" the sergeant, Frank Looney, said to him.

"Report for the Captain."

"What's the matter with it?"

"Read the part at the end. About the guy in Yonkers who got the ticket that night."

"What ticket?" Looney said.

"Guy got a ticket on Bay Seventeenth that night."

"What is this ticket?" Looney said, grabbing the report. "I didn't hear about any ticket."

"I got it right here," Laughlin said.

Looney read the report. "What are you going to do?" he said to Laughlin.

"I've got the names of two Yonkers cops who know about him. I'm going to ask them to go over and interview the guy and see what they think."

"You're going to ask *them*?" Looney said. "Your ass. You're going to go up there and ask him yourself."

"Go to Yonkers?"

"You're damned right. Take somebody along for the ride with you. I want to know everything about him. Take two guys with you to make sure you do it right. Complete coverage."

"I'll call the local police there anyway," Laughlin said. "There's those two patrolmen I want to talk to, long as I'm going up there."

He dialed the number for the Warburton Avenue Station House and asked for Juliano or Charles. Charles answered the phone. Laughlin made an appointment for 10:30 a.m. When he hung up, he found Detectives Lisa and Haroldson getting ready to go with him. The sergeant had assigned them. It took an hour to get to the stationhouse in Yonkers. As the three Brooklyn detectives were getting out of the car in front of the small one-story frame station house, Lisa smirked. "Now this is what you call a real candy-store operation," he said.

They went inside and found two patrolmen sitting at one desk, and three plainclothesmen, detectives, at the other. "I'm Detective Laughlin, from the New York Police Department," Laughlin said. "And these are Detectives Lisa and Haroldson."

"I'm Lieutenant Campion of the Yonkers Detective Division," a heavyset man in plainclothes said. He waved his hand at the others. "These men are with me."

"I see," Laughlin said. "I had an appointment to see two patrolmen." He turned to the other desk. "You the fellas I called?"

"That's Officer Juliano and Officer Charles," Campion said. "What is it you fellas need?"

"We'd like to know about a Bernard Rosenfeld," Laughlin said.

"Anything we can do to help," Campion said. "We're very interested in him ourselves. In fact, we were just going to get a search warrant for his place."

"Well, we'd like to talk to him," Laughlin said.

"Sure," Campion said. "Now what about this ticket he got in Brooklyn the night the two kids got shot?"

"I got to get a pack of cigarettes," Laughlin said. He got up and walked outside. Standing on the sidewalk, he snarled, "The rat fuck!" People on the street turned to look at him. He went to the drugstore on the corner and bought a pack of cigarettes.

When Laughlin came back inside, Lisa was talking to Campion. Lisa was telling Campion how little he knew about Rosenfeld, and Campion, feeling superior, gave out a few small details. Campion kept reminding them that they were in Yonkers and that this was his territory, and even if they wanted to know about Rosenfeld, it was really his responsibility to check the guy out.

A few blocks away, in his apartment, Rosenfeld had been up since nine. He sat at his breakfront and printed, in the big slanted letters that were now famous everywhere, the start of a note: "Because Mort is Mort, so must the streets be filled with Mort (Death). . . ."

When Rosenfeld finished the note, he put it in an envelope and addressed the envelope to the Sheriff of Suffolk County. Suffolk County is the last county out on Long Island. The Hamptons are in Suffolk County. When the sheriff came to pick up the bodies at The Cave, he at least would know they were because of Mort, Bernard decided. He went downstairs with the letter, with the .45 in a duffel bag, and with the .44 in his pocket. When he got into his car, he saw the empty cranberry-juice jar sitting on the front seat. He decided he had better fill it up. He might be driving a long time. He tossed the duffel bag and the envelope onto the backseat and watched the duffel bag slip halfway to the floor. Then he took the empty jar and went upstairs and filled it with cold water. He paused for a moment. The apartment was soundless. From the yard in back of the apartment house, he heard a young child shriek and then there was a splash as the child jumped into the water of a small plastic swimming pool. Rosenfeld sat on his swivel chair with the jar of water in his hands and thought.

He was not going to go to the post office today, he knew that, but Sam was telling him that it was too early to go out to the Hamptons. And Mort was telling him the same thing. Mort was talking to him very nicely now, not yelling or screaming. He liked Mort now. He couldn't wait to go down the staircase of The Cave for Mort, and stand there with the Ranger Strike IV and start pumping away. Pumping big .45 slugs into the bodies with the twirling lights on them. At midnight he would do it. Or just a little after midnight. When Charley Weppler was dancing with his girl. He would try to put the same .45 through Charley Weppler and the girl. Death at once. Death for Mort, he thought. Bernard fidgeted in anticipation. Bodies and blood everywhere. He would become the greatest killer General Jack Cosmos had ever had. He was happy now. He would wait until evening, until it got dark, and then he would go out and do his job. He put the jar of water in the refrigerator and he sat and thought.

The conversation in the police station had been going on more than two hours when Laughlin said that he and his men, Lisa and Haroldson, were going to take a break for lunch. "Then we'll all go look for Rosenfeld," Laughlin said. "Okay?"

Campion nodded.

The three New York City detectives went outside, got into their car, and drove up Warburton Avenue. Laughlin had a map of Yonkers out on the front seat. He followed Warburton until he came to Jarvis Street. He turned right and took Jarvis up a sharp hill. At the second corner he turned into Hudson Terrace, down the hill to the new apartment house. He found a space and pulled in. He got out and looked around.

"Just wait here a minute," Laughlin said to Lisa and Haroldson.

Go to the cars, he told himself. He hit it right away. The cream-colored Galaxie was parked directly in front of the building. Laughlin took out his notebook and checked the license-plate number. That was it, all right: 773-YTD. He walked up to the car and looked in. There was a duffel bag in the back, half on the floor. What appeared to be the barrel of a shotgun was sticking out of a pile of dirty underwear and socks. Laughlin swallowed hard. On the seat, right near the duffel bag, was an envelope. As Laughlin looked at the envelope, as the large slanted printing came off the envelope and jumped right through the closed window at him, he turned into a piece of dry ice. He had to open his mouth to breathe. His hand went right to his gun. He stood there for several moments. He went back to his own car and told Haroldson he wanted to break into Rosenfeld's car. Haroldson went through the trunk of the car and took out a wire hanger. In a few seconds, Laughlin was inside the Galaxie. He picked up the envelope by its edges, opened it, and looked at the first line of the note inside: "Because Mort is Mort ..." The paper rattled in Laughlin's hand.

"I got the sonuvabitch," he said.

Haroldson reached in and lifted the duffel bag. He pulled open the top to reveal the .45 Ranger Strike IV semiautomatic rifle. "Look at this," Haroldson said.

"You go make some calls," Laughlin said. "Lisa and I stay here."

As Haroldson drove away, Laughlin and Lisa walked to a car across the street and took up a position behind it. They took turns watching the doorway of the apartment house and the streets in both directions. Anybody going near that car was going to be theirs.

Nothing happened in the hour Haroldson was gone. He was on the phone forty-five minutes. He was on hold while Sergeant Looney went to Lieutenant Fitzsimmons who went to Captain Finan who went to the chief of detectives. Commissioner Bracken was in on the call within twenty minutes. Ten minutes after that, the mayor was involved. Reluctantly, two very important decisions were made. The Yonkers police was going to have to be involved; so was the Special Task Force. Chief Maloney said he would be coming up himself with Inspector Carillo and Captain Finan and six detectives from Tenth Homicide and six more from the Task Force.

Maloney said it might take a couple of hours to get the group together and up to Yonkers. "Keep his car under surveillance," Maloney said. "Don't move in unless he comes to the car. Anything happens, call my office immediately. There will be someone there waiting for a call." In the meantime, Maloney said, Commissioner Bracken would contact the chief of police in Yonkers and arrange for Yonkers detectives to surround the apartment, a holding action.

By three o'clock, Haroldson was back with Laughlin and Lisa. He told them the arrangements. By four o'clock, Lieutenant Campion, the Yonkers detective, was at Laughlin's side.

"You fuck," Campion greeted him.

Laughlin smiled. "You were thinking the same thing," he said.

Campion ignored the remark. He said that he would have men on the roof and at all entrances to the building except the main entrance. He also had patrol cars at every intersection within two blocks of the building. He was sealing off the area, he said, as quietly as possible.

When a parking space opened up right behind the cream-colored Galaxie, Laughlin slid his car into it and moved up tight, pressing against the Galaxie, bumper to bumper. Haroldson then walked to the car in front of Rosenfeld's car, worked the window open, got the door open, and released the parking brake. Then he and Lisa pushed the car back, so that Rosenfeld's car was neatly sandwiched into its parking space. There was no way Rosenfeld could pull out in a hurry, if at all.

For over two hours, Laughlin and Haroldson and Lisa sat in their car and said almost nothing. When one of the others mumbled something, Gene Laughlin heard the voice of the mayor congratulating him. When he looked out at the setting sun, he began to squint in the light from the television cameras. And then, every so often, there would be this dark, sour juice running through him: he could get shot.

The Yonkers police brought Mort Cole to Laughlin's car, and Cole, as best he could, described Rosenfeld: heavyset, black wiry hair, a round goofy face. As Cole tried to fill in the description, Laughlin bit his lip in concentration.

By seven o'clock, the contingent from the New York City Police Department was on the scene. The detectives reinforced the Yonkers police and tightened the ring around the apartment house. Maloney, Carillo, and Finan waited in a car that their driver, a sergeant, had parked just three cars behind Laughlin's. They sat there for three hours, and in the silence, Carillo lived through a whole symphony of emotions. He was, he admitted to himself, thrilled by the prospect of the catch. He was delighted for the people of the city whose fears would be calmed. Yet he was sorry for all the men in his command who had trusted him and who would be bitter because they had not been called in for the kill. And he was angry because he now knew that his questions about parking tickets had drawn unsatisfactory answers, hurt because he could feel Maloney elbowing him out of the case, and disappointed because his Task Force, despite all the time

309

he had spent thinking and planning, had not come up with the name Bernard Rosenfeld.

At 10:20 p.m., somebody in Laughlin's car hissed, and Laughlin turned his head in time to see the glass doors of the apartment house swing open and this chubby guy with dark wiry hair come out. Laughlin's left hand went to the driver's door. He had his pistol in his right hand. He heard the bodies in his car rustle. "That's him," Lisa said.

Laughlin said nothing. He just held up his hand holding the gun, motioning for silence, for a little more patience. He watched Rosenfeld walk out to the curb and unlock his car door. As Rosenfeld bent toward the car, Laughlin moved. He was out of the car, he had no feeling of opening the door and touching the ground, and he was moving toward Rosenfeld, moving, moving, moving. He almost didn't realize that Lisa, coming out of the back door, was floating past him, floating at Rosenfeld. Lisa was not making a sound and he was controlling his body, and he had his gun up in the air and he descended just as Rosenfeld, his body curled up and defenseless, was slipping into the driver's seat.

Lisa had it timed perfectly. As Rosenfeld slumped into the seat and his head came up, Lisa reached in and put the muzzle right against Rosenfeld's temple.

Behind Lisa, all the nerves came out of Laughlin in a rush. "Police! Don't move!" he shrieked.

It was a sound which went out into the night air like a trumpet.

Suddenly, wherever Bernard Rosenfeld looked, through the windshield, through the passenger windows, through the rear window, there were guns aimed at him. Pistols, shotguns, submachine guns, an arsenal. And pressing against his temple, pressing hard, was this .38 Police Special.

Rosenfeld's eyes went up and looked at Lisa. Rosenfeld smiled. "Well, you got me," he said.

He looked at the crowd swelling around him, and his eyes stopped on Dominick Carillo. "Hello, Inspector Carillo," Rosenfeld said.

When they pulled Rosenfeld out of the car, Laughlin lunged past Lisa and grabbed for the bulge in the pocket of Rosenfeld's jeans. Laughlin brought out the .44-caliber Bulldog Special. Now he could share the spotlight with Lisa. He held the gun up as if he were saying mass with it.

"What the fuck is his name?"

"Rosenfeld," the man from the *Times* said. "Bernard Rosenfeld."

"You're shittin' me."

"No, it's on the wires already. Lives in Yonkers."

"Yonkers?"

"Yeah."

The conference room on the third floor of the police headquarters building was beginning to fill with news people. It was after 1:00 a.m. now, and the news of the arrest in Yonkers had broken more than an hour earlier. There had been sufficient time to summon reporters and columnists and photographers and even television crews. This was not like covering a shooting where all the elements of the story might be gone before you got there. This was hurry-up-and-wait. Go to the police headquarters; the story will meet you there. The man who has killed six young people and wounded seven others is in custody. He is being held at police headquarters. Have your cameras ready and you may even get a picture of him. The *Times*, with its usual show of strength, had dispatched a team of ten. There were almost as many reporters from the *Dispatch*, and perhaps half a dozen from the *Express*. ABC, NBC, and CBS each had at least three full crews on hand, some tape and some film, representing both local and network interests, and the new president of ABC News had shown up himself to direct his people's operation. He used to be in charge of ABC Sports. He used to supervise ABC's coverage of the Olympic Games. He found the atmosphere at police headquarters familiar, a blend of news event and carnival, a lot of glitter surrounding legitimate drama. He had been at Munich, too, at the time of the massacre.

Almost everyone who had covered any aspect of the case was at police headquarters, including many who had not been assigned but had been drawn by curiosity, by the hold a major event, especially a disaster, exerts on people in the news business. Danny Cahill showed up at ten after one. As the recipient of the letter from the killer, Cahill was an acknowledged authority on the case; other reporters looked to him for inside information. He affected possession of that information.

The only journalist missing who had been closely involved with the case was Gil Rodgers. He did not know what he was missing. His assignment desk had tried to reach him as soon as the first tip came

311

in. The man running the desk in the newsroom pressed a special button on his telephone, then dialed the three-digit number of Rodgers' beeper, the electronic device all reporters were expected to carry on their person so that the desk could contact them at any time. As soon as the man on the desk dialed the number, he began hearing a beep . . . beep . . . beep . . . coming from the far corner of the newsroom. The desk man got up and walked toward the sound and found the source of it on top of Rodgers' desk. Rodgers had left his beeper there. When he had taken the new news and feature assistant out for a drink after dinner, he had intended to return to his desk before going home. He had underestimated his own charm. They had gone straight to her place. She had a fine stereo system and a decent choice of records; they had not bothered to turn on the radio or the television.

"How do you spell Rosenfeld?"

"R-o-s-e . . ."

"Didn't the cops say all along they figured he was a Catholic?"

"Yeah."

"And didn't they say he probably lived in the Bronx or Queens?"

"Yeah."

"And they still caught him?"

"Yeah."

"How?"

Up on the thirteenth floor, Bracken, the police commissioner, and Maloney, the chief of detectives, and the mayor and a squadron of aides and public-relations specialists were at work, orchestrating the news conference that would soon take place. "Let's bring in all the weapons that were found in his car and in his apartment," Abe Wise, the mayor's press secretary, suggested.

"And the envelope with the printing," Larry McDermott, the deputy police commissioner for public affairs, said. "Don't forget that. That stuff about 'Mort is Mort, and Mort is Death.' We want that."

"Good," Wise said.

"Who talks first?" McDermott said.

"You do. You introduce the Mayor. We can't have him go first because the cameras may not be rolling. We sure as hell don't want them to miss his first few words, not with that election coming. The Mayor's only going to make a brief statement about the people of the city being able to sleep soundly again, and then he's going to introduce Commissioner Bracken, and Bracken can introduce Chief Maloney. The Chief, the way I see it, will make a brief statement and then he'll introduce two of the detectives who made the arrest and they can show the evidence they confiscated. They won't have to say anything, just hold up the guns and the ammo, that'll be enough."

"What about Carillo?"

They talked about him as if he weren't in the room. He had worked sixteen- and eighteen-hour days, six and seven days a week, for months, and they looked at him like he was an embarrassment. "Oh, the press guys who want him'll get ahold of him after the news conference," Wise said. "That'll be better. It won't break up the flow of the conference."

He had been the man out front, the man taking all the heat through all the shootings, and now, on pay day, he was supposed to fade into the background. Don't worry, they told him, you'll get a promotion, you'll be the top Italian Inspector on the force. Full Inspector. You'll be a hero. Hey, it wasn't your fault it wasn't one of your guys who came up with the killer.

Playing their games, he thought. The mayor is running for re-election, and the primary comes up in a few weeks. The timing is beautiful for him; he couldn't be happier. If we had caught the guy two months ago, the impact would have worn off before the election. Maloney. Bracken. A pair of heroes. Irish heroes. He smiled to himself. At least it was an Italian, Lisa, who made the collar. That was something. And Rosenfeld greeting him by name, that was something, too. "Hello, Inspector Carillo," Rosenfeld had said. Carillo liked that. Fuck the brass and fuck the politicians. He had worked his ass off, he knew that.

"It's one-thirty," someone said. "Should we go down?"

"No, give it another half an hour," McDermott said. "I'll send word down that the news conference'll start at two. That way, we won't miss anybody. All the papers, the radio stations, the networks, the wire services, the news magazines — hey, nobody's going to get tired and go home. And at this hour, we're not going to lose any audience by holding off for another thirty minutes. There's bulletins on the air now, and people watching the late movies can see words crawling across the bottom of the screen telling them to keep watching. They will. Nobody who's stayed up this late is going to go to sleep now."

"Should we show them Rosenfeld?" someone said.

"It'd be beautiful," one deputy mayor said.

"It'd be beautiful, but we can't do it," another deputy mayor said. "I don't give a damn about the legal ramifications, about his rights, but all we need is a Jack Ruby standing there with the press. That's all we need. The mayor can kiss re-election good-bye, and all of our asses will be in a sling."

"Shit," the first deputy mayor said. "We'd be better off if there were a Jack Ruby. How many millions you figure we'll spend trying to put this guy away for the rest of his life? And then how many millions more will we spend keeping him away? And we're cutting back on cops and firemen because of the budget crisis."

Rosenfeld was on the same floor, in an interrogation room in the back. A dozen detectives were in with him, most of them from the Special Task Force. Every man on the Task Force who wasn't there was on his way in. They all wanted to see Bernard Rosenfeld. They wanted to touch him. They wanted to figure him out. Some of them wanted to strangle him. They took turns in the conference room, looking at him and asking him questions, and almost every detective came out of the conference room surprised by the way he felt.

"I swear to God," Detective Doyle said, "if anybody had told me I'd feel anything but hatred for this bastard, I'd have told him he was full of shit. I thought I'd kill him with my bare hands, but how the hell can you hate this guy? He's a marshmallow. He's gone, completely gone. He's a fruitcake. He don't have a sane bone in his body."

Bernard Rosenfeld still had that half-smile on his face. He was polite. He was cooperative. It was almost as if he thought the traffic ticket was his only real problem and, by being nice, he could get out of it.

"What's your name?"

"Bernard Rosenfeld."

"Where do you live?"

"Yonkers, Seven-forty-three Hudson Terrace."

"Did you kill Connie Bonventre?"

"Yes, sir." No change in tone. No change in expression.

"And Laura Davidson?"

"Yes, sir."

"And Michele Hudson and Edward Nodari and Linda Tomasello and Mitzi Levinson?"

"Yes, sir."

314

"How do you know their names?"

"I read them in the newspapers."

"Why did you do it?"

"Because Sam told me to." Same tone. Matter of fact.

"Who's Sam?"

"He's a six-thousand-year-old man."

"A six-thousand-year-old man told you to kill these people?"

"Well . . ." Bernard sort of shook his head. "He didn't tell me himself."

"What do you mean?"

"His dog told me. That's the way he got his orders to me. Through the dog."

Rosenfeld's eyes were the only ones in the room that weren't popping.

"The dog told you when to kill?"

"Yes, sir."

"How often did you go out looking for, ah, people to shoot?"

"I went hunting every night."

"But most nights you didn't shoot anyone?"

"That's right."

"Why not?"

"Because Sam didn't tell me to." Rosenfeld hesitated. "I'm not authorized to make those decisions myself."

"Bernard, did you write that first note to Inspector Carillo?"

"Yes."

"What did you call yourself?"

" 'The Chubby Behemoth.' "

"And how did you sign the letter?"

"I think, uh, 'Mr. Monster.' "

"What did you say about the girls of Queens?"

"That they were the prettiest. Sam told me that."

"Did you want to fuck those girls?"

"Oh, no, Sam just wanted me to kill them."

"Do you hate girls?"

"Oh, no, I like girls. I had nothing against those girls. I was just doing what I had to do."

"Did you know any of them?"

"No, see, don't you understand? I was ordered to kill them. Sam Thornton ordered me to kill them."

315

"Sam Thornton?"

"Yes. He's six thousand years old, and he's a demon, and he lives in Yonkers. On the corner of Evergreen Street. 'Evil King Evergreen.' That's Sam Thornton."

As new waves of detectives came in, Rosenfeld answered the same questions over and over. His answers were consistent, and he did not seem to mind being asked the same questions. When he was pressed for details, he tried to think of them. He was very good at describing the shootings. He did not hate the police, he said. He admired them. He had wanted to be a police officer himself at one time.

"I'm glad I'm here," Rosenfeld said.

"Why?" Johnny Dwyer said.

"Because it's nice and quiet here. I can't hear the dogs."

Dwyer came out of the room with a half-smile, like Rosenfeld's, on his face. "He's nuts," Dwyer said. "I don't mind that. But there's something still bothering me: he says he ran after each shooting. He didn't walk. He ran. He wasn't crazy enough to hang around, and he wasn't crazy enough to walk, and he wasn't crazy enough to leave any clues. He's crazy, all right, but I know a lot of sane people who wouldn't be so careful like he was. I've heard that expression, you know, crazy like a fox. Well, that's him. Smart crazy."

The interrogation of Bernard Rosenfeld continued on the thirteenth floor when the mayor, the commissioner, the chief of detectives and all their troops went down to the third floor for the news conference. The conference was a theatrical success. The mayor was brief and to the point.

"I am delighted to announce," he said, "that the police have apprehended the man whom they believe is the Son of Sam, the forty-four-caliber killer. The police are confident, and so am I, that more than a year of terror is over, and New Yorkers can once again sleep soundly."

The mayor beamed. The commissioner beamed, too. So did the chief of detectives. A couple of reporters noticed that Inspector Carillo did not appear as happy as everyone else, but they assumed that was merely because he was tired. The press was delighted. The conference was worth waiting for. The statements were good. The accoutrements were perfect: the weapons and the ammunition and the poem printed in that distinctive style that had marked the letter to Cahill:

BECAUSE MORT IS MORT
SO MUST THE STREETS
BE FILLED WITH MORT (DEATH)
AND HUGE DROPS OF LEAD
POURED DOWN UPON HER HEAD
UNTIL SHE WAS DEAD.
    YET, THE CATS STILL COME OUT
AT NIGHT TO MATE
    AND THE SPARROWS STILL
    SING IN THE MORNING.

A majority of the newspeople left after the conference; some be-cause they had to, they had to get to studios and to newsrooms; and some because they felt they had all they needed of the story. Some reporters did not leave. Henry Glenville did not leave until he found out from a detective he had been cultivating about Sam Thornton. Glenville made a wise move; he went straight to Yonkers, and, before the rest of the press closed in, he persuaded Thornton to let him photograph the letter that had been written to him, in a sloppy scrawl, about his dog. Thornton also permitted the *Express* to photo-graph him and his daughter with their dog. The dog still had a slug in his thigh. Sam Thornton said he was positive it was a .44-caliber slug. The pictures of Thornton and his dog and his letters appeared in the *Express* the same day. So did pictures of Rosenfeld's apart-ment, with its litter and its strange graffiti. There was a hole in the wall where Bernard had fired at Mort Cole, and next to the hole Rosenfeld had written:

Hi
My name is
MR Williams
And I live in this hole
I have several
children who Im TURNing
Into killers WAIT
TiL they grow up.

how do you like your blueeyed boy
Mister Death

Danny Cahill did not leave after the press conference, either. He walked off with Carillo, and Carillo described to him, in great detail, the arrest. Then Carillo took him upstairs where all the detectives were. There were bottles of scotch and rye and beer floating around the thirteenth floor, all courtesy of the mayor's office. The detectives who came out of the interrogation room in the back went straight to the whisky and then some of them went to Cahill. He kept pretending to drink scotch while he soaked up the information he needed to write a column about the questioning of Bernard Rosenfeld. Cahill kept looking at the clock on the wall because he knew there would be one last special edition going to press at 5:00 a.m. He had to make the edition with his column, or the city editor would chop off his fingers. The earlier press runs had been cut back. Hundreds of thousands of copies of that final edition were going to flood the city. Cahill heard all about Sam Thornton and about the dogs that told Bernard Rosenfeld when to kill. Cahill stayed on the thirteenth floor till three-thirty, and then he knew he had to go and start writing or he would blow the edition.

"C'mon," he said to Carillo, "let me just see the guy for a minute. Just a quick look. And let me just ask him one question. Maybe two."

Carillo smiled and shook his head. "Forget it," he said. "There's no way you can talk to him. Just walk with me, and when we go past that room in the back, take a look through the open door. Maybe you'll catch a glimpse of him, maybe you won't." Then Carillo raised his voice. "Come on," he said, "I'll walk you to the elevator. I've got to get some sleep tonight, you know, I've got to get out to the One-oh-nine tomorrow."

"Hey, Inspector," Dwyer called out. "Everybody's going to be out at the One-oh-nine tomorrow. We got a party there starting at five o'clock, that all right, Inspector?"

"Sure, sure," Carillo said. He started with Cahill, and he took him the long way to the elevators, past the interrogation room. As they went by, Cahill turned his eyes through the open door, and he saw the guy sitting on a chair, with a half a dozen detectives grouped around him. The stragglers were still asking him questions. He was trying to help them. He was pudgy. He looked soft. He didn't look as if he could hurt anyone.

"Sonuvabitch, he looks familiar," Cahill said. "I know I seen him, somewhere."

Carillo stopped. "I saw him, too," he said. "I saw him every night, before I went to bed, and I saw him every morning, as soon as I got up. He just didn't look like that, that's all."

318

All of the members of The Moment of Truth had gathered in the gallery on Waverly Place. They had been up all night, listening to the radio interviews, watching the television reports, then reading every word in the *Times* and in the *Dispatch*, passing the papers from hand to hand. Early in the afternoon, they had seen the *Express*, too, with the pictures of Sam Thornton and his dog and the letters written to him. The more they saw and the more they read, the more positive they became. "We were right all along," Mitchell Block said.

"Of course," Selma Sagerman said.

"Sam, the demon, is the real killer, not Bernard Rosenfeld," Block said.

In a corner of the room, two of the girls hugged each other and moaned.

Aaron Castle spread open the *Express* to the photo of the letter presumably written by Rosenfeld to Sam Thornton, complaining about Thornton's dog. Then Castle spread open an old copy of the *Dispatch*, showing the letter presumably written by Rosenfeld to Danny Cahill. The handwriting in the letter to Thornton was a mess; the printing in the letter to Cahill was exquisite. They did not look as if they could possibly be the work of the same man.

"These letters corroborate our theory," Castle said. "The letter to Sam Thornton, I would say, was written in Rosenfeld's normal hand. The letter to Cahill was written by the demon, using Rosenfeld's hand. There is precedent for this: people possessed often speak in languages they could never have learned. This is the same thing, Rosenfeld writing in a literary style that he had never mastered."

None of the members of The Moment of Truth was tired. Their eyes were bright, their suspicions confirmed. "It is clear what we must now do," Lionel Silver, the leader of the group, said. "We must go to the proper authorities and we must persuade them to allow us to perform an exorcism. We must drive the demon Sam from Bernard Rosenfeld's body."

Everywhere in New York City, people were reacting to the arrest and identification of Bernard Rosenfeld with immense relief and matching curiosity. As great as the fear had been, that was how great the interest was, in Rosenfeld, in his background. Everybody wanted to know what blend of environment and heredity had produced this pudgy mutant who could kill and smile, who could appear so calculating and so guileless.

There were more personal reactions, too. The father of Vinny Masone said that neither he nor his son felt any bitterness toward Bernard Rosenfeld. "It's really sad," Lou Masone said, "that a human being should be so twisted, so sick." The mother of Mitzi Levinson was not so compassionate. She said that capital punishment should be reinstated. The father of Marie Perrotti said he felt the same way.

The only reaction that was absent was doubt. No one doubted for an instant that Bernard Rosenfeld was Son of Sam. For once, no one suspected a frame-up, an arrest to get the police department off the hook. Most of the time, cynical New Yorkers would think of that first thing, but not now. The evidence was too overwhelming; the ballistics test, confirming that Bernard Rosenfeld's .44-caliber Bulldog was the one that had fired the bullets found in the victims, ended all discussion. No one argued that Bernard Rosenfeld had not committed the killings, not even Bernard Rosenfeld.

Danny Cahill, who had not slept in two days, found two guys in the Bronx who had served in the army with Bernard Rosenfeld and through them, Cahill pieced together a column about Bernard's military life — his experiments with LSD, the hallucinogen, and with Fundamentalist religion, with fire-and-brimstone Christianity. Rosenfeld had popped acid in Okinawa; he had become a regular, later, at revival meetings in Kentucky. Both trips, Cahill pointed out, had taken their toll. Cahill got his column finished in the early afternoon and then, before going to the 109th for the victory party, he took care of a pressing practical matter.

"Dear Bernard," Cahill began typing. "When you wrote to me several months ago, you said that if we ever met, you would tell me all about Sam and introduce me to him. I would like very much to take you up on that offer. I would like to come visit you. There are a lot of things I would like to discuss with you. . . ."

Cahill turned and picked up a container of Sanka and took a sip. Then he put it down, took out one of his Villiger cigars and lit up. His eyes gleamed.

27

Inspector Carillo walked into the squad room and saw the beer and the cigarette butts and the crumbs on the floor and, out of force of habit, turned to Detective Dwyer and said, "Hey, come on, let's get this place straightened up."

More than one hundred people, cops and auxiliaries and reporters, swirled around Dwyer, most of them in varying stages of inebriation. Dwyer looked at the people, looked at the mess, looked at the inspector and, with the middle finger of his right hand, informed Carillo that he would not be cleaning up the squad room today. Carillo smiled and walked through the laughter and the debris to his own small office. He could not remember when he had last slept, but the adrenaline churned up by the arrest and arraignment of Bernard Rosenfeld was still surging through his veins, still keeping him going, emotionally and physically. He would tolerate a little sloppiness now. Guys from the 109th Precinct, from downstairs, guys who had nothing to do with the Task Force, were soaking up the booze, cases of beer and scotch, and gobbling the egg rolls and the butterfly shrimp and the spare ribs sent over from Lum's. Three television newscasters were trapped in the middle of the party, trying to conduct coherent interviews with incoherent cops. The detectives who had met Rosenfeld, who had questioned him and listened to him, were explaining to anyone who would listen what he was like, explaining their own feelings toward him.

Herbie Klein was sitting on top of a desk, his feet on a basketful of the most recent artist's sketches — based on lengthy interviews with the girl who had had the good look at him — that did not at all resemble Bernard Rosenfeld. Klein was flanked by the brunette social worker and the blonde from the phone company. The blonde, normally aloof, was celebrating the capture of Bernard Rosenfeld by keeping open the top four buttons of her blouse. Every cop in the place was fantasizing about diving into her cleavage, except Johnny Dwyer, who was too busy switching from beer to scotch. Not long after seven o'clock, the scotch ran out, and when Herbie Klein suggested, "Let's go to Lum's," Dwyer thought it was a sensational idea. He didn't even mind being joined by the brunette, whose name was Patricia Ann, and the blonde, Vivian. Cahill showed up at Lum's, too. He had a glass of water. The girls got screwdrivers from Harry the bartender. Klein got bourbon. Dwyer concentrated on scotch and on telling Cahill what a terrific cop he was. Everybody was feeling very good. Everybody except Herbie Klein. This is the last night, he was telling himself. Tomorrow, I start going home early again. He ordered another bourbon.

Patricia Ann, the brunette, reached over and touched his arm. "You know," she said, "I'm going to apply for the Police Department. I really like the work. I like the atmosphere. I like the people."

"Yeah?" Klein said. "You sure?"

"Sure, I'm sure," she said. She looked at her watch. It was nine o'clock. "I have to get going," she said.

"Hey, it's early," Klein said. "You don't ever leave this early."

"I have to do something special," Patricia Ann said.

She smiled and said good night to everybody in the bar. The blonde, Vivian, was sitting between Cahill and Dwyer. They were leaning across her chest, talking to each other about the case. Her tits were practically in their faces, and all they cared about was Bernard Rosenfeld.

"Would you walk me to my car?" Patricia Ann said to Klein. "I know, the guy's been caught, but, still, I'd feel better."

"Sure," he said. He turned to Dwyer. "I'll be back in a couple of minutes," he said.

Outside, Klein and Patricia Ann turned left, turned left again on Union Street and walked back toward the precinct. "My car's in the lot," she said.

He opened the car door for her.

"It's a nice night," she said. "Would you take a ride with me, just to relax?"

Klein could feel himself shivering. It wasn't cold. "Sure," he said.

She handed him her car keys, and she slid into the passenger seat. As he backed out of the lot, she reached over and let her hand fall on Klein's thigh. She pressed it and blew him a kiss.

He drove. He drove with one hand guiding her ten-year-old Plymouth along the Van Wyck Expressway from Flushing to Forest Hills and with the other holding on to her hand, pressing her hand against his leg. When he reached Queens Boulevard, he turned off and drove to Rego Park. He drove right up to Pablo Birani's apartment house, but he did not stop. He went one block farther, to the park with the fountain and the benches and the shade trees. He parked under the trees. It was only nine-thirty. There were no other cars near him.

Herbie Klein flipped off the engine, turned to the future police officer and put his hands, trembling, on her waist, under her blouse, then slid them up till they cupped her breasts. She reached for him, too, and undid his holster belt, slipped off his .38, and let the pistol fall to the floor.

And then they made love, and perhaps thousands of other New Yorkers made love the same night, in the same way, in cars parked in lovers' lanes, but theirs — without fear, without preoccupation — was the best, theirs was the sweetest.